THE TUDORS

The King, the Queen,
and the Mistress

Also Available

The Tudors: It's Good to Be King
Final Shooting Scripts 1–5 of the Showtime Series

THE TUDORS

The King, the Queen, and the Mistress

A NOVELIZATION OF SEASON ONE OF
The Tudors FROM SHOWTIME NETWORKS INC.

CREATED BY *MICHAEL HIRST*
WRITTEN BY *ANNE GRACIE*

SIMON SPOTLIGHT ENTERTAINMENT

NEW YORK   LONDON   TORONTO   SYDNEY

This book is a work of fiction. Any references to historical events, real people, or real locales are used fictitiously. Other names, characters, places, and incidents are the product of the author's imagination, and any resemblance to actual events or locales or persons, living or dead, is entirely coincidental.

SSE

SIMON SPOTLIGHT ENTERTAINMENT
An imprint of Simon & Schuster
1230 Avenue of the Americas, New York, NY 10020
Copyright © 2007 by Showtime Networks Inc. and
Peace Arch Television LTD
"The Tudors" © 2007 TM Productions Limited/PA Tudors Inc.
An Ireland Canada Production. All rights reserved.
Showtime and related marks are registered trademarks of
Showtime Networks Inc., a CBS Company.
All rights reserved, including the right of reproduction
in whole or in part in any form.
SIMON SPOTLIGHT ENTERTAINMENT and related logo are
trademarks of Simon & Schuster, Inc.
Designed by Gabriel Levine
Manufactured in the United States of America
First Edition 10 9 8 7 6 5 4 3 2 1
Library of Congress Control Number 2007932202
ISBN-13: 978-1-4169-4778-3
ISBN-10: 1-4169-4778-7

ACKNOWLEDGMENTS

The true creator of this book is Michael Hirst. To take such a huge story as the Henry Tudor and Anne Boleyn story and to compress it into a few hours of riveting entertainment takes enormous talent. From Michael Hirst came the vision, the story, the characters, and their words: to him belongs all credit.

Thank you to my agent, Nancy Yost, and to Terra Chalberg, Tricia Boczkowski, Emily Westlake, and Cara Bedick of Simon & Schuster.

Chapter One

Whitehall Palace, London

"It must be war, have you heard?"

Thomas Tallis looked up. The man was addressing him. "No, I didn't know." He'd been working out a new harmony in his head, to a work as yet unwritten.

"The French—they've murdered the Earl of Devon."

"Ah." Tallis looked around vaguely.

"Not here, man, in Italy!"

"Ah." He nodded, still at sea.

"The Earl of Devon, the English ambassador, Edward Courtenay—the king's uncle! Murdered! In cold blood and in broad daylight."

"Oh." Tallis nodded, now paying attention.

"The king cannot swallow such an insult. It must be war! Which means I'll *never* get my petition heard."

Tallis grimaced in sympathy. Gossip was all the petitioners and hangers-on had . . . leftovers from the real court, where the real decisions were made.

"We poor folk must seek the light of great men," an elderly petitioner had told him when Tallis had first arrived at court. "It is our fate, as it is the fate of the moth to seek the flame." The man had tapped his arm ponderously. "But take heed of the moth, young Master Tallis; if we venture too close, we risk burning our wings."

Tallis had thought it very wise at the time. But his wings were not what the problem was now. It was his stomach. The real food was in there, in the court. The hangers-on ate the court leftovers, only Thomas was not adept at shoving his way in early, so he was often left hungry.

Nor was he sufficiently adept at catching the eye of the king's secretary, Mr. Pace. Tallis touched a hand to his doublet and felt the crackle of his letter of introduction from the dean. If it was to be war, he didn't suppose they would have time to notice an obscure musician.

The door next to him cracked open an inch, just enough for Tallis to hear a voice say, "His Majesty wants council this afternoon to be brief. He's due to play tennis." It was Richard Pace, the king's own secretary. Tallis leaned closer.

"Where is the king?"

Mr. Pace responded, "He's gone down to his house at Jericho."

Tallis heard a tut of disapproval, then, "How is he?"

"With regard to . . . ?"

The older man said with barely leashed impatience, "With regard to Italy. What the French are doing in Italy. What other regard is there?"

"His Majesty is counseling patience."

"Yes, but you are his secretary. You see him every day."

"He's mad with grief. Almost inconsolable." There was a pause. "It was his uncle they murdered, after all!" The doors opened.

"Here he is now!" The urgent hiss rippled through the crowd as the tall, confident figure of Richard Pace, secretary to His Majesty, King Henry VIII, appeared. Behind him stood an older man dressed plainly in black. It was the famous humanist, Thomas More, one of the king's most senior advisers.

For one precious, hopeful second, Tallis managed to catch Pace's eye. He clutched his letters of introduction, but the mass of vociferous petitioners surged forward, and Tallis, and the moment, were lost in the crowd.

"Sir, sir! Sir!" men called, waving papers to draw his attention, but Richard Pace cleaved effortlessly through, and passed into the king's private apartments. The yeomen of the guard, armed with long battle-axes, slammed the oaken doors shut in his wake. Tallis's stomach rumbled.

"My lords," Henry, King of England, addressed a dozen or so members of his council in his private chambers. "We meet to consider questions of great moment." The councillors stood in a semicircle around the seated king. They were the great lords of England, the heads of the richest and most noble families in the kingdom.

Beside the king stood Cardinal Wolsey, noting everything. Information was power. The scion not of any noble family (though none dared say it to his face) but of a cattle dealer and butcher, he was now one of the richest and most powerful in the land, and all through his own efforts.

The king continued: "The king of France has demonstrated to the world his aggressive policies. His forces have already overrun five or six city-states in Italy. He's a threat to every Christian nation in Europe—yet he bullies the pope into declaring him the Defender of the Faith!" He paused to let his words sink in.

"On top of that, to prove that nobody can touch him, he arranges to have our ambassador in Urbino—my uncle!—murdered in cold blood."

The assembled men nodded in agreement.

"My lords, speaking personally, I believe all these actions are causes for war," Henry concluded.

His audience's response was unified. "Aye!"

"Indeed they are!"

"Ample and just causes, Sire!"

The king turned to the Duke of Buckingham, who had not joined in with the rest of the men. "Buckingham, what say you?"

If anyone resembled the son of a butcher, Wolsey thought, it was England's highest-ranking nobleman, Buckingham, with his fat, red face. Buckingham, whose blood claim to the throne was closer than the king's.

Wolsey eyed Buckingham's ostentatious outfit. To wear raiment so much richer and more bejeweled than the king's was folly indeed. Henry liked to win. In everything. But then, Wolsey reflected, so did his grace, the Duke of Buckingham.

Buckingham finally spoke. "Your Majesty certainly has every reason to prosecute a war. Indeed, I warned you a year ago about French ambitions—though it has taken this personal tragedy for Your Majesty to accept my word!"

Henry frowned at the open criticism. He turned to another of his trusted advisers, the Duke of Norfolk, the head of the powerful Howard family. "Norfolk? What say you?"

Norfolk nodded enthusiastically. "I agree. We should attack France with all our might. The king of England has an ancient and historic right to the French throne, usurped by the Valois. It's time we kicked them out!"

At this, there was some laughter. More heads nodded. Henry, quietly pleased, looked slowly around at his councillors. He paused at Thomas More, who was writing a note. *Or pretending to,* thought Wolsey.

Finally the king asked, "What do you say, Wolsey?"

"I concur with Your Majesty. They are indeed just causes."

The king smiled and clapped his hands together. "Good! Then the matter is settled. We shall go to war with France. Your Eminence will make all the necessary arrangements."

Wolsey inclined his head. "Majesty."

Henry rose. "And I can go—at last—to my tennis match." Everyone bowed as he hurried from the room, a spring in his step, anticipating the coming match.

The councillors fell into their own small cliques, whispering together, as they left the room. Wolsey didn't move. More gathered up his papers, waiting until all the others had left. Then he looked at Wolsey, his face troubled. "Do you really think we should go to war?"

"I think we should try to do what the king wants us to do," Wolsey said.

"What if the king doesn't know what's in his best interest?"

"Then we should help him to decide."

*   *   *   *

"Hah!" The tennis ball slammed off the black painted back walls in an unreturnable shot. From the crowded galleries came a burst of clapping. Henry smiled, enjoying the applause. He looked well, playing tennis, he knew. The ladies could hardly take their eyes off his strong thighs and muscular arms.

Henry, as usual, was winning today, paired with his close friend Charles Brandon, against cohorts Anthony Knivert and William Compton.

Henry had a passion for tennis; it was a fast, hard, aggressive game and he excelled at it. He'd had the tennis courts constructed some years earlier, along with a bowling alley, a cockpit, and a pheasant yard. His pleasure buildings, he called them—perfect for when the weather was too wet or cold for hunting or hawking or jousting.

"And what took you to your house at Jericho last evening?" Brandon murmured as he positioned himself behind Henry for the next serve. "Or need I ask? Assuaging your grief, I believe." He hit a return and added, barely missing a beat, "And how does Lady Blount?"

"She 'does' most satisfactorily, though she's fretting."

"Fretting?"

"Her husband is jealous. He's threatening to send her to a nunnery."

"A nunnery?" Brandon swore under his breath. "What a waste!"

"Indeed it would be—if I allowed it," said the king. "Play!"

They played several more points before Henry paused to wipe the sweat from his forehead with a handkerchief. He cast a speculative eye over the spectators. "The pretty little blonde, behind Norfolk," he said to Brandon. "I haven't seen her before."

Brandon followed his gaze. "Lady Jane Howard. Norfolk has just brought her to court, as a lady-in-waiting to her Majesty. Ready?"

Henry nodded and they played on. "Have you had her yet?" Henry asked.

Brandon grinned. "She has the sweetest, plumpest breasts . . . and she sighs when you kiss them."

Laughing, Henry returned the serve in a winning shot. "Our game, I think, Anthony."

Knivert made mock obeisance. "Your Majesty knows we're just letting you win!"

"Actually, I'm playing as hard as I can!" Compton puffed. Henry grinned. "Play!"

"Now, there is someone I have to try," Brandon murmured a short time later. "Look over there: middle gallery, blue dress. See her? See that exquisite, virginal face?"

Henry nodded. *A sweet morsel indeed.* "Who is she?"

Brandon cracked the ball, unplayably, off three angles, to more applause. He gave Henry a grin. "Buckingham's daughter."

Henry glanced up at the sweet face of the girl who sat next to her proud and haughty father, unaware that the king and his best friend were discussing her. "A hundred crowns you don't succeed."

"Done," Brandon accepted. "Play!"

A carriage drove through the arched entrance set into the five-story redbrick gatehouse flanked by octagonal towers and came to a halt in the great courtyard. The visitors alighted and looked around, impressed. Hampton Court Palace, the home of Cardinal Wolsey, was one of the most beautiful houses in England. Reputed to have more than two hundred beds hung with silk constantly made up in readiness for guests and a staff of over five hundred, it was a grand sight, with its mullioned windows gleaming in the sun, its red brick turrets and crenellated walls, surrounded by ornately designed gardens.

Cardinal Wolsey's secretary ushered the guests inside, leading them through a maze of rooms hung with valuable paintings and tapestries.

Wolsey received them in a magnificent book-lined chamber, a setting of wealth and subtle display. Not for him the restrained, moderate clothing of Thomas More. Cardinal Wolsey, as always, wore a scarlet cassock in heavy, sumptuous fabric—silk-lined velvet today—and, around his neck, his heavy, gold chain of office, studded with jewels and bearing a cross that hung midway down his chest.

"His Excellency the French ambassador and Bishop Bonnivet," the secretary introduced.

Wolsey rose from a desk piled with business and official papers. "Gentlemen, welcome." He held out his hand, and in turn each distinguished visitor kissed it.

"What happened in Urbino—the butchering of our ambassador—was most unfortunate." He paused. "Especially for me." Wolsey fixed the French Ambassador with a hard stare. "Your Excellency is well aware of my sentiments toward your country. I have labored long and consistently in French interests. But how am I to explain this?"

The ambassador made a faintly apologetic moue. "Frankly, it was not done on my master's orders. And those who have committed the crime have already been punished."

"No. You must understand, we are already beyond that," Wolsey continued. "King Henry is a young man. He has a young man's appetite for war—witness his love of the tourney. He would like nothing else than to ride at the head of a great army and win back England's lands in France. It will be hard to appease him."

The ambassador made a Gallic gesture. "Then, by all means, let us have war."

Wolsey looked at him. "With the greatest respect, Your Excellency, you don't mean that. You are already fighting a war against the emperor. Now you would have to fight on two fronts—even though your king is already complaining, privately, of being short of money and supplies."

The Frenchmen exchanged glances. Wolsey's knowledge of such secret information was a shock to them, he saw, concealing his satisfaction. Really, did they think he was so simple?

Bishop Bonnivet spoke at last. "May I ask Your Eminence why you invited me here today? I am a man of God, after all, and not a diplomat."

Wolsey said smoothly, "But I too am a man of God. I believe that faith can drive diplomacy. I asked you here because I wanted your advice."

Bonnivet looked surprised. As well he might, thought Wolsey. The bishop stumbled to find the right words. "Well . . . I believe . . . I believe that everything humanly possible should be done to avoid a war between our two countries." He darted a quick look at the ambassador, and hurried on, more confidently. "It would do England no good to get involved in our European squabbles. Far better she stands above them. Why become involved when you don't have to? I am sure Your Eminence has ways of pacifying the—your Lion," he finished with an ingratiating smile.

Wolsey inclined his head. Of course he did, but that was not the point. Why should he? That was the question they'd failed to consider. With Henry, one did not plant notions lightly. An idea—any idea—once planted in the king's head, was damned near impossible to root out. A prudent man, an ambitious man would do so only when all avenues had been considered. And Wolsey was nothing if not prudent. And very ambitious.

Wolsey came to the point. "Excellency, I'm not going to make any demands. This is the outline of a new peace treaty." Wolsey pushed a sheaf of papers across the table. "Take a deep breath before you open it."

The ambassador reached for the papers. "May I?"

Wolsey put a hand over his, stilling the move to open the document. "No. I want you to go away and read it carefully. I believe it introduces something new into the world of diplomacy. If your king accepts it, in principle, then he can sign without any loss of face. On the contrary, he can rejoice. My master can rejoice. We can all—rejoice."

The room was silent.

The ambassador hesitantly touched the document, as if it were a poisoned chalice, then looked at Wolsey. "In which case, what does Your Eminence want in return?"

"Nothing."

"Nothing?"

"Nothing from you," Wolsey said meaningfully. He looked at the bishop. "What I want, Your Grace . . . only you can give me."

"I—I don't understand," Bonnivet stammered.

Wolsey gave him an enigmatic smile. "Ah, but when you come to think of it, when you pray . . . when you ask God . . . I'm sure the answer will come to you."

In the king's private apartments, dinner was being served to King Henry and Queen Katherine. Each dish was carried in by servants, tasted for poison by the official taster, then passed to the gentlemen of the privy chamber, who in turn passed it to the nobles who waited on the king and queen. This day, the Duke of Buckingham had the honor of serving the king while Lady Blount served Queen Katherine.

Flutes, recorders, a trombone, and a harp played from the gallery as the dishes passed before them; tender haunches of venison from the royal deer parks, roasts of beef, pheasant glazed with rose water, coneys roasted whole, and platters of vegetables, especially artichokes, for the king was fond of them.

Henry, as always, ate with good appetite. He'd passed a very active day. He glanced sideways at his queen. She merely picked at her food, waving most of it away. He'd once thought her the most beautiful woman in England; now she looked old, so much older than he did. Such was the trouble when a young man married an older woman.

Of course the miscarriages had exhausted her. So many children, and only one still living.

"How is our daughter?" Henry asked her.

"She is well." Despite her many years in England, she still spoke with a marked Spanish accent. Once, Henry had found it charming.

"Her tutors say she has exceptional talents, especially for music." She smiled at him. "Like her father. Your Majesty should be proud."

Henry smiled back. "I am, sweetheart. You know it. Mary is the pearl of my world." He gestured to Buckingham.

"Majesty." Buckingham bowed and presented another dish: a whole baked turbot with saffron sauce—Henry's favorite.

"Will you have some?" Henry asked his wife. She shook her head. He sliced into the succulent flesh and ate it delicately with knife and fingers.

"You have not answered my nephew's letters," Katherine said quietly.

Henry pretended not to have heard her.

She persisted. "Why have you not answered his letters?"

"Just because your nephew is the king of Spain, does he think I have nothing better to do?"

"You know he advises you to sign a treaty with the emperor recognizing France as your mutual enemy."

Henry, his mouth full of fish, didn't answer.

"He also advises you not to heed everything Wolsey tells you, since Wolsey is so biased for the French."

Henry snorted. "Since when are you a diplomat?"

She raised her head proudly. "I am my father's daughter!"

Henry clenched his fist and answered in an undertone. "You are *my* wife! You are not my minister, or my chancellor, but my *wife*." There was a pause, and, aware that ears were craning to hear the soft, furious exchange, they both smiled.

Katherine leaned across and whispered in Henry's ear, "And I should like to be your wife in every way. Will you not visit my bedchamber again, as you used to?"

Henry stilled, his appetite suddenly gone. He stared down at the turbot's glassy eye for a long moment.

"This fish is not fresh," he declared, and pushed the plate away.

Later that evening, as Henry was being readied for bed, her words came back to him. He lifted his arm for one of the grooms of the bedchamber to tie up his nightgown. Another pulled back the curtains around the ornately carved tester bed while a third removed the warming pans.

A priest presented a jeweled crucifix to him. He kissed it, said a silent prayer, and crossed himself.

His gaze wandered to a side table where there was a silver bowl containing various fruits. An attendant, anticipating his wants, seized the bowl and offered it to him. Henry wasn't really hungry, he was more . . .

restless, but he reached out absently and found he had selected a pomegranate, perfectly ripe.

He sliced the fruit in half. For a moment he stared at the rich, moist, ruby flesh inside, plump with glistening seeds. . . .

"Fetch my gown."

"Yes, Your Majesty."

As Henry sucked out the fruit with relish, the servants fetched a dressing gown. Two more servants took flaming torches from the walls and led Henry into the secret passage that connected his private apartments to Katherine's.

How long had it been? Henry reflected as he strode down the corridor. A year? More? No matter. He had chosen a pomegranate, which was Katherine's emblem, and it was ripe. God willing, old as she was, tonight he would get a son on her.

When Henry threw open the door that only he ever used, the queen's ladies fell into a flutter. As one, they dropped into a low curtsy. Among them was Lady Jane Howard, last seen applauding him at tennis.

The ladies rose, babbling, clearly flustered.

"Your Majesty, we did not kn—"

"Welcome, Your Majesty. The queen did not expect—"

"Where is the queen?" Henry addressed Lady Jane. Up close she seemed even younger and more beautiful.

"Her Majesty is still at prayer, Your Majesty."

Henry paused. He stood, staring down at her. Her skin was like silk, luminous, milky white, her hair thick and glossy. From the tight, smooth bodice, a pair of pert breasts pressed eagerly. Fresh. Young.

Henry took a deep breath and came to a decision. "Tell Her Majesty that I came to offer her my love and devotion, as her true husband." He turned away, but as he did so, he caught the eye of one of his own servants, who understood immediately.

As Henry returned through his private door, the man hurried over and whispered in Lady Jane's ear.

A short time later, Lady Jane was escorted into Henry's bedchamber.

She came to him, eyes downcast, slightly flushed and nervous, sank into a low curtsy and remained there. Henry made one swift gesture, and the servants instantly withdrew to the outer room.

He turned to Lady Jane and gently lifted her to her feet. "Jane," he said softly. "Do you consent?"

Her blush deepened, flooding the milky breasts with a delicious pink. "Yes, Your Majesty."

Henry stroked her cheek, and pulled her closer. He kissed her gently, first on her mouth, then moving slowly to her cheek and down her throat. She arched back, and he tore open the front of her gown. Her pert young breasts sprang free, sweet and round. He bent and kissed each breast in turn.

Lady Jane arched, closed her eyes, and sighed.

Alone in the small, beautiful Queen's Chapel, Queen Katherine knelt on the hard stone floor, as she did for many hours each day, praying for a son. All around her, slender beeswax candles burned, each flame a symbol of hope, of yearning. On the altar in front of her stood an exquisite image, blessed by the pope himself, of the Holy Virgin holding the baby Jesus in her arms.

The queen gazed at the Holy Virgin, her lips moving in silent, ceaseless prayer.

In the communal chamber of the palace, Thomas Tallis readied himself for yet another night of sleeplessness, hunger, and discomfort. He'd eaten only an end of dry bread and a knob of hard cheese, washed down with some sour ale. It sat ill on his stomach.

Snores, farts, and drunken mumblings filled the air, the sounds of failures and hangers-on. Some fallen on hard times, and some, like Tallis, men who would never find fame or fortune at court, men who were now too poor to afford a bed or room.

Like Tallis, they were too proud to leave, too proud to go back to wherever they came from with their tail between their legs.

Tallis pressed a withered bunch of herbs to his nose. He'd brought them from home, tucked them into his doublet in a last-minute sentimental gesture. The scent was faint, and not enough to block the noxious odors of the room, but he took comfort from it, all the same.

He checked inside his doublet to see that his precious letter was safe, then, his back propped against a stone pillar, closed his eyes against an unfriendly world and tried to sleep.

CHAPTER TWO

The crowd roared inside the tiltyard. Two huge warhorses carrying knights in full armor—one in black, one in silver—hurtled toward each other down either side of a wooden barrier.

The huge horses thundered faster and faster. The ground shook. Each knight lowered his long wooden lance, aiming at the breastplate or helmet of his opponent. The courtiers and the crowds in the public galleries cheered on their favorite.

Queen Katherine sat under a colored awning watching the spectacle with several of her ladies.

Crash! The black knight's lance shattered against the silver knight's helmet. Splinters of wood flew everywhere. The silver knight crashed to the ground.

The crowd gasped. Waited. The fallen knight lay in the center of the yard, unmoving. Then slowly they saw it, blood bubbling through the eye slits of his helmet. Several men ran toward him. One bent and lifted his head. Blood gushed out beneath it, pooling and soaking into the sand of the tiltyard.

The black knight, victorious, removed his helmet, and the cheers rose again. It was the Duke of Buckingham. He inclined his head graciously toward the spectators' galleries, accepting the applause as his due.

It took three strong men to lift the fallen knight. He groaned as they moved him. A groom kicked fresh sand over the bloodstains, and the jousting started again.

King Henry and his friends Brandon, Knivert, and Compton waited eagerly to enter the list. Henry's armor was magnificent. Descended from a long line of famous warriors, Henry was a king worthy of his blood.

Laughing and joking, they passed the time criticizing the preceding jousts and speculating about the various ladies in the queen's pavilion. Brandon had a particular interest in the newest of the queen's ladies. There was, after all, a bet on.

"Ah, my turn at last," Brandon said, casting a glance at the Queen's Pavilion to see who was watching.

"Good luck, Charles," Compton said.

"I don't need luck, my friend. Not like you do."

Compton grinned. "Have it, anyway."

Knivert laughed and jerked his head in the direction of the ladies. "He always 'has it, anyway.'"

The heralds' horns sounded, and Brandon rode up to the dais on which Katherine and her ladies were sitting. He bowed to the queen. "Your Majesty." Then, deliberately he let his search settle on Lady Jane a moment, pass on . . . and settle on Anna, daughter of the Duke of Buckingham.

"My Lady, would you do me the honor of letting me wear your favors today?"

Anna nodded shyly. She stood up to give Brandon a piece of material dyed with her colors. Without taking his eyes from hers, Brandon tied the material around his arm, then bowed.

He rode away to the lists, well satisfied. Behind him he could hear the ladies whispering and giggling.

At the end of the list, his page handed him his shield, helmet, and lance. Brandon took his place and lowered his visor. Now he could see only a sliver, just enough to see his opponent. It was all he needed. He waited for the signal to start.

Brandon could feel Anna's gaze burning into him. The signal came. He spurred his horse to action and thundered down the list.

* * * *

Far from the roar of the tiltyard, Cardinal Wolsey sat working at his desk. It was piled high with documents.

Affairs of state did not wait for sports and tourneys to be finished. Not that Wolsey had a taste for such things. Jousting was a game for the nobility.

Wolsey had worked hard to get where he was, and the higher he rose, the more work there was to do. He sometimes woke before dawn, at four or five, and worked through the day and late into the night. The king knew it too, and appreciated it.

His secretary knocked. "Eminence, Lady Blount is here."

Wolsey's first reaction was irritation. He had no time for dealing with the whims of the king's mistress. He hesitated. Bessie Blount was no fool. "Very well, show her in."

Lady Blount entered the room and sank into a deep curtsy.

"Your Eminence."

"What can I do for you, Lady Blount?"

She hesitated, twisting a ring around her finger. "I am—with child, Your Eminence."

"So? It is not an unusual state for a woman." Wolsey picked up his quill.

"It is—it is His Majesty's child."

Wolsey put down the quill. He gave her a searching look. "Are you quite certain?"

"Yes."

Wolsey thought for a moment. "Have you told the king?"

She shook her head.

"Good. In due course I will inform His Majesty. But for the time being you will say nothing to anyone—*on pain of death*." He gave her a hard look. "Do you understand?"

She nodded.

"When you can no longer disguise your condition, you will be removed to a private place for your lying-in. There you can give birth to your bastard."

He picked up the quill again. The audience was at an end. "Thank you, Your Eminence."

Wolsey did not respond. He was once more engrossed by his correspondence.

Lady Blount quietly left the chamber and, as the door closed behind her, heaved a sigh of relief. She had been right to seek Wolsey's assistance. She needed someone to help protect the interests of her child. The king had lost all interest in her, and her husband would talk only of locking her away in a nunnery.

It had been worth coming here, even though the queen had been displeased with her for missing the tourney, she told herself.

The crowd roared again as another knight crashed to the ground. Applause rang out as the man was helped to stand and took himself off, bowing mockingly to the crowd.

Henry and his friends were sweaty, dusty, and covered with gore, but their bloodlust was afire and they wanted more.

"Who's next?" Compton asked, craning his neck.

"The black knight—Buckingham," Brandon said.

"What?" Knivert exclaimed. "He's won ten courses already! What's he trying to prove?"

"Let me go against him," Compton pleaded.

"No," said Brandon. "I will. I'd love to damage that man's insufferable pride."

"Out of the way!" Henry ordered, and Brandon drew back as Henry rode into the list.

The crowd hushed. As it always did, the very appearance of the king of England, in armor, on horseback, in the flesh, elicited an audible thrill of excitement.

As he rode over to the dais, Compton leaned closer to Brandon. "What is it between those two?"

Brandon looked around to see who might overhear before he answered. "Buckingham has a better claim to the throne than Henry. And they both know it."

Henry gave a courtly bow to the queen. "My Lady."

Katherine smiled and tied her colors to his arm. As she was tying it, Henry caught Lady Jane's eye. He held her gaze a moment, and she blushed. He gave no sign, but bowed once more to Katherine and cantered back to the end of the list.

His helmet was placed carefully on his head. A servant passed him his shield and lance. He closed the visor and suddenly through the two narrow eye slits he saw his target, Buckingham, a tiny distant figure. Henry's blood, the blood of warriors, quickened.

The Tudor claim to kingship was not based on bloodlines, but on blood. His father had won the throne on the battlefield—Bosworth Field—seized it, and held it, founding a Tudor dynasty that would live forever. If Buckingham had forgotten, he would learn his lesson afresh today. And Henry Tudor, son of the victor of Bosworth Field, would be his tutor.

Henry's horse, also bred for war, caught his mood, snorting and prancing restlessly. At the signal, Henry spurred it to action. The hoofbeats thundered as the horse picked up speed, faster, faster. The crowd roared. The tiltyard became a blur of speed. Henry's sole intense focus was on the tiny slit of light that contained his quarry.

He lowered the tip of the lance, seemingly miles away, and difficult to aim because of its length and weight, and the movement of the horse. His muscles locked and the lance steadied, pointing straight at his foe.

Buckingham's horse hurtled toward him, growing bigger and bigger in the narrow slits of the helmet. Henry stared down the line of the lance and braced himself.

CRASH! There was an explosion of noise. A sickening sound as wood and metal collided. Henry lurched. Something shattered. His helmet rang.

He reeled, steadied himself, and gathered his wits. His lance was shattered. Henry threw it aside. He wrenched his horse around to see what had happened. Buckingham lay sprawled on the ground, ignominiously defeated. The people yelled in delirious celebration.

Henry was their king. Chosen by God to rule over England. Again, a Tudor had emerged victorious.

Henry rode back and watched impassively as Buckingham's pages removed his helmet. There was no blood. Grunting with the effort, they managed to sit him upright. From the dust, Buckingham glared up at Henry, dumb with sullen fury and humiliation.

The king gave him a cold, warning look, then wheeled his horse around and rode off to enjoy his triumph.

Henry sat back in the royal barge and watched England, his England, drift past him. He would be dining with Thomas More en famille at More's home in Chelsea. He much preferred to travel by barge than to brave the dirty and congested London streets.

Thomas More and his family stood at their private landing stage to greet the king. Henry leaped ashore and embraced More. "Thomas." He was fond of his old tutor.

As they strolled in the sun, Henry asked, "Why won't you come and live at court, Thomas?"

"You know perfectly well why: I don't like it. I have my legal practice and my life here. The court is for more ambitious men."

"You didn't say much in council."

"About what?"

"About going to war with France."

After a pause, More said, "As a humanist I have an abhorrence of war. It's an activity fit only for beasts, yet practiced by no kind of beast so constantly as by man."

Henry frowned. "As a humanist, I share your opinion. As a king, I am forced to disagree."

More gave a faint smile. "Spoken like a lawyer."

Henry snorted. "You should know. You taught me!"

"Not well enough, it seems."

Henry playfully grabbed More around the neck. "Are you finished?" Laughing, More admitted that he was. Henry let him go, and walked on ahead.

"Harry!" More called out, and hurried to catch up. "No, I'm not finished. Instead of spending ruinous amounts of money on war, I think you should spend it on the welfare of your people."

Henry looked at him. "Thomas, I swear to you, I intend to be a just ruler. But tell me this: Where's the *glory* in education and welfare? Why is Henry V remembered? Because he endowed universities and built alms houses for the destitute?"

Henry made an emphatic gesture. "No! It's because he won the Battle of Agincourt. Three thousand English bowmen against sixty thousand French! The flower of French chivalry destroyed in just four hours!" He looked at More. "That victory made him famous, Thomas. It made him *immortal*!"

The court was crowded, and getting noisier by the minute. They'd feasted well and drunk even better. The dukes of Buckingham and Norfolk stood to one side, observing. Buckingham drained a goblet and held it out to be refilled. "He has no right to any of this," he told Norfolk, his speech slightly slurred. "His father seized the crown on the battlefield; he had no real claim to it, only through a bastard on his mother's side."

Norfolk said in a soothing tone, "Your Grace's family is more ancient."

Buckingham nodded emphatically. "We are. I am a direct descendant of Edward II. It is *my* crown, and this is *my* court. Not *his* crown, or *his* court."

Horrified, Norfolk looked around. "Lower your voice! That's treason, Your Grace."

"But it's true, isn't it, Norfolk? It's the truth. And one day we shall make it come true." He looked at Norfolk.

Norfolk said nothing.

Buckingham moved off, followed by a small entourage of his followers. As they walked through the court, courtiers bowed and made way for him. One or two even leaned forward to kiss his hand. He made an impressive figure, a living portrait of a king-in-waiting.

He passed from the court and made his way to his private apartments. As he opened the door he could hear in an adjoining room the very loud, unmistakable sounds of a couple in the throes of lovemaking.

He strode to the door and flung it open. There, on his bed, was that swine, the king's low-born companion, Brandon, naked and bucking atop Buckingham's own daughter, Anna.

With a howl of rage, Buckingham drew his sword.

Brandon rolled off Anna, then froze as the point of a sword touched his throat.

"What is this?" Buckingham snarled.

"This is what it looks like, Your Grace," Brandon replied coolly.

Buckingham pressed the point a little deeper. "You have violated my daughter."

"No. No, she begged." Brandon gave him an insolent look.

"You've taken her honor!"

"I swear to Your Grace I have not. Someone else was there first." At that, there was a muffled giggle from the bed.

Buckingham almost exploded with rage. "Son of a whore!"

Brandon gave an indifferent shrug. "Yes, that's true, Your Grace."

Balked and frustrated, Buckingham lowered his sword. "Get out!"

Brandon left. Buckingham walked over to the bed. Anna crouched there, waiting, knowing what would follow, ice-pale and terrified.

"Look at me," he growled.

Anna looked up. Her father stared down at her for a long, long moment, then hit her as hard as he could across the face. Blood spurted from her nose.

Holding an orange hollowed out with spices and herbs to his nose to protect himself against the stench of humanity, Cardinal Wolsey proceeded through the palace. Petitioners swarmed around him. His servants pushed them back.

His usher walked in front, shouting, "Make way for His Lord's Grace. Make way there!"

The petitioners called out, "Eminence, I beg you, read my petition!"

Standing among the petitioners, starved, and feeling quite ill, Thomas Tallis watched hopelessly as the cardinal stopped to talk with Mr. Pace, the King's secretary.

"I trust you are keeping a good eye on my interests, Mr. Pace?" Wolsey said.

"Of course, Your Eminence. Like an eagle."

Wolsey raised an eyebrow. "I don't want an eagle, Mr. Pace. They can soar too high." He added with a shrewd look, "Be a pigeon: Shit on everything!"

Pace gave a quick smile. "Yes, Eminence."

Wolsey moved on. "Where is the king?"

"Out hunting."

"Good. It keeps him in good humor. Send word when he returns."

"Yes, Eminence." Pace bowed as Wolsey walked away. The petitioners continued to call out. Pace's gaze wandered dispassionately over the men calling out to him, then he stopped. His gaze returned to a thin, drawn, pale young man.

Tallis felt his heart stop in his chest. Mr. Pace was staring straight at him. As if he recognized him. He stared dumbly as the king's secretary lifted a hand and beckoned.

Tallis stumbled forward.

Mr. Pace looked him up and down. "You've been here a long time. What is it you want?"

Tallis fumbled inside his shirt. "I—I have letters of introduction, sir. I—" He pulled them out and handed them over.

Mr. Pace glanced at them, frowned, and examined them more closely. He looked up. "But—these are from the Dean of Canterbury Cathedral!"

"Yes, sir."

Pace regarded him a moment, then shook his head. "Come with me." Ignoring the pleading calls of the other petitioners, he led Tallis to the Chapel Royal, where a group of young choristers was rehearsing under the guidance of a grizzled, elderly man. Pace nudged Tallis. "That is the choirmaster, Mr. William Cornish."

Tallis nodded. The music was sublime, the harmony of pure, perfect notes filling the hushed chapel with glory. Tallis's battered soul soaked it up like balm.

They stood and listened for a few minutes. Suddenly, to Tallis's horror, Mr. Pace cleared his throat, very loudly.

Irritated, William Cornish looked around. Seeing the King's secretary waiting, he stopped the rehearsal and came over.

"Mr. Pace, what can I do for you?"

"This young man has letters of introduction. From the Dean of Canterbury Cathedral."

William Cornish took the letters and examined them. As he read, his eyebrows rose. Finally he peered at Tallis over the top of the letters. "Thomas Tallis."

"Yes, sir."

"And you play, it says, the organ and flute, and can sing more than moderately well."

Tallis nodded and felt himself flushing.

"Anything else?" William Cornish asked.

Thomas swallowed. "Yes, sir. I—I compose a little."

Cornish's brows rose again. "Indeed? Well, if the dean commends your talents—we shall have to see. . . ."

The moon rose over London, turning the city into a place of silver and shadows. In the king's private outer chamber, Henry met with Cardinal Wolsey and Thomas More to discuss the preparations for the war. Even after a day's vigorous exercise, Henry had energy to spare. He strolled about the room, munching on an apple.

"I trust Your Majesty enjoyed good hunting today," Wolsey said.

Henry nodded amiably. "How are the preparations going?"

"Very well. Both your army and fleet are assembling. Provisions and stores are being laid in. You could go to war in a matter of weeks."

"Excellent! I knew I could depend on you. When have you ever failed me?"

Wolsey inclined his head. "I am grateful to Your Majesty. There is just—" He broke off, looking faintly troubled.

The king stopped. "What is it?"

With the air of someone delivering a reluctant truth, Wolsey said, "Your Majesty, wars are expensive. To pay for them, you must raise taxes. That's not always popular."

There was a pause in which the names of Richard Empson and Edmund Dudley hung silently in the air. Henry's father had brought a battered kingdom to a state of prosperity by a program of rigorous taxation. Empson and Dudley were the ministers who'd carried out this taxation program. They had been hated by the people.

One of Henry's first actions when he succeeded to the throne at the age of eighteen was to have Empson and Dudley executed, he forgot on what charge.

It had made him immensely popular.

Wolsey continued, "What if Your Majesty could gain more glory and prestige by other means?"

Henry gave him a shrewd look. "Other means?"

"Peaceful means."

Henry pulled a face. "What! No battles? No glory?"

"I think Your Majesty should hear him out," More said.

Reluctantly Henry threw himself in a chair. "Go ahead, then."

Wolsey explained. "In the last few weeks, on Your Majesty's behalf, I have conducted an intense round of diplomatic talks. Not just with the French ambassador, also with representatives of the emperor, and envoys from the Italian States, Portugal, Denmark—"

"What for?"

"To make a treaty."

"What kind of treaty?" Henry demanded, looking anything but happy.

More stepped in. "It's a new kind of treaty. Something never before envisaged."

Henry's brows rose. "Which is?"

Wolsey took a deep breath. "A Treaty of Universal and Perpetual Peace."

Henry, despite himself, was intrigued. "A Treaty of Universal and Perpetual Peace." He rose from his chair and resumed his pacing. "How is such a thing to be effected?"

Wolsey answered. "In several stages. In the first place there will be a summit meeting between the kings of France and England. During the summit, Your Majesty's daughter will be formally betrothed to the French dauphin. And at the end of the summit, you will both sign the treaty."

More added, "The treaty will be quite new in the history of Europe, committing all its signatories to the principle of collective security and universal peace."

Henry's quick mind was spinning. "How would it be enforced?"

Wolsey answered. "Should any of the signatory countries suffer aggression, all the others would immediately demand that the aggressor withdraw. If he refuses, within one month all the rest would declare against him, and continue until peace is restored."

"The treaty also envisages the creation of pan-European institutions," More added.

Henry's pacing picked up speed. "In some ways I like this! I know what it is. I recognize it. . . ." He looked at More. "And so do you, Thomas."

More nodded. "Yes, Henry. It's the application of humanist principles to international affairs." He turned to Wolsey. "Your Eminence is to be congratulated."

Wolsey spread his hands in a gesture of humility. "I don't seek praise. Your Majesty will be seen as the architect of a new and modern world. For me, that will be reward enough."

Henry embraced him. "Always, *always*, be assured of our love."

Wolsey smiled. Henry, in good spirits, was clapping More on the back when a nervous groom entered.

"What is it?" Henry asked, displeased with the interruption.

"Your Majesty, the Duke of Buckingham insists upon an immediate audience."

Henry pulled a face, then reluctantly gave his assent. Wolsey gave a low bow and began to withdraw, but Buckingham, not prepared to wait, pushed rudely past him and strode into the room. He flicked a disdainful glance at Wolsey, as if he were something the dog had brought in, then, when Wolsey had left, he turned to the king.

"Your Grace," Henry said coolly.

"Your Majesty ought to be made aware that I have discovered Mr. Charles Brandon in flagrante delecto with my daughter!"

Henry arched an eyebrow. "And you interfered?"

There was a shocked silence. The duke's face spasmed, puce with ill-controlled rage. "Mr. Brandon has brought shame to my family. I demand that Your Majesty banish him from court—with whatever other punishment Your Majesty sees fit." He stood toe-to-toe with the king, glaring belligerently.

The king said coldly, "There will be no punishment. Unless your daughter accuses Mr. Brandon of raping her." He eyed the duke shrewdly. "Does she so claim?"

There was no response. Buckingham visibly struggled with his anger.

Henry repeated in a hard voice, "Does she claim that Mr. Brandon raped her against her will?"

"She doesn't need to! The offense is against me and against my family!"

Henry shrugged. "As far as I know, there has been no offense. Therefore no need for any punishment."

Buckingham's breathing was audible. He seemed about to explode, but managed to collect himself enough to give a short, jerky bow. "Majesty," he ground out, and stalked from the room.

Henry watched him leave, a faint smile on his face.

Thomas More emerged from the shadows. "Be careful of Buckingham, Harry," he said quietly. "He may well be stupid, but he is richer than you are, and he can call upon a private army." He added, "Even your father never crossed him."

Henry turned and gave him a long, inscrutable look.

Later that night, in the shadowy corridors of the court, Wolsey was walking in company with Bishop Bonnivet, speaking quietly where no ears could hear and no eyes could spy.

"I'm very happy that the king of France has agreed to sign the treaty and host the summit," Wolsey told the bishop.

Bonnivet spread his hands in a gallic gesture. "His Majesty is delighted there will be no war. As we all are."

"And what about the other matter we spoke of?"

After a moment, Bonnivet responded, "Which 'other matter,' Your Eminence?"

Patent disingenuousness. Wolsey seized the bishop around the neck and slammed him against the wall like an insect. The bishop choked, his eyes bulging with shock.

In his ear, Wolsey hissed, "I saved your master's arse. I want my reward. And you can arrange it. Do you understand?" He banged the bishop against the wall again.

Unable to speak, the bishop nodded.

At the same time, the English ambassador to the court of France, Sir Thomas Boleyn, was responding to an invitation to visit the Duke of Buckingham in his private rooms within the palace.

He walked through the duke's heavily gilded rooms, each one more lavishly and ostentatiously decorated than the last, escorted by one of Buckingham's retainers, a man called Hopkins. Boleyn noted the display of princely wealth. And thus, power.

In one room he saw a pretty young girl with a bandage over her nose, reading a book. Buckingham's daughter, Boleyn thought, but what had happened to her face? Seeing his regard, she turned away self-consciously.

Hopkins beckoned to Boleyn and showed him into a room.

"Your Grace, Sir Thomas Boleyn."

Buckingham, dressed magnificently in a slashed and embroidered doublet of silk and velvet, jewels sparkling all over his person, greeted him with a languid gesture. "Sir Thomas, I hope you didn't find my invitation presumptuous. I heard you had been recalled from France."

"I'm here for a short while, Your Grace," Boleyn said.

"They tell me you are an excellent ambassador."

"Then, whoever they are, they are very kind."

Buckingham dismissed his servants. After the door had closed behind them, he said, "You come from an old family."

Boleyn acknowledged the compliment. "Indeed. Though not as ancient, or as grand, as Your Grace's."

Buckingham, clearly pleased, waved the compliment aside. "Nevertheless, we have much in common. I understand—" He paused significantly. "I understand you dislike parvenus and upstarts as much as I do."

Boleyn knew who Buckingham meant. He responded cautiously, "I— I think I might follow Your Grace's argument."

Buckingham nodded. "The king chooses to surround himself with commoners, men of no distinction, new men, without pedigree or titles. How does that help the prestige of his crown?"

Boleyn was in dangerous waters. And walls had ears. "Your Grace, I—"

Buckingham made a scornful gesture. "His father only acquired the crown by force—not by *right*!"

Boleyn said carefully, "Your Grace, no one wants to return to the evil days of civil war. What is done is done. The king is the king."

For a long moment Buckingham scrutinized Boleyn's face, then he gave a faint nod. "And Wolsey is his handmaiden! The son of a butcher! A man of the cloth with a mistress and two children! Tell me, Boleyn, how do you like this fellow?"

Boleyn was relieved to be let off the hook. It was one thing to talk open treason, another to criticize Cardinal Wolsey. "Not at all," he said.

Buckingham smiled and rubbed his hands together. "Then, together, we shall destroy him!"

Chapter Three

The arrangements for the Treaty of Universal and Perpetual Peace were moving ahead apace. And Henry deemed it time to write personally to his cousin, Francis, King of France. As his barber shaved him in his private chambers Henry dictated a letter to his secretary, Richard Pace.

"My dearest royal cousin . . . No. Make that *My beloved* cousin. We send you our love. We love you so much, it would be impossible to love you better." He caught Pace's eye and saw the hint of a smile.

"Let us make all necessary arrangements so we may meet face-to-face. Nothing is now closer and dearer to my heart than this Treaty of Universal Peace."

Henry paused, angling his head to allow the barber to shave under his chin. "As a token of my goodwill, my commitment to this treaty, and my love for Your Majesty, I have decided—"

The king stroked his clean-shaven jaw, thought for a moment, and dictated, "I have decided not to shave again until we meet. My beard will be a token of universal friendship, of the love between us." He caught Pace's eye again and laughed.

Bishop Bonnivet arrived at Hampton Court Palace, Cardinal Wolsey's home, big with news. He came straight to the point. "I have some news for Your Eminence. His Holiness, Pope Alexander, is desperately ill. It cannot be long before he is summoned to God's House."

"How very dreadful," Wolsey said smoothly, and crossed himself. "Let us pray." He bowed his head for a moment and, when he had finished, looked at Bonnivet.

The bishop, feeling like a mouse being eyed by an owl, said hastily, "In view of Your Eminence's well-known piety, as well as your great learning and diplomatic skills, I can assure Your Eminence of the support of the French cardinals at the conclave to elect a successor."

Wolsey affected an expression of faint, gratified surprise.

Bonnivet finished, "With the votes of your own cardinals—and if it is pleasing to God—you will be elected pope, Bishop of Rome, our new Holy Father."

The muscles of Wolsey's face barely moved, but somehow he exuded total satisfaction. He crossed himself devoutly again, saying, "Thank you, Your Grace. You make me feel truly humble."

Queen Katherine was in a strange, somber mood. She stood in her apartments, being undressed by two of her ladies, Lady Blount and Lady Jane. The queen must always speak first, and tonight, since she didn't speak, they disrobed her in silence. The two ladies were somewhat relieved by the queen's silence; both had lain with the king. The question was, did Katherine know?

They removed first the detachable oversleeves of heavily embroidered brocade, then the undersleeves of patterned velvet. Lady Jane unlaced her bodice, then Lady Blount removed it. As the queen stepped out of the velvet overskirt, she rested her hand lightly on Lady Jane's shoulder for balance. As Lady Jane crouched to lift the skirt, Katherine stared down into the fresh young bosom, then averted her eyes.

Lady Blount unlaced Katherine's tight corset, and slipped it from her body. She bent to remove the queen's slippers and then rolled down her stockings.

Lady Jane waited for the queen to lift her arms and don her nightgown. She'd seen the expression in the queen's eyes as she watched Lady Blount. The queen gave her a sharp look, and Lady Jane blushed.

The two ladies collected the petticoats and began to fold them. Suddenly Lady Blount gasped and put a hand to her belly. A sudden cramp.

Katherine noticed. "Are you ill, Lady Blount?"

"No, Your Majesty. I shall send these to the laundress, shall I?" She made to leave.

"No, stay," said the queen.

Lady Blount froze.

"Kneel beside me, Lady Blount. Lady Jane, you may leave." Lady Blount knelt beside the queen and waited.

After what seemed like forever, Katherine gave a heavy sigh. "Lady Blount, I have not talked to anyone for a long time. Cardinal Wolsey dismissed my Spanish confessor and most of my Spanish ladies, in case they were spies. And I cannot trust my English confessor."

She fiddled with her rosary. "I can trust you, though, can I not, Lady Blount?"

"Yes, madam."

Katherine sighed again. "Do you know something: If I had to choose between two extremes, I would always choose extreme sadness rather than extreme happiness. Does that shock you?"

It did, but Lady Blount remained silent.

"You may ask, what is my sadness?" the queen continued. "It is this: that I cannot give the king a living son. That is my pity. That is my suffering."

Lady Blount swallowed.

The queen went on. "I once gave birth to a baby boy, a sweet boy, who died in my arms, after just four weeks of life." Her voice cracked. "The king blames me, I know. He does not know how much I suffer, how much I pray. . . ." She looked down at Lady Blount, her face shining with tears. "And now he does not come to my bed. Not for one year! He does not come because he thinks me repulsive!"

Lady Blount's eyes filled with sympathetic tears.

"Look at me! Am I not old? Am I not fat and repulsive?" Katherine railed in self-loathing.

"Gentle madam, no," Lady Blount said softly.

At that, Katherine broke down, weeping bitter, scalding tears. Lady Blount could not bear to watch. She could not even put her arms around the queen. It was not seemly.

And her own guilt gnawed at her.

She lowered her eyes and said no more. The queen sobbed. They were both trapped, powerless. It was always so for women.

"My son, my daughters, have you finished your reading?" Thomas More had shocked society by educating his daughters to the same level as his son—even teaching them to read and write in Greek and Latin.

"Yes, Father." More's adolescent children—four by his first wife, and one stepdaughter—came forward to bid their father good night.

Smiling, he embraced each in turn. "God and His angels bless you and keep you this night, and always."

Alice curtsied to her husband, and ushered her children out of the room. She turned back, hesitating.

"God be with you, Alice. Sleep well," he said, and she left the room. More then entered his own private closet. The small room looked more like a monk's spartan cell than a bedroom. There was an iron cot, a wooden table, a washstand, and nothing else. A large silver crucifix dominated the room, glowing in the candlelight.

He removed his jacket, doublet, and his white lawn shirt. Beneath it he wore a hair shirt. He never took it off, except when he whipped himself. The hair shirt was filthy and lice-ridden. The skin around it was lacerated and raw with weeping wounds.

But the flesh was weak, and must be mortified for the sake of the soul. More knelt to pray.

King Henry's thoughts had also turned to prayer. In his private chapel in the palace, he sat slumped in the small, dark confessional. He looked troubled.

Through the carved wooden screen, the priest waited for him to speak. And waited.

Finally Henry spoke. "I have been thinking about my brother, Arthur. He died. Of a fever. He'd only been married for six months."

He was silent for a long moment. In the chapel a candle guttered.

"My brother was married to my wife! When he died, it was decided that I should marry her. I think my father didn't want to lose the dowry. Or the prestige of a Spanish marriage."

He fiddled with his rosary beads. "In any case, Katherine swore that her marriage to Arthur had never been consummated, that he was too weak and ill. That's why a papal dispensation was granted giving us permission to wed."

In the darkness, Henry could hear the soft, close breathing of the priest.

"So I married her. And since then she has had five stillborn children, a boy who lived for just six-and-twenty days, and a single living daughter." He bent over, gripping his head in his hand as if in pain. The priest waited.

"What if she lied? What if their marriage was consummated?" His voice was anguished.

The priest said, "She has sworn before God that it was not."

"But I have just heard a different story. From a servant of Arthur's, who was there! He says that in the morning my brother left the bed-chamber in good spirits. He said, 'I need a drink. Last night I was in the midst of Spain!'"

His words seemed to hang in the silence. The priest said nothing, but shifted uncomfortably.

"What does it say in the Gospels? If a man should marry his brother's wife . . ." Henry banged his hand on the wood of the confessional, making the priest jump. "Tell me!"

"In Leviticus it says: 'If a man marries his brother's wife, they will die childless. He has done a ritually unclean thing.'"

Henry clenched his fists. The priest continued, "But you *have* a child."

"But not a *son*! Not a son. Can you not see that it is Divine Justice for my offense against God!" He rested his head bleakly against the wooden screen, then banged it in frustration.

Henry strode through the court accompanied by a gaggle of courtiers and servants. The doors to the queen's private chambers opened, and a pretty, dark-haired little girl of about six emerged with her governess. Henry's eyes lit up.

The child and the governess both curtsied formally, but with a great roar of delight he swept the little girl up in his arms and swung her around, laughing, showing her off.

"This is my daughter, Mary! Isn't she beautiful? Tell me! Isn't she—so—bea-u-ti-ful?" He kissed her with each word.

"Papa! Papa!" Mary smiled and kissed him back enthusiastically, much to everyone's delight.

Katherine appeared at Henry's elbow. "May we talk?"

Henry handed his daughter back to her governess. "Good-bye, sweetheart. Be good. Do everything you are told." He followed Katherine into the queen's private chambers.

She said abruptly. "I don't like it, Henry."

He frowned. "What don't you like?"

"Your beard."

He grinned ruefully and rubbed his hand across his stubble-covered chin, the result of several days' growth.

In a tight voice Katherine added, "Nor do I like what it means."

"Now, Katherine," Henry warned her, all amusement gone from his face.

"You are giving my daughter away to the dauphin and to France! You did not even consult me. The Valois are the sworn enemies of my family!"

Henry stiffened. "She is mine to do with as I see fit. It is a great marriage."

"It is *not*! She is marrying into a cesspit! I see Wolsey's hand behind this!" With difficulty she reined in her anger, and in a low, intense voice said, "Though I love Your Majesty, and am in every way loyal to you, I cannot disguise my distress and unhappiness."

Henry regarded her frigidly. "I am afraid you will have to."

The plans for the summit were continuing apace. It was to be a huge endeavor. Each country was hoping to outdo the other in magnificence.

In his private chambers, Henry was playing chess with Sir Thomas Boleyn, his ambassador to France. The game was well advanced.

Henry moved his bishop to threaten Boleyn's queen and sat back in his favorite, heavily carved chair. "Tell me about King Francis, Sir Thomas," he asked.

"He is twenty-three years old, Majesty," Boleyn replied.

Henry raised his brows. "He is younger than me."

Boleyn smiled. "Your Majesty would not think so, to look at him."

Henry looked pleased. He glanced at the board and moved one of his knights.

"Aha . . ." Boleyn nodded. It was a good move. He leaned over the board, contemplating his options.

Henry continued "Is he tall?"

"Yes." Boleyn's hand hovered over a piece. "But ill-proportioned." He moved a pawn.

"How about his legs? Has he got strong calves, like mine?"

Boleyn looked up. "Majesty, no one has calves like yours!"

Henry laughed, and brought up his queen. "Check! Is he handsome?"

Boleyn moved his king to safety. "Some people might think so. He certainly thinks so himself."

"He's vain?" Henry inquired eagerly.

Boleyn gave him a dry look. "Your Majesty—he's *French*!" They both laughed. Henry moved his bishop to attack.

Henry asked, "What about his court?"

Boleyn pursed his lips. "It has a reputation for loose morals and licentiousness, which the king, by his own behavior, does nothing to dispel." He countered Henry's bishop with an aggressive move by his own queen.

"Good move! Very good! You mean Francis himself encourages such behavior?"

"Majesty, it is openly said that Francis has such slight morals that he slips readily into the gardens of others and, er, drinks the waters of many fountains."

Henry glanced at him, then took Boleyn's rook. "You have two daughters. How do you protect them?"

"I keep a watchful eye on them. But I also trust in their goodness and virtue." He moved a pawn to block the bishop.

"You will return immediately to Paris," Henry told him. "I am entrusting you with all the diplomatic negotiations for the summit."

Boleyn inclined his head. "Thank you, Majesty."

Henry moved his knight. "Checkmate, Sir Thomas."

Boleyn flung up his hands. "You are too skilled a player for me! An excellent game, Majesty."

"You asked to see me, Eminence," Thomas More greeted Cardinal Wolsey in his home, Hampton Court Palace.

"I did. To talk about the summit. Come, let us walk together." He and More strolled through the beautifully decorated rooms. "And since you have been appointed the king's principal secretary while you are both in France . . ."

More inclined his head. "I believe I must thank Your Eminence for my appointment."

Wolsey acknowledged the debt, but hurried on. There was a great deal to be done. "It is vital that His Majesty does as he is told. I have drafted rules governing all matters of precedent and etiquette. They are to be observed *at all times*."

More nodded.

Wolsey continued: "It has also been agreed that in order to preserve the honor of both nations, neither king will take part in any joust or combat."

More gave a wry smile. The king would not be very happy about that. "I see. So what *can* the king do?"

Wolsey lifted a cautionary finger. "Never say so. You must always tell the king what he *ought* to do, not what he *can* do."

There was a short silence. Wolsey stopped and fixed him with a look of deadly seriousness. "You see, Thomas, if the Lion ever discovers his true strength, then no man will be able to control him."

The English ambassador, Sir Thomas Boleyn, had just returned to his Parisian mansion. He summoned his daughters, Mary and Anne. They were eager to hear about his trip.

"I have exciting news," he told them. "There is to be a summit between King Francis and King Henry near Calais." He paused and added, "And I am to arrange it."

The girls clapped their hands with excitement. "Papa, that is wonderful!"

"That means you will both have the opportunity to meet . . . the king of England!" Boleyn observed his daughters with a dispassionate eye. Mary, the oldest, was by far the prettiest. Anne was not as pretty, but what she lacked in beauty she more than made up for in cleverness. His eyes darted between them, assessing . . . surmising.

Each in her own way would play their part in furthering the cause of family promotion. What else were daughters for?

He poured out some wine for them and raised his glass to his prettiest daughter. "Mary."

He gave her a long, significant look, then added, "And Anne." He smiled knowingly and brought the glass to his lips. *"Salut!"*

Back in London, Henry was selecting a new wardrobe to be made especially for the summit. His private chambers swarmed with tailors and tailors' assistants, as well as the usual crowd of courtiers.

Henry looked eagerly through mounds of clothing and accessories. He had the reputation of the best-dressed sovereign in Europe and was eager to maintain it. The fabrics were beautiful, expensive, and richly colored. There were doublets, jackets, robes, coats, cloaks, and mantles made of silk, satin, and deeply slashed velvet. They were embroidered with gold and silver thread, and finished with furs such as sable, ermine, or miniver. Many were decorated with real jewels, some so heavily encrusted with gold work, diamonds, amethysts, and rubies that the fabric beneath was barely visible. In the midst of the chaos, a servant announced, "His Eminence Cardinal Wolsey."

Wolsey entered and bowed. "Majesty."

"Good! I want your opinion." Henry gestured him over. "Do you like this cloth?" From a pile of clothing he lifted a magnificent suit of cloth-of-gold and silver, and held it against himself.

Wolsey, a man of acknowledged taste, studied the effect through narrowed eyes. "It suits Your Majesty well. May I suggest you wear these with it?" He picked out some accessories carefully: gloves, shoes, chain, and an over-jacket lined with black fur.

"Excellent!" Henry said, pleased. "Do you think Francis will have anything as fine as these?"

"Only if he steals them."

Henry laughed, clapping Wolsey on the back. "Come. Let's eat together. We can talk." They strode from the room, all the courtiers and servants bowing as they passed.

There were even more people in the next, larger chamber, where the dining table was laid and the food ready to be served.

The Duke of Buckingham stood waiting, his face a mask of cold impassivity. He was to hold the silver basin for the king to wash his hands in. His mind still full of the new clothes, Henry absentmindedly dipped his fingers into the basin, then turned away to dry them.

Buckingham was about to take the basin away, when Wolsey said, "Hold a moment," and put his own fingers into the basin.

Buckingham's face reddened as he swelled with outrage. Bad enough that he, the scion of one of the most ancient and most noble families in the land, the man who by rights should be king, should have to wait on Henry

Tudor like a servant, but to be holding the basin for a butcher's son!

He tipped the whole basin of water over Wolsey's shoes.

Everyone froze. There was a shocked silence in the room.

"Your Grace will apologize," said the king.

Buckingham didn't move.

The king repeated in a hard voice, "I said, you will apologize."

The silence stretched. Not a soul in the room seemed to move or breathe. Buckingham's face was working, almost purple. The veins on his neck stood out with the physical effort to bring his rage under control.

Eventually he managed to grind out the words. "I—I apologize if I have offended Your Majesty."

There was a tense hush, then the king gave a small nod and the whole room exhaled.

"Your Grace may leave us," Henry said in a hard voice.

Buckingham gave a stiff bow and withdrew.

Henry looked at one of his grooms and snapped his fingers. "Fetch the chancellor a pair of shoes!" The groom ran off.

They sat down at the table, wine was poured, and the food was served. Henry, acting as if the incident had never happened, seemed in great spirits. He turned to Wolsey. "Tell me, Chancellor, how go the preparations for my summit?"

"Everything is ready, Majesty. It will take place in the Pale of Calais—which, as you know, is English territory—in a valley known as the Val d'Or—the Valley of Gold."

Henry, chewing on a leg of pheasant, nodded.

Wolsey went on. "A thousand laborers have constructed a palace there for Your Majesty. They have called it the Palace of Illusions. Some say it is the eighth wonder of the world!"

He addressed himself to his food, and the rest of the table buzzed with the news, exchanging gossip and speculation. Valley of Gold! Palace of Illusions! The eighth wonder of the world—how exciting!

Under cover of the chatter, Wolsey leaned closer to the king and said, "Lady Blount is with child."

Henry frowned and gave him a sharp look. "Lady Blount?"

Wolsey nodded. "She came to see me. She is carrying Your Majesty's child."

Henry picked up his glass and drank from it.

"If you want her to keep the child," Wolsey continued in a low voice, "I will arrange for her to be moved to the house at Jericho. I will also deal with her husband."

The king said nothing, which meant tacit approval.

Lady Blount dealt with, Henry moved on. "I can't wait for this summit; it will change the world forever."

"That is my dearest hope. My ultimate belief."

Henry nodded. "Nothing will ever be the same. You and I will be immortal."

Wolsey dipped his head, humbly.

Buckingham stormed into his private apartments, slamming the door behind him. His rage had only grown. His humiliation at the hands of Henry Tudor and the butcher's son was the last straw!

"Hopkins!" he shouted.

His servant, Hopkins, hurried to his side. "Your guests are here, Your Grace," he said, indicating an inner chamber.

Buckingham nodded, took a deep breath, mastered his fury, then stepped into the room. Awaiting him were the Duke of Norfolk, Sir Thomas Boleyn, and two other councillors.

Buckingham met each man's gaze. "The time is ripe," he told them.

He turned to Hopkins. "Listen! You are to purchase as much cloth of gold and silver as you can find. It is a better thing to bribe the guards with."

"Yes, Your Grace."

"Then I want you to proceed to our estates and do as we discussed, just making some noise that we're only raising men to defend ourselves."

"Yes, Your Grace."

Buckingham picked up a thin dagger from his table and stared at it.

After a long pause he said, "My father once told me how he had planned to assassinate Richard III."

Abruptly, he seized hold of Hopkins with a rough hand. He stared at him malevolently, as if Hopkins had turned into Richard III.

In a soft, savage voice Buckingham continued: "He would come before him, with a knife secreted about his person."

He suddenly dropped to his knees before Hopkins. The knife was now hidden among the folds of his clothes.

"Your Majesty!" Buckingham purred.

Hopkins tried valiantly to play his part in the charade and moved to raise Buckingham, but there was real fear in his eyes. Norfolk, Boleyn, and the two councillors shifted uneasily, watching with growing alarm.

Then, with an abrupt, savage movement Buckingham rose and thrust the dagger into Hopkins's chest!

Boleyn made a sharp sound. The others gasped. For a long moment nobody moved.

Then Buckingham opened his hand. It was empty. He shook his sleeve, and the dagger dropped out. Buckingham grinned maniacally into Hopkins's shocked face, lifted the dagger—and stabbed it into the table.

CHAPTER FOUR

Val d'Or (the Valley of Gold) in English-occupied Calais, France
Henry's horse breasted the grassy ridge first. Flanked by yeomen of the Guard, and under the banner of the Lion Rampant, he was followed by his courtiers and great nobles, led by Buckingham, Boleyn, and Norfolk.

Below them in the valley was a truly fantastical sight: Spread over a grassy green valley lay a vision; a city of brightly painted tents—small tents colored green, blue, or red, and trimmed with gold; pavilions and marquees adorned with the king's badges, or painted with heraldic beasts. Pennants and brilliantly colored banners fluttered in the breeze. Called the Field of the Cloth of Gold because of the huge amount of cloth-of-gold used, in the center of all stood a fairy-tale palace: the Palace of Illusions.

Wolsey and his assistants had seen to everything: It had taken six thousand laborers and craftsmen three months to prepare the site.

There were cooking tents and dining tents—Henry's own dining hall was a huge tent made of cloth-of-gold, and contained his privy kitchen. There were enormous bread ovens and specialist kitchens—a wafery, a pastry house, huge cauldrons, and spit roasts. Enormous quantities of foodstuffs had been transported there—more than two thousand sheep, a thousand chickens, calves, deer, beef cattle, a dozen herons, thirteen swans, thousands of fish and eels, bushels of spices, mountains of sugar, and gallons of cream, not to mention vast quantities of wine and beer. It was all necessary—more than five thousand people had accompanied the king from England.

There were chapels, even a tiltyard, and gardens and pathways with statues and fountains. And in the center, with banners fluttering in the breeze, sat the pièce de résistance—the Palace of Illusions, a large canvas palace, constructed purely for the summit.

"The Valley of Gold," Henry announced.

The French had nothing half as splendid: They were housed in a small town of four hundred small tents, also made of cloth-of-gold with a few large pavilions.

Henry surveyed the scene with satisfaction. Everything was set for his historical triumph. As they watched, riders appeared on the ridge opposite. The Fleur-de-Lys fluttered above them. Compton pointed. "Your Majesty, look! The French."

At the head of a party made up of Swiss Guards and his own courtiers rode Francis, King of France: tall, young, dark and handsome, despite the famous long nose.

The two parties stared across at each other, warily. The echo of generations of enmity hung in the air between them.

"What is the plan?" Compton asked.

"I am to ride down alone to meet Francis."

The French began to descend through the trees in files.

"What if it's a trap?" Knivert said quietly. "What if they mean to lure you down there and kill you?"

Henry's banner flapped noisily in the breeze. Henry stared across at Francis, ignoring Knivert's statement, then urged his horse forward. "Stay here! All of you!" he shouted. "On pain of death! Stay!"

He rode out alone as Francis and his guards emerged from the trees.

The king's companions watched edgily, then heaved a sigh of relief as Francis galloped away from his guards and met Henry alone, at the entrance to the magnificent French pavilion. Buckingham tightened his jaw with ill-concealed disappointment.

*   *   *   *

That afternoon, the first of the formal receptions began in the French camp, which was situated at some distance from the English. It was a glamorous affair. The inside of the pavilion was lined with blue velvet embroidered with fleurs-de-lys. The French sat on one side, and the English on the other. All were dressed in their finest, most expensive clothes, displaying their most ostentatious jewels; a war of a different sort.

No one dazzled more than the two kings. Henry, dressed in cloth-of-gold, gorgeously embroidered and ablaze with precious jewels, sat directly across from Francis, dressed in blue velvet embroidered in gold and silver thread, also laden with jewels.

Alongside Henry sat Queen Katherine, Wolsey, More, and other members of English nobility. Francis sat with his beautiful young wife, Queen Claude, and several dukes and princes of the church.

Trumpets sounded. An English herald proclaimed, "Hear ye! Hear ye! I, Henry, by the Grace of God, King of England, Ireland, and France, do hereby—"

"Stop!" Henry said loudly. He looked at Francis. "I cannot be that while you are here, for I would be a liar. So during this summit I am simply Henry, King of England." He smiled, and applause rippled through the pavilion.

"And I am just Francis, King of France—and Burgundy," said Francis instantly. The audience applauded, and, like two fencers circling each other, the two kings exchanged smiles.

Cardinal Wolsey stepped forward. "Your Majesties, may I ask you each to place a hand upon the Holy Bible, and swear before God and these princes and lords here gathered, that you will be true, virtuous, and loving to each other." He held out a large, gold-tooled Bible. Henry and Francis placed their hands upon it simultaneously.

"I so swear." Henry declared.

"Oh, I swear too. Of course," his cousin added. The audience applauded; the two kings smiled, embraced each other again, and moved away.

Wolsey said, "And now the queens' majesties."

Katherine and Claude approached, then hesitated. Katherine said under her breath, "We are supposed to kiss the Bible. But which one of us first?"

The French queen whispered back, "You do it. I don't mind."

Katherine shook her head. "No, I couldn't. Why don't you kiss it first?"

"I don't want to." The two queens stared at each other. "What shall we do?"

"Kiss each other!" suggested Katherine at last, and happily, the two queens kissed cheeks. The audience applauded, laughing heartily to cover their awareness that an incident had been averted. Henry and Francis joined in, and the signal was given to hand drinks around.

A short time later Cardinal Wolsey returned, accompanied by Katherine and Henry's daughter, six-year-old Princess Mary. From another entrance Cardinal Lorenzo Campeggio brought in the eight-year-old dauphin of France.

"Princess Mary, may I introduce Prince Henry Philip, your future husband," Wolsey said. The crowd applauded, smiling at the two pretty children, dressed in fine, adult clothes.

The little princess looked at her future husband up and down with unaffected curiosity. "Are you the dauphin of France? If you are, I want to kiss you."

A ripple of genial laughter greeted her announcement. Mary tried to kiss the small boy, who, terrified, tried to escape from her clutches, crying, "Mama! Mama!"

Disgusted by this performance, Mary gave him a shove, and the heir to the French throne sprawled on the floor. The crowd's amusement turned to horror. Francis swore. The weeping dauphin was swept away by doting courtiers.

"Mary, Mary," Henry murmured in token disapproval and tried to hide a little smile of satisfaction.

*   *   *   *

Next it was the English turn to host a reception. It was held in the Palace of Illusions. A magnificent palace designed in the Italian manner, one entered through an ornate gateway surmounted by a scallop shell pediment, two large Tudor roses, and a golden statue of Cupid. A Roman-style fountain spouted what looked like wine. Chained to the fountain were silver drinking cups.

Henry surveyed the scene with pride. He looked around at his companions and said, "What do you think?"

Thomas More shook his head. "It's—it's incredible. It looks so real," he said, gesturing to the stone wall behind Henry.

Henry laughed, put his hand against the solid-looking stone wall, and shook it! "Only painted canvas."

Brandon walked over to the fountain. He cupped his hands and drank from the free-flowing liquid. "But the wine is real!"

Everyone laughed and crowded forward to sample the wine. White wine, Malmsey wine, and claret would be free to all comers, day or night, throughout the summit.

Inside the palace, the hall had a ceiling of green silk studded with gold roses, the walls were decorated with gorgeous tapestries, and the floor bore a taffeta carpet. In the central hall the two kings, their queens, and the most important nobles sat at long dining tables, the courtiers standing behind them. The space that separated the tables housed English and French soldiers demonstrating their fighting prowess with staves and pikes.

Frequent bursts of laughter did not disguise the sharp competitive undertow. As the contests finished, Henry caught Francis's eye, raised his cup to him, and rose from his chair.

"Brother, I have a gift for you." At his signal, Norfolk carried the gift to Francis and presented it with a bow.

Francis said, in French, "You know, I fear the English, even when they bring gifts!" His courtiers laughed.

He opened the box and revealed a fabulous collar of rubies. Francis smiled graciously at Henry. "Thank you, brother. And now I have a gift for you."

Henry opened his box—a magnificent bracelet of diamonds—worth more than Henry's gift. Henry managed to smile graciously. "You embarrass me, brother. Your gift is much more splendid. And all I can offer you in return is—this pastry." He gestured, and his chef carried a large brown pie across to Francis. Its crust was shaped like a cockerel.

A pie! Some of the French courtiers audibly snickered. The chef bowed, placed it before the French king, then offered him a sharp hunting knife.

Amused, puzzled, and a little wary, Francis took the knife and cut into the elaborate pastry. The crust cracked open, bright wings fluttered, and a dozen small ortolan birds burst from the pie and flew around the tent. The pavilion rang with laughter and applause for Henry's little trick.

"Very amusing!" Francis said, sounding anything but amused.

Wine continued to flow freely, and the thoughts of young men turned to young women. The French ladies seemed younger and more beautiful. Certainly French fashions were more revealing.

As Brandon, Compton, and Knivert eyed the French ladies, Francis leaned on Henry's shoulder and said softly, "You see that young woman over there? Dressed in red and gold?"

Henry saw the girl he meant and nodded.

Francis continued: "Her name is Mary Boleyn, and she's the daughter of your ambassador. I call her my English mare because I ride her so often." He laughed softly and, having scored a point, moved away again.

Sir Thomas Boleyn threaded his way through the milling crowd in the huge French pavilion. It was evening, and in the far reaches of the candlelit pavilion the atmosphere was quieter, less boisterous, more . . . seductive. People were playing cards, drinking, laughing, touching, and whispering. Long lingering looks were exchanged.

His eyes fell on one beautiful young lady, the center of attention of three handsome bucks. Boleyn smiled, and drew her from the men's orbit.

She kissed him. "Papa."

"King Henry noticed you today," Boleyn whispered. "He wants to see you." He began to draw her through the crowd.

"Wait!" she said. "I must go and tell Anne." She disappeared into the crowd, searching until finally she spied her younger sister, Anne, surrounded by admiring Frenchmen, one of whom was kissing her neck.

"Anne," Mary called, and whispered the exciting news into her ear. Anne smiled.

Boleyn escorted his daughter to meet Charles Brandon, and then went in search of Cardinal Wolsey.

He met up with him in a private apartment. "In my presence he has railed against Your Eminence, calling you a necromancer, a pimp, accusing you of using evil ways to maintain your hold over the king," Boleyn told Wolsey.

"Go on," Wolsey said.

"He made it clear that the affairs of England would be handled better if he, and not you, were at His Majesty's right hand."

"And what did Lord Buckingham say about the king?" Wolsey asked.

"He told me he has a greater claim to the throne, and that as His Majesty has no male heirs, and will have none, that he, Buckingham, will succeed to the throne." Boleyn hesitated, then added, "But he also told me once that he has considered bringing that eventuality forward more quickly."

Wolsey leaned forward. "In what way?"

"By assassinating His Majesty."

The words hung in the air a moment, then Wolsey nodded. "You have done well to come to me." He offered his hand, and Boleyn kissed it. "Say nothing of this to anyone," Wolsey added.

In the king's apartments a pure and glorious voice was singing unaccompanied. Thomas Tallis was singing to the King while Henry was having his symbolic beard shaved off and waiting for Charles Brandon to come to him.

Tallis's song finished. The king awarded him a sovereign and he left, escorted by a groom. Tallis clutched the coin, awestruck. He had come a long way from the hungry young man waiting to speak to the king's secretary.

The despised beard now gone, Henry examined his reflection in a handheld looking glass. A movement caught his attention and he turned. Brandon, at last, bringing a young woman in a cloak, the hood drawn up to conceal her face.

Brandon nodded in response to the king's unspoken question, smiled, and withdrew, leaving them alone. "Approach," he said.

The woman glided forward and sank into a curtsy. The king gently pushed back the hood. "Lady Mary."

"Your Majesty," Mary Boleyn said softly.

He caressed her beautiful face with the back of his hand, letting it trail downward. "I have heard many things about you, Lady Mary. You have been at the French court for two years. Tell me, what French graces have you learned?"

She looked at him for a long moment. "With Your Majesty's permission?" she said, and sank to her knees. To Henry's surprise she unfastened his codpiece, removed it, and lowered her mouth to him.

Henry was shocked and a little disgusted, but also thrilled. He closed his eyes and moaned in pleasure.

At the evening feast the aristocratic diners and onlookers were entertained by wrestling matches between English yeomen of the Guard and French Bretons. Slowly, under the influence of the wine, the mood of camaraderie changed. Ancient habits of mistrust and suspicion began to surface, and the throng had drifted into two separate groups: French and English.

A huge Breton, naked to the waist, tossed a brawny yeoman out the ring like a straw man.

King Francis crowed delightedly. "You see that, brother? The truth is, in most things, we French excel you. Why deny it? We have the greatest painters, the greatest musicians, the greatest poets, the most beautiful women." He gave Henry a sly, sidelong glance and added, "Even our wrestlers are better than yours!"

Henry stiffened. "Are you sure?" he said belligerently.

More leaned forward. "I beg Your Majesty to consider—"

Henry ignored him. "Are you sure *all* your wrestlers are better than mine? Do you want to prove it?" He stood up, and the room stilled, all eyes drawn to the kings.

"What are you suggesting?" Francis asked.

"I am suggesting—I am *challenging* you to a wrestling match. You and me, *brother*," Henry said with a sneer.

Francis's advisers surrounded him, shaking their heads, pleading with him in soft, urgent French not to respond.

"Harry—for the love of God!" More tried.

But Henry was beyond appeal. "You're a coward!" he accused Francis.

Francis cursed and sprang to his feet. "I accept your challenge. Let's do it now."

The two kings strode to the ring. The crowd watched incredulously as their grooms stripped them of their gorgeous raiment. Both men were fine physical specimens, and they knew it. The pavilion fell silent as, almost naked, the French and English kings strutted into the ring and faced each other.

A nervous herald declared, "Your Majesties . . . gentlemen . . . the rules of the game are as follows: The first man to throw his opponent to the ground will be declared the winner. Are you content?"

They nodded.

"Then fight!"

As the two kings began to circle each other warily, the pavilion exploded with noise. All decorum abandoned, the English and French roared and bellowed support for their king.

"Come on," Knivert said. "What bet will you lay?"

Brandon had to shout above the noise. "His Majesty is going to win."

Thomas More heard him and shook his head. "Whatever the outcome of this match, King Henry is not going to win."

The two kings feinted, striving for a hold, eyes locked, panting, a sheen of sweat making their fit bodies gleam. Contact! They grappled, muscles straining. The crowd yelled.

The two queens watched, white-faced, clutching each other's hand unconsciously. Across the ring, Boleyn caught his younger daughter's eye and smiled at her knowingly.

Wolsey watched Buckingham's face like a hawk.

Francis was taking the blows harder. Henry, scenting victory, closed in and seized the French king in a deadly grip. The crowd screamed. The contest looked all but over, but just as Francis seemed about to be hurled to the ground, he found a last reserve of inner strength. He bucked, powering his body upward.

Henry, caught off balance, lost his grip on Francis's sweaty flesh. They teetered, straining, and grunting, then Henry crashed to the floor.

The English onlookers stared, appalled, disbelieving. The French went wild in delirious joy.

As the grooms and servants of both kings surrounded them, Henry surged furiously to his feet. "A rematch! I want a rematch!" He tried to shove his way through the throng to Francis, shouting, "Can you hear me? I want a rematch. Or are you afraid?"

"Of what am I supposed to be afraid?" Francis drew himself up proudly, regarding Henry with all the scorn of the victor for his well trounced opponent.

"Then we'll have a rematch," declared Henry.

A tall Frenchman stepped between them. "*Non.* As His Majesty's physician, I absolutely forbid it." He held up an authoritative hand. "It would not be right for His Majesty to further risk serious injury, in the name of sport."

Henry fumed as Francis was hustled away by his retinue and applauded and fawned upon by his supporters.

He turned to More. "I don't want to sign the treaty!"

"That's understandable," More began. "But, still—"

"No, I won't sign it. Go and tell them."

More looked at him, hard, and said in a low voice, "If that's what you want. But perhaps Your Majesty—"

Henry raised his voice angrily. "I said go and tell them."

More regarded him in silence, then inclined his head. "All right." He held his king's gaze and added in a voice that only Henry could hear, "If you want the world to think that the king of England is easily changeable, shallow, intemperate, incapable of keeping his word—then, of course, I'll go and tell them. I am, after all, merely Your Majesty's servant."

Henry glared at him in frustration, turned on his heel, and stormed out.

The peace teetered on the brink of disaster for four days until, against all advice, King Francis took himself to Henry's chamber while the king was sleeping. When Henry awoke, Francis offered to help him wash and dress, a sign of respect that mollified Henry somewhat, and enabled him to sign the peace with what passed for good grace.

Henry watched as Wolsey called on the king of France to step forward and sign the treaty. Across the room, Henry caught the eye of Thomas More, and his gaze hardened. He might have managed to swallow the French insults, but he had not yet forgiven More.

"And now I ask His Gracious Majesty, the king of England, in good faith, to also sign the Treaty of Universal and Perpetual Peace," Cardinal Wolsey said.

Henry signed the treaty and was embraced by a smiling Francis as the audience applauded. Wolsey handed both men small copies of the gospels, bound in velvet with gold leaf, and embraced them both as the applause swelled. It was done. The treaty was signed. Universal and Perpetual Peace was established.

Inside the Palace of Illusions, King Henry stood alone in his beautiful apartment. He stared down at the velvet-and-gold-bound Gospel in his hand, and his face contorted. He hurled the precious book across the chamber, where it smashed the looking glass.

He seized an ornamental ax from the wall and deliberately, frenziedly set about destroying his apartment. In a cold fury he tore the chamber to bits, wreaking havoc with every blow of the ax. At the sound of destruction, grooms and servant came running, but the King hacked so recklessly at everything in sight that no one dared approach him.

He did not stop until everything was destroyed.

The trees were almost bare, and the chill of approaching winter crept through Whitehall Palace. Henry strode to the leaded window and stared out, brooding. Wolsey watched, well aware of what was disturbing the king: Charles of Spain, the queen's nephew, had been elected head of the Holy Roman Empire.

"Now he is no longer just Charles V, King of Spain, but also the Holy Roman emperor. His dominions are vast, his wealth extraordinary." Henry turned. "And he's only twenty years old!"

He looked at Wolsey. "You will make arrangements to visit him at Aachen. Personally. It may suit us more to do business with *him*, rather than the French. Don't you agree?"

Henry's gaze dared Wolsey to argue, but the cardinal didn't blink, even though he knew that any alliance with Spain would destroy the Treaty of Universal and Perpetual Peace.

It would also lose Wolsey the crucial French vote in the papal election. And thus his heart's desire.

Wolsey showed no sign of it. "Yes, Majesty."

Henry resumed his pacing. In a more confidential voice, he said, "What have you discovered here?"

"The Duke of Buckingham is raising an army. He tells everyone that it is to protect him when he tours his Welsh estates, since he is unpopular there. But," he said with significance, "he's also been borrowing large amounts of money."

Henry considered the information. "Invite him to court, for the New Year. But don't say anything to alarm him."

The Shrine of Our Lady of Walsingham, in Norfolk, had been a place of holy pilgrimage since before the arrival of William the Conqueror.

It was now the most famous shrine in the kingdom. Rich or poor, highborn or lowly, they came to pray, to be blessed, to be granted a miracle.

A coach drew up about half a mile from the small Slipper Chapel, the last pilgrim chapel on the way to Walsingham. It was a bitter day. Rain fell in steady sheets.

The coachman let down the steps, and a lady made her way down into the road. She removed her shoes and, barefooted and bareheaded, despite the icy rain, began to walk the half mile to the chapel.

Katherine, Queen of England, had come to pray, yet again, for a son.

By the time she reached the chapel she was drenched, her feet bruised and frozen, but she did not care. The hardship would give her prayers strength.

She crossed herself and sank to her knees on the stone floor, staring up at the compassionate face of Mary, holding her son, the baby Jesus, in her arms. Tears spilled down Katherine's cheeks as she prayed, "My Lady, full of Grace, I pray you . . . I beseech you . . . in all humility . . . for the love I bear you, and your son, Jesus Christ . . . I pray you . . . give me a child. A son to fill my empty womb. I beg you . . ."

Weeping, she pressed her face against the cold, unforgiving stone.

A hundred miles south, in the palace at Westminster, Katherine's husband, the king, lay in bed, naked, deep in thought.

"Majesty," his companion whispered.

The king ignored her.

Mary Boleyn pouted and began to rake Henry's chest gently and teasingly with her fingernails, her hands drifting lower. . . .

Henry grimaced. Though a virile man, he preferred both discretion and simplicity in his lovemaking, and he considered Mary's Frenchified habits unseemly. "Leave," he ordered.

In the king's private house of Jericho, outside of London, Cardinal Wolsey had called to see Lady Blount, installed there some months before. A large stone house screened by high brick walls and surrounded by a moat, Jericho had long been used by Henry for secret trysts and private assignations. The moat was connected to the River Can, and thus easily accessible by boat.

"Your Eminence," Lady Blount greeted Wolsey.

Wolsey's eyes dropped to her belly. "You are well?" She was big with child.

"As can be expected. Have you some message from His Majesty?"

"No, none," Wolsey said. "But I do have a message from your husband."

She stiffened. "My husband?"

"I have spoken to him. He finds that he is reconciled to your condition."

She closed her eyes briefly. "Then he won't send me to a nunnery?"

Wolsey shook his head. "He will be made an earl, and given estates."

"And my child?"

"That is for the king to decide—whether or not he will recognize the child. I cannot give you any more encouragement."

Wolsey sent for Thomas More. "I wanted you to know: I am being sent to meet the new emperor. The king has asked me to draw up a new treaty, uniting us against the French."

"You must be very sad," More said.

Wolsey shook his head. "I am very realistic."

"Then I am sad."

"Our dreams were unrealistic." Wolsey told him. "Like your Utopia."

"Probably. And yet I will continue to dream them, even if I am alone in doing so." After a moment, More said, "I fear His Majesty no longer trusts or cares for me as he once did. His love grows a little cold."

"Thomas, let me offer you some advice," Wolsey said. "If you want to keep the love of a prince, this is what you have to do: You have to give him whatever it is that you care for most in the world."

Thomas considered the idea. "But the thing I care for most—is my integrity." He looked at Wolsey. "And what is it that you care for most in the world, Your Eminence?"

Wolsey changed the subject. "Have a care for Henry while I am gone. Buckingham is gathering an army together. He is planning to kill the king."

Chapter Five

It was the New Year, when every member of the royal family, every courtier, even the servants, gave the king a gift. In return, Henry gave them a gift, usually a cup or bowl in gold or silver plate, marked with the royal cipher and weighted according to rank.

Henry stood beneath a cloth-of-gold canopy with Queen Katherine in the presence chamber at Whitehall Palace, receiving the nobles of the kingdom. They presented their gifts in turn, each striving to outdo one another, impress the king, and earn his goodwill. Each gift was displayed, then removed by the palace chamberlain and placed upon a table with the rest, for comparison.

It was not customary for the king to be so closely flanked by his friends, but on this occasion Brandon, Compton, and Knivert stood by. As Buckingham entered the chamber with his man, Hopkins, in attendance, they stiffened.

Thomas More glanced at Wolsey. Wolsey gave a small, discreet signal and guards moved quietly and unobtrusively into position just outside the doors.

The gift-giving proceded. Buckingham was the last. As Buckingham sank to his knees, Brandon, Knivert, and Compton eased closer to the king, watching like hawks.

"Watch his hands," Brandon hissed.

"Your Majesty." Buckingham's hand moved. Everyone tensed, ready to spring, but he was only gesturing to Hopkins, who presented a gold-plated clock, its casing inlaid with jewels.

Henry adored clocks. They rated among his most prized possessions. Clocks were a luxury few people could afford.

"It has some words engraved on it," Buckingham told him.

Henry read the engraving aloud, "'With humble, true heart.'" He looked down at Buckingham. "Your Grace overwhelms me. Your words are the greatest gift; greater than any riches."

Buckingham rose. Henry's men braced themselves for action. Brandon even took a step forward, but Henry gave an imperceptible shake of his head and Brandon stopped.

Buckingham bowed and moved away to join his friend, Norfolk. The ceremony was over.

Several hours later, in the freezing predawn light, Buckingham and his large group of retainers rode out of the palace gates. Buckingham paused a moment, gazing back upon the towers of the palace in the dawn. He looked at Hopkins. "Not long now, Hopkins. Not long."

Spurring on his horse, he rode off, his large retinue of men streaming out behind him.

They rode through a landscape of field and ancient oaks, the only sounds the creaking of leather, the hoofbeats thudding dully into the frozen earth, and the occasional clink of metal against metal.

Without warning, another party of horsemen appeared through the trees, riding hard to cut them off. They wore the king's colors. Knivert and Compton rode at their head.

Buckingham was not concerned. He had more men, and he outranked Knivert and Compton. "What do you want?" he demanded as his party was surrounded.

"Your Grace is arrested on suspicion of treason," Compton told him. "I am ordered by the king's majesty to take you to the Tower."

"Let us pass," Buckingham said. His men drew their swords.

"You shall not pass," Knivert said coolly. "And if any of your men should strike one of His Majesty's servants in pursuit of his duty, that is treason too—as Your Grace knows."

Buckingham reluctantly gestured for his men to put away their swords. He said contemptuously, "You are unversed in the ways of the nobility. You know nothing. If I am accused of treason, I must be tried by a jury of my *peers*—not by the dogs of *butchers*." He gave them an arrogant look and added, "There is no lord in England who will ever find against me!"

"I have instituted a Court of High Steward to judge Buckingham's case," Henry told Wolsey. They had met in Henry's private chambers. "Twenty peers will be appointed to the court. The Duke of Norfolk will lead the jury." He signed a document, sealed it with the royal seal, and handed it to Wolsey.

Wolsey took the paper. "Majesty . . ."

"What?"

"It would be dangerous to find the duke guilty of treason."

Henry arched a brow. "Even if he is?"

"Yes. Even if he is." Wolsey chose his words carefully. "He could be found guilty of some lesser offense, heavily fined, and banished from court. In that way, he would be disgraced, but his allies and friends would have no cause to rise against you."

"And that would be the best outcome?" Henry said.

"I believe it would."

"And you could make the court come to that decision?"

Wolsey inclined his head. "I have every confidence."

"As I have in Your Eminence." But as Wolsey left, Henry's face hardened. He sent for Brandon.

"Wolsey will set up the court," he told Brandon. "Norfolk will head it. Remind Norfolk of his responsibilities."

Brandon bowed. "I will, Majesty."

The next day, Brandon found Norfolk with his young son and several servants, showing his son the sights of the Palace.

Brandon approached the party and bowed. "Your Grace."

The good humor melted from Norfolk's face. "What do you want?"

"Only to pass on His Majesty's love," Brandon said. "His Majesty appreciates the role you will play at Lord Buckingham's trial, and for all the care you have for His Majesty's well-being."

Norfolk regarded him through narrowed eyes.

"He also sends you this." Brandon handed Norfolk a small package.

Norfolk opened it, then froze as he saw it contained a large, gold ring bearing a ruby seal. He glanced at his son, then drew Brandon aside. "This was my father's ring," Norfolk said. "He was executed—by His Majesty's father."

Brandon gave him a bland look. "His Majesty thought you might like to wear it." He looked over to where the young boy was waiting. "Is that your son?"

"Yes," Norfolk said in a tight voice. "He is to be received by his god-father, the king."

"Your Grace should have a care for his inheritance," Brandon said softly. "It would be terrible, for example, if some action of yours should deprive him of a father, a title . . . and a ring." He let his words sink in, then bowed. "Your Grace," he said, and walked away.

Norfolk stared after him, Brandon's words ringing in his ears. He looked at his young son gazing around the court with bright, eager eyes, and his hand closed convulsively over his dead father's ring.

The day for Buckingham's trial had come. The court was arraigned. The great nobles of England, with Norfolk in their midst, had heard testimony from a number of witnesses, the most damning of whom had been some of Buckingham's own officers, who bore grudges against him. The verdict was about to be announced.

Buckingham was brought in. He approached his peers, looking confident and easy as he took his seat. He glanced around at the gallery, saw Wolsey watching, and his lip curled slightly.

He looked back at Norfolk and gave a faint smile in anticipation of Wolsey's defeat. Norfolk avoided his gaze. Buckingham's brows drew together.

Norfolk, the leader of the Jury of Peers, nervously declared, "Your Grace has been accused of treason, and with imagining and plotting the death of the king's majesty." He paused, looking down, shuffling through his papers. A tear ran down his cheek.

Buckingham sat up. He tried to catch the eyes of his other peers. None would look at him.

Norfolk continued. "This, this Court of High Steward, after reviewing all the evidence against Your Grace, finds Your Grace . . . finds Your Grace guilty of the charges against you." More tears trickled down Norfolk's cheeks.

"No!" Buckingham gasped.

Norfolk went on. "And so . . . and so . . . sentences Your Grace to death, at His Majesty's pleasure." He broke down, weeping, as the court erupted with noise.

Buckingham, white with shock and fury, leaped to his feet, pointing at Wolsey. "This is your doing! You butcher's dog! It's all your doing!"

Wolsey shook his head. Yeomen of the Guard came forward and removed Buckingham, still protesting. They marched him to a small, dark cell in the Tower of London and pushed him roughly through the door.

It had all happened in an instant. In shocked disbelief, Buckingham heard the key grate in the lock. It couldn't be true—it just couldn't! But their footsteps faded implacably away, leaving him alone.

How could the highest noble in the land be brought so low by the son of a butcher? How?

Eventually, Buckingham became aware of a faint ticking. A clock? Here? He followed the sounds and in the dim light of the cell, he found the clock and lifted it to peer closely at it.

Not just any clock, it was the clock he had given to the king. He had thought the inscription he'd chosen was so clever, so subtly ironic: *With humble, true heart.*

On the day of Buckingham's execution, the king went to Jericho. Dressed all in yellow, the color of rejoicing, Henry galloped off on a splendidly accoutred mare.

In the dim cell deep in the Tower of London, Buckingham knelt in prayer, trying to control his shaking limbs, as a priest prayed aloud for him in Latin.

Outside, the key turned in the lock. The heavy prison door swung open. "It's time, Your Grace," called the constable of the Tower.

Buckingham turned to him, his face working silently, a gray rictus of terror. He still could not quite believe that he was to die a traitor's death.

The yeomen of the tower ignored his frantic mumbling. They lifted him to his feet and half-walked, half-carried him out of the Tower, onto Tower Green.

A small crowd of people had come to watch the execution. Buckingham stumbled past them, oblivious. Ahead was the raised platform, where waited a black-hooded executioner, the bishop, and more priests.

He was not ready for death.

He dragged his feet but was forced onward. Trembling violently and hanging from the arms of the guards, he was brought to the platform almost in a state of collapse.

Sunlight glinted on the executioner's ax as he knelt before Buckingham and asked, "Do you forgive me?"

Buckingham's mouth opened, but no words came out. He was cold in his shirt, and afraid. His eyes were full of tears.

He looked away from the executioner, at the faces of the people who had come to see him die. He found his daughter, Anna. She was weeping. Their eyes met.

Buckingham could not bear it. He looked away.

Behind him the priest concluded his prayers, then, after a pause whispered, "Your Grace must kneel."

Buckingham groaned, but did not move. He had to be helped to kneel and to place his head upon the block.

The executioner told him, "When you spread out your arms, I will strike!" He raised the ax.

Buckingham could not bring himself to move his arms. The moment stretched and stretched. Finally, with a muttered curse, Knivert stepped forward, seized Buckingham's hands, and pulled them into place.

The ax crashed down, and the Duke of Buckingham was no more.

At Jericho, King Henry entered the bedchamber where two midwives stood by a wooden cradle covered with a velvet cloth.

They sank to their knees, but the king ignored them. He had eyes only for the cot. Without expression, he stared at the newborn babe, then slowly made the sign of the cross. "I have a son," he said. He lifted the child, naked, from the cradle and examined him. The child was whole and hale, lusty, and beautiful.

Louder and with jubilation, Henry said, "I have a son!"

The birth of a healthy son—even a bastard—so overjoyed the king that he ordered that public celebrations be held.

The court was filled joyful with music, and the finest dishes were brought forth for a great feast. Wine flowed as people talked, ate, danced, and played merry games. Sweetmeats and coins were distributed to the poor, and in the outer court, jugglers, acrobats, and fire-eaters performed. Outside the palace, crowds gathered to watch the streams of people entering the court, the great lords and beautiful ladies in their magnificent gowns. At night, to the *oohs* and *ahhs* of the crowds, fireworks exploded in the sky over the palace.

Henry drank and laughed with great gusto, well pleased with everything. All his friends and all the great men of the kingdom were there to share his triumph. It was a magnificent occasion.

Wolsey entered the gallery and searched the crowd with his eyes. There was no sign of Lady Blount. He made his way toward the king and bowed. Henry greeted him genially.

"Your Majesty is to be congratulated on this happy event," Wolsey said.

"Thank you, Your Eminence." The king drained his cup, then added, "You will find the lady through there." He waved a hand toward an adjoining room, then, as Wolsey moved away, turned to slap Brandon on the back.

Grinning, Henry said, "Well? A son, finally!"

"Congratulations, Majesty."

"I always knew it wasn't *my* fault."

"No," Brandon agreed. The noise of the celebrations suddenly dimmed.

Queen Katherine had entered the far end of the gallery, accompanied by two of her ladies. They curtsied. Katherine's eyes were tragic, but she was regal to the backbone. With all eyes on her she took a glass of wine and raised it toward Henry in a toast. She sipped, handed back the glass, and left.

Wolsey found Lady Blount in a dim, private chamber, sitting bolt upright on a chair, her hands folded; alone, untended, waiting.

Wolsey said, "His Majesty has decided to recognize his son. He will be known for the present as Henry Fitzroy, and he is to have his own establishment at Durham House, with a chaplain, officer, and retinue befitting his station."

Lady Blount's face twitched with emotion. "Thank you, Your Eminence."

"You must write and thank His Majesty," Wolsey said. "I only do his bidding." He left her, sitting alone in the semidarkness, listening to the celebration of her son's birth.

The celebrations continued. The wine continued flowing, and the mood got more raucous. Henry simply roared for more drink and food to be served.

Meanwhile the press of people outside the chamber had grown, visibly and audibly. Faces were pressed against the windows, and the guards were having trouble keeping the crowds away from the doors and guests. The watching throng was so dense, so excited, that people entering or leaving had difficulty passing through.

Suddenly the king shouted, "Let them in! This is a celebration for everyone!"

The guards hesitated. Such a thing was unheard of—the great folk, mingling with the lowly.

"I said, let them in!" Henry bellowed. "Come in! Come in!" He waved to the commoners.

The guards stepped aside, and people streamed inside. At first it caused great laughter as nobles and commoners rubbed shoulders. However, some of the nobles—Norfolk, for one—were appalled by this breach of decorum. Thomas More also took the opportunity to slip away.

But nothing could stop the king. He was beloved of his people, he knew. He watched them eyeing their surrounds and suddenly shouted, "Take something! Everyone should take something. As a souvenir to remember my son's birth. To celebrate."

The common people looked at one another uncertainly. Could the king possibly mean such a thing? There was more wealth here than they would see in a lifetime.

Henry shouted again, "Go on! Take what you will!"

Wolsey murmured a warning. "Majesty, I—"

"Hush! Hush!" Henry told him loudly. "These are my people!" The watching nobles and courtiers laughed as the crowd began to swarm around the gallery, grabbing anything and everything that came to hand. In minutes the room was stripped bare, but, intoxicated by the unheard-of opportunity, the commoners got carried away.

First one tugged at a silver button, then another at a cap, and then, suddenly, they all started to pull at the clothes of the noble lords and ladies. The ladies squealed with fright, and tried to escape, but Henry and his friends, who had been drinking for most of the day, roared with laughter. They watched the spectacle as, with more and more impudence, the common people stripped the nobility of their clothing. It was like a plague of human locusts.

Only the king and Cardinal Wolsey, standing slightly apart, were not approached. The king and the Church—untouched and untouchable.

Wolsey was horrified. "Your Majesty! Stop this!"

But Henry just watched. It was a madhouse. Nobles screamed and shouted as they were stripped naked by frantic, greedy hands. Knivert, stripped naked, clambered up a pole to escape the grabbing of sweaty hands. A naked young woman screamed and screamed as the mob pawed at her.

Wolsey cried out, "Your Majesty! For the love of God!"

Henry started, as if waking up. He shouted, "Guards! Guards! Where the hell are you? Guards!"

The guards piled in, scattering the mob and driving them from the palace, leaving the court shocked, and reeling.

In the Vatican, Pope Alexander was receiving the last rites. He lay, attended by cardinals and bishops, four great candles burning at each corner of his bed and a gold crucifix between his folded hands.

As the priest chanted, Cardinal Campeggio whispered to Bishop Bonnivet, "What was your deal with Wolsey?"

"The French vote—in return for England not going to war with France," Bonnivet whispered back.

"The fact is, Wolsey has gone to Aachen to meet the new emperor," Campeggio said. "He obviously means to break the treaty with your king."

The priest administering the last rites turned to Campeggio with a wafer. "Will Your Eminence bless this wafer, which is the body of Christ?"

Campeggio, frowning irritably, said a few quick words in Latin, made the sign of the cross, and gave the wafer back.

"In which case," continued Bonnivet, "we are no longer obliged to deliver our side of the bargain."

Campeggio nodded. The priest meanwhile put the wafer on the pope's tongue. The pope didn't move.

"Your Holiness *must* swallow it. Please," the priest pleaded. If the wafer was not swallowed, the pope's soul would be endangered. The pope tried, but he was too weak. The priest began to weep.

"In any case, we don't want an English pope!" Campeggio declared. "We had one once. He was insane! Never again. The pope must be an Italian. That is God's will."

He looked across at the priest, who was openly sobbing and begging the dying man, "Please, Holy Father. Please."

"Push it in!" Campeggio snapped.

Shocked, but desperate, the priest pushed the wafer down the pope's gullet. Alexander's mouth twitched, he made a small sound and died.

Campeggio and Bonnivet removed their caps, crossed themselves, and knelt with great devotion beside the corpse. Outside, the bell began to toll.

Thomas More was walking through the inner court at Whitehall Palace when he saw Lady Blount approaching. He was about to bow, when a door opened and the chamberlain announced, "The queen!"

Queen Katherine, accompanied by several of her ladies, was on her way to chapel. More watched as both women caught sight of each other at the same time, and froze momentarily. Behind Katherine's eyes he could see terrible pain, and also great bitterness.

Lady Blount swept a low curtsy. "My Lady."

Without responding, the queen swept past, her head held regally high. Lady Blount rose, her eyes also reflecting pain and bitterness.

More sighed and continued on his way. He needed to speak to Wolsey. Inside Wolsey's chamber, he checked briefly, surprised to find the cardinal standing with his back to the door, looking out of his windows, as Wolsey was usually at his desk.

Without turning his head, Wolsey said, "There has been an incident of the sweating sickness already in the city. You know how afraid the king is of catching it."

"Yes," More agreed. Henry had an abhorrence of filth and a terror of disease, particularly the sweating sickness. With so many at court, the cesspits soon filled up and the court had to move on.

Wolsey said, "This place stinks! In a few weeks' time the court will quit this palace for Hampton Court."

"I had heard," said More. Wolsey had spent a fortune in preparing his house for the king's visit. Wolsey had still not turned around. More said, "How is the king?"

Wolsey turned and resumed his place behind his desk. His eyes were red with tears. More understood their cause immediately. The news from Rome.

He recalled Wolsey's words to him so many months ago. *If you want to keep the love of a prince, this is what you have to do: You have to give him whatever it is that you care for most in the world.*

"I was sorry to hear of Cardinal Orsini's election as pope," More said.

"You are perpetually sorry, More," Wolsey told him.

"I wasn't simply being polite."

Wolsey fiddled with a document. "Weren't you?"

"No. As long as there is such blatant corruption in the Church, then that heretic Luther will continue to gain followers." More added, "If Your Eminence had been elected pope, you would have worked tirelessly to cleanse and rid the church of all its evil practices." He shrugged. "It's no different from sluicing out His Majesty's palaces when they are full of shit."

Wolsey looked up. "Perhaps you think too highly of me, Thomas." He paused. "Perhaps, in a way, you think too highly of the whole human race."

In Boleyn's quarters in the palace, Norfolk and Boleyn were meeting, quietly and discreetly. A slender, dark-haired young woman entered, and dropped to her knees in front of Norfolk: Anne Boleyn, newly returned from France, eighteen and in the flower of youthful beauty. She greeted her uncle, and a few moments later he left.

Boleyn turned to his daughter. "Do you know why you are here?"

"No, Papa. In Paris, no one explained."

"Good," said Boleyn. "It is better that way."

She tilted her head and gave him a curious look. "What's happened?

Boleyn shook his head. "His Majesty is tiring of his French alliance." He paused. "It seems he is also tiring of your sister. He no longer invites her to his bed."

"Poor Mary." Anne tried to sound sympathetic, but could hardly conceal a grin.

Boleyn corrected her sternly. "Poor us! When she was his mistress, all our fortunes were made. Now most likely they will fall." He paused and looked at his daughter. "Unless . . ." He stared into her deep, brown intelligent eyes.

Anne understood at once. "Even if he had me," she said slowly, "who is to say he would keep me? It's not just Mary. They say that all his liaisons are soon over. That he blows hot and cold."

Boleyn smiled. Anne had always been the clever daughter. He said, "Perhaps you could imagine a way to keep his interest more . . . prolonged? I daresay you learned things in France? How to play his passions!" He touched his daughter's cheek. "There is something deep and dangerous in you, Anne. Those eyes of yours are like dark hooks for the soul."

He paused to let his words sink in, then said in a soft, implacable voice, "Make sure he takes the bait."

The court was on the move. The palace was suddenly, completely, and eerily empty, for it wasn't just the hundreds of people who moved, but a lot of the furniture as well. It was a huge amount of work, overseen by the Knight Harbinger.

Beds were dismantled and packed, Henry's throne and other chairs of estate, as well as other items of furniture, were transported. Carpets, tapestries, and hangings were taken down, and clothing and linen cleaned. Everything was packed in chests and wrapped in canvas, and whatever wasn't taken was locked away.

All that remained back at Whitehall Palace were the gangs of servants working under the supervision of the Keeper and the Office of Works. For the palace had to be cleaned. Almost overcome with the stench, servants lugged buckets of water to swill out the notorious "house of easement" with its long benches with seat holes cut so that many could move their bowels at once.

In the halls and public areas, where young Thomas Tallis once had waited to be noticed, the filthy rushes, stinking of human and animal urine, bits of rotting food and all sorts of rubbish, were forked up from the floors, just as in the stables the grooms forked up stable refuse. Outside, carts carried all the soiled straw and detritus away.

And finally the floors, the paneling on the walls, and even the ceilings were washed.

Henry, far away from all these arrangements, rode in the first carriage with Wolsey. "How was your meeting with the emperor?" he asked Wolsey.

"Good. Constructive." He flexed his fingers. "He does not bother to disguise his antipathy for the French. He wants to go to war with them, and is desperate for an alliance with Your Majesty."

Henry nodded thoughtfully. "And in return for our alliance?"

"There will be a joint invasion of France for the overthrow of King Francis."

The overthrow of King Francis! Henry remembered being overthrown in the wrestling match with Francis. The memory festered.

"And I shall claim the crown," Henry said. "And once more truly be King of England, Ireland, and France, like my forefathers!" As he spoke, Hampton Court appeared at the end of the avenue. Sunlight glinted off all the windows of the great house. It looked magnificent.

Henry eyed it thoughtfully. "Your Eminence, you have built a most beautiful place here."

Wolsey smiled. "Thank you, Your Majesty."

"It's probably the finest palace in England." Henry sighed loudly. "I have nothing to compare. Nothing to show more fair."

Wolsey's smile faded. Henry smiled gently at Wolsey and waited.

Wolsey gazed at his beautiful and beloved house one last time, then fell to his knees in the carriage. "Majesty, it's yours."

"With the furnishings?" Henry asked immediately.

Wolsey gave a strangled laugh, and Henry joined in as the carriage rolled on, toward the king's newest home, the magnificent Hampton Court Palace.

Chapter Six

The Dover Road was pocked with potholes, and the carriage that bowled along it lurched and bounced. Inside, three men clung to the straps that hung from roof and sides of the coach; Thomas More and two envoys from the Emperor Charles V, the nephew of Queen Katherine.

"We are most grateful to you, Mr. More, for coming to welcome us in person," Mendoza, the smaller envoy said. He was short, with shrewd, dark eyes, and he carried himself with immense dignity.

"No, it's my honor, " More said. "His Majesty regards your visit as a thing of great moment."

"When shall we have an audience with His Majesty?" the second envoy, Chapuys, asked. He was large, handsome, and bearded.

"After you have had one with his chancellor," More told them. "At least let me advise Your Excellencies on this: There is only one way to reach the king's ear, and that is through the good offices of Cardinal Wolsey."

The envoys looked at each other, then back at More. Mendoza said quietly, "We heard rumors, Mr. More, that the cardinal advocates French interests."

More met his gaze squarely. "Only when he believes them to be in our interests also."

The coach jolted along. English landscape slipped past: mostly wooded, with little signs of human habitation or even agriculture.

Ostensibly to pass the time, but also because it was a pet subject of his,

More inquired, "Tell me, what is the emperor's attitude to the spread of the Lutheran heresy through some of his territories? My friend Erasmus tells me that in Germany it's spreading like a forest fire!"

Mendoza spread his hands. "His Highness does everything in his power to suppress it. But, as you know, Luther himself is the guest of one of the German princes unfortunately beyond his control."

More nodded. "My king is writing a pamphlet demolishing Luther's arguments, and defending the Papacy and our faith."

The envoys exchanged astonished looks. Chapuys leaned forward. "You mean—he is writing it himself—with his own hand? No!" Very few kings were more than basically literate—such menial tasks were usually left for their subordinates.

More permitted himself a smile. "Ah, Excellency, there are a great many things my king can do!"

Finally the weary travelers arrived at Hampton Court Palace. Cardinal Wolsey waited, magnificently dressed in his robes and surrounded by servants.

"Your Excellencies," he greeted them, smiling warmly as the envoys kissed his hand. He continued, "This is indeed a happy day. We have planned many festivities in honor of this most welcome visit. And it's my devout hope that, together, we can finalize the details of a treaty which will link your master and mine in perpetual friendship."

Chapuys inclined his head graciously. "That is very much our hope too, Your Eminence."

Wolsey smiled and gestured for them to go with him into a side chamber. Thomas More stepped forward to follow, but Wolsey put up a hand, saying quietly, "Not you, Thomas," and closed the door on More.

Wine was poured, then the servants were dismissed and Wolsey's gracious manner disappeared with them. "I don't want to waste my time, or yours." he said. "Before we drink, tell me if the emperor is sincere about this treaty." He looked them in the eye, rather unnervingly.

Chapuys looked back. "He is."

Wolsey nodded. "Then to cement it, I propose that we also announce the betrothal of the emperor to Princess Mary, the king's daughter."

The envoys exchanged guarded looks. Mendoza said carefully, "It is our understanding that she is already betrothed to the dauphin."

"But she will now be betrothed to Charles," Wolsey told them. "Unless you have some other objection?"

Mendoza glanced at his colleague, then said, "On the contrary."

"Good, we are agreed."

Chapuys cleared his throat, then said very quietly, "The emperor told us to inform Your Eminence personally that he wishes to bestow upon you a very generous pension. He will also throw his weight behind your ambitions to be pope."

Wolsey gave no sign he had heard. He raised his glass. "We shall drink to the success of Your Excellencies' visit."

"By all means," Chapuys agreed, and lifted his glass.

"Now, Your Eminence," said Mendoza when they had drunk the toast, "when do we meet the king?"

"You will see him," Wolsey said enigmatically. With a faint smile he added, "Tomorrow there is a pageant in your honor. It's called *Le Château Vert*, the Green Castle. Devised, written, and produced by Master William Cornish, a gentleman of the Chapel Royal. I believe some of the music has been composed by young Thomas Tallis. But William Cornish put the whole thing together. The man is a genius. You have heard of him?"

The envoys shook their heads, bewildered as to why they were being told about a devisor of entertainments—however talented—when they had enquired about meeting the king.

"No? We think of him very highly." Wolsey added, "His Majesty will be present at the entertainment."

And with that, the envoys had to be satisfied.

"Poor Buckingham." Norfolk shook his head sorrowfully. "I warned him. I told him that even those who recognized his right would not choose to fight for him." The morning sun sparkled on the damp grass as Norfolk strolled with his kinsman, Sir Thomas Boleyn, through the grounds of his country estate. Ahead of them a couple of Norfolk's dogs sniffed eagerly following the scent of a hare or perhaps a fox. Boleyn nodded.

Norfolk continued, "It was his mistake that he could not be satisfied with being Buckingham—but he must be king! But Buckingham was enough for any man." He gazed out at the view of the vast estates that surrounded him and spread his arms in an expansive gesture. Norfolk was clearly satisfied to be Norfolk.

They walked on, brooding on ambition, family advancement, and the quicksands of royal favor, on which all depended.

After a while, Norfolk said, "So, you will find some way to put my niece before the king?"

Boleyn nodded. "Yes, Your Grace. It's already arranged. A most ingenious and intriguing arrangement, if I may say so."

"Good." Norfolk snapped his fingers to his dogs. "After she has opened her legs for him, she can open her mouth and denounce Wolsey." He looked at Boleyn and laughed. "They do say that the sharpest blades are sheathed in the softest pouches."

"Quiet! Quiet everyone! Take your positions," William Cornish called softly. The members of the cast moved quickly into position, onto a stage bearing a specially constructed castle with three towers, all painted green.

Rows of tiered benches had been constructed around the great hall. They were packed with dignitaries, courtiers, and nobles. There was an audible air of anticipation.

As Chapuys and Mendoza were led to their seats of honor, they looked in vain for the king. "You said your king would be here," Mendoza said.

Wolsey gave an inscrutable smile. "You will see him soon enough."

The envoys exchanged glances. Henry was known to enjoy dressing up in disguise and taking part in pageants and masques, and entertainments. His absence in the audience could mean only one thing.

Musicians began to play, and all attention turned to the stage. An allegory was being performed; eight young ladies in white satin gowns were prisoners in the towers of a castle.

"They are the Graces," More explained to the crowd. "They have names like Kindness, Honor, Constancy, Mercy, and Pity. They are prisoners in the castle." He pointed. "That tall, fair lady is His Majesty's sister, Princess Margaret, soon to be married to the king of Portugal."

The Graces were imprisoned by ladies in black, representing things like Danger, Jealousy, Unkindness, Scorn, and Disdain. The audience happily hissed them. William Cornish, dressed as Ardent Desire, led eight lords up to the castle. "Youth, Devotion, Loyalty, Pleasure, Liberty, and others!" Henry was a lord, but the audience could not see which, as their faces were hidden. The lords demanded the Dark Ladies release their fair prisoners. They refused, and a mock battle took place.

To the sound of gunfire and drums, and with smoke billowing up and martial music, the Dark Ladies strove to repel the gallant knights by throwing rose water, comfits, and sugared sweets at them. The audience rocked with laughter. The lords, in return, threw dates, oranges, and fruits at the Dark Ladies. The audience cheered their efforts and applauded as the Dark Ladies were overcome and fled.

"Come! Let us free the Graces!" Henry shouted, and climbed the steps up to one of the towers. At the top, he came face-to-face with his destiny—a very beautiful young woman with jet-black hair. He stopped, with a sharp intake of breath, like an arrow through his heart, and stared.

From dark, expressive eyes, she gazed back at him. Like all the Graces, she was dressed in layers of gauzy white, with a stomacher embroidered in gold. She wore a tiny gold and white cap, with her name embroidered on it in gold. Henry read it. "Perseverance?"

"Yes, sir."

"You are my prisoner now," Henry told her.

Lady Perseverance modestly lowered her eyes as Henry took her hand. He led her down the stairs, and a different sort of music filled the air, sublime . . . emotional.

Thomas Tallis had composed it for the occasion. He conducted as the lords led their captive ladies back to the ground floor, where they unmasked themselves, to fresh and delighted applause.

But the king seemed unaware of the applause. He stared at Lady Perseverance, as though suddenly rendered incapable of speech.

The musicians then began to play a stately pavane, and the lords and ladies began to dance in formal patterns, constantly changing partners.

Henry could hardly tear his eyes away from Lady Perseverance, but his sister Margaret intruded into his private world. "I must speak to you!" she said urgently.

"I trust you have settled all your affairs here, Margaret?"

She responded, frustrated, "Yes, but—"

Henry said quickly, "The king has written of his love for you, his great eagerness to set eyes upon you, having seen your portrait." The dance forced them apart, and Henry desperately looked round for Lady Perseverance. She avoided his gaze.

The dance brought his sister back, so Henry continued, "He's sent you a fine gift."

"I'm grateful. I only wish—"

Henry shook his head as they were swept apart again.

The moment they were together again, Margaret said, "I beg you, plead with you, as your sister—don't make me marry him. He's an old man!"

"Enough! I won't hear any more!" Henry turned deliberately away from her distress. His searching gaze found Lady Perseverance again, dainty and graceful in floating white gauze. He watched her like a hawk as she danced tantalizingly close, then drifted away again.

Finally she came close enough for him to whisper, "Who are you?"

She gave him a faint smile, danced on, then drifted back, and whispered, "Lady Anne Boleyn."

With that she was gone again, and the dance drew to a close.

The crowd applauded wildly. The entertainment had been a rousing success.

Behind the Green Castle, in a dim corner, William Cornish was having a quiet drink. A shadowy figure slipped in beside him: Sir Thomas Boleyn. He looked at Cornish, smiled, and dropped a small pouch of money into his hand.

"Thank you, Master Cornish. I'm very grateful to you."

As the Spanish envoys were finally taken for an audience with King Henry, and Richard Pace, the King's secretary, led them past the queen's private chambers, Katherine emerged.

"I know you have an audience with the king," Katherine said in Spanish. "I just couldn't let you pass without seeing you." Pace frowned, but was powerless to interfere.

"Majesty," Mendoza responded. "Your nephew the emperor sends you his love and filial regards. Always."

"Tell him, if he loves me, he should write to me more often!" Katherine said. "But I am happy from the bottom of my heart that you are here, and that there is going to be a treaty." She glanced at the listening Pace, leaned forward and whispered, "Just beware of the cardinal."

The doors to the king's chambers opened and the chamberlain said, "His Majesty will receive you now."

Chapuys bowed to the queen. "Madame."

The envoys followed the chamberlain past the heavily armed yeomen of the Guard and into the Presence Chamber, where Henry and several of his noblest councillors, including Norfolk and Derby, waited.

Henry sat on a Chair of Estate beneath a canopy of cloth-of-gold. Richly garbed, magnificently presented, tall, and self-confident, he presented the very picture of a formidable and awe-inspiring ruler. "Gentlemen, I welcome you to my kingdom," Henry said. "I know you will succeed in your efforts to negotiate a successful treaty. You may trust in everything that Cardinal Wolsey says; he speaks for me directly in all matters."

He continued: "For my part, I should like to invite the emperor to pay a visit here, as soon as it can be arranged. The visit would give pleasure both to me, and to my queen." Henry smiled, signaling that the audience was at an end.

The envoys rose and bowed themselves back out of the room.

The doors shut, and Henry rose energetically. "Right, I'm for hawking. Have Brandon join me." He strode from the room.

In the park, Henry and Brandon squinted against the sunlight, watching as a dove flew across the sky. Then, in a blur of speed, Henry's falcon swooped in a swift, savage kill. The hapless bird plummeted to the ground, lifeless. A game dog was unleashed to fetch it.

Henry whistled, and with a whoosh of wings, the falcon returned to its master's glove. Henry stroked it with pride. "A jewel of a bird," he said. "Swift, powerful, without mercy." He handed the bird back to his falconer, who slipped a hood over its head, then Henry and Brandon rode on.

Henry told Brandon, "I have some business for you, Charles."

"As Your Majesty desires."

"My sister is to marry the king of Portugal. I want you to escort her and her dowry to Lisbon, and give her away in my name."

There was a short, stunned silence. "Why me?"

"I need to send her with someone I can trust."

Brandon grinned "You trust me with a beautiful woman?"

Henry reined in sharply and gave him a haughty stare. "With my sister, yes! Of course I trust you. Why shouldn't I?" He gave Brandon a hard look, and Brandon, rather shamefaced, lowered his eyes.

Henry rode on. He continued. "In any case, you're already betrothed to . . . ? Which one is it? It's hard to keep up."

"Elizabeth Grey," Brandon said. "She's a cousin of the Marquess of Dorset."

"Exactly."

After a moment, Brandon said, "I'm honored by Your Majesty's trust, but there is still a difficulty. I'm not important enough to give away the sister of a king—and the king of England too."

Henry smiled and puts a hand on his shoulder. "That's why I'm making you a duke."

Brandon goggled. "A—a *duke*?"

Henry was delighted by his friend's surprise. "Yes, Your Grace! Duke of Suffolk. How does that please you?" Without waiting, he cantered away, laughing.

Brandon lost no time in searching out Princess Margaret. He learned she was in the gardens with her ladies, feeding bread crumbs to the fish in the pond.

He spied one of her young maids standing with her back to him at the entrance to the gardens. He reached out from behind and stroked her cheek. She jumped, and blushed when she saw who it was.

"May I see your mistress?" Brandon asked with a flirtatious smile.

"Yes, sir. This way." Excited and envious, in equal measure, she led Brandon into a green space, and the presence of the king's younger sister, Princess Margaret.

Tall, like her brother, and graceful, with reddish-gold hair, Margaret watched with a glacial expression as Brandon approached. She was still furious about this marriage, and nothing would please her. Especially not the man her brother had appointed as his representative. Brandon bowed.

"Mr. Brandon. You are not yet invested a duke, I think?" Her voice was laced with sarcasm.

"No, madam, I—"

She cut him off. "I shall be taking with me to Portugal a company of two hundred persons. They will include my chamberlain, my chaplain, my laundress, and all of my ladies."

"Yes, madam. I—"

"If you have anything to discuss, please do so with my chamberlain."

"Yes, madam."

Margaret gave Brandon a disdainful look and sniffed. "I am surprised my brother chose a man without noble blood to represent him. Even Norfolk would have been better."

"Yes, madam."

She gave him a sharp look. Brandon's face was impassive. She sniffed again.

* * * *

The envoys had completed their business and returned to Spain. The public occasions were over for the time being, and this night, Katherine and Henry dined together in a more intimate setting than they had for some time, in one of the smaller rooms.

Without the distraction of guests at the table, the atmosphere was awkward. Katherine was in renewed spirits, happier now that the treaty with her nephew had been made, and looking forward to the prospect of the Emperor's visit.

She was trying hard. Too hard. Henry resented it.

Dinner was punctuated with long, uncomfortable silences.

"Did the envoys leave in good cheer?" Katherine asked him.

"They were in excellent spirits."

"And my nephew will come? We will wait for news."

"Wolsey will find out."

There was another long silence. Henry could hardly look at her.

Katherine leaned closer and said, "I had a dream. And in my dream, you came to me again, and held me in your arms, and you whispered that all would be well. That all would be well, and all manner of things would be well."

Henry pretended he did not hear.

Katherine's dark lashes glittered with tears. She knew his doubts. His doubts after all these years of marriage.

"Henry. Sweetheart. Husband . . ."

He said nothing, sat like a rock, his face turned away from her.

She placed her hand over his. "You must believe me. I never knew your brother in that way. He was so young. And he was ill. He was already sick when we married."

There was no response. She continued. "I was still a virgin when I married you. I have known no other man, nor ever want to. I am yours, as you are mine. Look, these cups bear the symbol of our union!" She lifted one of the cups toward his eyes so he could see the intertwined letters, H and K.

"Dearest husband, I love you."

Henry said not a word. The moment dinner was over, he strode from the room. He prowled through the court like a caged and angry young lion, followed by his attendants. Courtiers bowed before him, ladies curtsied. His eyes flickered over them indifferently, brooding, restless.

His eyes fell on a group of young women standing talking together. His gaze singled out the prettiest one, and he looked from her to one of his retinue. The man knew exactly what he meant.

As Henry strode on toward his own chambers, the servant walked across to the young woman and whispered into her ear.

Henry disrobed in his outer chambers, quaffing wine impatiently, then walked through into his candlelit bed chamber. He flung himself down on a Chair of Estate and stared broodingly into the darkness.

After a moment the young woman slowly appeared in the glow of the candlelight. She wore only a thin, flimsy robe. As she unfastened it, it slipped from her shoulders to the ground.

"My Lord, how like you this?" she whispered.

The gardens of the palace rang with explosions. Henry was experimenting with gun powder. He loaded an arquebuss, a large gun, while his arms master looked anxiously on. Wolsey stood by, patently uninterested in the weapon.

"So when's he coming?" Henry asked.

"At the end of this month," Wolsey answered.

"So soon?" Henry considered the news. "If he needs allies for his attack on the French, that can only mean that he intends to attack shortly."

"Indeed," Wolsey agreed. "The envoys told me in confidence that the emperor will strike first against the French occupation of Italy. He has a claim to the duchy of Milan."

"And then?" Henry raised the heavy gun and stared down the barrel at the target.

Wolsey continued: "And then, after he has driven them out of Italy, with your help, he will invade France itself."

Henry looked increasingly excited. "You will prepare all our forces for a joint invasion." He aimed and fired, staggering back with the recoil. The harsh sound shattered the silence.

Wolsey waited for the smoke to clear. "Yes, Your Majesty."

"And I want another warship." Henry handed the spent weapon gun to his arms master and held out his hand for another.

Wolsey hesitated. "Majesty, we have only just launched the *Victory*."

"Then order another. Even greater. What we lack in men we can more than make up for in ships. We're an island race. I swear we have the best and bravest sailors in the world—and I will have the best navy!"

"Ships are expensive," Wolsey warned.

Henry dropped his voice. "My father was a careful man. A shrewd man. A businessman. He left me a great deal of money, Your Eminence. And I intend to spend it!" He loaded and primed the next gun, fired at an archery target, and blew it to pieces.

Wolsey left, passing Sir Thomas Boleyn on the way. "Majesty?" Sir Thomas said, with a gently inquiring note. The king had sent for him. Boleyn knew perfectly well why, but he was not going to let on.

"I—I feel I have been remiss," the king told him. "I never showed you my gratitude for all your diplomatic efforts on my behalf."

"Your Majesty had no need. I am simply content to serve you, in whatever capacity I can be of use."

Henry smiled, not quite with his usual confidence. He was feeling his way. "Nevertheless, I do intend to reward you. It pleases me to make you a Knight of the Garter. And I am also appointing you comptroller of my household."

Boleyn managed to appear suitably surprised, even humbled, as if he had no idea why he should be chosen for elevation.

"I think Your Majesty has a better opinion of my talents than I have."

"I will be the judge of that." Henry fiddled with the gun, as if unsure of what to say next, then said, "We shall talk more later." It was a clear dismissal.

Boleyn bowed and began to back out. He was almost gone before

Henry called him back. "Oh. I forgot. Your daughter. The one who performed in our masquerade."

"Anne?"

"Yes. Um . . ." There was a long silence.

Boleyn ended it diplomatically. "As a matter of fact, she is soon coming to court, as a lady-in-waiting to Her Majesty."

Henry nodded and returned to examining the pistol, as if uninterested in the news. Boleyn left and Henry raised the pistol, sighted down the barrel, and shot the target.

As he left the gardens, Boleyn caught Norfolk's eye. Norfolk raised one eyebrow. Boleyn smiled.

The moment he was alone, the king laid down the pistol. He closed his eyes. "Anne," he sighed, and the single word expressed all his pent-up longing and yearning.

> *"And will you leave me thus?*
> *Say no, say no, for shame.*
> *To save you from the blame, of all my grief and grame?*
> *And will you leave me so?*
> *Say no, say no."*

Thomas Wyatt, tall and handsome, with dark curly hair, looked at the lovely, black-haired girl in despair. They were in the beautiful walled garden of Hever Castle in Kent, the Boleyn family home. The ancient fruit trees were garlanded in blossom.

He leaned back against a bough and continued reciting his poem.

> *"And will you leave me thus*
> *Who has given you his heart*
> *Never to depart*
> *Neither for pain or smart*
> *And will you leave me so?*
> *Say no, say no."*

He looked down at Anne, who was stretched out upon the grass, to see the effect of his verse on her. She chewed thoughtfully on a sweet stem, apparently unmoved.

Wyatt recited the final verse:

> *"And will you leave me thus*
> *And have no More pity*
> *Of him that loves thee?*
> *Alas, your cruelty!*
> *And will you leave me so?*
> *Say no, say no."*

He waited for a moment. "Well . . . do you like it?" He jumped down from the branch and knelt beside her.

She looked up into his face with a smile. "Should I like something that accuses me of being cruel?"

"You *are* cruel, Mistress Anne."

"Am I?" Her eyes and lips were like an invitation. Slowly, Wyatt lowered his face towards hers . . . but Anne, at the last moment, turned her head away with a small laugh.

"You have no claim on me, Master Wyatt."

"I have the same claim as every other lover to whom a woman's heart has been freely given."

She said airily, "You are a poet. I am a woman. Poets and women are always free with their hearts, aren't they?"

Wyatt's expression grew serious. "Anne." He reached out to stroke her hair.

She trembled a little, then shook her head and sat up. "You mustn't. Stop it, Tom!"

He looked at her. "Then I was right?" he said. "You are leaving me?"

She didn't answer him, but got to her feet, brushing grass from her skirts.

"Why don't you answer me?"

Anne looked at him. "You're married."

He rolled his eyes. "You know I'm getting a divorce." He gave her a pleading look.

There was a short silence, then Anne said, "You must never ask to see me again. Do you promise?"

"Why should I? When I have just learned what promises are worth!" She turned away.

"Is there another?" he asked. "Is that it? Do you love another?"

Anne looked back at him. Her beautiful eyes were hooded and dangerous, like a falcon's. Her voice was cold and hard as she said, "Never ask of me. And *never*, if you value your life, speak of me to others. Do you understand?" She waited.

Wyatt was almost too stunned to respond.

"Never," she repeated, with utter finality. She turned her back on him then and walked back up the path with a straight back.

"Lady, have you no pity?" Wyatt called after her.

She made no sign that she heard, and passed through the gateway, out of his sight.

Chapter Seven

Late at night a letter was brought to Cardinal Wolsey's quarters. His secretary brought it to him; the cardinal was at his desk, working late into the night, as was his habit.

Wolsey looked up at the interruption.

"From France," his secretary said.

Wolsey took the letter. He warmed the seal over the flame of a candle until it softened, and then sliced it skillfully and invisibly open. As he read the letter, his face filled with anger.

"King Francis has already discovered our rapprochement with the emperor. He feels betrayed and angry and is making threats against our interests."

His secretary frowned. "Who told him?"

The question hung in the air.

"'What serpent was ever so venomous as to call the Holy City of Rome "Babylon" and the pope's authority "Tyranny," and turn the name of our Holy Father into "Anti-Christ"?'" Thomas More read aloud from the manuscript Henry had written that had so impressed the Spanish envoys in which he had denounced the heretic, Martin Luther. "It's very good. Strongly worded—but good."

Henry beamed. "You're sure?"

"You might consider toning the polemic down, just a little. Here, for example, where you describe Luther as 'this weed, this dilapidated, sick and evil-minded sheep.'"

Henry frowned. "Tone it down?"

"For . . . diplomatic purposes. I think you should touch more . . . slenderly on the pope's authority, for the pope is a prince, as you are. At some time in the future you may not be so in agreement."

Henry shook his head firmly. "No, never. I swear to you that no language can be strong enough to condemn Luther, or gracious enough to praise His Holiness." His words gave him an idea. "In fact, I will dedicate a copy to the pope and you can take it to Rome."

More looked surprised. He placed the manuscript down on the table in Henry's study. "Why me?"

"If there is anything good or true in it, then it's due to you," Henry told him. "I could never have written it, or anything else, Sir Thomas, without your guidance and unfailing honesty."

More was touched by the tribute. He was also puzzled. He said, "Why did you call me that? *Sir* Thomas?"

The King smiled. "A knighthood is the least I can do for you."

"But a great deal more than I deserve."

Henry gave him a dry look. "Now, don't be too modest, Thomas. You're not a saint." He laughed and clapped More on the back, then went on: "There is something else I want you to do for me. Seize all the copies of Luther's works you can find—and burn them."

In May, Henry's book defending the Church against the attacks of Martin Luther was put on exhibit at Paul's Cross. Not far away, a great book burning was held, where Luther's works, and thousands of manuscripts and books inspired by him, were destroyed, including Tyndale's heretical translations of the Bible into English.

The event was conducted by Sir Thomas More, accompanied by a gathering of bishops and priests. As More tossed the books and manuscripts onto a huge bonfire, a gorgeously robed bishop held a gold cross high and chanted Latin orisons over the flames. A large crowd watched as fire consumed the heretical words. Sparks and flakes of ash spiraled up into the night sky.

After months of discussion and preparation, the Spanish king, the Holy Roman Emperor, Charles V, began his state visit to England.

The skies over the Port of Dover blazed with fireworks, showering iridescent trails of gold and silver across the velvet dark skies and gleaming water. From Dover Castle, huge cannons boomed across the harbor—in welcome.

Cardinal Wolsey waited on the docks as the king's representative, along with the king's secretary, Richard Pace, the Duke of Norfolk, and other councillors. Above them, richly embroidered banners whipped in the wind; the emperor's Black Eagle banner and England's Lion Rampant.

The formal reception was to be held inside the great hall of the castle. Lines of courtiers waited eagerly for their first glimpse of the emperor, craning their necks toward the open doors and the darkness outside.

As Charles V stepped into the light, there was a ripple of surprise. Just one-and-twenty years of age, he was small and not at all imposing to look at, especially for a populace who was used to their own tall, magnificent Henry. Even the French King Francis was tall, handsome, and well built. Charles, on the other hand, was rather weedy-looking, with the prominent, misshapen jaw of the Hapsburgs, over which he'd grown a black beard. His eyes were pale and watery, and his complexion was dead-white. Still, he was the most powerful man in the world, so the applause was loud as he walked between the lines of people, smiling and bowing to all sides.

Wolsey, enjoying the occasion, the fruit of all his hard work and planning, escorted the emperor toward the High Table, which was magnificently set with gold plate and intricately wrought gold cups.

Suddenly Richard Pace stepped in front of Wolsey. "Your Eminence, a moment!"

Puzzled and irritated, Wolsey paused and looked back. There was a fresh stir at the back of the hall, a loud and excited murmur, the sound of people quickly making way. The crowds parted, and suddenly there was Henry, striding forward, smiling widely.

"I could not sustain the anticipation," Henry told the emperor. "I had to come straight down to Dover to meet you."

"Then I am most truly honored." The two princes embraced and kissed—to fresh and sustained applause.

Henry said, "Tonight we shall feast and dance. Tomorrow you will see my ships. Come!" He waved a hand. "Music! Let's celebrate!"

Minstrels started playing in the gallery. Henry walked arm-in-arm with the emperor to their seats at the High Table, followed by the other guests. As Richard Pace moved to take his place, a guard stepped in front of him. "This way."

Puzzled, Pace went with the guard up the steps to the gallery. There he found Wolsey standing waiting for him, with several other guards.

Wolsey said, "Mr. Pace, you knew, of course, that His Majesty was going to pay this surprise visit?"

"Yes. As his secretary, I would obviously—"

Wolsey cut him off. "And you knew, of course, that the imperial envoys had come, privately, to make a treaty with His Majesty. After all, Mr. Pace, you speak Spanish. Almost as well as you speak French."

Pace frowned in confusion. "Yes. I—I don't understand, Your Eminence."

"I think you do, Mr. Pace. I really think you do. Because I think you not only spy for me—you also spy for the French!"

Pace blanched. "No! It's not true!"

"You are removed from all your positions."

"No, wait! I swear to you—I swear by everything that's holy, it's not true! His Majesty—"

"It is treason to plot against His Majesty," Wolsey said in a hard voice.

Pace looked suddenly very frightened. "What are you saying?"

But Wolsey had said all he intended to. He made a signal to the guards, who seized Pace by the arms. Too shocked to offer resistance, he was escorted from the room through a private exit.

Richard Pace entered the Tower of London by way of Traitor's Gate on a dark and dismal day. He sat huddled in the boat, in a daze. He still could not believe what had happened. It was a dream, surely—a nightmare.

A voice shouted, "Prisoner to the steps! Prisoner to the steps!" Rough voices shouted orders. Rough hands bundled him out of the boat. He stumbled as he was pulled forward by his chains.

He stared at the constable of the Tower. "I'm an innocent man. I don't know why I have been brought here."

The constable had heard it all before. He jerked his head, and Pace was dragged on, up the steps, toward the Tower.

Pace turned his head and screamed, "I'm innocent!"

The Constable, unmoved, spat into the river. "Put 'em out," he said, and with a hiss, the blazing torches were extinguished in the dirty waters of the Thames.

Pace was thrust into a dark, dank cell. The door slammed behind him. He listened as the guards marched away. He was alone—more alone than he'd ever been in his life.

Exhausted, he slumped against the wall. It was damp. He was so close to the water line, he could hear water sloshing up against the wall outside.

He looked around him. There was just one stubby candle; the light would not last long. There was hardly any furniture, just a rough bench and some dirty straw on the floor.

Under his horrified gaze, the floor moved, seeming to twitch. Cautiously he pushed at the straw with his foot and a rats' nest exploded. Rats ran everywhere, over his feet, up his legs.

He screamed in horror and revulsion—he had an abhorrence of rats.

He rushed to the door and banged on it with all his might. "It was Wolsey! Not me! It was Wolsey!"

Rats scuttled and squeaked all around him. He redoubled his efforts, banging and banging on the door, yelling, "Listen to me! It's Wolsey who has a pension from the French! Ask him! Ask him! It's not me! I didn't do anything! I'm innocent! It was Wolsey!"

He banged on the doors until his hands bled, and still he did not, could not, stop. "It was Wolsey! Wolsey. Wolsey," he sobbed. "He told them! Wolsey told them. Listen to me! It was Wolsey. . . ."

His terrified voice drifted out across the cold, silent waters of the river . . . unheard.

"Come on, what are you standing here for?" A young courtier grabbed Thomas Tallis's arm in excitement. Other young men rushed past them. "The queen's new ladies have arrived. Come on!" The young courtier pulled Tallis with him, and they joined the small stampede of young males, through the rooms toward the queen's private chambers.

They arrived just in time to get a glimpse of about twenty young ladies, escorted by the formidable-looking Sir Ashley Gross, headed into Queen Katherine's rooms. One glance from beneath Sir Ashley's bushy brows halted the young men in their tracks.

His fearsome looks did not, however, prevent them from trying to catch the eyes of the young women—one or two bolder fellows even making vulgar signs to the ladies.

Tallis was embarrassed by the whole business. Then he noticed a young lady he had seen somewhere before, a dark-haired lady with dark eyes. He frowned, trying to place her.

It took him some time to recall where it was, but eventually it came to him: He'd first seen her in France, at the Palace of Illusions. Her sister had been the king's mistress for a time. And more recently she'd acted a part in the entertainment he'd worked on for the Spanish ambassadors. Lady Disdain?—no, Lady Perseverance.

The name came to him at last: Mistress Anne Boleyn.

* * * *

"And now, Charles, have you ever seen such a monster?" King Henry ushered the Emperor Charles V into a large, bare room in the palace. They'd only just arrived in London, and Charles was yet to greet his aunt, Queen Katherine, but Henry was impatient for the emperor to see this marvel first and had made a detour.

Charles stared, then said quietly in Spanish, "My God!" He came closer. "What is it?"

Henry beamed, well pleased by the Emperor's awed reaction. "It's a Cannon-Royal. An 8.5 inch bore, firing a seventy-pound shot. There's not a cannon like her in the world." He laid a hand on the massive barrel. "I'm putting ninety-one of them into my flagship, the *Mary Rose*. She's being refitted right now, having her weight increased from five hundred to seven hundred tons."

Charles shook his head in wonder. "I am an emperor, but I—I have nothing like this."

"You have vast armies!" Henry said. "Together, we shall be invincible. How could the French withstand us?"

Charles nodded thoughtfully. He had already been given a tour of the English war fleet in Dover, inspecting the well-armed warship, the *Henry Grâce à Dieu*. And now, another warship armed with ninety-one of these guns. He told Henry, "With you beside me, there is no boundary or frontier or world we could not conquer."

"Indeed there is not," Henry agreed.

"You know, you and I are united by an indissoluble tie," Charles commented. "Since you are married to my mother's sister, you are really my uncle."

"It's an affinity that delights and pleases me—nephew," Henry responded. They laughed, and as the doors to Katherine's apartments opened before them, they walked into a crowd of loveliness; the queen's newest ladies-in-waiting gathered in the queen's outer chambers.

Henry checked, his eyes flickering over the ladies, who had all sunk into deep curtsies. He could not see Anne Boleyn, though he knew she must be among them. He'd seen her name on the list.

He gestured to Charles. "Go ahead, Your Highness; your aunt is waiting!"

Charles bowed and proceeded through the doors. Henry's eyes returned to the ladies-in-waiting, searching for just one face. He espied Anne just as she turned away to follow Charles inside with the others.

Charles saw his aunt, the queen, waiting. Plump and matronly, she still looked radiant, dressed in gold lined with ermine, strings of pearls wound around her neck. Smiling, the Holy Roman Emperor walked toward her and, with no warning, sank to his knees before her, saying, "Majesty, I ask for your blessing, as a nephew to an aunt."

Katherine, with tears in her eyes at the honor he had shown her, gave him her hand to kiss, then gently raised him to his feet and kissed him. "I give you my blessing freely, my dear Charles, as I give you my love."

"Your Highness," Katherine said, "allow me to present my daughter Mary, your future bride." Nine-year-old Mary Tudor stepped forward and curtsied beautifully.

"Bravo." Charles applauded. "Come!" He gestured her closer. He knelt before her, kissed her cheeks, and looked at her solemnly. "We must wait. To be married, I mean. Do you think you have the patience?"

Mary nodded eagerly. "I have a present for Your Highness. Do you want to see it?"

"I love presents," Charles told her. "Show me!"

Mary took his hand, drew him to the window, and pointed. "There!" she said. "Look out there!"

Charles looked into the courtyard and saw six beautiful horses being paraded. "Are they for me?" he asked.

Mary nodded. "And I have hawks for you as well," she confided. "Do you like my gifts?"

"They're the best present I've ever had! Thank you, Your Highness." He smiled at the little girl, who beamed happily.

A reception was held, with music, feasting, and, later on, dancing. The tables groaned with the weight of all the finely wrought gold plate and huge platters of food. Candlelight glinted on the many jewels, and the gold and silver embroidered clothing of the ladies and gentlemen, and in the rich tapestries that hung from the walls. In the gallery, musicians played recorder and lute, trumpet, and trombone, virginal and harp. Many of the pieces they played Henry had composed.

Henry and Charles sat with Katherine and Princess Mary at the high table, where they were served the finest delicacies by the Duke of Norfolk and other great nobles on their bended knees.

"As soon as possible, you must both come and visit me," Charles said to Henry and Katherine. "I want to show you especially the treasures of Montezuma, the king of the Incas, that General Cortés recently discovered in Mexico."

"We should love that," Henry told him. "We have only heard a little about those lands across the sea that people call the Indies."

"I tell you, that's where the future is," Charles said. "So much undiscovered land. So much wealth of gold and silver, salt and minerals."

As Charles described some of the wonders of this new world, Henry listened, fascinated by his commentary. He glanced idly up and saw Anne Boleyn, standing just a few feet away, speaking to her father, not paying Henry the least attention.

His heart stopped. For a few seconds he could see nothing but her.

Katherine, glancing at her husband, noticed his look. She watched him watching as Anne nodded in response to something her father had said, then moved gracefully away. Only after she had disappeared into a group of women did Henry come back to himself.

Henry saw Katherine watching him and Charles looking quizzically across. He smiled and placed his hand over Katherine's. "Sweetheart," he murmured. She tried to slip her hand out, but he gripped it tight, smiling as he turned the conversation to war. "How are your preparations?" he asked Charles.

"We are recruiting more German mercenaries. But everything is going well. I shall take Milan by next spring."

"And then?" Henry prompted, releasing his wife's hand.

"And then," Charles said, "together, we shall invade France and bring an end to the adventures of that libertine monarch, King Francis."

Henry grinned. "That will make me very happy."

"It will also make you the king of France!" Charles told him.

Henry savored the thought.

The musicians began to play dance music. Charles smiled at little Princess Mary and said to her, "Will you dance, Your Highness?" He added, to Henry, "With Your Majesty's permission?"

Henry waved graciously. Applause broke out as the emperor led his diminutive bride-to-be on to the dance-floor.

Henry soon followed with his sister, Princess Margaret, who took the opportunity to pour into her brother's ear her continuing opposition to the marriage he had arranged for her.

"I've heard he also has gout," she whispered vehemently when they came together in the dance. "They say his spine is deformed. He walks like a crab."

But it was just like the night of the performance. Henry was uninterested in his sister's woes. He could think of nothing but Anne Boleyn. He scanned the dance floor, searching for a glimpse of the elusive Mistress Boleyn.

Margaret interpreted his abstraction as a stubborn refusal to listen to her. "All right," she said finally. "Promise me something. I'll agree to marry him—but on one condition: After he's dead—which can't be long—I can marry whom I choose!"

She waited. Henry said nothing.

"Agreed?" she prompted him. "Henry, do you agree to that? To let me choose?"

Henry, irritated, nodded and Margaret was satisfied. They danced on.

Katherine sat at the high table, watching her little daughter dancing with Charles—a ludicrous, yet touching sight.

As the dance came to a finish, Anne Boleyn appeared beside her and curtsied as she removed a last dish from the table. "Madam."

For a moment, Katherine held her gaze, looking at the beautiful young woman with a kind of infinite sadness. Then she waved her away.

As Anne moved off, she did so in such a way that her path was blocked by Henry. Lowering her eyes demurely, she curtsied again.

"Lady Anne?" Henry said.

"Yes, Your Majesty."

He just stared at her, saying nothing. She raised her eyes and met his gaze. His eyes were lost in hers. After a long silence, Henry murmured, "Forgive me," and stepped aside to let her pass.

Thomas Boleyn watched the brief encounter with satisfaction.

Queen Katherine watched it also, with bitter pain. The King had once gazed at her in that way. She leaned toward her nephew, Charles, and said softly, "I am so glad to see you. It is often so lonely here."

Charles gave her a look of surprise. "Lonely?"

Katherine said, "Things are not well between us; with His Majesty."

Charles frowned. "But I saw with my own eyes how attentive he is to you. He looked at you with such devotion, it seemed, with such love."

"I fear that was for your benefit. Henry is a good masquer." There was a pause while she tried to master her emotions. Eventually she said, "I fear sometimes that he will ask me for a divorce."

"A *divorce*?" Charles exclaimed. "No, that's impossible!"

"Is it?" Katherine said sadly. "Even though he is without the heir he so desperately wants, he has not visited my bed for almost two years."

Shocked, Charles stared back at her.

That night, Henry dreamt of Anne. . . . He pursued her, chasing her through chambers and down the shadowy corridors of the palace, catching a glimpse of pale skin and dark hair, or the movement of a skirt whisking round a corner. His blood sang as he strode after her. He was the huntsman; Anne was his quarry, his dainty, dark-haired doe.

Finally, she was cornered, panting, in a shadowy chamber. She sank to the floor in obeisance, her pale nape exposed to his gaze. He bent down and gently raised her. She was so close to him, he could breathe the fragrance of her skin, feel the soft warm puffs of her breath, almost taste the rosy lips she moistened with her her tongue, nervously.

"Will you?" he asked.

She smiled, but shook her head. "No," she said, and her voice was soft and sweet, like wild honey. "Not like this."

"How?" Henry asked her.

"Seduce me . . . write letters to me. And poems. Ravish me with your words. *Seduce me.*" And then she'd disappeared.

Distressed, Henry called out, sitting bolt upright in bed. He even woke the groom, who slept at the foot of his bed. He jumped up, reaching for his sword. "Majesty! What is it?"

"Just a dream," Henry told him, but he knew now what he had to do.

The time had come for the new treaty between Spain and England to be signed in front of witnesses. The leading nobles of the kingdom had gathered to watch the occasion. Brandon sat with his friends and Boleyn with his.

On a dais sat the two kings, Queen Katherine, and Princess Mary. Wolsey presented the new treaty to their Majesties, saying, "For Your Majesties to sign this treaty between you of perpetual amity and concord, and to confirm with your seals and before these witnesses the betrothal of Charles, Holy Roman Emperor, to Her Highness Princess Mary, upon her reaching the age of twelve."

He paused, then continued, "I say to you again, in my power as papal legate and chancellor of England, that you should sign this treaty of friendship, one to another, and never break it, so help you God."

Henry and then Charles came forward, signed the document, and applied their seals to the manuscript. They then embraced, to great applause.

Afterward, Charles bowed to Katherine and kissed her hand. He whispered to her, "I swear to you my honor and my allegiance. You must always trust in me. Always." He met her gaze steadily.

As the meeting broke up, Henry looked around, mildly puzzled, then drew Wolsey to one side. "Where is Mr. Pace?" he asked Wolsey. "He should have been here."

"Majesty, I have discovered, shamefully, that Mr. Pace did not deserve Your Majesty's trust. So I have removed him from his offices."

Henry looked surprised. "You're sure?"

"The French were paying him a pension."

Henry looked shocked. "I see." After a moment, he added, "I trust you will find me a suitable replacement?"

Wolsey bowed, and Henry moved away. He passed the Duke of Norfolk, who waited until the king had passed before he drew Thomas Boleyn aside. He murmured in Boleyn's ear, "Well? How do our affairs proceed?"

"Very well, Your Grace," Boleyn told him. "The king makes no obvious declaration of interest . . . but it's possible to detect it in the way he glances at her—as if, in his mind, he could see her naked."

Norfolk nodded. He stared across at Wolsey. "But when can we bring an end to that insufferable prelate?"

Boleyn followed his gaze. "All in good time. One thing will follow another." He hesitated, nodded toward Brandon, then suggested quietly, "Perhaps it would be a good idea to include the Duke of Suffolk in our schemes."

Norfolk was disgusted. "Duke? He is barely a gentleman."

"He is the king's closest friend," Boleyn reminded his kinsman. "And I believe he hates Wolsey as much as we do. He would be a natural ally . . . at least for a time!" He smiled.

After the signing of the treaty there was jousting and in the evening, fireworks and plays, and feasting and dancing. The king, tired but exuberant after a successful day in the tiltyard, stood with his friends, talking and laughing while the musicians played their most joyful tunes, and people danced, and ate and drank their fill.

In amongst all the noise and activity Henry suddenly noticed a man standing quietly, waiting for Henry to notice him.

Eagerly, Henry approached him and directed him toward a private antechamber. "Well, goldsmith," he said when they were alone. "Do you have those pieces I asked for?"

The goldsmith bowed. "Yes, Your Majesty." Very carefully he took out a piece of velvet cloth, and opened it out upon a nearby table. Inside were four magnificent gold brooches. The first was of Venus and cupids. The second had a lady holding a heart in her hands. The third brooch portrayed a gentleman lying in a lady's lap. The last was of a lady holding a crown in her hands.

CHAPTER EIGHT

"His Holiness expressed astonishment that you had found time to write the pamphlet. He knows of no other king who would, or even could do such a thing." Sir Thomas More had just returned from his trip to Rome and come straight to the king's private chambers to give him all the news.

Henry was delighted. "Is that true?"

More nodded. "Indeed it is. And there's more. To show you his gratitude, the pope has decided to give you a new title. In fact, he has given you three choices, Most Orthodox, Angelic, or Fidei Defensor."

"I like Fidei Defensor: Defender of the Faith. It is an honor," Henry added, clearly moved.

"It will be conferred on you by papal bull. Er . . . Your Majesty should know that Martin Luther has also responded to your work."

Henry's eyes narrowed. "What did he say?"

"He accused you of raving 'like a strumpet in a tantrum.'"

Henry looked shocked. "*What?* He said *that*, about *me*?"

"I know. Listen to what else he says." More took out Luther's pamphlet and read from it. "'If the King of England gives himself the right to spew out falsehoods, then he gives me the right to stuff them back down his throat.'" He paused. "There is more of that sort of thing."

"How dare he! Spew out falsehoods, do I? Like a strumpet in a tantrum?" Henry picked up a large plate and hurled it across the chamber. As it shattered into a hundred pieces he shouted, "He ought to be *burned*! *Burned*!"

The question of Anne Boleyn was upsetting Henry greatly. Never had any woman affected him so—he could not even seem to get near her. As one of the queen's ladies, she ought to be close and on hand, yet instead, she was strangely elusive.

Even in church, when she came in attendance on the queen, she would not, could not, meet his eyes. After weeks of stolen glances, passing glimpses, and a word or two spoken in public, Henry was wound as tight as a spring.

He'd sent her the brooches. He'd originally intended to send her them one by one, like a tale unfolding. *Seduce me,* she'd said in the dream.

But he'd become impatient and sent them all at once, beautifully wrapped in cloth-of-gold, with instructions to his servant that he be discreet in delivering it only to the lady's hands when she was alone. And still he'd heard nothing from her. She had so far given no word, no sign that his gift had pleased her.

He was unable to settle to anything. Even hunting had lost its edge. Anne Boleyn: He paced about his private chambers like a newly caged lion, unable to do or think of anything else.

The door opened, and the chamberlain appeared, saying, "Your Majesty, Lady Anne—"

Henry whirled, his heart missing a beat.

"Lady Anne Clifford," the chamberlain finished. A rosy-cheeked young woman entered and made her curtsy. She was carrying a folded package of cloth-of-gold.

"What is that?" Henry asked, frowning.

"Your Majesty." Shyly she handed the king the package, then dropped her eyes and stood there in silence.

With a curt gesture, Henry dismissed her. He unfolded the cloth, knowing what he would find: the four gold brooches he had commissioned for Anne.

There was also a letter. He tore it open and took it to the window so he could read it better.

> *Your Gracious Majesty,*
> *It causes me such pain and grief to return the gifts you gave me.*
> *Alas, they are too beautiful, and I unworthy to receive them. I*
> *think I never gave Your Majesty cause to give them to me, since I*
> *am nothing and you are everything. Give them, I pray you, to a*
> *lady more deserving of Your Majesty's affections.*

Henry's hand shook slightly as he read.

> *I am leaving now for my family's house at Hever. I shall think of*
> *you on the journey there.*
> *Your loving servant, Anne Boleyn.*

Henry read the last part again, aloud: "'Your loving servant, Anne Boleyn.'" He stared at her handwriting and traced her signature with a gentle finger.

Then he pulled out his writing materials. *Seduce me with your words,* she had said in his dream.

Anne Boleyn sat in a cozy corner of the kitchens at Hever Castle. It was the warmest place in the house, with a huge open fire and rows of ovens radiating heat.

She read the letter aloud to her brother, George: "'I was distressed you would not accept the brooches. They were made for you, not for anyone else. And why are you not worthy when I deem you so? For certain, it must be plain to you now that I desire to find a place in your heart. . . .'"

"Wait! Give it to me!" George, a few years older than Anne, tried to snatch the letter.

Anne jerked it out of reach, then laughing, relented and gave it to him.

George read on: "'. . . a place in your heart and your grounded affection.'" He looked up at Anne. "'Grounded affection'?"

He gave an appreciative whistle and continued reading: "'Tell me at least that we can meet in private. I mean nothing more than a chance to talk to you.'" He raised a mocking eyebrow. "'I beg you, come back to court. Soon. And meanwhile, accept this new gift . . . and wear it, for my sake.'"

He looked at Anne again. "What gift? And where is it?"

With a graceful wave of her hand, Anne indicated her neck. Around it, she wore a double string of pearls with a small, solid gold cross, inset with a diamond.

George Boleyn stared. "Holy Jesus!"

At the Port of Dover, burly sailors and liveried palace servants were busy loading the heavy oaken chests bound with brass containing Princess Margaret's clothes and the rest of her dowry, onto the ship that was to carry her to Portugal.

The princess's eyelids were swollen from weeping. She'd farewelled her brother Henry in London, and reminded him of his promise that the next time she married, she could chose her husband. He had not acknowledged her reminder, only exhorted her to do her duty and love her new husband, whom she dreaded meeting. She was still angry with Henry.

She was also angry with Brandon. He'd promised the king that he would look after Margaret as if she were his own sister.

Brandon offered her his arm to escort her onto the vessel. She accepted it with haughty disdain.

"Here is your stateroom," he told her. "I hope it meets with Your Highness's approval."

It was large, for a ship's cabin, with fine wooden paneling and good furnishings, richly decorated. Margaret gave it a cursory glance. "It will serve," she said indifferently.

"The beds are narrow, but adequate," Brandon said. "And if there is action all this paneling will be removed."

She looked at him. "Action?"

"If we are attacked," he said, matter-of-factly.

"Who will attack us?"

"Pirates," Brandon told her, his face impassive.

The princess suddenly saw his game. She said tartly, "It seems to me, Your Grace, that we have more to fear from some pirates already on board!" She turned her back on him and started to organize her ladies.

He sauntered away, a faint smile on his face.

That night Margaret lay in her narrow bunk beside her stateroom, dimly illuminated by a swinging lantern. She was finding it hard to get to sleep. The ship pitched and rolled slowly in the swell, and the creaking of the timbers was most unsettling.

Through the thin partition that divided her stateroom from the captain's cabin she could hear male voices, laughter, and the clink of glasses: another world. She lay on her bunk, listening.

She could hear the captain, two of his officers, and Brandon. Brandon's voice in particular was very clear. The men were playing cards, gambling and drinking and laughing.

Margaret listened, staring blankly at the paneled wall that divided them, picturing it all in her mind. Suddenly she realized there was a small knothole in the wooden paneling. Perhaps she could see? Her curiosity got the better of her.

She got up to investigate. She couldn't see the whole room, but she could watch Brandon and the captain as they played.

The captain played a card. "There we are, Your Grace. My king has your queen."

There was a short pause, then Brandon shrugged and said, "I was rather hoping, Captain, that the knave would get the queen."

The men laughed, but Brandon raised his eyes and looked directly at the wall, as if, somehow, he knew that Margaret was watching him from the other side.

She sprang back, her cheeks hot with embarrassment.

* * * *

Cardinal Wolsey considered the question of Richard Pace's replacement. His eye fell on one of his clerks working diligently at his desk, writing down lists of figures.

Thomas Cromwell. Wolsey had employed him for some time. Hard working, soft spoken, young—in his thirties—with both intelligence and a subtle acuity, he might be just the man Wolsey needed.

"Mr. Cromwell!" Wolsey said.

Cromwell looked up from his work. "Eminence?"

"I have long noticed your aptitude for work and your diligence in carrying through my affairs . . . as well as your discretion."

Cromwell said humbly. "I am grateful to Your Eminence."

"You are from obscure stock," Wolsey said, "but then, so am I. It should not be held against you." He paused, weighing it up. "I may have a proposition to put to you."

"Thank you, Your Eminence."

Wolsey glanced at his clock. "The king is waiting for me. We shall speak of it later." He left, aware of Cromwell's eyes on his back.

"By the terms of our treaty with the emperor, we are obliged to support his war effort financially. At present his armies are fighting the French in Italy. Near Milan." Wolsey glanced at the king, who was pacing around the room, showing no interest. "Unfortunately, I have calculated that to honor our obligations we shall be obliged to raise taxes."

Taxes had always been a sensitive issue for Henry, but still he didn't respond. Wolsey went on, "A bill will be presented to Parliament in its next session."

Henry nodded absently. "Good. Good."

"I trust the bill will be approved."

Henry said, "I am sure, Your Eminence, that with your guiding hand it will be."

"At least our alliance with the emperor is popular. I ask myself, sometimes, why that should be so?"

Henry looked at him. "Because he's not French!" Henry didn't even smile at his own joke. He moved away restlessly.

Wolsey tried another tack. "The new warship is commissioned at Portsmouth." But even this didn't bring the king around. He prowled the room, bored and irritable. Wolsey thought for a moment.

"I forgot to tell Your Majesty: We have a new visitor at court, Princess Marguerrite of Navarre. I received her yesterday and thought her indeed a very beautiful young woman, with a very sweet—and yielding—disposition." He noticed a faint glimmer of interest in Henry's stance and added, "She confessed a great admiration for Your Majesty."

He observed the king's profile. He seemed to be half-listening, at least. Wolsey said delicately, "Shall I arrange—?"

"Yes. Do it!" Henry said impatiently. "What else?"

"With Your Majesty's permission, I mean to appoint a new secretary, instead of Mr. Pace."

Henry gave an uninterested nod.

The constable of the Tower of London unlocked the door to Richard Pace's cell and entered. A single, feeble light burned, faintly illuminating the gaunt figure inside. His courtier's clothes were dirty and threadbare, but despite the endless months that had passed, the man still carried himself like a gentleman.

"Mr. Pace," the constable greeted him.

Pace bowed. "At your service, sir."

"You are to be released." He waited.

"I don't know anything," Pace said. He plucked at his clothes, his hands like living creatures.

The constable frowned. "What's that? I said, you are to be released."

Pace continued as if he hadn't spoken: "I told my wife. I told her: I don't know anything. Anything at all." He shook his head back and forth, his long, dirty fingers worrying at his clothing.

"You . . . told your wife, Mr. Pace? When?"

Pace nodded. "Yes, sir, hush. She's there—over there sleeping." He laughed softly. "We talk together. I thought she had died giving birth to our son. I was sure I went to her funeral, and wept. But now I see she is alive, and as well as I." He hesitated, and his fingers stopped their fretful motion. "Can you . . ." His face twitched. "Can you not see her?"

Disconcerted, the constable held the candle up to Pace's face. Pace's eyes stared back at him blankly. Richard Pace, the king's erstwhile secretary, had gone quite mad.

The constable put the candle down, saying quietly, "Yes, Mr. Pace. I see her."

Pace, reassured, smiled broadly. His hands resumed their plucking.

"Your Majesty," Wolsey said, "may I present Princess Marguerrite of Navarre."

"Madame." Henry greeted her.

The princess curtsied, her dress cut so low that Henry could not fail to appreciate her very large breasts.

He raised her gently. She fixed him with a gaze that was almost feral. *"Majesté,"* she said.

"You are here on a visit?" Henry asked her.

"Yes, *Majesté*, the count, my husband, had to stay behind in France"— she peeked at him under her lashes—"regrettably."

Henry raised a brow. "Indeed? Very regrettable, madame. But you must be compensated. You must enjoy some . . . pleasures while you are here."

The princess smiled.

Norfolk watched the exchange sourly from a distance. Thomas Boleyn quietly joined him, murmuring, "I have some news which may interest Your Grace."

Norfolk glanced around, then nodded for Boleyn to go ahead. "As the king's new treasurer," Boleyn explained, "I have discovered some, shall we say, curious facts concerning the financial affairs of a certain prelate." They both looked over to where Wolsey was standing.

Norfolk leaned closer. "Tell me!"

"It appears that he has been using some of the king's money to invest his new college in Oxford, and his own personal foundation."

"What?"

Boleyn explained. "He closes down the worst monasteries, strips them of their assets, as he is supposed to do, but instead of transferring all the profit to the privy purse, he makes the profits disappear."

Norfolk stared. "Incredible! How much richer does that man want to be?"

"There's more," Boleyn told him. "The Bishop of Winchester died six months ago. Winchester is the richest parish in England. Wolsey is supposed to appoint his successor." He paused for effect. "And he just did. He appointed himself."

Norfolk spluttered with outrage. "You must tell the king! Right now! Tell him! Wolsey will be destroyed."

"No." Boleyn said. "Pardon me, Your Grace, but we must judge the time exactly! Such is Wolsey's hold over the king that—whatever the evidence against him—the king won't believe it. He'll ask Wolsey to tell him the truth; and he'll believe Wolsey's lies. But"—he held up a finger and gave Norfolk a shrewd look—"there will come a point. An exact point. When the king's belief in his minister will hang in the balance. And then, Your Grace, we shall drop our truth into the scales. And the scales will fall."

At a distant table, Thomas Tallis was seated with the servants, taking part in the meal for once, instead of preparing the musical entertainment. Yet his food sat untouched while he scratched annotations onto a piece of music. He was, as usual, a world away from the intrigues of the court.

Two young twins, ladies-in-waiting, watched him, and whispered and giggled in the way of young girls. "Thomas? . . . Thomas Tallis?"

Tallis looked up reluctantly. "What?"

The twins, who were very pretty, smiled warmly at him. "How are you, Thomas?"

"I am well."

The first sister said, "We just wanted to tell you how much we love your music, Thomas."

Tallis looked down and muttered, "Thank you."

The girls slid closer along the bench until their lithe young bodies pressed lightly against his. The second sister said softly, "We share a room. Do you want to come back with us, Thomas?"

There was a pause. Tallis looked from one to the other. They smiled back, very pretty, very confident.

"No thank you," he told them seriously. "I want to finish this song."

They pouted. "You could finish it tomorrow."

Tallis shook his head. "No, I'll have forgotten it by tomorrow."

"You'll forget us, too, won't you?" the second sister said.

Tallis smiled apologetically. The girls moved away and without another thought, Tallis returned to his musical annotation.

A shadow fell over the paper and he looked up, thinking it was the girls returning. Tallis's eyes widened as he saw who it was. William Compton, one of the king's best friends, stood inches away, looking down at Tallis. Compton nodded, then, without word, continued on his way to join the king.

Tallis stared after him, his song momentarily forgotten. He shook his head and turned back to his music.

Compton saw at once that Henry and Knivert had been drinking for some time. Henry was in an odd mood, apparently jovial, but with an edge. "What do you think of Princess Marguerrite of Navarre?" he said.

Knivert and Compton looked her over. "She's well built," Compton said. "But her top decks look a little heavy." They laughed.

"She's King Francis's sister," Henry said. "I happen to know that." He winked, and they laughed again.

Henry spotted Sir Thomas More moving through the crowds. He rose to his feet, embracing More warmly, seemingly rather drunk.

"Dear Thomas!"

"Majesty."

"Come on, stay at court. I need you. I'll give you excellent chambers. Compton has excellent chambers. You can have his!" He laughed.

More smiled. "Much as I love Your Majesty, I like my chambers to have my family inside them."

Henry smiled, then was abruptly distracted again as he noticed a young man with curly dark hair arriving in court. He made a beeline toward the young man.

Knivert said to More, "I swear His Majesty loves you above everyone, Mr. More." Compton nodded in agreement

More grimaced. "That may be true, gentlemen, and yet, if my head could win him a castle in Spain, I think he would cut it off." With an enigmatic smile, he moved on.

The man Henry had spotted in the crowd was the poet Thomas Wyatt. "Mr. Wyatt," he announced. "You are a poet."

Wyatt bowed. "I write poems, Majesty. I don't know how to 'be a poet.'"

"I have read some of your poems," the king told him. "I like them."

Wyatt inclined his head. "I don't know what to say."

There was a long pause, then Henry said abruptly, "Were you in love with Anne Boleyn?" Suddenly it was apparent that the king was not drunk at all.

Wyatt, caught off guard, hesitated, "I, er . . ."

"Wolsey told me you were almost engaged."

Wyatt shook his head. "No! It's not true."

Henry gave him a hard stare. "Did you love her?"

Wyatt weighed his response up carefully. "Lady Anne is so beautiful that it is the duty of every man to love her. Of course I loved her—but from a distance." He added, "I have a wife."

There was a tense silence, and then Henry waved a hand in dismissal. "Very well," he said, seeming to accept Wyatt's explanation. He drained his cup of wine. "I'm for bed," he said, glancing at Knivert. Knivert gave a discreet nod.

*   *   *   *

In the outer room of the king's bedchamber, the king's grooms and servants sat, not looking at one another, their faces blank and stolid as they could make them. Every sound from the king's bed was audible. The king's big wooden bed shook with a violent rhythm, and the princess was very vocal and unabashed about the pleasuring she was receiving.

"Oui, Henri . . . C'est ca, Henri . . . oui, Henri . . . Ohh . . . C'est ca . . . Mon Dieu!"

The listeners, hardly able to contain themselves, bit their inner cheeks to prevent laughter escaping.

The bed rocked more violently. *"Mon Dieu, Henri . . . ou . . . ou . . . Mon Dieu . . . ah, oui . . . ah, oui . . . Henri . . ."*

One of the listening grooms smothered a guffaw. It set off the others.

In a soft voice, one of the grooms began to mimic her strangulated English. *"Ah, oui . . . Henri."* And they were all laughing, but doing their best to keep it quiet.

A second groom joined in, *"C'est ca . . . oh . . . ah . . ."*

The pitch of the princess's voice rose from the other room, and the first groom said, *"Mon Dieu, Henri!"* and waggled his eyebrows.

They heard a final shriek, then it went quiet.

The second groom said softly into the silence, *"C'est fini!"* and the room filled with the sound of muffled laughter.

In the state cabin of the ship bound for Portugal, Princess Margaret could hear Brandon moving about on the other side of the partition. She was already in her nightdress. He was getting ready for bed. She stared at the knothole in the wood, then looked away. She lay down on her bed, but after a few moments, she could not help herself.

She climbed up and put her eye to the knothole. She watched as he removed his shirt and lay on a bunk, just beneath her eye level. His naked torso was almost close enough for her to touch. He was strong, young, well muscled. She stared, her mouth dry, feasting her eyes on him, and pressed her eye closer to the knothole.

* * * *

"A messenger from the emperor, Your Majesty," Knivert announced. He led a rider into the court. The man, covered from head to toe in mud, looked utterly spent as he sank to his knees in front of the king.

"Well," said Henry impatiently. "What is it?"

"The emperor has won a great victory against the French," the messenger said.

Henry's eyes lit up, but he could hardly believe what he was hearing. "What are you saying?"

The man, recovering his strength a little now that his mission was almost completed, recited, "At the Battle of Pavia, five days ago, the emperor's armies totally overcame those of the French. The French army was destroyed."

"My God! Is this true?" Henry grinned around at the listening court.

"Not only that!" the messenger said, his eyes lit with triumph. "The French king himself was also captured on the battlefield."

It took a moment for his words to sink in. "Francis?" Henry exclaimed incredulously. *"Captured?"*

"Yes, Your Majesty. He is now the emperor's prisoner."

Oblivious of the man's muddy state, Henry bent down and embraced him. The king was jubilant, almost laughing. He told the messenger, "You are as welcome here as if you were the angel Gabriel!"

He turned to Knivert and the others in the chamber. "What great news is brought to us this day! Let there be feasting and dancing—celebration of this most excellent occasion!"

Along with the feasting and dancing, there was, inevitably, jousting: the theater of war. The tiltyard looked like a carnival site. Pennants fluttered in the breeze, and everyone came dressed in their finest clothes.

In the Royal Pavilion, Queen Katherine watched beneath a royal canopy of cloth-of-gold embroidered with the Tudor rose and Katherine's own symbol, the pomegranate, and her initials and Henry's, interlaced. Sitting next to her, in a place of honor, was the messenger who had brought the good news to the king.

Great crowds cheered and clapped as Knivert and another knight ran a course, and their lances shattered. On his way back, Knivert passed Compton, who was preparing to enter the list.

"Well done," Compton called.

Knivert said grimly, "I tell you, William. I will be called a knight before this day is through, or I never will be." Knivert and Compton were both envious of Brandon's title.

Wolsey and More were among those watching as Henry rode out into the tiltyard. Wild applause erupted, for it was a special event to see the king of England ride into battle.

Henry approached the royal pavilion, and the cheers became deafening as Katherine rose and tied her colors to his lance, indicating that he was her champion.

Wolsey watched the little ceremony sourly. Since the French defeat, he had not been his usual congenial self. He leaned across to More and said contemptuously, "You see how popular she is with the people! Even though she can't even say Hampton Court properly. She still calls it 'Antoncort'!" He snorted. "But for all that, the people have taken her to their hearts."

More responded, "Eminence, she is the daughter of Isabella and Ferdinand, so perhaps they think she is what a queen should be."

They turned, distracted, as the crowd stirred with speculation and amusement. Under Compton's direction, two servants carried a long tree trunk into the list. They were husky fellows and yet they staggered under the weight of the tree trunk.

Intrigued, the king lifted his visor and trotted over to Compton. "What is this?"

Compton grinned. "Just a trick! Watch!" He handed his lance to his page. The two servants heaved the heavy timber over the saddle so that Compton could hold the end just like a lance. However, this was longer and weighed a great deal more.

The watching crowd became more and more curious, then amazed. Novelties of every kind were always welcome, and feats of strength commonplace, but this was something new!

They watched, open-mouthed, as Compton gave the signal and took the whole weight of the trunk. Grimacing with the effort, the veins standing out from his neck, he rose slowly from the list.

The crowd gasped. All eyes were on Compton and the massive tree trunk.

Katherine chose this moment, while all eyes were on the list, to speak quietly to the Spanish messenger sitting beside her.

"Don't look at me," she said in a low, urgent voice. "But I ask you privately to do something for me. Take this letter to the emperor." She slipped the letter to him in a discreet movement and it vanished, equally discreetly, into his clothing.

"You will do this for me—and not show it to anyone else?" she whispered to him. "Or say a word about it to anyone?"

He nodded, almost imperceptibly.

Boleyn and Norfolk sat together, watching Compton dispassionately.

"When will you bring my niece back to court?" Norfolk said quietly.

"Soon, I think," Boleyn said. "Now his appetite is whetted." They exchanged smiles.

The applause rose as Compton approached the end of the list. His face was drawn, the veins in his neck knotted with the strain. His muscles started to tremble. The tension was visible to the crowd, who watched avidly as he strove to keep his arm locked and steady. He grunted in pain, but the crowds were cheering him on now, willing him on. And he made it!

His goal achieved, Compton dropped the trunk with relief. He took the salute of the crowd as he rode triumphantly around, his helmet off, and grinning widely. He passed Henry who was waiting to enter the list again. Henry grinned and nodded at him.

Henry put on his helmet, took his shield and lance from his page and rode out to ringing cheers and applause.

At the other end, his opponent, Knivert took his place.

Henry spurred his horse.

Suddenly the crowd started screaming with a new tone. Something was wrong.

"Look!" Boleyn pointed. "The king's forgotten his visor!"

"Hold! Hold! HOLD!" the crowd screamed. "The king! THE KING! HOLD!"

But Henry couldn't hear the cries beneath the tumult of noise, the thundering of hooves . . . and Knivert, his own visor down, had no chance to see. They thundered toward each other. Closer, closer. They horses closed at full pelt. The crowd held its collective breath.

Crash! Knivert's lance struck the front of the king's helmet, snapping his head backward with a sickening sound. The horrified crowd gasped.

The lance was shattered. Henry put his hand to his face and slumped forward. There was a sudden, shocked silence, broken only by the fluttering pennants snapping in the breeze, and the sound of the horses blowing and stamping.

Katherine rose to her feet in alarm, and suddenly the lists were filled with action as grooms, servants, and almost every noble in the country ran toward their stricken king.

Gentle hands lifted Henry from his horse. Knivert, horrified, dismounted, tossing his helmet aside.

They carefully removed Henry's helmet. His face was bloody, the skin gouged with splinters. With exquisite care, Boleyn plucked out the seven or so splinters that still protruded from the flesh of his cheeks and forehead.

"I'm not hurt. Give me a cloth!" Henry demanded groggily. He was given one. He wiped the blood away with his own hand, then grinned at their appalled faces.

"You see?" he said. "No serious damage."

Knivert, with tears in his eyes, bowed his head. "Will Your Majesty ever forgive me?" he said brokenly.

"It was all my own fault," the king assured him. "And to prove to you—and to the people—that no harm has come to me, I shall run again."

Everyone looked at him in stupefaction.

"Come, Anthony!" Henry insisted. "Run against me!"

His companions were astonished, but he was the king, and not to be gainsaid. Henry walked, a little gingerly, over to the dais, to Katherine, who was still in a state of shock.

"Madam, have no fear for me," Henry told her. "It was an accident, and I intend to show you and everyone that I am perfectly well and unharmed."

"If you must—but I would much rather you did not. I pray God no other harm can come to you, my beloved husband."

Henry's mouth twitched with distaste. He forced a smile and walked back to his horse.

Slowly, people began to realize what he intended, and from a slow and worried murmur, the noise grew and grew into wild cheering.

Henry, enjoying himself, called across to Knivert, "Come, Anthony! Arm yourself," and rode to the top of the list.

Knivert, still shaken by the lucky escape, rode to the far side. They each took a fresh lance, and prepared to ride.

The crowd fell silent. The whole atmosphere was different now: Their king had almost died moments before. It had reminded everyone that this was not merely a game—it was life and death.

Henry and Knivert thundered toward each other. *Crash!* Their lances glanced off their shields.

They turned again. The volume of noise began to rise again, as people grew in confidence. Their God-given king was invulnerable.

They charged again. Henry's lance shattered against Knivert's shield. Knivert's lance missed completely. Even to the crowd, it looked deliberate.

From the top of the list, Henry raised his visor and shouted, "An honest charge, Anthony. No fears. No favors."

Knivert seemed to nod. Henry was given a fresh lance—and charged. They pounded toward each other and their weapons clashed loudly.

Knivert's lance glanced harmlessly off Henry's shield—again, a deliberate miss, but Henry's lance struck Knivert's helmet. From inside there was an explosion of blood.

Blinded and unable to control his horse, Knivert swayed sickeningly in the saddle.

"Help!" Henry shouted. "Help him! Help him!" People rushed toward Knivert. He slumped over in the saddle as blood poured out of his helmet and down his horse's flank.

Chapter Nine

Brandon stepped into Princess Margaret's oak-paneled stateroom on-board the ship bound for Portugal. Lushly furnished with velvet and silk, the cabin almost resembled one of the smaller rooms at court. Margaret was seated at a table, playing patience.

He waited. Margaret continued playing cards. "Your Highness asked to see me."

She turned a card over. "Only to ask how much longer we must be at sea."

"If the wind continues fair, two more days."

Margaret didn't respond. Brandon bowed again, and turned to leave, but she said, "Do you play cards, Your Grace?"

"Sometimes . . . Your Highness."

Margaret made a gesture for him to sit. She gathered up the cards and, for the first time since he'd arrived, she looked at him. "What game shall we play?" she asked. Their eyes locked.

"You choose," Brandon said.

She thought for a minute, then said, "French Ruff."

They began to play, picking up cards from the pack, discarding others. Neither one was concentrating on the cards.

After a time Margaret asked, "Wine?"

"As you please."

She gestured to one of her ladies, who poured two glasses. The game continued. "Your Highness must be looking forward with great anticipation to your wedding?" Brandon said.

Margaret shot him a warning scowl, but said nothing.

Brandon went on, "I heard that the king was a great horseman . . . in his time. And famous for his beautiful mistresses."

"Don't tease me. I don't like it."

"Will you like it when an old man tries to make love to you?"

Her eyes flared. "Your Grace goes too far. Already."

Brandon shrugged. "It says in the Gospels that the truth will make you free."

She jumped up from the table, and he rose too. "Now you are blasphemous!" she said. "My poor ladies should not have to hear you!" Margaret dismissed them, and her ladies filed out, shutting the door behind them.

Suddenly the cabin felt much smaller than it had before. They stood, staring into each other's eyes. Margaret was breathing heavily. Brandon swallowed.

Abruptly Margaret pulled Brandon toward her and kissed him passionately. She stared into his eyes and said, "I want you to leave." But she did not let go of him.

"Do you?" Brandon asked softly.

Her eyes were bright with lust. "Yes. Now!" She started pulling at his clothes, kissing him on the face and neck, pressing her body against his.

Their kisses became frantic. The cards spilled.

"A pity," Brandon joked. "I had a winning hand."

Margaret pushed at him. "Just leave." But her actions contradicted her words.

In answer, he crushed his mouth over hers, hauling her hard against his body.

The boat pitched and they stumbled, falling against the wall of the cabin. Brandon turned, holding Margaret between his body and the wall, pressing her against it as they kissed, and kissed, and kissed.

Their caresses grew more feverish. He started to lift her skirts.

"No . . . no . . . no!" Margaret moaned, but her lips tore at his and her arms pulled him closer, pulling his narrow hips into the juncture of her legs.

Brandon entered her, as passionately as he kissed her, and she wrapped her legs around him, wanting him, wanting the passion and the release and the oblivion.

The night after the accident in the tiltyard, Henry woke, roaring with pain. He sat up in bed, clutching his head. Grooms rushed into the bedchamber.

"Majesty!"

Henry grunted, and started to bang his head against the bedpost. One of the grooms tried to stop him. Henry thrust him away and continued banging his head.

"It hurts, it hurts," he roared.

"Fetch a physician!" a groom ordered. "Quick! Hurry!" The first groom ran off.

Henry remained in agony, banging his head, while three physicians were fetched. They stood around him, arguing in fierce whispers about the best way to treat their roaring sovereign.

All the time the king went thud, thud, thud against the bedpost. At last, agreement was reached and a physician timidly approached. "Your Majesty, we would like to bleed you a little to drain away the bile that is causing Your Majesty so much pain." He waited, then added, "With your permission?"

"Anything!" Henry said.

The physicians, observed by several councillors summoned for the occasion, for the king's health being a matter of state, prepared to bleed the King.

They rolled up Henry's sleeve and applied a tourniquet to his arm. A silver bowl was placed beneath the arm. As one of the physicians raised a sharp knife to cut into the king's flesh, the observers crossed themselves. The room filled with the soft chanting of prayers.

A silent argument broke out between the physicians: no one wanted to be the one to wield the knife. They passed the knife back and forth until, exasperated, one of them seized the knife and drew the blade across the king's distended vein. Blood spurted out, pumping into the silver bowl.

Henry himself lay back on the pillow, his face bathed in sweat, but clearly enjoying some ease. The three physicians peered into the bowl, examining the blood's color and consistency. Everyone in the room relaxed a little.

The next evening, Henry was completely recovered. He strolled through the court with Wolsey. "Send a message to the emperor," Henry ordered. "Tell him of our joy and contentment at his great victory at Pavia, and his capture of the French king."

"Yes, Your Majesty."

"Ask him what he intends to do with Francis. And whether or not, with Francis captive, it may not be a good time to think of striking at France itself. Tell him we have gold, men, and ships at his disposal, and that we are eager to do battle and share some of his glory."

"I shall." Wolsey caught the eye of a young man standing among the courtiers and nodded to him. Wolsey said to Henry, "Ah! Your Majesty, here is your new secretary."

Thomas Cromwell came forward and bowed before the king.

"Thomas Cromwell is a trained barrister, a scholar, and a diligent man," Wolsey said. "I pray he will prove most useful to Your Majesty."

Henry looked Cromwell up and down, and nodded. "Mr. Cromwell."

Henry and Wolsey moved on, entering a hall, equally crowded. At the far end of the hall he saw Katherine waiting for him, holding the hand of their daughter Mary. Henry nodded to Katherine and began to make his way toward her.

Then Henry saw Anne Boleyn. She was wearing his gift—the pearl necklace. "You are back at court, I see." He feasted his eyes on her a moment, then said discreeetly, "May I see you somewhere private?"

Anne agreed, and they made arrangements. Henry then moved forward to greet his wife and daughter. The little princess ran to him, and he swept her, laughing, up in his arms.

"Sweetheart." Henry kissed her. After a short conversation he kissed her again and put her down. As he did, he caught Anne's eye briefly.

Katherine narrowed her eyes at Wolsey, then fell into step with Henry as they proceeded through the hall. "Why does Wolsey open my letters?" Katherine demanded under her breath. "Am I not the queen of England?"

"Are you sure he does?"

"Yes."

"Then I shall stop it." Henry told her. "Sometimes the cardinal is too zealous. But it is always in our interest"—he glanced at her and added—"unless you have secrets!"

She met his look, but at the same moment, Henry caught sight of Anne. She was talking and laughing with a handsome young man. There was no doubting their obvious intimacy.

The sight jolted Henry, who forgot he was in the middle of a serious conversation with his wife.

Katherine watched his face. She could see the jealousy, the yearning . . . the love. Deeply wounded, she lowered her eyes. She said nothing. There was nothing to say.

Henry dropped her arm and walked into his presence chamber, where Norfolk and other courtiers were already assembled. Knivert stood among them. The wound near his eye was still livid, the area around it deeply bruised. "You nearly lost an eye, Anthony," Henry said.

Knivert shrugged. "I don't use that one much, anyway." Henry smiled, then gestured to Norfolk to come forward. Norfolk came, holding a velvet cushion upon which sat a ceremonial sword. He bowed, and Henry lifted the sword.

"Kneel," he ordered Knivert.

As Knivert knelt, Henry touched him on each shoulder with the blade of the sword. "Arise, Sir Anthony Knivert."

Knivert rose, and Henry embraced him. The doors opened again, and the chamberlain announced, "Mr. William Compton."

Compton entered. Knivert looked from him to the king and realized Henry still held the ceremonial sword. His jaw dropped.

Henry had no difficulty interpreting his expression. He asked, "Why so reproving a look, Sir Anthony?"

"Majesty," Knivert answered, "I almost lost an eye for the same result!"

Henry grinned, enjoying himself. "Ah, but you never carried a tree!" He laughed. "Pray kneel, Mr. Compton."

A short time later Henry detached himself from his courtiers and went off to meet Anne Boleyn.

She was waiting for him in the private chamber where they'd arranged to meet.

"I have dreamt of this moment a long time," he told her. "Anne, you must know that I desire you with all my heart."

She lowered her eyes. Henry gently cupped her chin and raised her face. "Who was he? The young man I saw you dallying with just now?"

Anne smiled. "I think you mean my brother George."

At her words, Henry relaxed. He caressed her cheek and gently drew her toward him. After the earlier difficulty he'd had in seeing her, he expected some resistance, but she gave him none. She glided into his arms as if she belonged there.

Henry kissed her, long and deeply. At last, at last. He gazed into her wonderful eyes, which seemed to shine with a light all their own, even in that dull passage.

"Kiss me again, my love," Henry said, and again they kissed and it was everything he had dreamed of, and more. He wrapped his arms around her and kissed her a third time, but there were footsteps in the corridor and they broke guiltily apart.

"I must go," she whispered. "Her Majesty expects me."

Henry, drunk with love, nodded, smiling. "We shall meet later, sweetheart."

Anne nodded, dropped a quick curtsy, and hurried away into the shadows, just as Knivert and Compton turned the corner. "Who was that, Your Majesty?" Compton asked.

"Just a girl," Henry said softly. "Just . . . a girl."

That evening, in a quiet part of London, visitors in dark cloaks slipped quietly from the shadows and knocked softly on the door of a respectable merchant's house.

Each time, a servant cracked open the door and waited for a softly spoken password before admitting the visitor. On admission, the men removed their dark cloaks. Their clothes were plain, and mostly dark, but the rich fabric showed that these were prosperous and important men.

In the main room of the house an assembly was gathered. The last stragglers seated themselves. A plainly dressed pastor had already begun to speak. He was Dutch, speaking English with a thick accent.

". . . the pope, far from being a descendant of Saint Peter, is a sinner and hypocrite, a handmaiden of the Devil, and the living Antichrist on earth." He looked around the room. "This is what Luther teaches us, in order to free us from false idols and false worship. . . ."

His audience listened with sober attention. They had not come here lightly, out of curiosity. Not for nothing did they risk themselves to hear one of Luther's followers preach what most in Roman Catholic England would call heresy.

They burned heretics.

Among the audience sat a young, thin man, dressed in plain, dark clothing. Thomas Cromwell, the king's new secretary, Cardinal Wolsey's newest protégé, listened with the rest, his face impassive.

The pastor continued, "Our message—of hope, of liberty, of truth—is already spreading throughout Europe, from one corner to another. Here in England, we have planted a seed that will, with prayer and with action, and perhaps even with sacrifice, one day grow to become a great tree whose branches will overreach the kingdom and destroy the putrid monastic houses of the Antichrist. And this tree will be called the Liberty Tree, and in its branches all the Angels of the Lord shall sing Hallelujah."

In the darkness just before dawn, Princess Margaret stood, staring out through the rear window of her stateroom. A sliver of lonely moonlight illuminated the ship's wake like a silver blade.

Slowly, too slowly, the moonlight faded. Through her other window, the town and harbor of Lisbon began to materialize in the faint predawn light. She stared at it bitterly and closed her eyes.

She could sense Brandon behind her. He put his hands on her shoulders and stood, looking out with her. "Your new kingdom," he murmured. She said nothing, just watched in silence as the dawn broke.

Brandon continued, "The king must be—"

"Don't! I forbid you to speak of that!"

He moved closer, the warmth of his body soaking into her. She shivered. "I should hate you!"

"But you don't," Brandon said. "I know you don't."

There was a long silence. Finally Margaret turned and looked at him, her eyes wet with tears. "What am I going to do?"

Brandon stroked her cheek sadly. There was nothing to say.

The next day, Princess Margaret walked into the Portuguese palace. Her path was lined by severe-looking monks and nuns who stared at her with no sign of welcome. Margaret walked with pride, but inside she was shaking. She took comfort from the fact that Brandon walked a pace behind her.

Inside, a reception party of Portuguese bishops, aristocrats, and officers in plumed helmets waited. There were a few women present, but most were elderly men. They watched her with cold eyes and hard expressions. There were no welcoming smiles, not so much as a friendly look. She felt like an insect on a pin.

The king of Portugal came forward, shuffling slowly, with a stick. She had been told he was in his sixties, but he looked much older. His frame was emaciated, and his thin hair sat on top of a skull-like face. He looked ancient, half-dead, but bizarrely, he had effected the dress of a much younger man.

As this apparition shuffled toward her, Margaret almost visibly recoiled. "Save me," she murmured under her breath.

But she was not to be saved. The king bowed to her, and the lascivious eyes in their bony sockets traveled slowly up and down her body.

With shaking knees, Margaret managed to curtsy. "Your . . . Majesty." She swallowed and tasted bile.

The king began to speak in Portuguese: "Margaret, you are even more handsome than your portrait. I feel fortunate that you are soon to be my queen. Everything here is at your disposal. I want you to be happy, and to make me happy."

Margaret blinked. She spoke no Portuguese, and no one had thought to tell her that her new husband spoke not a word of English. Someone came forward and quietly began to translate what the king was saying, and then she wished they hadn't, for what he said now was even more horrifying.

"And then we will make children together, you and I," the king continued. His rheumy old eyes brightened as they ran over her body again, and he licked his lips, which were already wet, and added, "Many children . . . with God's help!"

Margaret threw a piteous look at Brandon.

He stared ahead, his face expressionless.

Margaret's wedding ceremony commenced with a great pealing of church bells. The bride looked magnificent, except for her eyes, which were red and swollen from crying.

At the door of the cathedral the music swelled, playing a solemn march that felt to Margaret appropriately funereal. She began the long walk down the aisle with twenty-four ladies behind her holding up the heavy train.

Brandon, as King Henry's representative, walked with her, giving the bride away. She clung to his arm, shaking, but her head was held high.

The atmosphere was poisonous. The cathedral was packed with the cream of Portuguese society and the king's relatives, none of whom appeared to approve of this wedding. They stared at her with obvious hostility, and muttered loud comments in Portuguese.

"There she is—the king's English slut."

"There's the money-grabbing bitch!"

"I want to scratch her eyes out!"

Margaret did not know what they were saying, but their meaning was obvious. Even the children made rude gestures and stuck their tongues out at her. It took forever to reach the altar. As far as Margaret was concerned, it was over much too soon.

The king was waiting. As she approached, he turned and, cadaver-like, grinned at her with stained and broken teeth. She faltered, but Brandon propelled her firmly forward.

"What are you doing?" Margaret hissed at him.

"What the king ordered me to do!"

They finally reached the altar. The bishop signaled the bride and groom to kneel. The king managed with some difficulty—he had to be helped because of his gout.

In Latin, the archbishop began to marry them.

In English, Margaret began to pray.

The day crawled to a conclusion, and finally the hour of Margaret's wedding night was upon her. Her ladies prepared her for the marriage bed, like a sacrificial lamb, lacing pearls into her hair and spraying her with different perfumes. All the while a priest prayed over her in Portuguese. He annointed the bed with Holy Water, and blessed it. Margaret was placed inside.

Trembling uncontrollably, she waited. She almost jumped out of her skin as musicians struck up, accompanying the king on his journey into the bedchamber.

Margaret's new husband stood, feasting his eyes on the young princess as his attendants removed his dressing gown. Beneath it, he wore a brightly striped nightshirt. The bright colors contrasted shockingly with his waxen parchment of his face. His grooms removed the wig he'd worn to his wedding, to reveal sparse gray stubble thinly covering a bony skull.

He grinned at Margaret like a death's head as he dipped his fingers into the Holy Water and blessed himself. Slowly, he climbed into bed beside her. She lay there, rigid, as with great formality the curtains around the bed were slowly closed. And the court waited.

The broaching of a new bride by a king was a matter of state and must be witnessed.

Margaret lay stiff, filled with horror and dread. The old man in the bed stank of perfumes and musk pastilles, but underneath the perfumes lay the stink of a none-too-clean, goaty old man.

She winced when his shriveled old hands thrust under her nightdress, pushing it higher and higher. She lay with eyes screwed shut, willing her mind elsewhere as he panted and slavered over her body, exploring her flesh with little murmurs of delight.

He parted her legs, and she felt the press of him against her. He tried to thrust and thrust against her, panting louder and louder, but nothing happened. He scrabbled around on her body, trying different angles, using his dirty old feet against the bedposts to gain some leverage.

The bed curtains parted briefly as his feet slipped through, and Margaret caught a glimpse of a row of faces, observing solemnly. There was blood in her mouth; she'd bitten her cheek in an effort not to vomit.

The bed creaked, and creaked again, and soon it was creaking with an unmistakable rhythm, louder and louder. The sound of panting was joined by grunts, groans, and odd, falsetto whinnying sounds from the king.

It seemed to go for ages, then the king gave a shudder and a sort of trilling sound, and subsided. Margaret gave one solitary squeak to indicate she'd played her role in this horrific farce.

Then there was silence, except for the loud panting from the king.

Everyone waited, unsure of what to do. Then a colonel in the king's army stepped forward and pulled back the bed curtain.

Margaret lay there, her nightgown in disarray. The king lay on his back, red-faced from his exertions and breathing with difficulty.

The colonel addressed Margaret. "Did His Majesty . . . ?" He paused, discreetly. Everyone waited.

Margaret nodded. And immediately everyone in the bedchamber started to applaud. As the noise and applause grew, Margaret looked at her new husband.

The physical effort of making love to her had utterly exhausted him. He lay there, gasping like a landed fish, showing no evidence of awareness of his apparent triumph. He had to fight for every breath, she saw. His eyes were glazed, and one shriveled claw clutched at his chest. Clearly it wouldn't take much . . .

She might not have to endure this as long as she'd thought.

Anne Boleyn lay on her bed in her nightdress, reading the latest letter from Henry.

> *I beg you, name some place that we can meet, and where I can show you truly an affection which is beyond a common affection.*

She looked at the signature.

> *Written with the hand of your servant, H. R.*

She smiled and tucked the letter inside her bodice. A noise made her look up. Her father was standing in the doorway. He moved swiftly forward and snatched the letter. Quickly he scanned it, then looked at his daughter with obvious satisfaction.

"Excellent work, daughter! Now he is 'your servant.' With some subtle care, and the lure of your flesh, he may become something even closer." He patted her on the head, then blew out the candle and walked out.

Anne lay in bed, her eyes open. The smile had faded from her face. Misery engulfed her. She had not expected to feel like this, not at all.

It was a glorious sunny day, the first to follow in a long period of rain, and Henry had decided to go hawking. With Knivert, Compton, and other members of his immediate entourage, he set out, a collection of servants in close attendance.

A lazy buzzard circled in the afternoon sky. Henry's party cantered down a long field, strung out like a procession. As the first riders came to a wide, sunken ditch, they pulled up sharply. Compton called out to the others, "Hold! Hold!"

Henry trotted up. "What is it?"

Compton rode around, testing the ground. "The ground's too boggy for the horses. We'll have to go round that way." He pointed.

Henry frowned. "That's a long way. Why can't we go this way?"

"We can't jump that ditch," Compton told him.

Henry gave him a scornful look. "You mean you can't jump it!" He jumped off his horse and walked down to the ditch. Everyone waited while the king examined the ditch, and then, to their bemusement, examined a copse of young trees growing nearby.

He shouted for an ax to be brought and set to work himself, lopping off branches from a sturdy sapling of about ten feet high. The others exchanged bewildered looks.

Knivert dismounted. "What are you doing, Your Majesty?"

For an answer, Henry cut down the sapling. "What does it look like? I shall vault over this stupid ditch. I refuse to let it stand in the way of my sport." Everyone laughed.

"Are you sure about this?" Compton asked.

Henry grinned. "Watch, my friend, and see what the king of England can do."

Laughing and taking bets, they gathered to watch as Henry took a few paces back, measuring out his run. First he tested the flexibility of his pole, then he ran toward the ditch.

With the greatest agility he speared the pole into the center of the water and took off, soaring up in a magnificent leap, to the accompaniment of cheers and applause.

The pole snapped in midair and Henry fell headfirst into the heavy clay mud of the ditch.

Henry's head and shoulders had disappeared beneath the mud. His legs waggled about comically. His companions clutched their ribs and hooted with laughter.

It took one of the grooms, Edmund Mody, to realize the gravity of the situation. He ran forward and threw himself into the ditch, frantically struggling through the thick black mud to get to his master, buried alive. Desperately he began to dig, pulling at the king's body.

Too late the king's companions realized the king was drowning in mud. They flung themselves off their horses and got to the edge of the ditch just as Mody pulled Henry's face clear.

Horrified, they watched the man reach into Henry's mouth and scoop great chunks of mud from it. Still, the king didn't breathe. Mody again reached into his mouth to clear out even more mud from his windpipe.

Knivert and Compton and all the rest stared, frozen, utterly horrified. Then, with an appalling sound, Henry took a great, painful gasp, and air rushed back into his lungs.

His companions clustered around him, deeply shocked. They had stood by laughing while the king nearly died.

That evening Henry sat watching the members of his court dance. He was brooding. Katherine sat beside him. Henry could barely bring himself to look at her.

God had made it clear to him now. He had not given Henry and Katherine a living son—it was Henry's punishment for marrying his brother's wife. God had given him a healthy bastard son as a message: He could have sons, but not with his brother's widow.

Next, God had brought him Anne Boleyn, and Henry was in love for the first time in his life. And then he'd nearly died, ignominiously buried upside down in mud.

It all meant something. He sent for Wolsey.

"I almost died," Henry told him.

Wolsey nodded. He had heard. "Yes, Your Majesty."

There was a pause. "No!" Henry shook his head and strode up to stand face-to-face with the cardinal. He stared at him, their faces bare inches apart. "Not, 'Yes, Your Majesty.' I ALMOST DIED! DON'T YOU UNDERSTAND?" he shouted.

Wolsey was silent, unusually cowed.

Henry paced about. "Since that moment, I've done a great deal of thinking. If I had died, what would I have left? I have no heir—only a daughter, and a bastard son." He whirled and glared at Wolsey. "Do you understand, Wolsey? The Tudor dynasty—it's gone, all my father's work. It's all finished. And it's *my* fault. It's my fault."

He resumed his pacing. "I've lived too much for pleasure. I married my brother's wife, and God has punished me. I never thought about the future. I've been such a fool."

There was another silence. Henry moved slowly back to stand in front of Wolsey. "Everything has changed now," Henry said. "*Everything.* I want a divorce. And you will get one for me!" He gave Wolsey a hard look, then marched from the room.

There was dancing in Portugal to celebrate the royal wedding. The King's gout prevented him from dancing personally, so he and his young bride sat and watched the others dance.

Brandon approached, and bowed deeply to the king. "With Your Majesty's permission, may I dance with your wife?"

A courtier translated, and the king nodded brusquely. Brandon escorted Margaret onto the dance floor, and they started to dance.

After a time, Margaret asked him, "When do you leave?"

"Tomorrow."

Margaret gave him a panic-stricken look. "You can't."

Brandon smiled a little. "Why can't I? I've discharged my duty. Why should I stay? You have a life to lead."

"No!" she said vehemently.

They danced on. The king watched them like a hawk.

Brandon said, "It's strange, but some men, who seem at the peak of health, who are still young and full of life, suddenly collapse and die." They moved apart and then came back together. He continued, "And by the same counter, some old men, whose bodies look worn out, whose race seems run . . . they can go on for years . . . and years . . . and years." He waited and then said, "Don't you think that's strange?"

Margaret was silent, trying hard not to give anything away. She was only too conscious that a whole kingdom was looking at her, and not with friendly intent.

"Do you tease me because it amuses you?" she said at last.

"Why else?" he said lightly.

Margaret looked at him. "Because you love me."

Brandon suddenly had no reply. He stared into her eyes, and they danced without thinking, their familiarity with each other and their yearning unconsciously revealed.

The king watched them, becoming visibly more angry. "Who in Hell is that fellow?"

Dawn rose over the ancient city of London and while some in the city woke, they were mostly the poor; the servants, the beggars, those who must glean a living from a harsh world. Most of the aristocracy slumbered on.

Not, however, the king. He was bent over a letter, writing.

Perhaps you don't understand. But I can't sleep, I can hardly breathe, for thinking of you. Your image is before my eyes every waking second. I almost believe that I would sacrifice my kingdom for an hour in your arms. . . .

*   *   *   *

Margaret stared out of the window as dawn broke over the city of Lisbon. Riding at anchor in the harbor was an English ship, waiting to take Brandon back to England.

After a few moments she walked back to the bed. Her husband, the king, was asleep, but troubled. His breath came in shallow, painful gasps.

She stared down at him impassively. His face on the pillow seemed particularly skull-like. Almost as if he was already half in the other world.

Carefully and quietly, Margaret took a pillow and pressed it hard over his face. His limbs shook and kicked. His hands scrabbled at her body, and he made strangled sounds in his throat.

It sounded and felt much like it had when he had made love to her. She shuddered, recalling it. Never again. She kept on pressing the pillow until there were no more jerks, no more, quivers, no more sounds.

The king of Portugal was dead.

Chapter Ten

In the spring, Henry bestowed the title of Lord Rochford on Sir Thomas Boleyn. He also made his three-year-old son by Bessie Blount the Duke of Richmond and Somerset, and Earl of Nottingham. The child now outranked everyone in the kingdom, except his father.

Queen Katherine was outraged. She knew who was responsible for this: Wolsey! She sent a message for him to attend her immediately after the ceremony was concluded. She waited in her private chambers, seething, until one of her ladies announced Wolsey's arrival.

"I see His Majesty's bastard son is made a duke! Does it mean—" Katherine broke off, swallowing her rage. "Does it mean he is now next in rank to the king? Next in line to the throne? Above my daughter?"

"Yes," Wolsey said. "Technically. He is set above everyone, except a legitimate son."

Katherine furiously blinked back tears. "His Majesty loves our daughter," she said. "He has shown it on many occasions, in public and in private. I cannot believe he means to place his bastard child above her."

Wolsey said nothing.

"I don't believe His Majesty was personally responsible for this action. After all, our daughter is engaged to the emperor!" She threw him a challenging look.

Wolsey cleared his throat. "Then Your Majesty has not heard?"

"Heard what?"

"The emperor has married Princess Isabella of Portugal."

Katherine's jaw dropped.

"Apparently he decided it was not worth waiting for your daughter to grow up. And, who is to say, but perhaps he was influenced by the fact that the beautiful Isabella brought with her a dowry of a million pounds." He let the immense sum sink in. "He broke his word."

Katherine could not speak, she was so shocked, so betrayed. First by her husband and now by her nephew. Dumbstruck, she stared at Wolsey, as if at some loathsome toad.

He smiled serenely back at her.

Back at the king's house at Jericho, Lady Blount curtsied to her small son. "Your Grace." Then she smiled and opened her arms, and the little boy flew into her arms.

She kissed him, wiped away a tear, and looked at him sadly. Then, in an encouraging voice, she told him, "Now, Henry, listen to me: You are going to have your own house now, and lots of servants to help you and look after you."

The child nodded, unaware of the implications. "I know, Mama."

"You must promise me to be a good boy," his mother said, trying to keep her face serene. "Be thoughtful and kind to those around you. You may be set above them, but if I find you have grown too proud, I will be sad and displeased."

The little boy looked serious. "Yes, Mama. I promise."

Lady Blount said with a smile, "Good, and I promise to come and see you as often as I can. I am sure your new house will be very grand!"

Her emotions threatened to overcome her, so she hugged him tightly again and whispered into his ear so that nobody else could hear, "I love you, my darling boy. I love you."

Henry paced about his chambers, agitated. He clutched a document in his fist. "My poor sister!"

"Indeed," Wolsey murmured. "To be made queen for just a few days. It seems incredible. A tragedy."

Henry nodded. "Poor Margaret. When she returns, she is to be treated to every comfort and kindness while she mourns."

Henry put down the letter and looked at Wolsey. "And now . . ."

Wolsey knew what he meant. "As for the—the great matter of Your Majesty's annulment, I have set up an ecclesiastical court with Archbishop Warham to consider and decide on the matter. It will meet in secret, if Your Majesty agrees."

Henry gave a brusque nod. "Make sure it comes to the right decision quickly." He returned to his pacing.

Wolsey inclined his head. "I have some further news," he said. "Concerning the emperor." He waited. Henry gave him an impatient look.

"He has released King Francis," Wolsey told him.

Henry's pacing stopped dead. *"What?"*

"I have it on good authority," Wolsey said quietly.

"On what terms?" Henry demanded.

"I have yet to find out."

Henry smashed his fist onto the table. "He should have consulted me! We are supposed to be allies! What game is he playing? I want to see his ambassador!"

He suddenly opened his hand, looking anxiously at what it contained. But the silver locket in his palm was undamaged. "I will see the ambassador," he said slowly. "But, first, I have an appointment. . . ."

Henry rode fast down the hard-baked earthen road, escorted by two yeoman of the guard, their horses' hooves churning up clouds of dust. He had an appointment at Hever Castle, with a lady.

At Hever, he was directed to a galleried chamber. Anne waited on the far side.

"Anne," he murmured. He was almost shaking with passion. He stared into her eyes and repeated, "Anne." Then he crushed his mouth against hers greedily.

He was a man intoxicated. His arms encircled her, drawing her ever closer. "Anne," he said for the third time. He smiled lovingly at her, his eyes bright, confident.

"I want to say something to you," he told her. "If it pleases you to be my true, loyal mistress and friend, to give yourself up, body and soul, to me, I promise that I'll take you as my only mistress. I won't have a thought or affection for anyone else."

He waited for her to speak, then added, in case she hadn't understood, "If you will agree to be my *Maîtresse en titre*, then I swear I shall serve only you." He waited.

Anne stiffened. "*Maîtresse en titre?* Your official mistress?"

"Yes! And you will have everything you need. Everything within my power to give you." He caressed her cheek. "You need only ask—it will be yours!"

Anne turned away from him, her face downcast.

Henry frowned and snatched her hand to make her look at him. "What is it, sweetheart? What is it?"

She turned a reproachful face toward him and said sadly, "What have I done to make you treat me like this?"

Henry was confused. "Done? What fault have I committed? Tell me!"

"Your Majesty, I have already given my maidenhead into my husband's hands. And whoever he is, only he will have it."

"Sweet Anne—"

Anne shook her head. "No! For I know how it goes otherwise. My sister is called *the great prostitute* by everyone."

Henry looked at her, stunned. Confused emotions roiled around in him. No woman had ever refused, him, let alone deemed his intentions an insult. He said stiffly, "I am sorry if I offended you. I did not mean to. I spoke to you plainly of my true feelings."

Anne lowered her head again. "Majesty."

Henry had no option: He turned and stalked away. He strode down the long hall, red-faced and obviously embarrassed, and came across Thomas Boleyn waiting for him in the hall.

Boleyn stepped forward, looking surprised and concerned. Henry didn't so much as acknowledge him. He stormed out of the castle, mounted his horse, and galloped off.

Boleyn listened to the sound of the horses' hooves receding, and gave a small and satisfied smile. He went in search of his daughter and found her standing by herself in a dark little space.

"That was well done, my beautiful daughter," he told her.

"Was it?" Anne said quietly. Boleyn stepped forward and peered at her face in surprise. She had been crying. She stared at her father a moment.

"Was it?" she repeated bitterly, and fled the room, weeping.

When he returned to Whitehall, Henry summoned the ambassador of the Holy Roman Emperor to an audience. "Señor Mendoza, I am not pleased to see you," Henry told the ambassador bluntly before the man had finished bowing.

Mendoza feigned astonishment. "Majesty?"

"Your Master has broken all his promises," Henry said. "He has accepted our money, but used it against our interests. He has negotiated a separate peace with the king of France and His Holiness the Pope . . . whilst neglecting his ally and his friend. He has not kept faith!" He glared at Mendoza. "Charles has nothing but words for me! Deeds he keeps for others!"

Mendoza began in a soothing voice, "The emperor would never betray Your Majesty. Never! He regards you as his uncle. He—"

"His fucking uncle! How old am I?" roared Henry.

Mendoza said carefully, "Well, Your Majesty must consider that you, yourself, may not always have kept to your obligations. After all, we received only half the amount of gold that was promised—"

Henry furiously stepped off the dais and jabbed his finger at Mendoza's face. "Your accusations are totally false! Unacceptable! I will answer for my honorable conduct—whoever wants to contradict me!"

There was no arguing with a king. Mendoza hung his head and

managed to look embarrassed. After a short while, he was dismissed.

Moments later, looking far from sheepish, Mendoza walked through the court, his eyes darting here and there as if he was seeking someone. At last he saw him. He made a discreet gesture, and Sir Thomas Boleyn came forward.

Mendoza drew him aside into a quiet corner. "My Lord Rochford. The emperor sends you his warmest congratulations on your elevation," Mendoza told him.

Boleyn raised his brows. "And what does the emperor care about my elevation?"

"He cares to have friends at the English court," Mendoza said, adding softly, "and he pays for the privilege."

Boleyn gave him a shrewd look. "And does the emperor have many friends here already?"

"Several. Your Lordship would know them."

"And . . . what does friendship pay?"

Mendoza smiled "One thousand crowns a year."

Boleyn's eyes widened. It was a fortune. "I will certainly consider His Highness's gracious offer."

Mendoza smiled and moved away. Boleyn turned and found the Duke of Norfolk watching. Was Norfolk on the Emperor's payroll too? he wondered. And who else at court might be?

Norfolk approached him. "And how go the young lovers?" he asked quietly.

"He asked her to be his official mistress," Boleyn told him.

Norfolk looked intrigued. "But naturally she . . ."

Boleyn gave a smug smile. Norfolk nodded, pleased.

They stood for a while, watching the activities around them in silence. Norfolk asked casually, "How did you find the Imperial Ambassador?"

"Stimulating," Boleyn responded cautiously.

"Indeed. I have talked to him. I find him a man of great . . . principle," Norfolk said, and moved away.

*My lady, you have left me in distress, not knowing your true feel-
ings. With all my heart I beg you to give me an answer—whether
you favor my suit, or reject it!*

Anne lay curled up in her bedchamber at Hever Castle, reading Henry's
latest missive. Other papers lay scattered around her; several poems, a letter from a friend in France, and a tract by Martin Luther that she'd been
reading when Henry's letter had been delivered.

Henry's letter continued: *I tell you I pledge to you all my honor, love, and
service.* She closed her eyes at the heartfelt emotion in the words. She'd
never expected to feel like this about Henry. If she had . . .

But she had begun this course. Her family was depending on her.
There was no option but to see it through to the end.

Suddenly the letter was snatched from her hands by her brother,
George.

"No, George! Please. Give it back!" Anne begged him.

George skipped away from her, reading aloud. "'I have given you my
heart—now I desire—'"

Distressed, Anne tried again to reclaim the letter, but George evaded
her.

"Don't! Please!"

George continued, "'now I desire to dedicate my body to you.'"

Anne gave up, and slumped, dejected as George read the conclusion
of the letter.

"'Written by the hand of him who in heart, body, and will is your
loyal and most ensured servant, H. R.'" George peered at the letter and
grinned. "And look! He has drawn a little heart between the letter H and
R." He pointed, laughing.

He looked at his sister. Anne's face was red. Enjoying himself, George
whispered, "Just imagine: The king of England writing to my little
sister—promising to be her servant! It's incredible."

"Give me the letter," she said quietly.

George ignored her. "He's in love with you," he crowed.

"Give me the letter!"

Startled by the passionate vehemence in her voice, George stopped laughing. He handed the letter back to her and watched as she tucked it away out of sight.

George studied her profile. At last he said in a worried voice, "You're not in love with him—are you?"

Anne didn't answer.

On a warship bound for England, the newly widowed queen of Portugal lay on a bunk in the arms of Brandon, Duke of Suffolk.

On this return journey the gentle creaking of the timbers, and the rhythmic roll of the ship upon a placid sea now soothed Margaret. She wanted the journey to go on forever.

"It was a great death," Brandon said, and kissed her. "To die in the fulfillment of one's conjugal duties; what could be better? Your 'little death,' and then his larger, more permanent one." He smiled.

"Do you think they were suspicious?"

Brandon laughed. "Of course they were suspicious! Didn't you see the way his servants looked at you?" He gave an ironic smile. "But his son was overjoyed! I mean: His Majesty was overjoyed. After all, he had waited many years for the crown. The old man had clung on grimly."

Margaret gave an extravagant shudder. "Don't remind me of his clinging habits! I'm doing my best to forget them!" They laughed, softly, quietly, caressing, brushing lips.

After an interval, Margaret said, "What are we going to do?"

"Isn't this enough?"

"No! . . . Well, yes." She kissed him. "And no." She sighed. "We shall come to England eventually."

They thought about what might face them. There would be consequences, they both knew. Brandon turned her face toward him and looked into her eyes. "Marry me," he whispered.

"What?" She stared at him.

"You heard. Marry me!"

Margaret was stunned at the audacity of the suggestion. He'd given voice to the secret dream of her heart. But she was a royal princess—no, a queen—widowed but a short time, and he was a commoner . . . recently ennobled, it was true. . . .

But for Brandon to wed her without the king's permission was, technically, treason.

Compton made his way to a crowded London tavern. Why on earth would Brandon want to meet him here, in this unsavory location, when they could as easily have met at court? It was crowded, noisy, and stank of unwashed bodies, beer, wine, and damp wool.

He spotted Brandon, waiting, already drunk, judging by the number of wine bottles and empty glasses on the table. Brandon embraced him warmly. "My dear William. Come, have a drink." He poured two glasses and continued. "How good to see you."

"Yes," Compton said. "But why here? I don't understand." He added, "We've been expecting you back at court."

Brandon's smile vanished. He looked uncertain, even worried. "How is the king?"

"Anxious to see his sister," Compton told him. "And to share her grief."

"Ah . . . her grief . . . yes." Brandon drained his glass. He gave Compton a rueful, guilty look. "We're married."

Compton was confused. "What? Who?"

Brandon shrugged. "She . . . and me! We're married."

Understanding slowly dawned, and Compton goggled. "You and . . . ?"

Brandon nodded. "Yes. You have to tell him. You have to tell the king."

"*I* have to tell him? Why do *I* have to tell him?"

"It will be better coming from you." They fell silent, considering the enormity of the deed. Brandon could lose his head for it.

Compton emptied his glass, looked at his old friend again, and unexpectedly grinned. "What's the matter, Charles? Lost your nerve?"

Brandon slumped onto the bench. "It's no laughing matter."

"I know," Compton agreed. "So why did you do it?"

Brandon made an uncomfortable gesture. "You know me. I don't always think."

Compton snorted. "Yes you do! But not always with your head!"

It was Good Friday, and Queen Katherine was in church. The choir sang the *Stabat Mater*, while the ceremony known as Crawling to the Cross took place.

Barefoot, the men of the congregation crawled on their hands and knees toward an altar containing an image of the Virgin. The image held a large crucifix "marvelously finely gilt," which the men kissed reverently.

After the last man had kissed the crucifix, a monk lifted it and carried it to the lowest steps in the choir, placing it upon a velvet cushion. The austere, elderly Bishop of Rochester, John Fisher himself, who had been mentor to the young King Henry, crawled barefoot over to it and kissed it. He rose, bowed to Katherine and, with a gesture, invited her to follow him outside. As Katherine appeared, the waiting crowd broke into applause.

Fisher addressed them. "Good people of Lambeth. On this Good Friday, the Queen's Majesty will distribute the king's Maundy Money to these unfortunate but true and royal Subjects of Their Majesties . . . in the Christian spirit of charity and love."

Katherine approached the first thin and ragged man. He fell to his knees before her, trembling. One of Katherine's ladies passed her a golden coin, and she pressed it into the poor man's hand, whispering words of comfort into his ear.

Tears rolled down the poor man's cheeks. It was the greatest moment of his life. Far above the value of the money was the significance of being touched, and spiritually healed, by the queen. It was as if he'd been blessed by a saint.

Katherine moved on down the line, distributing the king's gift. Crowds watched her, smiling, weeping, feeling blessed.

One of the observers watched the ceremony with rather less evidence of joy—Mr. Cromwell, the king's secretary. His face was expressionless, but his nose looked faintly pinched, as if he'd smelled something rotten.

"He wants a *divorce*?" Sir Thomas More exclaimed, shocked. "I don't believe it!" He had received an urgent summons from Wolsey and, despite the late hour, had come immediately to Hampton Court. He stared at Wolsey, unable to take in the enormity of the king's demand.

Wolsey shook his head. "It's not a divorce. He wants an annulment on the grounds that he was never married in the first place." He saw More's look and added, "By marrying his brother's wife, he has offended both the laws of man and God. He simply wants that recognized."

"But the pope gave him a special dispensation to marry Katherine!"

Wolsey shrugged. "Indeed he did. No one denies it. But the king feels more beholden to God than he does to the pope. His conscience is genuinely stricken. He has disobeyed God's injunction, and nothing his Holiness can say or do will alter that fact."

More frowned. "But the pope is God's representative on earth. He does speak for—"

Wolsey tossed his quill aside. "Come, come, Thomas. What are you pretending? Kings get divorced all the time. And popes always find some excuse. I know you're an idealist, but you're not a fool. If Henry wants to annul his marriage, who's to stop him?"

More gave Wolsey a searching look. "All right. Let's play the realist. You talk of facts. Let me give you a fact: Katherine of Aragon is not only a great queen and the daughter of great kings, she is also immensely popular throughout the whole of the country. God forbid that the king abandon her—just to ease his conscience! I don't think the English people would ever forgive him!"

Wolsey seemed unmoved by his argument.

After a moment, More said in a low voice, "Does she know yet?"

Wolsey didn't answer.

Deeply troubled, More went to the window and looked out. Masses of dark clouds had gathered ominously over the moon. A storm was coming. It was appropriate, More felt. God knew what would come of this.

"Caught you!" Princess Mary jumped out from behind a chair and caught her mother around the waist.

"But, aha, now I've caught you!" Katherine lifted Mary and swung the child in a circle. The little girl shrieked madly. Katherine put her down and she staggered dizzily, giggling and exaggerating her state. All the ladies-in-waiting were laughing.

Suddenly their laughter died away. Katherine looked up and saw Wolsey standing at the door, watching. She froze.

"Come here, sweetheart," she told Mary who, puzzled at the abrupt change of atmosphere, gave her mother a worried look.

Katherine smiled reassuringly and gave her a kiss. "Go to your chambers," she told her. "I'll see you later."

"Yes, Mama," the child said obediently. One of the princess's attendants came forward and led her from the room.

Katherine gestured for all her ladies to leave. She looked disdainfully at Wolsey and said in a sarcastic tone, "Another visit, Your Eminence. You are always so . . . busy."

"I have some good news," Wolsey said mildly. "Since His Majesty has given the Duke of Richmond his own establishment, he considers it only right and proper that his beloved Princess Mary should also have hers."

Katherine's eyes narrowed. "What do you mean?"

"His Majesty intends to send the Princess to Ludlow Castle, on the Welsh Marches. She will be in the care of Lady Salisbury, her lady governess. Her tutor, Dr. Fetherston, will also accompany her, as well as three hundred members of the princess's household."

It took a moment for his words to sink in. "She—she is being taken away from me?"

"Not at all," Wolsey said. "His Majesty is according her the true honors of a princess."

"This is not His Majesty's suggestion!" Katherine said in a scathing voice.

Wolsey spread his hands in a helpless gesture. "Madam, I am often accused of things that are not my fault, or responsibility. Some folks are always prone to speak evil and report the worst without knowledge of the truth. And they might have poisoned Your Majesty's mind against me."

Katherine said bitterly, "You are taking my child—*my child*—my only source of happiness, the center of my world." Her voice rose to a grief-stricken pitch. "You are tearing her away from me as if you were tearing her from my womb!"

"I but do as the king commands," Wolsey told her.

Katherine stared at him with loathing. "Get out of my rooms!"

Wolsey bowed. "Majesty." He left, leaving Katherine staring after him, distraught, devastated. But she did not, would not weep. Not for him.

Katherine could hear the rain and the thunder as she knelt in prayer before her small shrine. She gradually became aware of a noise that was not part of the storm, and got up to investigate.

Her jaw dropped when she saw Henry entering the chamber through his private passageway. For a few seconds she thought that her prayers—after all these years—had been answered, that Henry was resuming his conjugal visits, but then she saw his awkwardness, the tension that radiated from him, and her hopes turned to ashes.

She dropped a low curtsy and waited.

Henry fidgeted awkwardly, paced back and forth a few times, and then said with uncharacteristic bluntness, "Katherine, I have something to tell you. As far as I am concerned, our marriage is . . . is at an end." He swallowed, then launched into what was obviously a prepared speech. "Actually, there is no need to end something that has never been. You and I were never truly married. There was a misunderstanding of . . . of scripture, and a . . . a papal misapplication of canon law. . . ."

Katherine heard the words, and her eyes began to mist with tears. Henry saw them. It caused him to stumble a little through the speech, but he was determined to finish.

"It's true I didn't know about this before. But now . . . now these things have been brought . . . brought to light by learned opinion. . . ."

Tears fell from Katherine's eyes, streaking her cheeks.

Henry averted his gaze and continued stiffly: "They weigh down my conscience. They . . . they force me to leave your bed and board once and for all."

He paused, the silence broken only by the drumming of the rain and the sound of the queen sobbing.

Henry continued. "It only remains . . . it only remains for you to choose . . . to choose . . . where you will live from now on, and . . . and . . . and to retire there as quickly as possible."

He waited for some response, as if that might help him, but Katherine merely wept, her tearful eyes staring at him.

Henry's throat closed. He hated this, hated having to do it. He wanted it over, gone, out of the way. In a coaxing voice, he said, "Please, Katherine, I beg you, keep this matter secret. And I swear to you . . . I swear to you that everything will be done for the best."

Katherine just looked at him with the eyes of deepest anguish, bereft, weeping piteously.

Henry, unable to stand it any longer, turned abruptly on his heel and walked out.

"Madam, Lady Salisbury is here," a lady-in-waiting told Katherine. A severe-looking aristocratic lady was ushered into Katherine's chambers.

With elaborate formality, Lady Salisbury curtsied before the queen. "Your Majesty. I have brought your daughter to say good-bye." She gave a signal, and another lady brought in Princess Mary.

The princess was dressed in very grown-up traveling clothes, like a stiff little miniature adult. She did not run into her mother's arms, as she normally did, but gave a stiff and solemn curtsy, as if to a stranger. She had obviously been rehearsed.

It broke Katherine's heart. "My baby," she murmured brokenly.

Lady Salisbury said in a cool voice, "Your Majesty must be reassured.

The princess will be well taken care of, as befitting her station. You will be sent regular reports of her health and accomplishments. And naturally you will visit her during the course of Your Majesty's progresses."

Katherine's face quivered, but she controlled her emotions, unwilling to expose her anguish to an inferior—or to distress her daughter. She said in as gracious a voice as she could manage, "Thank you, Lady Salisbury. And make sure she practices her music. She has—" Her voice cracked, but she recovered and said, "She has a great facility for music."

Lady Salisbury bowed again.

Katherine gazed at her little daughter and continued in Spanish: "Be strong, my beloved daughter. Remember who you are—the descendent of Isabella and Ferdinand of Castille, the *only* daughter of the king of England. Be strong, and be true, and one day . . ." She faltered, her voice breaking again. "One day you will be a queen." She kissed Mary tenderly.

Mary curtsied to her again. "Yes, Mama." And with that, the little girl was led away by Lady Salisbury, away from her mother, into an unknown future.

And then Katherine wept.

Chapter Eleven

"Is he sorry?" Henry scowled at Compton, with whom he was in private conversation. Compton had broken the news of Brandon's marriage to the king's sister.

"Does he repent of it?" Henry continued. "Tell me! Does he beg my forgiveness?"

Compton squirmed uncomfortably under his king's glare. "Your Majesty knows His Grace," he said at last.

Henry stared at him in disbelief. "You mean he does *not*?" he said in an ominous voice. Compton remained silent.

Henry made a furious gesture, then clenched his fists. "Send my sister here!" he snapped.

Compton hurried out.

Henry placed his fingers against his temple, as if his head was hurting him. A short time later, Margaret quietly entered. She made a deep curtsy, and kept her eyes lowered.

"You are not wearing black!" Henry observed coldly.

"No, Your Majesty."

"But you are in mourning. Your husband is dead."

Margaret didn't respond.

Henry said in a threatening tone, "I *said*, your husband is dead!"

She lifted her head, her eyes defiant. "No, he's alive!" she told him. "My husband is alive."

Henry marched up to and took her chin in his hand. "I gave you no permission to marry Brandon—nor would I ever."

Margaret jerked her chin out of his hand. "You gave me your promise! I was free to choose."

"I never gave you my promise. You're mistaken." He saw the defiance in her eyes and said angrily, "Do not *dare* to look at me! I am your lord and master! Not your brother!" He waited.

Sullenly, Margaret lowered her eyes, in a travesty of obedience, barely masking her deep resentment.

"The council demanded his head. I almost gave it to them—did you know that?"

Margaret did. It was Wolsey, she'd heard, who had convinced the king not to execute Brandon. Ironic, that, since her husband hated the cardinal.

Henry stepped back on the dais, beneath his canopy. "Both of you are banished from court," he told her. "You will relinquish your London houses. You will remove yourself from my sight. Do you understand?" He waited; then, as she made no response, he roared, *"Do you understand?"*

Margaret said between her teeth, "Yes, Your Majesty."

He looked at her, smoldering with rage at her defiance. "And Margaret?"

"Yes, Your Majesty?"

"I have yet to decide whether or not to make your new bedmate a head shorter," he said silkily.

Margaret's eyelids flickered. She stared at him in shock. He would not really behead her husband, his erstwhile best friend—would he?

In his own private chambers, Henry paced back and forth, a restless, frustrated lion. A groom entered.

"What is it?" Henry snapped.

The groom held out a small parcel.

"Who is it from?"

"The Lady Anne Boleyn, Your Majesty."

Henry nodded uninterestedly, took the small parcel, and dismissed the young groom. But the moment the man left the chamber, Henry tore open the package with shaking fingers.

Inside he found a most exquisite jewel; a trinket in the shape of a ship, with the tiny figure of a sole woman onboard, and with a pendant diamond. Henry stared at the jewel, turning it this way and that in his hands, trying to puzzle out its secret meaning.

"A ship, with a woman onboard," he muttered. "What is a ship? What, but a symbol of protection, like the ark that rescued Noah." He frowned. "And the diamond? What does it say in the *Roman de la Rose*? Yes. 'A heart as hard as diamond, steadfast . . . not changing.'"

He paced around, thinking—then suddenly it hit him. "She is the diamond," he exclaimed. "And I, the ship."

He stood there, breathing heavily. He saw his reflection in the looking glass. "She is saying yes!" he told it. His face suffused with joy. "She has put herself into my care."

Cardinal Wolsey cleared his throat, and the discreet hum of conversation in the room died. "Your Grace, my lords, I believe you know why we are gathered here . . . in private." He meant in secret. Almost all the dignitaries of the church were present.

"We are here at His Majesty's bidding. His Majesty has requested an inquiry into the nature of his marriage to Katherine of Aragon, for the tranquility of his conscience and the health of his soul." Not a soul in the room moved.

Wolsey went on: "For as it says in Leviticus, 'If a man shall take his brother's wife, it is an impurity; he has covered his brother's nakedness; they shall be childless.'"

Wolsey looked at his fellow prelates, trying to judge their immediate response. He met a mass of carefully hooded eyes.

"If, my lords," he continued, "we are able to agree between ourselves that the marriage was, in fact, never legal, and was proceeded with against both canon and religious law—as His Majesty, to his great regret, has come to believe—then it is my understanding that, as papal legate, I myself have the power and authority to dissolve and end it. But of course I would be grateful to hear Your Lordships' opinions on this great matter." He paused and looked at Archbishop Warham. "Your Grace?"

Warham said cautiously, "I am inclined to agree with Your Eminence—though I reserve judgment until I have heard all opinion."

"My Lord Fisher?" Wolsey turned to the elderly Bishop Fisher

Fisher sniffed. "I see no merit in the king's case, so expressed. None whatsoever. If there was any question of an obstacle to his marriage, then it was overcome by the pope's dispensation. The marriage was therefore legal, and as Your Eminence knows, divorce is disallowed by the church." He gave Wolsey a direct look and said firmly, "That is my opinion."

A murmur of agreement rippled through the room.

Wolsey looked thoughtful. There was no use in pulling rank, he saw at once—on a matter of principle, that would not be so easy. Looking at the faces in the room, he could see that this was not going to be at all the simple matter the king perceived it to be.

Sir Thomas More called on Bishop Fisher to discuss the matter of the king's marriage. "These are serious matters," More said. "It's important to know the true opinions of your fellow bishops . . . especially the archbishop."

Fisher nodded. "Warham has told me privately that he supports the queen."

More looked pleased. "Good. In that case, Wolsey will find it impossible to proceed. The case will have to be revoked to Rome."

"This case, it seems to me, has a wider context."

More nodded. "I know."

"The king threatens not to accept the pope's authority in the matter of the dispensation for his marriage. Such threats are becoming more and more common in Germany and other places, as you must be aware. There are Englishmen now living abroad—like Tyndale—who pour scorn on the traditions of our church."

More nodded again. "I know that, too. Can you believe that William Tyndale actually wanted to send me his English translation of the New Testament? As if I might approve such heresy!"

Fisher shook his head. "All these men are like little Lutherans. Ultimately they lack faith in the Holy Church. And—God forbid—if their word was ever accepted, it would see the utter ruin of the Christian faith."

"It's true." More clenched his fists. "I find that breed of men absolutely loathsome. So much so, that, unless they regain their senses, I want to be as hateful to them as anyone possibly can be."

Fisher looked at him with concern in his old eyes. "Sir Thomas, I pray and hope that His Majesty will always agree with you."

"King Francis is eager for a rapprochement with Your Majesty," Wolsey told Henry. He had come directly from the secret meeting with the other churchmen to Henry's private chamber in the palace. Henry seemed more restless than usual and alternated between prowling the room and hurling himself down to sit sprawled in his chair.

Wolsey continued. "He is disgusted by the treacherous behavior of the emperor toward Your Majesty. He understands it only too well, having suffered the same, and he offers you instead a genuine and mutual friendship."

"It's true that the emperor has betrayed our hopes," Henry said, staring at the jewel Anne had sent him, jiggling it distractedly in his hand.

"Perhaps he was never sincere," Wolsey suggested. "Even so, he still has friends at court."

Henry sat up. "Which friends?"

"My agents intercepted this letter." Wolsey passed it to the king. "It's a letter from the queen. She asks why the emperor does not write to her more often. She promises, always, to be his servant."

Henry scanned the letter, then he tore it to bits, angrily. Wolsey face flickered with unspoken satisfaction.

"His servant; not mine!" Henry snapped. He rose and began to pace around. After a few moments, he said, "Tell the French ambassador that we are in the mood for a rapprochement with King Francis. Let them send over delegates. Let us be allies against the emperor."

"Yes, Majesty," Wolsey purred.

"And now," said Henry, glancing down at the jewel in his hand, "I have another engagement."

"My own heart. My life. My Lady." Henry lay on a bed with Anne in his arms, kissing her passionately, with lingering wonder. She kissed him back, kissing first the corner of his mouth, then nibbling on his lower lip. She slid her fingers into his hair and kissed him back, opening her mouth to him and pressing her slender body against his.

He lifted his face to look at her, drunk with love. "I lay claim to your maidenhead," he said softly, and kissed her breasts.

Anne smiled and shivered with desire. "And I make you this promise: When we are married, I will deliver you a son!"

It was what Henry wanted to hear above everything. It inflamed his desire even more. "Sweet Anne. Oh, sweet Anne."

Their caresses became even more urgent and more intimate. Henry groaned deep in his throat and molded her against him, running his hands over her feverishly. This is what he craved, dreamed of, by day and by night, Anne . . . Anne.

His eyes asked a question. Hers gave assent; he could take her now, if he wanted to. Henry caressed her once more, then, with a deep breath, he rolled away from her, saying, "No."

For a moment, Anne didn't understand. Her senses were rioting. "What is it?" she breathed.

Henry lay beside her, fighting for control. Eventually he said, "I will honor your maidenhead until we are married. No less can I do for love."

Anne gave him a wondering look. "Oh, love. And by daily proof, I swear you shall find me to be to you both loving and kind."

Henry leaned back and kissed her, almost chastely, on the lips, then rose and quietly walked from the room.

*   *   *   *

"You said it would be all right!" Margaret threw a plate at Brandon. He ducked, and it smashed against the wall of the dining room at their country home. It was late afternoon. Earlier in the day, Margaret had returned from the court and her interview with her brother. No, not her brother, her lord and master, the king.

"You said he would forgive you!" Margaret shrieked. "You told me! You promised." A good many empty wine bottles lay scattered across the table. They'd been drinking since her return and were both quite drunk.

Margaret picked up an empty bottle to throw at him. "For the love of God, wife—" Brandon began.

"Don't call me wife!" Margaret snarled. "I don't want to be your wife. I hate you!"

Brandon moved around the table, trying to get closer. "No, you don't," he told her.

For answer, she threw the bottle, and only just missed his head. It smashed. "Yes, I do!" she said. "If it wasn't for you I'd still be queen of Portugal! Now what am I?"

"You're drunk," her loving husband told her. "And you're foolish." He added in a coaxing tone, "Of course the king will forgive us. He's just standing on his pride. We wounded his vanity, that's all."

Brandon grabbed hold of her, and continued. "Believe me."

"Why should I?"

Brandon pulled her closer and began kissing her. At first she tried desperately to resist, to break away, but then slowly the rigidity faded from her body. She melted against him and kissed him back passionately.

Margaret pulled back and looked at her husband in despair. "I don't know if you're really brave—or just a fool."

Brandon smiled. "Neither do I." He reached for her again.

She resisted, kicking and slapping him as, nonetheless, he pushed her toward the table. She kicked and bit him passionately, tearing at his clothes.

Brandon shoved her onto the table, sending bottles and glasses flying as they kissed and caressed each other wildly. He shoved her skirts high. Her legs opened and locked around him, and, sprawled across the table, they made love with wild abandon.

As they climbed toward their climax, Brandon paused in his exertions and looked down at his wife. "I'm still only a duke!" he said, and grinned. She slapped him again and pulled him closer.

"I ask you again," Bishop Fisher demanded. "If the king is so troubled by his conscience, why has he waited so long to bring this matter to a head?"

Wolsey had convened another secret meeting of the religious leaders of England.

"Because of his love for the queen, he has denied to himself the truth," Wolsey explained. "But her failure to produce a living son is proof of it."

Archbishop Warham spoke. "Then he wants to remarry?"

"If his marriage is annulled, then, yes, I am certain he will remarry, in the hope of producing an heir," Wolsey said.

"He has an heir!" Fisher snapped.

Wolsey shook his head. "I do not believe for a moment that the English people will accept his bastard son as a legitimate heir. Nor does the king."

"He has a legitimate daughter!" Warham pointed out.

Wolsey's glance embraced all the men in the room, celibate men, men of the church, and said, "My lords, English history is littered with the tragedies of those who tried to pass their crowns on to a daughter." His words sank in. When the twelfth-century Empress Matilda inherited the throne from her father, the country had been plunged into a ruinous civil war. No man in the room wanted to see that happen again.

"Then . . . he has a new wife in mind?" Fisher asked.

"He has a mind to take one, my Lord," Wolsey said carefully.

Fisher shook his head. "It stinks!"

Wolsey looked at him. "I think your honor should be careful."

"As should you!" retorted the ascerbic old gentleman. "One of the great advantages of having a library, Your Eminence, is that it is full of books. And some of these books contain ecclesiastical law. And according to those books, you have no authority to judge this matter. It is for the pope alone—or those he appoints." He peered down his nose at Wolsey and said bluntly, "It seems that, in this case, Your Eminence, your reach has exceeded your grasp!"

Wolsey met later with Henry in his private quarters in the palace. "I have invited a French delegation to visit Your Majesty's court, to discuss a new treaty, binding us together in the face of the emperor's intransigence and aggression."

"Good. Excellent," the king said. As usual, he was pacing about the room, but this time he was in a good mood.

Wolsey continued. "And since the emperor has reneged on his promise to marry your daughter, it would perhaps be politic to resurrect her betrothal to the dauphin. Or, should the dauphin already be promised, then to Francis's youngest son, the Duke of Orleans."

Henry seemed to take it in, but his mind was on other things.

"What of your secret sessions?" he asked. "Is everything decided? How soon should I expect the annulment?"

Wolsey, knowing he was on thin ice, said, "Your Majesty should not be concerned, but we were not able to come to a conclusion."

Henry swung around and stared. "Not *able*?"

Wolsey grimaced ruefully. "The matter is a complex one."

Henry frowned. "Really? How?"

"It is my best judgment that we should apply to His Holiness, Pope Clement, for a ruling on this matter. I am certain that—since he loves Your Majesty so well—he will rule in your favor."

Henry, displeased, frowned at Wolsey. He was accustomed to Wolsey providing whatever Henry wanted. He had never failed him before. Henry did not like failure, particularly when the matter was so dear to his heart.

"I hope so," he said in a cold voice. "I certainly hope so, Wolsey. For your sake."

*   *   *   *

A dinner was being held to honor the arrival of the French envoys. The boys of the Chapel Royal sang to entertain them, Thomas Tallis conducting; it was one of his new compositions.

Not everyone was pleased to see the French in favor again. Katherine was one. She felt more alone than ever.

Boleyn and Norfolk, for very different reasons, felt the same. They looked contemptuously at the French delegates in their very different, and rather chic, clothes.

"You can always tell the French," Boleyn said sourly.

"Yes," Norfolk agreed. "They're ponces! And they probably read books!" It was one of his greatest insults.

They turned their attention to Wolsey who was, once again, master of ceremonies.

"But they never did anything so clever as giving Wolsey a pension," Norfolk growled. "He has never failed them."

Boleyn said soothingly, "We must wait and see. When the wheel of fortune has reached its zenith, there is only one way for it to go." He indicated with his eyes to where Henry was dancing with Anne.

It would have been obvious to a blind man that the two were in love. Henry couldn't take his eyes off Anne, nor she off him.

Katherine sat, watching the dancers miserably. She was waited on hand and foot, but nobody spoke to her.

Suddenly a loud commotion erupted outside the room. The doors burst open. A solitary knight, a handsome youth with distraught eyes, entered and fell to his knees before the king. Henry dropped Anne's hand, and the music faltered to a halt.

"Your Majesty, I bring most terrible and calamitous news. Rome has been captured and sacked by the German and Spanish mercenaries of the emperor." The audience gasped in horror.

The young man continued. "They have plundered and befouled its churches, destroyed its relics and holy treasures, tortured and killed thousands of its priests."

Appalled by such unheard-of barbarity in the Holy City, people crossed themselves.

"Monstrous!" someone muttered.

"Worse than sacrilege."

But Henry's mind went straight to the core of things. "What of His Holiness?"

The knight shook his head sorrowfully. "The pope is a prisoner in the Castel Sant'Angelo."

"A prisoner of the emperor?"

"Yes," said the knight. "To do with as he pleases."

Henry looked shocked. Katherine sat up, also shocked, but looking marginally less miserable. The pope was in the hands of her nephew.

Henry would not get his divorce so easily now.

In shocked silence, people began to leave the feast table. One could not eat when such a dreadful thing had happened. It was an attack on everything they believed in. If the pope could be captured, if the Holy City could be sacked, if priests and bishops could be tortured and killed, what was the world coming to? Where was God?

The French envoys bowed to Henry silently and waited to let Katherine and her ladies leave first. Anne cast Henry a desperate look, for what chance did his divorce have with the pope in the hands of the Spanish?

Henry in turn stared at Wolsey as he departed. It was all up to Wolsey now.

Lady Blount walked slowly down a long stone passage in Ludlow Castle in Wales. She was dressed in black, with a black veil over her face. Behind her walked a small retinue, some holding flaming torches to illuminate the way. She shivered. It was the height of summer, yet the castle was cold.

She was led into a chamber. Candles burned around a bed of state, four large candles burning at each corner. Beside the bed, waiting for her, stood several physicians and priests, looking solemn.

In the bed lay a small, still figure.

"He caught the sweating sickness," a physician explained. "There was nothing we could do. He complained one morning of feeling ill. By the evening he was in the hands of God."

Lady Blount barely heard him. All she knew was that her son was dead.

Her face working with emotion, she moved slowly to the bed where her beautiful son lay still, as if asleep.

"Just a little boy," she whispered. She touched his cold hand, then leaned down and kissed his cold eyes . . . and then, only then, did she break down and cry out in her grief.

She wept, great wrenching sobs bursting painfully from her body. Her precious, precious child.

Henry sat alone in the gloom of his private chamber. A sole candle burned on a small table in front of him. He sat slumped, despairing. His eyes were haggard. In recent days he had suffered two terrible blows, and it showed.

He sat, staring at the two small objects sitting on the table in front of him: a little cap of estate and a duke's coronet, small enough to fit a child's head.

His son was dead.

Chapter Twelve

"I leave in three days," Wolsey told the king. "I shall go straight to Paris to meet King Francis and ratify the new treaty between Your Majesties. And to arrange the betrothal of Princess Mary to the Duke of Orleans."

"Yes, but what of the other matter?" They were in the king's private apartments, where Henry was being dressed by three of his grooms. One of the grooms held up a looking glass. Henry inspected his appearance carefully.

"Majesty, since His Holiness continues to be the emperor's prisoner, I have summoned a conclave of the cardinals to meet in Paris. It will be little matter to persuade them—in the pope's absence—to grant me license and authority to make a final judgment on Your Majesty's annulment."

Henry dismissed his grooms. "You leave with our blessing. And with anticipation of your success, Your Eminence. For which we are most impatient." He looked at Wolsey. "Have you talked further to the queen about this matter?"

Wolsey grimaced. "I have tried to persuade Her Majesty that it would be easier for all of us if she accepted Your Majesty's determination to end your marriage."

"What did she say?"

"I confess she took my remarks most dispassionately."

Henry sighed and dismissed him. As Wolsey was leaving, he remembered something. "Oh, I forgot. There is someone you should take with you: His name is Thomas Wyatt."

Wolsey looked puzzled. "The poet?"

"So he says!" Henry said darkly. "I don't like to see him. He once—" He paused. "He once possessed a jewel that I would have."

"Majesty." Wolsey bowed and left. As Wolsey emerged from the private chambers, he passed a group of men waiting to be called into the royal presence, and one woman—Anne Boleyn.

"Lady Anne, what are you doing here?" he asked her.

"I have an audience with His Majesty."

Wolsey smiled. "What would a silly girl like you have to say to a king?" Shaking his head, he moved, a man on important business, the "silly girl" immediately forgotten.

As he left, several of the men who had overheard his conversation with Anne Boleyn exchanged looks. Was it really possible that Wolsey could not know how the king was infatuated with Anne Boleyn?

In the meantime, Anne was immediately conducted through to the king's private chambers.

Henry greeted her eagerly. "Anne, sweet Anne." He took her in his arms, and they kissed. For a long moment Henry just held her close, smiling. He kissed her eyelids gently and stroked her hair.

"Your Majesty," she murmured.

"How much do I love you?" he said.

Anne searched his eyes. "Tell me he'll succeed."

"Who, sweetheart?"

"Wolsey. He will, won't he? He'll get an annulment?"

"Of course he will. You mustn't doubt it."

She smiled, then her face clouded over. Gently, Henry released her.

"What is it?" he asked.

She hesitated, as if trying to summon up courage. "Is it not strange?" she said finally.

"Strange? How, strange?"

"To, to trust so great a matter to just one servant—whoever he is— when Your Majesty has a thousand servants ready and willing to do your bidding. And when your very happiness hangs upon this resolution."

"Hush, my love." He kissed her. She opened her mouth to say something, and he stopped her mouth with another kiss. "It is nothing for you to be concerned about."

She gave him a sweet, penitent smile. "Forgive me. I spoke of things I should not."

Henry shook his head and pressed her hand to his lips. "No. I give you leave so that we can always talk freely together, honestly, openly and with our hearts. For me, that is a definition of love."

"Tomorrow I must go back to Hever," Anne said after a moment. "My father has requested it."

Henry's smile faded. "Very well," he said reluctantly. "I would never stand between a father and his daughter." He looked at her. "But come back soon, my sweetheart. Come back soon."

In the queen's private chambers, candles glowed on the array of icons and crucifixes. Katherine knelt in prayer.

She heard footsteps, and a long shadow fell over her. She rose to see it was Mendoza, the imperial ambassador.

"Forgive me, Ambassador, for receiving you here," she said.

Mendoza bowed. "I am at Your Majesty's disposal."

Katherine nodded over his shoulder toward the door. Walking over to it, she closed it quietly and discreetly. In Spanish, she explained, "Señor Mendoza, I need to get a message to the emperor. I have no other way. Wolsey opens all my letters. And now he has turned several of my women into his spies."

Mendoza was appalled. "Dear God. How can I help?"

"The emperor is the head of my family. I want him to know that the king is trying to divorce me. He wants to keep it secret—but he has already instigated proceedings."

"*No!*" he exclaimed, even more shocked than before. "It's impossible! Surely he needs the pope's permission?"

"He must!" Katherine agreed. "But the pope is still the emperor's prisoner, so how can he ever give permission?"

Mendoza took her meaning at once.

She continued. "Señor Mendoza, for the love of our savior, Jesus Christ, and the love of all that is sacred, tell my nephew what is being done to me here!"

Mendoza gave Katherine a reverent bow. "Leave it to me. I will find a way to evade the cardinal's spies."

"'Dear heart, I cannot say how much I miss you. I wish myself—especially in the evening—in my sweetheart's arms, whose—'" Anne broke off.

"Come along," Norfolk told her. "Pray, continue."

Anne was unhappy about sharing such an intimate letter with her father and uncle, but she had been ordered to read it to them. Flushing, she read: "'whose pretty breasts I trust shortly to kiss. Neither tongue nor pen can express the hurt of not seeing you. The only compensation is the thrill of anticipating our next meeting. . . .'"

She licked dry lips and continued. "'For what joy in this world can be greater than to have the company of her who is the most dearly loved.'" She folded the letter, lowering her eyes to hide her emotions.

"The king is plainly in love with you," Norfolk said scornfully. "To write like that! Like some lovesick boy who has never known love before and is now at the mercy of its torments. Don't you see, niece: It makes a man—any man—extremely vulnerable."

Boleyn smiled. "How do you like your charge, sweetheart?"

"I . . ." she hesitated. "At first, I confess I did not like it so much. I did not love the king at all. But now . . . now I . . ." She blushed, lowered her eyes again, and didn't finish the sentence.

"It is your duty to use his love for our advantage," Norfolk informed her bluntly. "By keeping his affections hot you may hope, in time, God willing, to supplant the queen."

Anne darted a frightened look at him, but the two men were busy smiling at each other in triumph at the success of their schemes, and missed it.

Boleyn continued circling her. "And in the meantime . . ."

"Yes, in the meantime, it is necessary for the achievement of all our ambitions that we go on seeking to bring down that proud prelate," Norfolk said. "It's insufferable for the king to lean upon a butcher's son."

Boleyn stopped in front of Anne and addressed her directly. "The cardinal stands between us and *everything*. And it is now in your power to do him a great hurt. And we expect you to do so."

Her father and her uncle stared at Anne. She nodded obediently. Her duty to her family was clear.

That evening, Anne's brother, George, knocked quietly and entered her bedchamber. Anne was sitting alone on her bed, the whole room in shadow.

"Anne," He said. "Why are you sitting in the darkness?"

She didn't respond.

George frowned and sat down on the bed beside her. "What's wrong?" he asked.

After a moment, Anne said quietly, "I have to go back to court tomorrow."

"So? What's wrong with that?" He peered at her. "I thought you'd be excited."

She sighed. "You don't understand."

"Of course I do!" George said airily. "I'm your brother, aren't I?"

She was silent, then shook her head. "If only you were still as you used to be. I remember I told you everything. All my secrets."

George stared at her curiously. "You can still tell me your secrets."

"I can't."

"Why not?"

"Because you'd share them," Anne said sadly.

He blinked, but didn't deny it. His silence acknowledged it. His eyes dropped; he couldn't even meet her gaze.

She turned away. "You see?"

After a long moment, he reached out, took her hand, and squeezed. "Are you frightened?"

She didn't answer.

*   *   *   *

"Tell me truthfully," More asked Wolsey. "What are your hopes for this mission?"

Wolsey put his seal to a document before replying. "I have many hopes. Firstly, to heal the wounds caused by years of Anglo-French hostility. And then to work toward a new balance of power in Europe. The sacking of Rome; the imprisonment of the pope. These things have destabilized the whole of Europe."

More raised an eyebrow, but nodded. "Admirable. And the Church?"

"The Church, too, is in need of mediation," Wolsey answered. "At the special conclave we shall lay plans for a general council to deal—in the pope's absence—with the urgent issues of reform and heresy."

"Equally admirable, Your Eminence." More considered the implications. "And the king's matter?"

"That will also be dealt with," Wolsey said shortly. "But as one matter among many others."

"I see." More pretended to peruse some of the volumes on a table. "You think the cardinals will give you authority to deal with it?"

"Yes."

More looked over at him again with a little smile. "Then you will be de facto pope."

Wolsey didn't reply.

More continued, "And since His Holiness may never escape captivity, then you will be p—"

"Idle speculation!" Wolsey cut him off. "Now, if that is all, I have much work to do before I leave for France, Sir Thomas." And he returned to his documents.

The French court welcomed Cardinal Wolsey almost as if he were a royal visitor. Flowers were strewn in his path; great French nobles and their ladies bowed and curtsied.

More, following behind, could see very well how delighted Wolsey was by his reception, nodding, smiling, and blessing those around.

He'd brought quite a retinue with him: not just More and the usual secretaries, assistants, and servants, but the poet Thomas Wyatt, and a collection of the finest English musicians, including Thomas Tallis, who was growing in fame.

The king and queen of France waited to greet Wolsey. "We salute you, Cardinal of Peace." Francis embraced Wolsey. "My dear Cardinal, my friend, my brother."

Queen Claude offered her hand. "Eminence."

Wolsey kissed her hand, almost sensuously. *"Madame, enchanté!"* He continued in French: "You are so beautiful that it is as hard for me to look you in the face, as it is to look up at the sun."

Queen Claude smiled, amused and touched. "You are very gracious, Monsieur Cardinal. Like a Frenchman."

"See!" declared Francis. "We treat you as a brother, for that is what you are: a true and loyal friend of France. We welcome you"—he made a large gesture with his arm to include everyone—"and all those with you, into our court and into our hearts."

"Your Majesties do me a great honor. I am deeply touched," Wolsey said.

Francis smiled. "My dear Cardinal—this is nothing. I intend to invest you with the Order of Saint Michael—the highest order of chivalry in France."

Wolsey beamed. "Then, Majesty, my cup overfloweth!"

Francis took Wolsey's arm and led him toward some waiting dignitaries. Those from the English court were then free to mingle and relax.

Thomas Wyatt moved to stand beside Tallis. They exchanged greetings. "I've been thinking," Wyatt said. "Perhaps one day you would set a poem of mine to music."

"I would be honored," Tallis told him. "Do you have one ready?"

"I'm working on one. I have the first line."

Tallis smiled. "Then you have almost everything!"

Wyatt laughed and moved away through the throng, casting an appreciative eye over some of the beautiful French women. He came across More, already casting a jaundiced eye over the proceedings.

He followed the line of More's gaze to where a group of lavishly dressed and bejeweled French nobles were bowing over Wolsey's hand with exaggerated flourishes. Wolsey was lapping it up.

"I've been observing you," Wyatt murmured. "You don't like the French much, do you, Sir Thomas?"

More smiled a little. "Oh, I don't mind them, Mr. Wyatt. It's just . . . whatever they do . . . they're somehow, always so very . . . French!" They both laughed.

Queen Claude was talking to Wolsey. "How is Queen Katherine, Your Eminence? I am so fond of her."

"She is as gracious as always, Your Majesty," Wolsey told her. "But although the king loves her, he accepts that their divorce is inevitable."

Queen Claude gave him a distressed look. "It is very sad, is it not?"

Wolsey didn't respond.

Some days later, in the dormitory in France where all the visiting English musicians and servants slept, Wyatt moved quietly, looking for Thomas Tallis.

Wyatt lifted a candle high, peering around at all the sleeping shapes. "Tallis? . . . Tallis!" he called quietly.

"I'm here," Tallis responded sleepily.

Wyatt crouched down beside him. Tallis blinked at the candlelight and sighed. "What is it? Do you poets never sleep?"

"I've written the first lines. Can I read them to you?"

Tallis nodded and sat up.

Wyatt read from a piece of paper.

> *"They flee from me that sometime did me seek.*
> *With naked foot stalking in my chamber:*
> *I have seen them gentle, tame and meek,*
> *That now are wild, and do not remember,*
> *That sometime they put themselves in danger*

To take bread at my hand: And now they range
Busily seeking with a continual change . . ."

He put down the paper. "That's all there is so far." He looked at Tallis anxiously, and waited for his response.

Tallis savored the words in silence for a moment. "It's wonderful," he said at last. "There is music in it. But what's it about?"

"A girl," Wyatt said. "But I haven't got to her yet."

"What girl?"

"Let's just call her the brunette," Wyatt said. "I loved her once. And I thought she loved me. Indeed, she once wrote in my book, 'I am yours, you may well be sure / And shall be as long as my life endures.'"

"But now she belongs to another?"

Wyatt shrugged. "So it seems." He leaned in close and whispered in Tallis's ear, "'Touch me not, for Caesar's I am!'" He continued, "She may just be a girl, Mr. Tallis, but I tell you this: If she gets her way, she will set our whole country in a roar." He started to get up.

Tallis caught his arm. "Wyatt—who is she, that she could set our country in a roar?"

Wyatt shook his head. "It's more than my life's worth. Just take my word."

Tallis was curious. "Yes, but . . . whoever she is: Did you sleep with her—or was it just platonic?"

There was a long silence. Then Wyatt said, "Good night, Thomas Tallis. Sweet dreams." And he disappeared into the shadows.

Thomas Cromwell, now Henry's secretary, made his move while Wolsey was in France. He handed the king a sheaf of official papers for him to sign and, as soon as that was done, he laid before him a great bundle of letters.

"Letters from His Eminence Cardinal Wolsey," he explained.

Henry almost groaned aloud. He gave a great sigh, pushed them away a little, and sat back in his chair.

For a moment, nobody spoke. Then Cromwell said quietly, "Your Majesty should know that His Holiness, Pope Clement, has escaped from the Castel Sant'Angelo."

Henry looked up, surprised. "He's escaped?"

"Apparently he dressed himself as an old blind man and walked out through his captors," Cromwell told him.

"Where is he now?"

"According to my information, in an Italian town called Orvieto, in the bishop's palace there, with what remains of his court. Of course, he is still within the power of the emperor."

Henry sat up, frowning. "And yet he is free? It would be possible . . ." He shot an upward glance at Cromwell. "It would be possible to send someone to him? To get a message to him?"

"Indeed it would be possible, should there be reason."

Henry considered his secretary, whom he'd taken for granted until now. "How do you know these things? Did Wolsey . . . ?"

"No, Majesty," Cromwell said smoothly. "I have my own sources."

Henry rose from his chair and, increasingly excited, started to pace around. "Let us say I wanted a message carried to His Holiness." He looked at Cromwell. "Is there someone you would trust? With your life?"

Cromwell nodded. "My source, Dr. Knight. He's a friend, a diplomat." He looked at the king. "He's a man of God. And a true Englishman."

Henry considered the recommendation, then said decisively, "Bring him to me."

Cromwell nodded and fetched Dr. Knight from an outer chamber. Dr. Knight was a middle-aged, scholarly-looking individual. He bowed deeply to the king.

Cromwell and Knight watched as Henry sealed two separate parchments and thrust them at Dr. Knight. "Here! We rely upon you, Dr. Knight, to deliver these two bulls to his Holiness, at Orvieto. They were written by our own hand."

"Majesty." Dr. Knight bowed and was shown out.

* * * *

Cromwell was not the only person taking advantage of Wolsey's absence in Paris. In his private study in the palace, Sir Thomas Boleyn, now comptroller of the king's household, was poring over inventories, lists, and account books.

He laboriously scrutinized long lists of payments and receipts, mostly noted against the names of religious houses. Many of the amounts involved were very large. Of particular interest to the comptroller of the king's household was anything connected with the name of Wolsey.

Boleyn frowned at something he noticed on a list. He checked it, then compared it with a different list, then, with increasing excitement, checked it again.

He drew out more documents and compared payments made to Cardinal College, Oxford, against receipts, making calculations in the margins. And suddenly it all came together. He smiled, sat back, and gazed down at the mass of figures with satisfaction.

"So that's how he does it!"

Henry was bored. He was playing cards with Compton, and losing heavily. With bad grace, Henry tossed him some money and pushed the cards away. "I hate cards! I hate the court." He stood up and began to pace. "I hate time itself."

"Your Majesty," Compton said. "If I could make a suggestion? Forget the court. Let us go out hunting—the way we all used to."

Henry stopped and gave him an arrested look. "Yes!" His eyes narrowed, knowing that Compton was suggesting something more. "But *not* Brandon."

"But Charles is—" Compton began.

"I said no!" Henry cut him off. "I haven't forgiven my Lord Suffolk. I can't forgive him. He never asked my permission to marry my sister. It was insufferable and grievous arrogance on his part."

He glared at Compton, aggrieved. "What did he expect? I don't say he's banished forever—only for as long as he breathes!" He gave a cold smile. "Otherwise, let it be as it used to be."

A short time later, Henry and Compton rode slowly along a track, with dogs, and servants walking behind carrying guns.

But Henry was not riding alone. A velvet-covered saddle had been fixed on behind his, and Anne was sitting on it.

Anne rode easily, her hands resting lightly around Henry's waist. She had a bow slung across her shoulders, and a quiver of arrows. From time to time she leaned her head against Henry's shoulder.

Henry half-turned to look and smile at her, radiant with happiness. He looked back at the sole figure of Compton and gestured him to ride up to join them. Henry smiled at him, teasingly. "So you see, William: Nothing can ever be as it used to be!" Then he urged his horse to a canter and rode on ahead with Anne.

They had a good day's hunting. They killed a young hart, and later, the hunters sat beneath a canopy of stars, enjoying a warm and peaceful evening.

A haunch of venison had been roasted over a large, open fire, and the scent of it on the breeze sharpened already keen appetites. Servants worked to carve and serve the meat. A lutist played soft music. Lanterns glowed, throwing pools of golden light. The fire crackled, the flames dancing and causing the shadows to dance with them.

Henry had no eyes for anyone but Anne. They sat close, sipping wine from each other's cups, murmuring soft words and laughing low and intimately.

Compton sat alone a good distance away, staring moodily at the couple. A servant handed him his food. Compton took it, and muttered. "I think our Harry is in love." The servant moved on, and Compton added, "Poor Harry."

Henry and Anne ate the flesh of the hart with their fingers. Henry leaned close and pushed a tender morsel between her lips. Then Anne did the same to him.

They gazed into each other's eyes, feeding each other the warm, tender morsels of flesh, kissing, nibbling, licking at each other, their fingers and mouths wet with the juices.

Henry licked Anne's fingers clean. She licked around his mouth, then kissed him, lingeringly. Both were oblivious—or careless—of who might be watching. It was as if they were quite alone.

They could hardly be more intimate—even if they had been making love, naked in a bed. But they were not naked in a bed, and Henry muttered: "Oh, God . . . Oh, God . . . Oh, God" over and over, in desire and eternal frustration.

Compton watched, alone, lonely . . . and troubled.

A servant opened the door to a chamber and announced the visitor to his master. "Lord Rochford."

Brandon looked up, startled. He had few visitors in his country exile, but Thomas Boleyn, recently entitled, Lord Rochford, was the last person he would have imagined would make the journey all this way to visit him.

"My lord?" He greeted Boleyn.

"Your Grace."

"To what do I owe this . . . pleasure?" Brandon said.

Boleyn's gaze quickly surveyed the room. "May I speak frankly?"

Brandon nodded and dismissed his servants. He poured two glasses of wine and handed one to Boleyn. "Your health, my lord."

"And yours." Boleyn drank, then sat. "Norfolk has sent me," he told Brandon.

Brandon frowned, even more surprised. "But Norfolk hates me. I am, after all, a new man. And he is far too grand for me."

Boleyn gave an ingratiating shrug. "I suspect he despises us all for the same reason; and yet he has interests to protect and to further, like the rest of us. He must deal with us as he finds us." He took another sip of wine and looked at Brandon over the rim. "And, after all, there is someone he hates even more."

Brandon knew who he meant. "The cardinal."

Boleyn inclined his head. "Of course."

"But what is that to me?"

Boleyn sat back, crossed his legs, and glanced out of the window, and asked, with seeming irrelevance, "Do you miss the court, Your Grace? Perhaps you don't. Down here, in this green space, you must have so much leisure to enjoy. So many idle pastimes." He paused.

"But I have heard it said by some," he continued after a moment, "that the king's presence is like the sun . . . and when you are away from it, there is only eternal night." He examined his wine, swirling it, admiring the fine color.

Brandon smiled a little. "You're very clever, Boleyn. People say that about you. They say you are charming . . . and clever. But I suspect you are even cleverer than that." He drained his glass and said quietly. "What does Norfolk want?"

"He wants you to help us destroy Wolsey," Boleyn told him. "And in return, he will persuade the king to forgive you, and welcome you back to court."

Brandon considered the proposal. "Thank you, my lord," he said, but made no further comment.

Boleyn bowed and departed.

Immediately another door opened, and Margaret entered. "What did you hear?" Brandon asked her.

"Everything," Margaret said. "What will you do?"

Brandon looked at her. "What should I do?"

"You told me once that sometimes Wolsey had been kind to you."

He looked at her in surprise. "Did I?" he said. "I had quite forgotten."

They both smiled.

Chapter Thirteen

The bound treaty between England and France lay open and ready for signing. Wolsey stepped forward to sign the treaty on behalf of King Henry. King Francis then signed. As he did so, Wolsey whispered to him, "It would be a good thing for Europe if we could also make peace with the emperor."

Francis gave him a look, and as the two men embraced for the benefit of the applauding audience, he snarled in Wolsey's ear, "How can you say that? He made me his prisoner! He squeezed my balls! I had to pay him millions in ransom. And my oldest son is still his captive."

The two men stepped back and smiled to the audience. Francis added from the side of his mouth, "How can I make peace with that devil? That hypocrite! That piece of shit!"

And the applause rang out for the signing of the treaty, giving the signal for the celebrations to begin. The kitchen staff staggered back and forth under great platters of food, while the servants with wine and ale jugs never stopped running. Music played almost constantly and there was much merriment and dancing. Entertainments of all sorts had been planned, from acrobats, magicians, jugglers, fools, and fire-eaters to masques and plays. The festivities lasted all day and well into the night.

More touched the Order of Saint Michael hanging on a ribbon around Wolsey's neck. "Your Eminence must be gratified by the progress you have made so far?"

"I am," Wolsey agreed. "Though I find it a burden to drag my old, cracked body from country to country."

"You would rather be at home?"

Wolsey shook his head. "I fret sometimes, about the king being influenced by others, when I am not there."

More looked at him. "Do you think he is so malleable?"

"I think he still needs guidance. All men, in my experience, can be seduced by malice, just as all women by promises."

More said soothingly, "After the conclave you can stop fretting. You will have the power to please him."

There was a short silence. Wolsey said quietly, "Pleasing our king is like playing with tame lions. Mostly it is harmless. But there is always fear of harm." He shot More a piercing look. "And then it can be fatal."

In a different part of the feasting hall, Wyatt, a little drunk, was reading his poem to Tallis.

> *"Thanks be to fortune, it has been otherwise*
> *Twenty times better; but once in special*
> *In thin array, after a pleasant guise,*
> *When her loose gown from her shoulders did fall,*
> *And she me caught in her arms long and small,*
> *Therewith all sweetly did me kiss,*
> *And softly said, "Dear heart, how like you this?"*

Wyatt, almost too emotional to go on, paused and put down his paper. After a moment, Tallis said softly, "I think you really did love her."

"Yes. It's true, I loved her," Wyatt said heavily. He sighed, then said in a different voice, "But just think. In a few more years, she'll be old and ugly. And then she'll be dead and forgotten. But if you set this poem to music, it might endure forever."

He arched an eyebrow at Tallis and added, "So not she, but I will be remembered. And I will have my revenge."

* * * *

"The king!" a herald announced. Henry walked through the court, accompanied by his usual retinue.

Anne watched him approaching. His eyes were fixed on her, even as he acknowledged bows right and left. For both of them, it was as if no one else existed.

The courtiers watched as Henry paused in front of Anne. Queen Katherine watched too.

"My sweet love," Henry murmured.

Anne smiled, then made to move away.

"No, wait! Wait! Only a moment. Stay!" Henry said. She paused. He looked at her and said the first thing that came into his head. "I sup this evening with your father and uncle."

"My father says it is all beyond his deserving," Anne said softly.

"No," Henry said. "For when I am with them, I am still close to you." He moved closer to her. "Here. Another token of my affection. Take it. From your humble servant." He slipped a small package into her hand, stared at her neck, and sighed. "Your neck. Ah. I love your neck."

He moved on abruptly, and Anne sank into a curtsy. A buzz of conversation rose after the king had passed, and some of it Anne could not help but hear.

The king had always been discreet in his amours—until Anne. The court was abuzz with the new, brazen behavior of Henry and his mistress.

Anne, walking through the crowd, was skewered with every step by probing, judging eyes. It was with some relief she saw her brother, George, approaching.

"I have something for you," he said with a grin. He took a piece of paper from his pocket and opened it. Inside was a beautiful drawing of a bird of prey pecking at a pomegranate.

"You see?" he continued. "The falcon is your crest and"—he glanced over at Katherine—"the pomegranate is hers!" He laughed.

Anne snatched the paper and screwed it up. "You still don't understand, do you? It's not a game, George! It's dangerous!" She stared at him, trying to make him understand, then saw that Mr. Cromwell was approaching, and moved a little away from her brother.

"Mistress Boleyn," Cromwell said, bowing

"Mr. Cromwell. He moved closer, and said in a quiet voice, "I have some news. The king has dispatched a good man, Dr. Knight, to see the pope, with letters about the divorce."

Anne smiled. "I know Dr. Knight. He was my tutor."

Cromwell inclined his head and said enigmatically, "Indeed. All things connect." He bowed again, and moved off.

Anne continued on her way. Finally she turned a corner and found herself briefly alone. With quick, eager fingers she unwrapped the package and found inside a beautiful necklace, set with sapphires and diamonds. She smiled as she rewrapped it.

Henry walked through to his private chambers to find that Katherine had gone ahead of him. He checked, then walked up to her and kissed her cheeks. "Sweetheart."

Katherine scanned his face. "You told me that everything would be done for the best. You tell me you love me. But you never show it."

Henry grimaced uncomfortably and glanced around, as if hoping someone else would come through. "Nothing yet has been decided," he said awkwardly.

Katherine looked at him. "What does that mean?"

Henry stared at her, unable or unwilling to explain.

In the queen's private chambers that evening, Katherine read her Bible quietly as Anne and two other ladies tidied her chambers, bringing in clean linen and a jug of water.

Despite the state of affairs between the king and queen and Anne Boleyn, Anne had not been released from her duties as lady-in-waiting to the queen.

Anne was quiet and demure as she performed her tasks, but in an act that was bound to provoke attention, she had chosen to wear the beautiful new necklace that the king had given her earlier.

Katherine read, as if absorbed in her Bible, but from time to time, her eyes would flicker up and fasten on the young girl folding linen and the magnificent necklace she wore.

Her ladies bid Katherine good night and began to withdraw, but she signaled to Anne to wait behind. As soon as they were alone, Katherine said, "That necklace. Who gave it to you?"

Anne stood with downcast eyes, saying nothing.

"Answer me!" Katherine ordered.

Anne's eyelids fluttered, and slowly she raised her gaze and stared directly at Katherine with those extraordinary eyes. "His Majesty," she said. There was no sign of the demure girl of a moment before.

Katherine sniffed. "You are surely expensive . . . an expensive *whore*." She used the Spanish word for it, but Anne understood her full well.

Anne's eyes flashed. "I am no *whore* . . . Your Majesty. I love His Majesty. I believe he loves me."

Katherine made a dismissive gesture. "He is infatuated with you, as men often are by new things. Soon he will see you for what you really are. Then he will tire of you . . . like all the others!"

Anne stared at the older woman confidently. "And if he does not?"

"I did not ask you to speak!" Katherine told her angrily. "You are a servant! Go now! Go!" With the stress of her emotions, her accent had become more thickly Spanish.

Anne curtsied and left, and as the door closed behind her, Katherine collapsed back against her chair. Now, finally alone, finally private, the proud, dignified face crumpled. She was so weary, so tired. But she could not give up. She would not allow Henry and some snip of a girl to make her life—her love—into a lie. But oh, she was so tired. . . .

"My lords, let's drink to the resolution of the matter which is uppermost on all our minds." Henry lifted his glass. He was dining with the Duke of Norfolk and Thomas Boleyn. They joined him in the toast.

"In a very short while we shall have an answer," Henry told them.

"I would trust to hear it more from Dr. Knight than Cardinal Wolsey," Norfolk said.

There was a brief silence. Henry gave him a sharp look. "Why do you say so?"

Norfolk said, "I fear it is not in the cardinal's interest to succeed."

Henry's eyes narrowed. "But his interest and mine are the same—surely? Wolsey is my servant."

Again, nobody spoke for a moment.

Boleyn said carefully, "His Grace means that the cardinal has some prejudice against my daughter."

Henry reflected on that, then nodded. "I know. He called her a silly girl. She told me."

Norfolk and Boleyn exchanged glances. Norfolk said, "There is . . . another matter. It is something you should be made aware of. My lord did not want to tell you. But I have insisted."

Henry put down his glass and looked at Boleyn. "Well?"

Boleyn took a deep breath. "Majesty, by your great bounty I was appointed comptroller of Your Majesty's household."

Henry inclined his head, acknowledging his gratitude.

Boleyn continued, "And in such a capacity, I have . . . I have discovered that, when corrupt religious houses are closed down, instead of all their assets going to your exchequer, as they should have . . . they are often diverted elsewhere."

Henry frowned. "Elsewhere? Where is elsewhere?"

"Into Wolsey's private foundations," Boleyn told him. "Into the creation of his great college at Oxford."

There was a short, incredulous silence. Then, "He *steals* from me?" Henry exclaimed.

Boleyn silently confirmed it.

Henry, his face troubled, signaled to a servant to refill his glass. "Your intimations shock me," Henry said. "They hurt me. As well as my chancellor. Wolsey has always been my friend."

"In this world, Majesty, a true—and loyal—friend is the greatest boon any man can have," Boleyn said. "For in everything else, there is a strange habit of forsaking."

They fell silent again. Henry was having difficulty taking it in.

After a while, Norfolk spoke again, seeming to change the subject. "The Duke of Suffolk has come to see me."

"Brandon?" Henry looked up.

"He said he would crawl on his hands and knees to beg your forgiveness, " Norfolk said. "He loves you."

Henry didn't respond.

The carriage swayed and rocked as it made its way through dappled French woodlands. Inside the carriage, Dr. Knight slumbered. He had come a long way; there remained a long journey ahead. They were bound for Orvieto in Italy.

He was woken by shouts. And a shot.

"Woah! . . . Woah there!"

The carriage lurched, throwing Dr. Knight almost to the floor as his coachman hauled the horses to a stop.

Recovering his dignity, Knight peered out of the window to see what was amiss. Several armed horsemen had accosted the carriage. Was it bandits? He groped stealthily for his weapons, but before he could do anything, one of the man had climbed into the carriage.

To Dr. Knight's astonishment, the man addressed him in English. "Dr. Knight? Forgive us, sir. We must just ask you to break off your journey for a day or two."

Dr. Knight stared at him. "Impossible! I am on the king's business."

"Yes, sir, we know," the horseman said. "That is why you must come with us."

Bemused, but having no choice in the matter, Dr. Knight sat back as his carriage was directed down a different path, accompanied by an armed escort.

He was taken to the French court and after much fruitless questioning of his escort, and more frustration at having to cool his heels waiting for who-knew-what, he was finally ushered into the presence of Cardinal Wolsey.

He blinked and stood, amazed at the sight of the cardinal sitting at his desk, turning over papers.

Wolsey looked up. "Ah, Dr. Knight. Come in."

"Your Eminence, I . . ." Knight did not know what to say. Wolsey gave him a shrewd look. "I make it my business to know the king's business. Did you suppose you could go to Orvieto without my knowing all about it?"

Dr. Knight lowered his eyes, accepting defeat.

Wolsey gestured to the papers in front of him. "You were to take these two bulls to His Holiness?"

"Yes."

"They are quite extraordinary documents," Wolsey said. "Do you know what is in them?"

Dr. Knight nodded. "A little. Yes."

Wolsey raised his eyebrows. "And you still agreed to carry them?"

Dr. Knight said nothing.

Wolsey consulted the papers again. "The first document," he began, "asks His Holiness, on behalf of Henry, King of England, to permit him—once divorced from Queen Katherine—to marry any woman he chooses; even one who would normally be forbidden to him because of a prior relationship with one of her relatives!"

"This was written in the king's own hand." Wolsey fixed his gaze on Knight and said, "I don't understand. What woman is he talking about?"

Knight gave him an incredulous look. Was Wolsey trying to trick him? Could the man who knew everything that was happening in England— and Europe—really not know this? Apparently not.

"Mistress Anne Boleyn," he told Wolsey.

Wolsey struggled to take it in. "Anne Boleyn? The King . . . loves *Anne Boleyn*?"

"Yes, sir."

Wolsey pointed to the document. "And this . . . legal caveat: about a prior relationship? That his new marriage may be forbidden?"

Dr. Knight spoke more in sorrow than in anger. "Surely Your Eminence knows that His Majesty had carnal relations with Anne's older sister, Mary. Perhaps even with their mother. So it is rumored." He added austerely, "I give no credence to the fact . . . as far as the mother is concerned."

There was a long silence. Wolsey had never bothered keeping track of the king's many mistresses—the women came and went and had no effect on affairs of state.

Now he realized the depth of his own ignorance. He had made a serious error in judgment. He turned to another document and gave a shudder. "This second bull. Have you read it, Dr. Knight?"

"No, sir."

"You are fortunate," Wolsey told him. "I would not like to be in the position of the man who presented it to the descendant of Saint Peter."

Dr. Knight stared at the document but said nothing.

Wolsey put him out of his misery. "It asks this: If no way can be found to declare the king's marriage to Katherine illegal or invalid . . . then the pope must simply agree to allow him a second wife." He paused to let the words sink in. Knight's face showed no change.

Wolsey said, "Do you understand? It asks the pope to sanction bigamy!"

Knight swallowed. Wolsey briskly rolled up the two documents and handed them back. "Since the king commands it, you must go on your way, Dr. Knight. . . . But with neither hope of success, nor honor."

He signaled Dr. Knight's dismissal and returned to work.

After Dr. Knight had been sent on his way, Wolsey sought out Thomas More. He found him in a stable yard and told him what he had learned. "What was I supposed to do?" Wolsey asked.

"I don't know," More said. "But I agree with you. It was unacceptable and crude. I'm disappointed in His Majesty."

"Will you accept the judgment of the cardinals?"

More shrugged. "What does it matter? The pope is free now. There is no need for a conclave."

"On the contrary. There is more need than ever. The pope is still in the power of the emperor and unable to exercise his authority over the Church. So someone else must do so—and I ask you again: Will you accept the judgment of the cardinals?"

More was silent.

Wolsey looked at him. "You don't want to get your hands dirty," he said. "I understand. But, unfortunately, you don't have a choice. The dyer's hand is always stained by the element he works in."

They walked on. And still More remained silent.

Wolsey continued, "More, if you are not for me now, then you are against me. The stakes have grown higher. Mr. Cromwell tells me that the king now dines with Norfolk and Boleyn."

More raised his eyebrows.

"They are my bitter enemies," Wolsey explained. "They constantly seek my downfall. And if you will not help me, then you will help them."

More said nothing, but Wolsey knew he was facing a crisis and he was beyond his usual polite urbanity. "We have known each other a long time, Thomas. I know very well you have often complained about my methods, my way of dealing. But underneath all that, I believe we still share many things. We are still humanists, though the world batters our beliefs and compromises our actions."

And then he resorted to an uncharacteristic crudity, adding, "And what's more, you owe all your advancement in this world to me."

More looked at him. "Nothing—no earthly thing—not even a prince, will *ever* compromise my actions." He turned, plunged his hand into a horse trough, and scooped up a handful of water. He continued, "Here is my element. The spiritual element. The higher element."

They both watched as the water drained out of his hand and back into the trough. Then he showed his hand to Wolsey. "Tell me: Am I stained by it?"

Wolsey said nothing. He stood in the stable yard, his crimson robes standing out like a splash of blood against the gray cobblestones of the yard, pondering the thought of how deeply he had been stained by his profession.

Henry sat in his private chambers, staring ferociously at something on the floor. It was Brandon, kneeling humbly before him, his head bowed.

Henry sneered. "I heard you crawled all the way here!"

Brandon bristled and raised his eyes. "Something like."

Henry stared back at him, hard, forcing Brandon to lower his eyes again. "Snaffle your tongue!" Henry snapped. "It's always too busy."

"Yes, Your Majesty."

"Did you come to beg my forgiveness?"

"Yes, Your Majesty."

Henry rose and walked slowly toward the prone figure. "Then beg for it," he told Brandon.

"With all my heart, with all my soul, with every ounce of my being. My king, my sovereign, my dread lord, I beg you to forgive your miserable servant, your humble, worthless, thoughtless servant, who deserved so little and, through your bounty and Grace, was given so much. Ungrateful wretch that I am. Unworthy of Your Majesty's love."

After a moment, Henry said, "Come here!"

Brandon looked up. Henry, still looking thunderous, sat at a small table. He propped his elbow upon it in the position for arm wrestling. Brandon blinked, not quite understanding.

"If you can beat me," Henry told him, "you can come back to court."

Was it a threat—or a promise? Brandon rose to his feet and sat opposite his king. He propped his own elbow on the table and clasped Henry's hand.

His mind was spinning. What should he do? Did Henry truly want him to try to win? Did Henry really want to lose? He hated losing. If Brandon won, would he win—or lose?

"Ready?" Henry continued. His face gave nothing away.

He started exerting pressure and pushed Brandon's arm toward the table rather easily. But then Brandon reacted and, stiffening his sinews, he slowly forced Henry's arm back upright. The two men's arms shook with the strain.

The tension was palpable. Brandon had no idea of the right thing to do: Win, or let the king beat him. His whole future depended on making the right choice. But which was the right choice?

Henry's face gave him no hint; it was blank, hostile. His eyes were full of fierce determination. He began to push again, harder. Harder. He forced Brandon's arm down, down.

Again Brandon felt a surge of resistance and fought back. The muscles on both men's arms were corded, straining, their faces contorted with effort.

Never once did Henry's eyes leave Brandon's. He stared into Brandon's eyes with black determination.

They were both panting with the exertion. Henry, with a grunt of pain, started to force Brandon's arm back up. Now, if he wanted, Brandon could probably allow himself to be beaten, without too much disgrace. He had to decide now.

With a gulp, Brandon decided. With all his might he pushed back, and forced Henry's arm down toward the surface of the table. The last few inches were an absolute agony for both of them, their arms, almost their whole bodies, convulsively shaking.

Suddenly Henry's will broke, and Brandon slammed his arm down. He'd won.

Or had he?

He waited, his stomach a cold pit of anxiety as Henry angrily freed his hand and stared with malice at Brandon. He got up and, turning his back on Brandon, started to walk away.

Terror flickered across Brandon's face. Oh God, he'd made the wrong choice.

Henry was almost at the door. Brandon was crushed by anguish. Then Henry stopped abruptly, paused, turned around, and with a wide grin, said, "Welcome back."

* * * *

In Paris, Wolsey was facing utter failure for the first time in his life. He gave no sign of this as his servant assisted him in the divestment of his outer robes.

King Francis was shown in. "My dear cardinal," he exclaimed. "What could I do? Your Eminence knows I cannot order my cardinals around. They only take orders from his Holiness."

Wolsey acknowledged the king's words with a barely perceptible bow. Francis looked at him, hesitated, then left.

Wolsey sat down heavily in a chair and stared out the window. He watched as day turned into night before his eyes. It was symbolic, really. A servant looked in, saw the cardinal sitting in the gloom, and began to light candles. Wolsey waved him away.

That was how Thomas More found him when he'd come after hearing of the outcome of the cardinals' meeting. He stared at the unmoving Wolsey. "What will you say?"

Wolsey didn't respond. There was no point. There were no words that could explain utter and complete failure—not to Henry.

"We leave for London tomorrow morning," More told him, and left.

Wolsey didn't move.

Wolsey made his way toward the king's private apartments. Cromwell saw him and bowed, blocking his way.

"Mr. Cromwell," Wolsey said sharply.

"Your Eminence, the king awaits you, but . . ."

"But what?" Wolsey snapped.

Cromwell said apologetically, "He is not alone."

Wolsey frowned and gave Cromwell a hard look. His audiences with the king were *always* private. "Not alone?" His question hung in the air, unanswered.

Cromwell opened the doors to the private chambers. Wolsey walked in and came to a sudden halt when he found Henry waiting for him—with Anne Boleyn. She stood, quite relaxed, beside the great fireplace.

Wolsey bowed, suddenly tongue-tied. He had no idea what to say to the king in front of this girl. He was shocked at the visible evidence of how much had changed while he was away. Surely the king didn't intend this—this *girl*—to be privy to important affairs of state?

"Well?" Henry prompted.

"Your Majesty, I was hoping—" He paused, and his gaze flickered to Anne.

"You can speak freely in front of Mistress Boleyn," Henry said. "She knows everything."

Wolsey looked at Anne and caught the faint look of triumph in her eyes. A girl, he thought. Just a girl. And yet . . .

For a moment, Wolsey said nothing.

The king gave him the opening he'd been dreading. "So! You have come back from Paris! Tell us of your triumphs!" He smiled. "Tell us all your news. We are so eager." He waited.

Wolsey swallowed.

Henry said impatiently, "For the love of God, do I have my divorce?"

Chapter Fourteen

Sir William Compton lay asleep in his bed in his mansion at Compton Wynates. Though the night was not warm, and no fire burned in his room, sweat beaded on his brow. A thin film of sweat had also formed above his lips.

The sounds of the early morning filtered into the darkened chamber: birdsong; hooves on the cobbled yard; the stirring of servants going about their duties.

In the orchard, a beekeeper opened up a hive. Behind him, a groom led a horse in from the meadow; the world was waking up to another day. Almost as if he had heard something strange, the beekeeper paused in his labors and looked toward the great house. Bees flew around his head, disturbed.

The indoor servants, moving quietly about the house, cleaning, preparing for the day, paused as moans and groans came from the bedroom. They exchanged glances: The master had gone to bed alone.

Finally, two servants entered the room. The groans were much louder. Alarmed, one of them ran to pull back the curtains so they could see. As the light struck Compton's eyes, he screamed and clutched his head.

The servants were horrified. "Christ Jesus!" exclaimed the first one.

"Sir William!" the second one cried. "Sir William! What is it?"

But Compton was beyond speech. His body kept convulsing; he was doubled over by gripping intestinal pains. His teeth chattered, and he shook violently as if he was chilled to the marrow. His eyes were screwed shut, and he rolled around on the bed, alternatively clutching at his guts and his head, as if plagued by terrible pains in both.

The servants stared at him and then at one another in rising panic. "Go and fetch the physician!" the first one yelled at those who had gathered around the door.

The watching servants goggled through the door in silent horror, staring at their afflicted master. Nobody moved.

"I said, go and get the physician!" the servant shouted. "NOW!"

They scattered and ran.

By the time the local physician was fetched, Compton was in a bad way. He lay, wracked with shudders, almost unconscious. His body was drenched in sweat. All the bedsheets were wet.

The physician approached, covering his nose with his hand, for the sweat stank. He touched the body and recoiled at the heat of the fever. He turned on the nearest servant. "Good God, man! Why did no one wake him? Don't you know sleep in these cases is almost always fatal?"

Compton's other servants and maids pressed into the doorway, trying to see what was happening.

"Keep away! Keep away, fools!" the physician shouted at them. "Your master has the sweating sickness!"

People started to vanish in a trice, but the physician stopped two servants. "You two! You stay! We must try to treat him . . . poor fellow. Turn him over!"

Frightened and disgusted, trying to cover their noses and mouths against the stinking smell, the servants approached Compton with the utmost reluctance.

The physician opened his bag and removed a surgical knife. He snapped at the shrinking servants, "For the love of God, get on with it! We may yet save him, although—" He broke off as the men turned the sweating, slippery body facedown.

"What will you do?" one of the servants asked.

The physician tore open the back of Compton's drenched nightshirt.

"Cut into his back," he said brusquely. "I have heard it sometimes works, for it draws off some of the toxins. Hold now!" The physician drew the knife across Compton's back.

Blood ran down between Compton's shoulder blades.

For the third time Wolsey checked his robes and smoothed back his hair. Again, he inspected his private reception room in Hampton Court Palace, checking that all was as he'd ordered. He was not accustomed to being nervous. It was not a feeling he enjoyed, but since he'd returned from France, he'd found everything resting on a knife edge. . . .

At last he could hear his visitors arriving. A sound behind him made him turn. He stared at Joan, his mistress, all dressed up in her finest gown.

"What are you doing?" he said, shocked.

Joan looked dismayed. "May I not meet the king?"

"No, of course not!" the cardinal exclaimed. "Go! Go!" He signaled her frantically to disappear, and just as the door closed quietly behind her, the main doors opened and Henry strode in, followed by Anne Boleyn.

Wolsey greeted them warmly. "Your Majesty. Mistress Anne. You are both gladly welcome."

They sat down to dine. Wolsey had gone to a great deal of trouble to ensure he entertained them royally, with roast pheasant, a whole carp, dressed with shrimps and many other delicacies.

He was an attentive host, ensuring the many servants posted around the room kept his guests' glasses filled with the finest of wines, and their plates heaped with the choicest morsels.

Throughout the meal Henry and Anne exchanged intimate glances, as lovers did, in their own world.

At one point, Anne smiled at Wolsey, saying, "I must thank Your Eminence for the magnificent brooch you sent me."

Wolsey inclined his head graciously. "I am so glad you liked it. It is Italianate, and the craftsmanship I thought superb."

But Anne wasn't listening. She was once again staring into Henry's eyes.

Wolsey hesitated, then continued: "Your Majesty will be more than pleased with the gifts sent by the king of France: a golden chalice! Gold silk altar cloths! And tapestries worth 30,000 ducats!"

Henry tore his gaze from Anne and looked at Wolsey. "Then we are allies with France once more?"

"Yes. And we are both officially at war with the emperor."

"Good. It pleases me," Henry said. Then his expression darkened. "Just as it pleased the emperor to reveal to the world that he has just had a son!—and by the princess he jilted my daughter for!"

He stared, brooding at the table, then caught Anne's eye. Her lips silently mouthed the words, "You too shall have a son," and his anger melted.

Wolsey, who had seen the exchange, cleared his throat. "More shrimps, Lady Anne?" He knew they were her favorite.

Anne smiled. "Thank you, Your Eminence. No more. You are too generous—in everything."

Wolsey, whose belief was that you could never be too generous, inclined his head with a modest smile.

After a moment, Henry asked, "What of our . . . personal matter?"

"Majesty, I have arranged to send two of my colleagues—two young lawyers, Stephen Gardiner, my secretary, and Edward Foxe, to see the pope at Orvieto, near Rome, where he still resides." He added casually, "Apparently in wretched discomfort."

Henry and Anne sat up, suddenly very attentive.

"What will you have these lawyers do?" Anne asked him.

Wolsey, offended by being questioned by a woman, disguised the fact, and said with a smile, "My lady, they will press upon His Holiness, by every means, the necessity of his cooperation. He must recognize, in both canon and civil laws, the invalidity of Your Majesty's marriage."

"And of that, there is no shadow of a doubt," Henry declared. "I have been reading countless books on the matter; sometimes reading them well into the night and giving myself terrible headaches."

He paused and gave a short laugh. "But I am more than ever assured of the legal and spiritual justice of my case. My conscience is clear!" He said the last words emphatically, his eyes drilling into Wolsey's.

"As it should be," Wolsey said smoothly. "And Your Majesty should rest assured, these two gentlemen, these two restless lawyers, will not leave Orvieto until they have received satisfaction."

Evening shadows fell across the house of Compton Wynates. A pretty young woman with a sweet and gentle face slowly entered Compton's chambers. It was Ann Hastings, Compton's common-law wife.

Tapers burned at each corner of the bed, cleansing the room of evil humors. Dr. Linacre, the King's own physician, bowed to her. "Mistress Hastings."

Ann was surprised to see him there. "Dr. Linacre?"

"As soon as he heard the news, the king sent me here," the doctor explained, adding, "Alas—to no avail."

"I . . . I came to see him," Ann said, trying to look past the doctor.

"Of course," said Dr. Linacre. "And yet, if I had the power to do so, I would not let you." He stood firmly between her and Compton, deliberately blocking her view of the bed.

Ann said sadly, "I loved him."

Dr. Linacre's face softened. "That does not surprise me. He was in every way, a most lovely and loving man. His Majesty will miss his companionship a great deal."

"Let me see him," she begged.

Dr. Linacre frowned, looking troubled. "There is a grave risk of infection—about which we know so little."

"Please." Ann gave him a piteous look, and with a sigh, the physician relented, and stepped aside.

Ann approached the bed and stared at the body of her lover. Compton was dead. His skin was deathly pale, marred by horrid bluish patches on his skin. And although his eyes were closed, his mouth remained open in a silent, frozen scream of agony.

Tears filled her eyes. She crossed herself. "My poor, sweet darling," she murmured brokenly.

Compton's hands were already folded over his chest. Ann took from her bosom a silver cross and gently eased it between his fingers. She started to pray.

"Forgive me," Dr. Linacre interrupted her prayers. "You must burn all his bedding and clothing. He must be in the ground first thing."

Ann gave a sad little nod. "I thought to have a lifetime with him. At least give me these few seconds."

Dr. Linacre nodded sorrowfully and left the room. Weeping in earnest now, Ann kissed and caressed the body of her dead lover. "Good-bye, my love. . . . May God bless you and keep you until we meet again. . . ."

"Gentlemen," Wolsey said, "here is a personal letter from the king, thanking His Holiness in advance for attending sympathetically to his suit." Wolsey had explained the intricacies of their assignment to the two clever young lawyers he'd selected to present the king's case to the pope at Orvieto.

The lawyers, Gardiner and Foxe, exchanged glances. "How is His Holiness likely to respond?" Gardiner asked.

"To be honest with you, Mr. Gardiner, I am not absolutely sure," Wolsey told him. "The pope was an abused prisoner of the emperor's mercenaries. And even though the emperor reputedly allowed him to escape to Orvieto, his condition continues to be little better."

Wolsey continued, "According to every traveler who has visited him, he leads a most sad life there, shut up in a ruined palace. In which case"— he sat forward in his chair—"why should he favor the emperor, who has caused him nothing but *misery*, above the king of England, who has *never* caused him any harm?"

Foxe said dryly, "The trouble is, Your Eminence, the swords of the king of England are much farther away than the swords of the emperor. Diplomacy is nearly always settled by such proximity."

Wolsey smiled. "Spoken like a true lawyer! But remember this also:

The pope is set above temporary kings—or he is nothing! His judgments ought not to be so expedient and cynical as those of worldly rulers."

There was a short silence, and the lawyers realized their audience with the cardinal was at an end.

They bowed and prepared to leave, when Wolsey added, his voice suddenly more intense. "Yes, play upon that theme. But if everything else fails—use threats!"

They blinked.

Wolsey continued, "Tell His Holiness that if the king can't get satisfaction from the papal court . . . then he'll find ways of satisfying his conscience and ridding himself of his present wife." He looked from one to the other. "Do I make myself clear?"

They nodded. "Yes, Eminence," Foxe said. "We understand."

Wolsey dismissed them with a curt wave. They hurried away.

"This was left to me by poor Compton's will," Henry told Brandon and Knivert sadly. He put the key into the lock of the small ivory chest and opened it. Inside, there was a small drawer filled with jewels, a chessboard, and a backgammon set.

Henry moved by the sight, shook his head. "Poor William! Is this all that remains, of an entire life?" He sighed. "We must give the jewels back to his unfortunate lady."

Brandon leaned over his shoulder and peered into the chest. "Backgammon!" he exclaimed. "Shall we have a game?"

Henry and Knivert stared at him, shocked.

Brandon hurriedly added, "To—to remember him by, I meant. Of course."

The others said nothing. Henry walked over to a large cupboard. "William died at his house in Warwickshire—a long way from here. God willing, the sickness won't spread. But you should fortify yourself against it, in any case." He opened the door of the cupboard, revealing shelves full of glass jars, herbs, spices, pills, lotions, ointments, sugars, plants of all sorts—a veritable pharmacology.

"You both know of my interest in medicine," Henry continued. "Some of these are some of my newest remedies." One by one he took items from the cupboard and explained their use and purpose to his friends. "These are plasters to heal ulcers. This is an unguent that cools inflammation and stops itching. And here are ointments that can help your digestion or soothe dry skin." He winked and added, "I have even developed one that comforts your member if it's sore."

Henry, smiling, gave Knivert a small pot of the latter. Then he took out some pills. "These are called pills of Rhazes, after the Arab who invented them. They are said to be good against the sweating sickness. But this infusion is even better."

He poured a little of a vile-colored liquid into a cup. Knivert looked at it uneasily. "What . . . is it?"

"A mixture of marigolds, *manus Christi*—a very efficacious herb—sorrel, meadow plant, linseed vinegar, ivory scrapings, all sweetened with sugar," Henry explained. He looked at Knivert. "Take some."

Knivert balked, hesitating. "You're . . . sure it won't taste vile."

"Trust me," his king told him.

Knivert closed his eyes and swallowed the infusion, shuddering as it went down.

"It should make you feel sick," Henry said.

Knivert gave him a desperate look. "It does," he said, gagging.

Brandon laughed, but Henry turned on him, saying severely, "You may laugh, but that mixture is a whole lot better than the sickness it prevents!"

Brandon immediately sobered.

In faraway Compton Wynates, Ann Hastings's women were weeping and wailing. Ann lay on her bed, still and bathed in sweat. But she was not breathing, and the sweat was cold.

A servant finished wrapping the winding sheet around her, covering at last her poor, pretty face. Her two ladies wept for sadness—and in terror, holding cloths to their noses and mouths as their poor dead mistress was carried away to be placed in the ground with her beloved William.

* * * *

"Majesty, there is a serious grain shortage," Wolsey told him. "Unless it is addressed, countless numbers of Your Majesty's poorer subjects will starve."

Henry was concerned by this news. "What should we do?"

"There are too many absentee landlords in your kingdom," Wolsey explained. "These great men regard it as more important to be at Your Majesty's court than on their own estates, supervising the harvest and feeding your people."

Henry frowned. "Which great men do you mean?"

Wolsey told him. Later, he made his way through the court with a satisfied air. He saw Norfolk, standing in the midst of a small knot of his supporters, and approached him. "Your Grace."

"What do you want?" Norfolk responded, not bothering to hide his antipathy.

"A word with Your Grace," Wolsey said smoothly. "If I might. In private."

Norfolk regarded him suspiciously. "Very well."

Wolsey led him to a quiet place.

"Well?" Norfolk demanded, folding his arms and planting his feet wide apart.

"Your Grace, you are commanded to return at once to your estates in East Anglia," Wolsey informed him.

Norfolk was astonished. An angry flush rose under his skin. "'Commanded'?" he said belligerently. "By whom?"

"Commanded, yes," Wolsey said softly. "By His Majesty. Of course." He produced a letter from the folds of his Cardinal's robes, and added dulcetly, "In His Majesty's own hand."

Norfolk snatched the letter from him. "What for?"

"His Majesty would like you to supervise grain production—and North Sea trade."

Norfolk exploded. "Trade? *Trade?* What do you take me for, a butcher's son?"

Wolsey didn't react to the taunt. "As you see, Your Grace, they are not my orders," he pointed out.

Frustrated, Norfolk glared at him, then stormed out. With barely masked triumph Wolsey watched him go.

In the parkland surrounding the palace, servants were laying a picnic out for Henry and his party. The palace chamberlain approached accompanied by a fussily dressed middle-aged Frenchman and two of his valets.

"Your Majesty," the chamberlain said, "may I present His Highness Jean de Bellay, Bishop of Bayenne, the new French ambassador."

Henry waved Bellay forward. "Welcome, Monsieur," he said in French.

Bellay kissed the King's hand. *"Majésté."* He continued in English. "Majesty, I am happy to present my credentials." He offered a roll of sealed parchment, which was taken by one of Henry's servants.

"And I am happy to once again be the friend and ally of your master, and thank him for all his precious gifts," Henry responded.

"It was the king's pleasure," Bellay assured him.

Henry took Bellay's arm and led him a little to one side. "Tell me, Your Highness, how is the war against the emperor proceeding?"

"Your Majesty has no cause for anxiety," Bellay said. "A French army and a fleet of our allies—the Genoese—have the emperor's soldiers hopelessly besieged at Naples. Sooner or later, Charles must surrender, and leave Italy altogether."

Henry smiled. "That is truly excellent news."

They fell silent a moment, and Henry glanced around, obviously looking for someone. "Ah!" he exclaimed, seeing a small group of figures walking toward them.

It was Anne Boleyn, her brother George, and a small retinue. Henry could hardly disguise his joy at seeing her. He hurried forward to greet her, managing not to run, but only just. He offered her his arm, and guided her to the ambassador.

"Your Highness, allow me to—"

Bellay anticipated him. "Is this not Lady Anne? *Enchanté, mademoiselle!*" He continued in French. "His Eminence, Cardinal Wolsey, has told me all about you. But he forgot to tell me how beautiful you are." He shook his head comically. "For a Frenchman, that is almost a crime."

Anne laughed and, also in French, responded, "But Frenchmen tell every woman she is beautiful. Is that not a crime too?"

Both Henry and Bellay laughed. Anne waved to her brother to approach. "I have a gift for you," she told the ambassador. George Boleyn came forward, leading a handsome greyhound.

"For me? No!" Bellay exclaimed.

"For you, Monsieur, yes! Absolutely. He is a very fast hound, and very formidable."

Bellay admired the animal, appreciatively. "What's his name?" he asked.

There was a short silence, then Anne gave a mischievous smile. "We call him Wolsey." Everyone laughed.

Henry took Anne's hand. "Sweetheart, you will be glad to hear that His Highness tells me the emperor will soon be defeated and driven out of Italy. So he will no longer be able to stand in the way of our happiness."

"God is good," Anne said softly, meeting his eyes.

"Indeed, He is," Henry responded. They stood, smiling lovingly at each other, when suddenly, from the woods, came a loud, angry shout.

"Go back to your wife!" a man shouted from the woods. His words echoed a little.

Angrily, Henry signaled to his guards and they rushed up into the woods to beat the forest for the man who had dared insult the king. The forest was endless, and there was little chance of finding the culprit.

Henry, angry and embarrassed, looked at Anne, who was also upset. "I'm sorry," he told her quietly.

She looked back at him.

Bellay pretended to look confused. "What was that? Did someone shout something? I didn't hear." But his attempt as diplomacy failed.

The incident had soured Henry's mood completely. He stared angrily into the trees, his fists clenched.

By the time the party returned, darkness was falling.

But all at the palace had changed. Fires were burning everywhere and smoke filled the air. As well, torches had been lit all around the palace. They stopped, shocked, staring at the silhouettes of figures hurrying back and forth.

Bellay sniffed the air, and almost gagged. "What is that—that vile stench?"

Henry said somberly, "Smoke and vinegar, Your Highness. Smoke and vinegar!" He had gone very pale.

The palace chamberlain hurried toward Henry. "What's happened?" Henry demanded, though he had an idea of what it was.

The chamberlain confirmed his worst fears. "There has been an outbreak of sweating sickness in the city. Three hundred deaths this day alone."

Henry closed his eyes briefly. "Fetch Dr. Linacre," he ordered. "And quickly!"

"Majesty." The chamberlain hurried off.

Bellay looked appalled. "My God, my God, what shall become of us?"

The valets lapsed into rapid, frightened French, saying, "They have the plague here! We shouldn't have come!"

"We're going to die! Everybody's going to die."

"Shit! Holy shit!"

More people came rushing up to the king, looking worried and protective. He just had time to say to Anne, "Don't be afraid. I will see you soon," before he was borne away into the palace.

Anne had no time even to respond. She watched him disappear into the palace. She stood there, alone, among the fires and the smoke, and the sense of menace.

The moment he reached his private chambers, Henry went straight to his medicine cabinet. Pulling the stopper off a jar, he shook out several of the pills of Rhazes and swallowed them, washing them down with wine.

Then he poured himself some of the infusion that had made Knivert feel so sick. He swallowed it. It made him gag too, but he controlled himself. He strode to the window and stood, looking out.

The world was lit by the red glare from the fires, and the black shadows of the smoke. It was like staring into the portals of Hell.

Servants carried a smoking brazier, attached to a long pole, slowly through the corridors of the palace. By swinging the brazier they filled the rooms and corridors with the burning herbs, destroying the evil humors that brought pestilence and disease. Anything to keep the sweat at bay.

In the king's private chambers, Henry discussed the outbreak with the finest physician in the land, the very learned Dr. Linacre. He was a tall, slightly stooped man with a heavily lined face and a wise, kindly expression. Henry had known the doctor all his life and trusted him completely.

"I find from experience, Your Majesty," Dr. Linacre said, "that in a great many cases, before any actual physical symptoms appear, the sufferers undergo a curious mental disorientation—a quick sense of fear and apprehension, a foreboding of pain and death."

Henry paced about, listening. Every now and then Henry pressed an anxious hand to his brow, just to check that he wasn't sweating.

Dr. Linacre continued, "Indeed, I have come to believe that this fear is a form of mental contamination that terrorizes the healthy into illness." Dr. Linacre was himself so enthused by his subject that he forgot he was talking to someone who was already more than apprehensive.

Henry had always had a morbid fascination for the very thing he was afraid of. It killed with amazing speed. First the victim would complain of an aching head, or pains in the heart, or stomach pains, shivering and sometimes a rash, but it always ended with a sudden outbreak of sweating, and within a few hours, most people were dead. A man could be "merry at dinner and dead by supper."

Dr. Linacre continued his lecture, "Carried away by the disposition of the time, people brood on the inevitability of infection even as they shut themselves away and struggle to avoid it. Every rumor sends them into agitated alarm; indeed, one rumor can itself cause a thousand cases of sweat." He shook his head sadly. "So thousands catch the disease from fear who need not otherwise sweat—especially if they observe a good wholesome diet."

Henry looked up. "A wholesome diet? Is that your best remedy, Dr. Linacre? Not . . . not infusions?"

Dr. Linacre smiled. "I hope Your Majesty trusts me when I tell you that there are countless remedies for the sweat, nearly all of them, in my opinion, medically useless."

"Even to ward it off?"

Dr. Linacre considered the question seriously. "Well, I heard of an interesting theory. A young gentleman of my acquaintance swears he can combat the disease directly by working himself into a natural sweat by exercise each night."

Henry stroked his jaw thoughtfully and added, "It's true that he has so far survived two attacks. On the other hand, His Eminence Cardinal Wolsey has survived four, his only recourse being pilgrimages to Our Lady at Walsingham."

Dr. Linacre shook his head and shrugged. "What I do know is that if a patient can survive the first full day and night of the sickness, he has a much greater chance of survival, although even then there is a good chance of further complications."

For a moment he pondered the problem in silence, then recalled himself, saying, "No doubt some day we shall find out the true cause and remedy. I myself should like to research the matter further—that is, if the disease spares me in the meantime!" He chuckled with what Henry considered rather ghoulish humor.

*   *   *   *

In a small, almost dark chamber, Brandon and a young woman were making love so violently that the whole bed creaked and shook. The headboard slammed rhythmically against the wall, dislodging little showers of plaster.

The woman groaned frantically, panting and writhing as Brandon drove into her as if he would never tire or stop. She climbed toward her climax for a second time, then a third, and then abruptly, he shouted, climaxed . . . and collapsed beside her.

They lay there panting heavily. After a moment he pulled back the curtain a little to let what remained of the light come in.

Brandon grinned. "What do you say? Isn't that the best way of working up a good sweat?"

She smiled. "Yes, Your Grace."

"The more you sweat naturally, the less likely you are to . . ." He didn't finish his sentence. He didn't need to. She knew what he believed.

Some put their faith in prayer; others in apothecaries' potions and the advice of physicians. As far as Brandon was concerned, you fought fire with fire, and the sweat with sweat.

"Bring out your dead! Bring out your dead!"

Through the dark streets of the city of London, a bell rang a somber note, calling to the citizens in their houses. A cart pulled by an old horse trundled slowly down the street, attended by three dark figures. The bell tolled relentlessly.

"Bring out your dead!

Here and there a door opened, revealing a patch of light. Weeping, the living brought out the dead bodies of their loved ones wrapped in sheets, and dumped them on top of the other bodies already in the cart. Some of the bundles were very small; the bodies of children.

With disaster hitting so fast and on such a scale, there was no time for any ceremony, only a hasty crossing of breasts, and a few stifled sobs in the darkness.

The cart moved on, and the wails of a woman in desperate distress pierced the night. Others held her back as her three small children were thrown onto the cart. A tiny skinny arm protruded from one winding sheet. The mother howled with grief.

The bell tolled. The cart rumbled on.

Chapter Fifteen

The kingdom, not knowing what else to do in the face of the plague, took refuge in prayer. Henry joined Katherine in a private daily mass.

Thomas More prayed daily with his family, and kept them at home, away from the worse contamination of London.

His words expressed the fears of many: "This plague that has come upon us is a punishment from God. We are all sinners, and God is displeased with us. Whether we live or die is entirely in His hands. All we can do is pray."

Henry was in a meeting with Wolsey when a note from Anne arrived. *"My poor maid has this day caught the sweat and died. I beg Your Majesty, what shall I do?"* Henry looked at Wolsey. "I want to see her."

Wolsey, who himself looked far from well, shook his head. "I would counsel against any contact with infected persons, or those who have had contact with them. You are the king of England."

Knowing he was right, Henry gave him an agonized look. "Yes, but what if? What if she . . . dies?" He paced about the room, trying to compose himself. "All right," he said after a minute. "Tell her that she must quit the palace, go back with her father to Hever—and by all means, shut herself up there! I will send her infusions to fortify herself—and I will write to her."

"And what of Her Majesty?" Wolsey asked.

"The queen should join our daughter at Ludlow. Pray God they will be safe enough in Wales."

"And you, Your Majesty?"

Henry thought for a moment. "I will shut myself up here," he decided, "and keep the sweat at bay with every means."

"Then if I may advise Your Majesty, keep around you as few people as possible, for in that way, you can reduce the risk of contamination," Wolsey said.

Henry frowned. Wolsey did not look at all well.

Katherine watched bleakly as her ladies hurried back and forth, packing Katherine's belongings for her sojourn in Wales. Henry came to say farewell.

"Are you pleased to send me away?" she said with quiet bitterness.

"You don't want to see our daughter?"

"Are you sending me away so that you can be with her?"

"No, she—" He broke off. "Do you mean Lady Anne Boleyn?"

Katherine sniffed at his disingenuousness. "Of course I mean Lady Anne Boleyn. You make no secret of her."

"She is going back to Hever. One of her maids died of the sweat."

"And your fear of the sweat is greater than your infatuation with your mistress."

Henry said with restrained asperity, "Katherine—she is not my mistress. I do not . . . I do not sleep with her. Not while you and I are still married."

"Do you tell her you love her? Do you make promises to her? Does she make promises to you?" Katherine gave him a clear look. "Will you not tell me since—as you say—I am still your wife."

There was an awkward silence. Henry finally said, "I wish. I wish, with all my . . . my heart, that you would accept that our marriage was based upon a lie."

She just looked at him.

"In the meantime, I still love you enough to want to save your life. That is why I command you to go to Wales."

Katherine saw the real concern for her in his eyes. She put a hand out to him. "When you speak like that, my love—"

But Henry stepped quickly back, as if her very touch might harm him, and the scales fell once more from her eyes. "You act as if I had the plague," she told him quietly. "As if love itself were like the plague."

Henry pretended he did not hear her. "I shall write to you," he said. "Tell Mary that the king, her father, sends his good wishes . . . and tender devotions." And with that, he took his leave.

"How do you feel, Anne?" Thomas Boleyn asked his daughter. They were in their carriage driving home to Hever Castle. Anne was looking increasingly wan and pale.

"I—I feel all right, Papa."

Boleyn frowned. "You're sure?"

Anne looked at him. "What are you saying? That because of my maid I am certain to be contaminated?"

"Of course not!" Boleyn said with unconvincing heartiness.

Anne looked away, staring out of the window and trying not to panic. She did feel unwell and was horribly sure she had the sweat. The more she thought about it, the more certain she became—and the more agitated. Her breath started to come in gasps.

"What is it?" her father asked.

"I can't breathe!" she gasped. "Please stop! I can't breathe! Please stop the carriage, I—" She started pulling frantically at her clothes.

Boleyn thumped the roof with a stick, shouting, "Halt!"

The carriage slowed, but before it had time to stop, Anne flung open the door and jumped out.

Boleyn watched her take deep breaths and try to control herself. Then she started to walk.

Boleyn called nervously from the carriage, "Are you all right?" but Anne didn't respond, just kept walking, her gaze fixed ahead.

Boleyn banged the roof of the carriage with his stick again. "On!"

The carriage rolled slowly on, keeping pace with the walking girl. She showed no awareness of it. Tears poured down her cheeks.

Or was it sweat?

* * * *

Within a day, the palace was virtually deserted. Henry walked from room to room, accompanied only by two armed guards, standing well back from the king. The emptiness was eery, unsettling. Smoke from fumigating braziers drifted through the shadowy silences, the smell of the smoke permeating everything.

Everywhere Henry looked showed evidence of hurried departures: abandoned books, clothes, partially consumed meals abandoned in mid-course. His footsteps echoed.

He reached his own chambers, where a single servant and a young page remained to serve him.

Henry felt trapped, helpless. The trouble with the sweat was that there was nothing you could do! He ate his evening meal in solitude, brooding. . . .

He'd taken his potions—not that Lineacre thought there was any point. It had been said by some that oranges were the key to prevention. Henry had eaten as many as he could. He'd also prayed morning, noon, and night for himself and his loved ones to be kept free of this terrible pestilence, and for the country to be rid of it.

He retired to bed early . . . but his sleep was plagued by terrible dreams. He lay awake in the semidarkness of his bedchamber, brooding.

What was it that Linacre had said about exercise? How someone the doctor knew tried to combat the disease by working himself into a natural sweat each night.

At least that was something active, Henry thought. Better than this endless waiting.

He climbed out of bed and began to exercise vigorously. The page boy sleeping at the foot of his bed woke and watched his master with some amazement. Henry exercised with fierce determination, working himself up into a natural, healthy—and, he hoped—health-giving sweat.

The next morning, after a night of fitful sleeping, interrupted by disturbing dreams and bouts of exercise, Henry took himself to confession.

Sitting in the small, dark compartment of the confessional he said, "Father, it is well known that sickness is a visitation from God and a punishment for sins. But why is my land so marked out for disfavor?"

He waited, but the priest didn't answer.

"What have we done that has so displeased Almighty God that so many are struck down?" Again, the priest said nothing.

Henry shifted uncomfortably. He wanted—needed—assurance, preferably divine, that it wasn't anything to do with him. Or his family.

The sweating sickness had plagued England since its first outbreak in the summer of 1485, the same summer that the first Henry Tudor had seized the English crown in the Battle of Bosworth, putting an end to the War of the Roses.

It had been suggested—never to Henry directly, though the whispers had inevitably come to his ears—that the dread disease was a judgment by God on England for allowing a Tudor to usurp the throne.

"I have searched my own conscience. Is it my fault that the Lord has visited plague upon England? But Father, I say this before God, my conscience is clear. . . ."

Nothing stirred on the other side of the screen. Maybe the priest did believe it was a judgment on a Tudor, and didn't want to say so out loud.

Henry said, "Father, I still ask forgiveness, even for sins unknown. And I ask for your blessing, Father. Not as a king—but as a man." He waited. "Please, Father."

Still no sound came from the other side of the screen. Very gently, Henry shifted aside the little dark curtain and looked into the priest's side.

The priest sat there, in silence, grinning at Henry. Grinning in a rictus of death, his face waxen and cold, his eyes wide and staring.

Henry recoiled and shot out of the confessional. He crossed himself, said a hasty prayer, and fled.

Orvieto, Italy

The two English lawyers, Gardiner and Foxe, looked askance at the so-called "Bishop's palace" at Orvieto. The place was a wreck—wretched and foul-smelling. The roof was partially collapsed, and much of the interior was open to the elements.

They were ushered into a chamber by a young priest. Gardiner and Foxe exchanged horrified looks as they waited. The "papal court" seemed to consist of a few shabby officials and hangers-on, and a couple of thin and mangy dogs.

Eventually, a scrawny-looking young priest in dirty ecclesiastical robes appeared. He greeted them in Italian, adding, "Are you the English envoys? This way." He led them into the next chamber, which was in slightly better repair and had a few more items of furniture.

The pope, Clement VII, formerly Giulio de Medici, was a small, intelligent-looking man. He was attended by several cardinals, also looking somewhat shabby and threadbare.

The pope greeted the envoys, wiping away tears. "Can you see how I am forced to live? Can you imagine your father's misery? The Spaniards are practically at my doorstep! I am in the power of the dogs!" He shook his head in despair.

Gardiner and Foxe frowned. It was difficult to know how to respond, not least because of their own complex—and contradictory—feelings toward the pope. Foxe came right to the point. "Your Holiness knows why we are here. We bring a letter from His Majesty, King Henry, the most dutiful and Catholic king of England, Ireland, and France." He offered Clement the letter.

Clement eyed the letter as if Foxe were handing him a live snake. He made no move to take it.

Gardiner stepped up to explain. "His Majesty thanks Your Holiness in advance for your support in his nullity suit. He knows that he and all his kingdom will be eternally bound to Your Holiness for what you are doing. He knows that you, Holy Father, will not object to our supplications." The two lawyers stared at hard at the pope.

There was a long silence. Finally, the pope took the letter and placed it, unopened, on a side table.

"I wish with all my heart to please and satisfy your master," he told them. "But I must say to you, in all honesty—as an honest man, and as God is my witness—that I have been advised that this suit is prompted solely by the king's vain affection and undue love for this woman, Anne Boleyn." His cardinals both nodded their heads as if to confirm his words.

The pope continued: "I have been told that the king of England desires his divorce for private reasons only, and that the woman he loves is far below him, not only in rank"—he met the envoys' eyes—"but also in virtue."

"Holiness," Gardiner said. "Who has told you these things?"

Clement shrugged and glanced again toward his cardinals. "There are rumors."

"What rumors?" Foxe demanded.

"Well, they say that Anne is already pregnant, and that the king urgently wishes to make her child his heir to the throne." Clement regarded them shrewdly.

The envoys smiled, as if amused by such nonsense. "Your Holiness has been badly misinformed—in *every* way!" Foxe told him. "Lady Anne is a model of chastity."

"Though very apt to procreate children—when the time comes," Gardiner added.

Clement continued to observe them with an expression of polite interest. His dark, intelligent eyes missed nothing.

Foxe continued: "Holy Father, Lady Anne impresses everyone who sees her or knows her with the purity of her life, her constant virginity, her soberness, meekness, humility, wisdom . . . her maidenly and womanly virtues."

"She is descended from high, very noble, and thoroughly regal blood," Gardiner said. "Indeed, of all the women in England, she above all is fittest to become queen."

Clement looked thoughtful. "But what of Queen Katherine?" he said at last.

"His Majesty is most insistent that she be treated with all manner of kindness, like a sister," Foxe informed him, "if she is persuaded to withdraw her opposition to the king's suit, and acknowledge the invalidity of her marriage."

"His Majesty hopes that, when Your Holiness has taken cognizance of the legal arguments we have brought with us, you will write to the queen to urge her compliance," Gardiner said, his tone becoming noticeably tougher. The cardinals shifted uncomfortably.

Gardiner gave them a hard look. He was, after all representing a most powerful, magnificent king, and this pope, though head of the Church on earth, was but a small, shabby creature without even a roof over his head.

Clement appeared not to notice. "Of course. But first I must read the arguments, must I not? Before coming to judgment."

He seemed about to dismiss them, so Foxe decided to add his might. "His Majesty also made it plain to us that, if you could not give him satisfaction, then he must look for a judgment elsewhere." He paused to let the threat sink in, then added, "He might be forced to live outside the laws of holy church, and beyond Your Holiness's authority."

The level of tension in the room suddenly rose. All pretense of supplication had been abandoned. Foxe had ripped the mask off.

It was a clear and direct threat to the pope as supreme head of the church, to whom all Christians owe their first allegiance. A defining moment. The whole room waited.

But Clement had not been born a Medici for nothing. With generations of diplomacy and intrigue at his back, he responded to the English envoys' threats with an artless smile.

He embraced the English envoys warmly, kissing their cheeks twice, in the Italian manner. "My sons, I will give this matter further consideration before coming to a decision," he said. His voice and manner carried the authority of generations of Medicis and popes. With a regal gesture he held out the hand bearing the holy papal ring, and suddenly the envoys stopped seeing him as a small, shabby, beleaguered Italian priest. He was the pope.

They fell to their knees before him in automatic obedience. "Thank you, Holy Father," they mumbled.

Gardiner and Foxe had been cooling their heels for what seemed like forever, waiting, and waiting for the pope's answer. Each day they would trudge from the run-down house where they had obtained lodgings only to trudge back again, having achieved nothing. There had been endless delays, diversions, and false hopes.

Eventually, they had been summoned back to the shabby, dilapidated room where they had awaited their first audience with the pope.

Finally he appeared, all smiles, and offered his hand for them to kiss. Beside him shuffled an elderly man in cardinal's robes. Gardiner recognized him. "That's Cardinal Campeggio," he whispered to Foxe. "He was at the Field of the Cloth of Gold. He's a very holy man."

They greeted the pope and Cardinal Campeggio and waited eagerly for the pope's response.

"My sons," Clement began. "I fear you will be disappointed in my answer. I am unable to make a judgment, here and today, concerning the king's suit."

Gardiner and Foxe's faces fell. Angrily, they began to rise from their seats. For this they had waited all this time in this shambles of a place?

Clement saw their anger and held up a pacific hand. "Wait! I have not told you that it is the end of the matter."

The envoys sat back, their faces suspicious. If this was another delaying tactic . . .

The pope continued. "I am resolved that it should be settled as soon as may be . . . but not here. You see how I am here!" He gestured to his crumbling surrounds. "And I am too far from England to make proper and fair judgment."

The envoys frowned again. The pope hurriedly gestured toward Campeggio, saying, "For these reasons, I am appointing Cardinal Campeggio as my official legate. Once the sickness abates in your country, he will travel to England and, together with Cardinal Wolsey, he will constitute a court to hear and decide upon the merits of the case."

He gave them a shrewd look and said, "If your king is as certain of his rightness as you say he is, then no doubt he will welcome the proceedings, which can only hasten the fulfillment of his desires."

He smiled. Gardiner and Foxe exchanged frustrated looks, then reluctantly bowed. The old fox had outsmarted them; he'd instituted yet another prevarication and delay. But what could they say?

* * * *

> *My sweetheart . . . I have sent you many remedies for the sweat. Please drink vinegar mixed with water. I . . .*

Henry heard a noise and looked up from his letter-writing. A young pageboy stumbled, banging his head against the wall. He walked on slowly and unsteadily toward the king. His face was now unnaturally white and sheened with moisture. He walked as if in a trance.

"Boy . . . ," Henry said warningly.

The boy came closer and closer, his eyes vacant and staring. The sweat was upon him.

Henry pushed back his chair, but as the boy reached his desk, he fell, his head crashing against it. He lay still, unmoving.

Henry stared, horrified.

Within an hour, Henry was gone from the palace, riding like the wind, with just four servants in attendance, fleeing from the scent and the sight and the threat of death.

They rode and they rode, passing over fields and through forests, moving farther and farther from civilization and the taint and the stink of death.

At last they came to a lonely tower etched against the skyline.

Henry rode toward it. Here he would stay until the outbreak of sweat had passed.

The business of ruling the country could not cease, however, and Henry's isolation was not complete. Precautions against the sweat were put in place. Letters were fumigated by being passed through the smoke of herbs, before they were presented to the king. Dr. Linacre supervised. A servant carried them along the corridor, left them on a desk for the king to take, knocked on the door and departed. Henry, as far as possible, stayed alone.

It was a very strange feeling for him. All his life he had been surrounded by people, when he slept, when he woke, when he bathed—the entire time. Now he was alone almost the entire time, communicating mostly through letters.

Wolsey's letters not only carried the scent of the smoke they had just been passed through, but also the faint tang of oranges. Ever since the first reports of the sweat had come to his attention, Wolsey had kept a large bowl of Spanish oranges—believed by some to be efficacious against the plague—on his desk. His habit was to slice open an orange and suck the flesh from it while he read his correspondence.

Henry ate Spanish oranges too. Wolsey's latest letter said:

> *Your Majesty should know that, His Grace, the Duke of Norfolk, having caught the sweat, asked to be allowed back to London, ostensibly to visit a doctor.*

Henry frowned and kept reading.

> *This permission I refused on Your Majesty's behalf.*

Henry gave an approving nod.

Three of Your Majesty's apothecaries have also fallen sick, and
three of your chamber servants have died. Your mason, Redman,
is also dead. The disease shows no sign of abating. There are now
40,000 cases in London alone. Lady Anne Boleyn is also sick—
yet still survives.

Henry froze. He stared at the letter and reread the lines. *Lady Anne Boleyn is also sick.* It struck Henry like a blow. He leaped to his feet, sending his heavy chair backward. "Dr. Linacre!" he shouted.

Linacre hurried in.

"Anne is ill!" Henry shouted. "Lady Anne Boleyn! Go to Hever at once. Now!" He shook the doctor slightly. "For the love of God, save her!"

Linacre gave him a doubtful look. "Majesty, if she is already ill, there is—" He broke off. The king was in no state to listen to his opinion. "I will go at once," the doctor said.

Henry watched him go, distraught. He looked around for someone to share his anxieties with. "Where the devil is Wolsey when you need him?" he snapped, forgetting he had sent Wolsey home.

Wolsey's desk in Hampton Court Palace was a mess. His papers lay scattered, his ink spilled, his tower of books fallen. Oranges lay scattered across the floor.

Among the oranges on the floor lay Wolsey. His teeth were chattering with cold, yet his face was sweating like a pig. He jerked as his abdomen knifed with pain. His eyes rolled back in his head.

Thomas Boleyn and his son, George, waited anxiously outside Anne's room. The door opened, and Dr. Linacre emerged, looking grave. He looked at them and shook his head. "In my opinion, there is no hope. The vital signs of life are weak and worsening."

George burst into tears.

"The priest should attend her now; it is time for the last rites. I'm very sorry," The doctor said and departed.

In the burying field outside London, the fires burned without ceasing. Cart after cart pulled into the field, where an immense ditch had been dug. The naked bodies of the dead were unceremoniously hauled from the carts and dumped into the pit. Men stood by to throw limed earth over the bodies to lessen the smell. Even so, the stench was indescribable.

Behind the open ditch lay equally long mounds of fresh turned earth, the remains of other ditches, containing thousands more bodies. It was a living nightmare. Hell on earth.

In Thomas More's house at Chelsea, More was poring over books with his seventeen-year-old daughter. Outside, they could hear the sound of a bell tolling, getting closer and closer. It was the sound of the death carts, moving through the neighborhood, collecting the dead.

More worked on, indifferent to the macabre sound. His daughter put down her pen and looked at her father.

"Are you not frightened, Papa?"

More stopped reading and looked over. "Of death? No. Why should I be? I have put myself in the hands of God, and I know with certainty that when I die I shall go to a much better place than this."

The bell sounded louder and louder as it came closer. His daughter shivered and crossed herself.

More said, "What you see around you, sweetheart, is not fear of death, but of what, for sinners, must surely follow it—a fear of hell." He closed his books, walked slowly to the window, and looked out.

"In truth," he said, "there is another disease I fear more than the sweat. Even now it is spreading everywhere, infecting thousands."

"Of what do you speak, Papa?"

"There is a specter haunting Europe. The specter of Lutherism. It spreads among the poor, those who see the church as rich and corrupt and decadent." He turned back from the window and said, "It has already ignited a peasants' war in Germany, which killed a hundred thousand people. Now the contagion has visited Salzburg, and Burgundy, and Montpellier, and Nantes. Every day brings more news of the virulence of this accursed heresy."

"But surely it won't come here?" said his daughter.

More shook his head. "It is *already* here. We know of secret meetings in the City of London, where Catholic priests and the Holy Father are held up to scorn and ridicule. Where the church is attacked and infamous books distributed."

Disturbed by such shocking heresies, his daughter crossed herself again. "What is to be done?"

"Let me ask you," said More. "What do you do to a house that is infected with sickness?"

She thought for a moment. "You purge it with fire."

He nodded in approval. "Yes. And so, in the same way, the sickness in the house of our faith must be purged with fire. I am personally against violence, as you well know. But I believe that Luther and his apostles should be seized, right now, and burned!"

His daughter stared, a little frightened by such a vehement outburst from her usually mild father.

The corridors of Hever Castle echoed with the sound of running feet. "Papa!" George Boleyn shouted. "Papa, come quickly!"

Thomas Boleyn followed his son into Anne's bedchamber. She was sitting up in bed, propped upon cushions. She looked thin and wan, her eyes shadowed and looking larger than ever.

Boleyn stared at her. "You're . . . alive!"

She gave a shaky smile. "Yes, Papa."

"Thanks be to God!" Boleyn fell to his knees beside the bed and grasped one of her hands. "Do you know what you have done, child? You have risen from the dead."

He kissed her hand, almost laughing for joy. "Now you can see the king again," he exclaimed happily. "It can be just as before!"

Anne stared at him in momentary disbelief, then quickly dropped her gaze, hiding the pain his words had caused. She sank back into the pillows and closed her eyes.

Slowly, as it became obvious that the outbreak of the sweat had passed, church bells started ringing all over the kingdom—the doleful, weary ringing of the dead cart bells was replaced with a joyful pealing, celebrating the abating of the plague and the triumph of survival.

Grief-stricken and devastated by loss, the living gave thanks for being spared and began the slow task of rebuilding their lives.

Henry, full of joy at Anne's miraculous recovery and relief at the abatement of the dread disease, was preparing to leave the tower, along with Dr. Linacre, and his small personal retinue.

Henry had written to Anne:

> *Thanks be to God, my own darling, you are saved . . . and the plague is abated. The legate which we most desire arrived at Paris on Sunday or Monday last. I trust by next Monday to hear of his arrival in Calais; and then I trust within a while to enjoy that which I have so longed for, to God's pleasure, and our own. No more to you now, my darling, for lack of time, but that I would you were in my arms, or I in yours, for I think it long since I kissed you.*

Henry mounted his horse and looked up one last time at the small window at the top of the tower—his refuge and his prison. He dug his heels into his horse's flanks and began the long ride back to London.

Wolsey had also miraculously survived the sweat. Still weakened by the toll the disease had taken, he sat in a chair at Hampton Court with a rug over his knees.

His mistress, Joan, entered, saying, "You have a letter—from Lady Anne Boleyn."

"Read it for me," Wolsey said weakly.

She broke the seal and read: "'My Lord, I am delighted to hear that you have escaped the sweat. All the days of my life, I am most bound, of all creatures, next to the king's grace, to love and serve your grace; I beseech you never to doubt that my opinion of you will ever change, as long as I have any breath in my body. Your humble servant, Anne Boleyn.'"

There was a short silence after she finished. Wolsey gave a faint snort. "Well, at least she has a sense of humor."

He looked at Joan. "Arrange for my pilgrimage to Walsingham. I must give thanks to Our Lady."

The choir of the Chapel Royal performed a requiem for the dead. Composed, arranged, and conducted by Thomas Tallis, it was the requiem he'd written for his friend William Compton.

The newly reconvened court sat and listened to the glorious, spiritual music. Henry sat with Brandon and Knivert. Queen Katherine had returned, bringing along her daughter, Mary. They sat beside the king.

Wolsey, still on pilgrimage, was absent, as was Norfolk, who had not yet been granted permission to return to court.

Many of the seats in the church were empty. On each empty seat rested a spur that had once belonged to a dead man. On some chairs other small items had been laid with the spur; a handkerchief, a glove, a tiny pair of shoes, representing members of the spur owner's family who had died with him.

The beautiful music soared, filling the church and listeners with emotion. Thomas Tallis conducted, his cheeks wet with tears. Few eyes in the congregation were dry.

Henry wept for his friend Compton and for his own mortality. Katherine, turning her veiled face toward him, laid her hand gently over his. He did not pull his hand away.

Shortly after the requiem concluded, a messenger approached Henry outside the church and whispered something to him. Henry, suddenly alert, hurried outside.

Anne Boleyn stood waiting for him. Henry broke into a run and swept her into his arms. He swung her round, exhilarated by love, relief, and desire. "Anne!" he explained. "My darling Anne!"

He rained kisses on her, kissing her mouth, her eyelids, her throat, her lips. "Anne!" he murmured between each kiss. "Anne . . . Anne." He crushed her against him, kissing her a thousand times, unable to think of anything else to say, except, "Anne . . ."

Chapter Sixteen

Wolsey had returned from his pilgrimage to Walsingham and, his health fully recovered, was back into his normal routine at Hampton Court Palace.

He'd been informed a guest had arrived and he rose to greet him. Wolsey blinked at the sight of his visitor, a bizarre-looking old man with a long, untrimmed beard and a dusty cloak. He leaned heavily on the arm of a young priest, shuffling with agonizing slowness, wincing in pain with each step.

Wolsey's secretary, Gardiner, formally announced him. "His Eminence, Cardinal Campeggio."

Wolsey gave the old man a sharp look of surprise. He hadn't recognized Campeggio at all. "Lorenzo, my friend, come and sit down."

"Your Grace must forgive my incapacity," Campeggio said once he had been made comfortable and they were alone. "God has given me gout, as a great trial. I try not to complain too much."

"My sympathy, Eminence," Wolsey said. "But you and I have another trial to attend to. His Majesty is keen that the legatine court be set up straight away to determine the case for his annulment. He has waited, as you well know, a considerable time already, and is anxious for a speedy resolution."

"Indeed, indeed," Campeggio acknowledged. "I have the pope's written commission to decide upon this matter. And from my decision, there can be no appeal. And yet . . ." He looked at Wolsey and took a sip of wine. Wolsey waited impatiently.

"We are old friends, are we not, Cardinal Wolsey? And we are both men of the world. I was married once. My wife died before I took Holy Orders. I even have a son who has traveled with me."

"And . . . so?" Wolsey was itching for the old man to get to the point.

"His Holiness wants to satisfy the king—however difficult that might be. But for all our sakes . . . would it not be better for you and I to try to persuade His Majesty to give up his divorce? Surely His Majesty's passion for this—this girl—will alter and fade with time, as all such passions inevitably do? His Holiness is certain that a reconciliation between their Majesties would be by far the most satisfactory resolution to this matter."

He gave Wolsey a shrewd look. "And he is prepared to offer certain inducements, if these are needed to ease the king's conscience."

Wolsey's expression grew stormy. "I fear Your Eminence has proceeded here in ignorance," he said. "Let me make certain things plain to you. If you do not grant the king his divorce, papal authority in England will be annihilated. Do you have no mind that, just as the greater part of Germany has already become estranged from Rome and the Faith, the same will not happen in England?"

Thrusting his face close up to Campeggio's, Wolsey continued. "If the king's desires are not met, what will follow, I assure you, is the rapid and total ruin of the church's influence in the kingdom; in short, the total ruin of the kingdom!"

In the king's private gardens, Henry was walking with Anne Boleyn. He was in an excellent mood.

"Is there any danger they may declare your marriage valid?" Anne asked him.

Henry shook his head. "I have Wolsey's assurance that the pope has already decided in my favor. The trial is just for the sake of appearances. It's a way of appeasing the emperor." He smiled at Anne.

"Then—we can start planning for the wedding?" she asked.

"Yes. Yes, my love." They embraced, kissing for a moment or two, then continued walking.

After a pause, Henry added, "And for—for the sake of appearances, there's—there's also something I have to do."

Anne was puzzled by his behavior. He seemed uncharacteristically awkward.

Henry continued, "For a while I have to share Katherine's table again and, sometimes . . . her bed."

Anne stopped dead and looked at him. "Her *bed*?"

Henry smiled and said in a coaxing voice, "It's nothing! I've just been advised by my lawyers that to do otherwise would risk a countersuit. I could be seen to be acting against her conjugal rights."

Anne stared at him. "You think it's *nothing* to go back to bed with your wife?"

Henry's face clouded over. "Yes! It is nothing." He added defensively, "What do you think is going to happen?"

She gave a hurt, angry shrug. "What usually happens!"

She tried to walk on, but Henry, also hurt and offended, grabbed her arm. "How little you trust in me!"

She swallowed hard, then said quietly, "I'm sorry. You know I trust you. I love you . . ." She tried to smile and give him a kiss, but Henry gave her a cold look and walked on, alone.

Cardinals Campeggio and Wolsey were shown into the king's outer chamber. Henry received them in an optimistic mood. Campeggio sat in a chair, looking enigmatic, but Wolsey stood, hiding his anxiety under smiles.

"Katherine is not to blame in this," Henry told Campeggio. "Nor am I. But the fact is, Excellence, we broke God's law, for which there can be no dispensation." He gave the elderly cardinal a sincere look. "You understand how deeply this matter touches my conscience—and how quickly I need it to be resolved?"

"I do," Campeggio said. "I sympathize—as does His Holiness. Naturally . . . but His Holiness also suggests to Your Majesty another . . . possible solution."

Wolsey darted him an angry look. "I have already made it plain to Your Eminence that His Majesty—"

Campeggio smiled and cut him off with a dismissive gesture. "No, no, no. Please. This is not the same, my friend. It's a solution that should very much please His Majesty."

Henry and Wolsey exchanged glances. "What is it?" Henry asked.

"His Holiness is aware of the queen's great piety," Campeggio began. "She herself has spoken of it. Her love for the Mother of God . . . for the saints . . ." He gestured. "And so on . . . So, he wonders if Her Majesty could be persuaded, like Jeanne de Valois, the sometime wife of Louis XII, to abdicate her marriage and retreat to a nunnery."

There was a long, stunned silence, then Henry said, "You will put this to Katherine?"

Campeggio shrugged. "Certainly."

Henry looked at Wolsey. "What do you think, Wolsey?"

Wolsey considered the suggestion from all angles. "It would certainly expedite matters. And it would save us the pain of a trial. And, since it was voluntary, it could not offend her nephew the emperor. Moreover, it would allow Her Majesty an honorable retirement!"

Henry grinned. "Excellent! Ask her right away!" he told Campeggio.

"Will Your Majesty at least consider the proposal?" Campeggio asked quietly.

Katherine gave him a gracious smile. "I will give you my answer in due course, after I have talked to the king, my husband." She suddenly noticed Wolsey approaching. She didn't want to have to talk to him, particularly not in front of Cardinal Campeggio, so she quickly offered Campeggio her hand, saying, "Father, will you hear my confession later?"

"Yes, my child." Campeggio gave her a concerned look.

Katherine, her eye on Wolsey's approach, tried to leave. Wolsey, determined to intercept her, moved quickly to block her way. Katherine gave him an unfriendly stare. "Eminence."

Suddenly, to her surprise and embarrassment, Wolsey fell to his knees before her and said, "I beg Your Majesty to yield to the king's will."

"And what is the king's will?" she asked.

"As His Eminence professes," Wolsey explained. "That you enter a religious community of your choice, and take vows of perpetual chastity."

Katherine was furious. "You talk to *me* of chastity? Do you not have a mistress and two children, Your *Eminence*?"

"Your Majesty is entering the third period of your natural life," Wolsey explained. "You have spent the first two setting a good example to the world. With this one act, you would set a seal on all your good actions." He waited humbly.

Katherine breathed deeply and brought her anger under control. In an arctic voice she said, "Please rise, Your Grace. It is not seemly that a man of your dignity should have to beg in public—whatever the cause." She swept away, leaving Wolsey to clamber awkwardly to his feet.

"So," Henry said to Katherine. "You talked to Campeggio?" As he'd told Anne he would, Henry took once again to sharing a table with Katherine. He made sure, however, to have enough people present to make it a semi-public affair.

"Yes," she said. "He talked to me." She ate a leisurely mouthful and, when she'd finished, said, "I told him that I could give him no answer without Your Majesty's permission."

A servant came and, on bended knee, presented a dish of carp. Katherine took some. Henry watched, chafing with impatience.

"And what answer will you give him?" Henry said as soon as the servant had moved away.

"I will tell him the truth."

Henry flushed, and ate some carp. It tasted like ashes in his mouth. "Katherine," he said in a low voice. "All the world now agrees that your marriage to me was unjust. Even you must acknowledge it!" He leaned forward and hissed in her ear, "So unless you agree to take the veil, I shall have to *force* you!"

Katherine sat in dignified silence, blinking hard, trying to fight back tears. After a long silence she said quietly, as if her husband had not just threatened to lock her in a convent for the rest of her life, "So, do I have your permission to speak to Cardinal Campeggio?"

Henry gulped down some wine. He felt angry and resentful toward her for putting him in such an uncomfortable position.

"I will not speak to him if you do not want me to," Katherine added.

Henry gave her a trapped look. He drank some more wine.

Master Richard Cromwell, the king's secretary, was shown in to Anne Boleyn's private apartments. Anne was sitting quietly by herself at the window, sewing.

"Lady Anne," Cromwell said quietly.

Anne brightened and put aside her work. "Mr. Cromwell. Do you . . . do you have a message from the king?" she asked with a mixture of hesitance and eagerness.

He shook his head, and lowered his voice. "I am sorry, my lady. I am here for a different purpose. A mutual friend, Mr. Simon Fysh, now living in exile in Holland, has sent me a gift for you." From the folds of his clothing, Cromwell produced a book.

Anne knew at once that he had brought her some literature from the followers of Martin Luther. Dangerous literature. Thomas More had burned books like this one.

"What is it, Master Cromwell?" she asked breathlessly.

"*The Obedience of the Christian Man*, by William Tyndale," he said. "It has many good criticisms of the papacy and the arrogance and abuses of priests. You will find it most illuminating."

Anne took the book. Cromwell continued, "But always and ever be cautious as to whom you show it. You know it might be accounted heresy just to possess it, and Wolsey is still keen enough to prosecute heretics— as we are called—who embrace the true religion."

"I will, and God bless you, Master Cromwell."

As Cromwell turned to leave, Anne thought of something. "Wait," she told him. She searched for a moment and found a beautiful piece of embroidery. She gave it to Cromwell, saying, "Please give this to the king, with my, with my love."

Cromwell hesitated, then took it.

"What is it you wish to confess?" Campeggio asked Katherine.

"Father, I wish to tell you about my first marriage, to Prince Arthur, His Majesty's older brother."

"I know of it. Go on."

"He never *knew* me," Katherine said. "I swear to you, under the sacramental oath, that I was untouched by Prince Arthur. I went to my marriage with King Henry a virgin, just as I came from the womb of my mother."

"I want to be absolutely clear," Campeggio said to her. "You say you came to the king's bed a virgin—intact and unviolated?"

"Yes, Father." After a moment, Katherine said, "Father, I say in all humility that I cannot accede to your request. I am the true and legitimate wife of the king, my husband, therefore your proposal is inadmissible. Come what may, I will live and die in that vocation to matrimony to which God has called me."

Campeggio sighed. "I understand."

"Furthermore," she added. "I give you permission to break the seal of the confessional and tell the whole world what I have told you!"

Campeggio nodded wearily. He waited until the queen had departed, then put his head into his hands. His solution was not to be. Neither Henry nor the queen would give way. Everyone would lose.

"I need to see Cardinal Campeggio," Wolsey told Campeggio's son. He moved toward the bedchamber, but Campeggio's son blocked his way.

"Forgive me. My father is indisposed," the son said. "In any case, there is nothing further he can do for the time being. He has sent some reports to Rome and must await the replies from His Holiness."

Wolsey's face reddened with anger.

"In the meantime, my poor father needs to rest and restore his strength." He met Wolsey's gaze coolly, making it clear he would not budge from his position.

Wolsey, enraged and on the edge of despair at the position this left him in, lifted a clenched fist. For a moment he seemed about to strike the younger man, but with a visible effort he mastered himself, turned on his heel, and stormed out.

Henry was holding an assembly at court. All around the palace, torches burned. Inside, the sound of music played as gorgeously attired ladies and gentlemen danced, feasted, mingled, gossiped, and plotted.

Thomas More and Campeggio were seated in a good vantage point, observing the glittering assembly. More was pointing out persons of note. "That is Princess Margaret, the king's sister," he murmured. "Recently returned to court. She's standing with the Duchess of Norfolk."

"And that striking-looking young woman?" Campaggio asked, pointing to a young woman who had just entered with several ladies in attendance. The young woman immediately went to greet Boleyn, now Lord Rochford, who was standing with the Duke of Norfolk. Courtiers began to gravitate toward her. "That would be Mistress Boleyn, yes?" Campeggio surmised.

"Yes. That is she," Thomas More said. "The girl for whom the king is prepared to sacrifice his marriage to a most gracious and loving queen."

Campeggio sighed. "I have tried to argue him out of his course, but I swear an angel descended from Heaven would be unable to dissuade him."

They watched Anne Boleyn smiling and receiving compliments. Campeggio leaned closer to More. "Do you suppose that they have taken things to the ultimate conjunction?"

More gave a faint distasteful look, indicating he thought the question beneath him.

Henry and Wolsey entered the court, Henry looking splendid in a gown of gold brocade trimmed with lynx's skin. For once, Wolsey did not seem to be enjoying the dramatic entrance. He looked anxious, a little shrunken, and less arrogant than usual.

Campeggio continued, "Wolsey is also threatening that if the king does not get satisfaction, it will alienate this realm from Rome."

More nodded. "That is my greatest fear, also."

Campeggio watched as Anne Boleyn tried to catch the king's eye through the crowds. She seemed desperate to meet his gaze.

He noticed Princess Margaret staring hard at Anne, with curled lip. *No love lost there,* he thought.

"I have received a petition from the Dukes of Suffolk and Norfolk and Lord Boleyn," Campeggio told More. "It says the divorce has the overwhelming support of the people of England."

More snorted and said in a savage undertone, "As Your Eminence would quickly discover, if you stepped outside these doors and saw the people—that is a manifest lie! On the contrary. The people love their queen—and they have every reason to do so." He stared at Campeggio a long moment, then bowed and moved away.

Henry moved through the crowd, talking to Wolsey but slowly making his way toward Anne.

"Her Majesty has refused the offer," Wolsey told him.

"Are you really surprised?" Henry said.

"Campeggio says the pope is prepared to consider legitimizing any children you might have with Mistress Boleyn, even if you are not married to her."

Henry swung around to stare at him. "Are you mad?" He frowned. "You must do better than that, Wolsey!" He moved to talk to Brandon, Norfolk, and Boleyn. They greeted him warmly. Wolsey watched, dismayed.

Campeggio watching, plucked the sleeve of Mendoza, the imperial ambassador. "Forgive me, Ambassador Mendoza, but I am new to this court." He pointed discreetly. "Who are these men talking to the king?"

"Lord Rochford is the father of Anne Boleyn, and Norfolk is her uncle. Like the Duke of Suffolk, they are Wolsey's sworn enemies—and everyone at court knows it. They would stop at nothing to bring him down."

"Yet the king still loves Wolsey?"

"Not so much as before, perhaps," Mendoza admitted. "But the cardinal should never be underestimated."

They watched as Henry detached himself from the group and moved toward Anne Boleyn. His eyes were fixed on her, and hers on him. It was as if neither could see anyone else.

"May I know what you think of the king's matter?" Campeggio asked quietly as he watched.

"I am surprised," Mendoza responded. "It seems to me that the king is a fool for love . . . and, for what? She is not the most beautiful girl in the world."

They observed, as Henry's sister Margaret stepped in front of him and curtsied, blocking his path. The king's sister greeted her brother, and Henry seemed about to pass on when something she said made him turn back angrily.

Campeggio watched the brief, vehement exchange, wishing he could hear the conversation between the king and his sister. He could guess, however. It was obvious that Princess Margaret did not approve in the least of her brother's infatuation with Mistress Anne Boleyn.

He turned back to Mendoza. "And the emperor?"

Mendoza shrugged. "It is no secret that the emperor is outraged at the king's behavior toward the queen, his niece. And I can tell you, in strict confidence, that he has also written to His Holiness demanding that the matter be settled in Rome rather than here."

Campeggio nodded. "He would not seek to . . . interfere . . . in any other way?"

"In what way?"

"If the queen was to be renounced, for instance, might he consider military intervention on her behalf?"

"He has not said so," Mendoza said carefully.

Campeggio gave him a shrewd look. "Has anyone asked him?"

Mendoza looked at him. "No . . . no, not yet."

Campeggio squinted back at the king just as he reached Anne Boleyn. She curtsied demurely, but even to an old man on the other side of the room, the look she and the king exchanged . . . burned.

They danced, only their hands touching, their eyes locked on each other, circling to the music in an ageless dance of seduction. Their bodies drew close, retreated, touched, withdrew, and all the time the music played.

Anne moistened her lips with her tongue. Henry watched as if he would devour her. Every breath Henry took was for Anne. Every sigh she made was for him. Their bodies flirted, brushed, touched.

They danced as if they were alone in the room, oblivious of the watching eyes, the whispered comments, the speculation.

Campeggio surveyed the room, observing the different faces watching the king and Anne Boleyn. He sighed, feeling suddenly ancient.

Katherine gazed out at the gardens in the still, gray morning light. Only the grip with which she crushed the gloves she was holding revealing her tension. She was waiting to meet the men who would represent her in the legatine court.

Her maid of honor ushered in two prelates in their clerical robes. "My lady, the archbishop of Canterbury, Archbishop Warham, and Bishop Tunstall are here to see you."

Katherine knew who they were. She also knew what they had been instructed to do. She gave them a warm smile, nevertheless. "My lords, I understand that you are among my council for the legatine court. As honorable men, as men whose first duty is to God and your conscience, you are welcome. Did the king send you here?"

Warham shifted uncomfortably. "Yes, Your Majesty."

"We must discuss your brief," she said briskly. "I have nothing against His Majesty—whom I love with all my being—only against his advisers, and a certain woman whose ambitions would ruin a kingdom."

"Madam," said Warham. "We are not here to discuss a brief, or any such."

"But—"

"We came to report, Madam, that rumors of plots against His Majesty's life are abroad, as well as plots against Cardinal Campeggio. If any such plots were to be successful, then clearly both you and your daughter would be suspected of involvement."

It was a clumsy and ludicrous threat. Katherine looked from one man to the other incredulously. "I cannot believe that the king gives any credence to such rumors, since he knows—and you know—that I value my husband's life much more than even my own."

Warham dropped his gaze.

Bishop Tunstall was not so easily cowed. "Madam, there is yet another complaint: that you are flippant and show yourself too much to the people. That you rejoice in their acclaim, nodding, smiling and waving at them. Therefore we suppose that you hate the king."

"Why should you suppose that?" Katherine asked calmly.

"Because you don't accept that you have all this time lived in sin with him. And even when the truth has been revealed, you refuse to accept the king's gracious offer to retire to a religious house."

Katherine made an impatient gesture. "Ah, that again! I have answered for that already. God never called me to a nunnery. I am His Majesty's true, legitimate wife."

"For the love of God—" Warham began.

"Yes! For the love of God!" she interjected angrily. "As you yourself, Archbishop, once professed! You told others that you knew my case to be true. So what changed your mind? Was it Wolsey?" She gave him a scornful look and added, "Tell me, do you prefer your place in this world to your place in Heaven?"

"You have not answered the charges."

"Sir, I think it hard enough to be accused and charged by my own lawyers! Where is the justice in that?" She regarded them with contempt. "I shall speak no more to you. You will not act for me! Bishop Fisher will, for he is a man whose faith is not for sale." With that, she swept regally back into her bedchamber. Her ladies closed the doors behind her.

At their country home, Brandon and his wife, Margaret, were discussing her recent quarrel with the king.

"His Majesty requests that you return to court. After all, you are his sister." Brandon had been drinking.

Margaret sniffed. "How can I return when he flaunts himself with that slut? I would be seen to be approving of his ridiculous liaison." She watched as her husband poured himself another glass of wine and shoved hers over for him to refill.

He said earnestly, "Margaret, you and I must stand in the king's good graces—or we are *nothing*. Let him marry whom he wishes."

"That was always your philosophy, wasn't it, Charles? So very cynical!" She sipped her wine. "Is that why you keep company with that devil Boleyn?"

"You liked him well enough once, when he helped us back to court." He gave her a narrow look. "Or were you just being cynical?"

Margaret shook her head. "I didn't see all of his game, then. Now I do. And I despise him."

"So do I!" he said. "But I hate Wolsey more. It's a marriage of expedience."

She gave a bitter laugh. "Just like ours? "

"No. I loved you," Brandon said quietly. He moved closer to her and tried to cup her cheek, but she drew back, avoiding him.

"You don't know the meaning of the word, Charles," she told him. "You can love, perhaps, for a year, or a month; a day, even an hour. And I do believe that in that hour, you love as well and deeply as any man."

She looked sadly at him and added, "But after that hour, you love not. You love another . . . and then another . . . and another." Her eyes shimmered. "Your love is most generous . . . where it is most hurtful."

Brandon saw the tears in her eyes and clumsily tried again to embrace her.

Margaret held him off. "Don't! Don't play the fool, Charles. It doesn't become you." Biting her lip, she ran from the room.

Brandon swirled the wine in his glass, staring moodily into it. He drained it in one gulp, then refilled his glass.

Katherine's ladies were in the middle of putting the queen to bed, when the secret door connecting her rooms to the king's opened and Henry appeared, in his nightshirt. The queen's ladies stared in surprise—it had been such a long time—before recalling themselves and dropping into a curtsy.

Though all Katherine's ladies-in-waiting were young and beautiful, Henry merely gave a cursory glance at them before climbing into bed with the queen.

At a signal from Katherine, the ladies filed out, leaving Henry and Katherine sitting up together in bed.

Silence fell. After a time, Henry said, "Katherine, why do you go on denying me justice? Why?"

She said nothing. He went on, "You're so heartless. So full of hatred. I can't persuade myself any longer that you love me. I think you must despise me."

"No! I do love you," she told him. "I've never ceased to love you. You know that."

"I don't know it," he replied. "I'm sure you hate me. Perhaps you should be kept away from our daughter . . . or you will poison her mind against me."

"How can you say these things to me?" Katherine said bitterly. "After all this time. After all we have meant to each other."

"I'm only asking you to be reasonable."

"I am being reasonable. It's you who's not being reasonable."

They sat there, side by side, not looking at each other.

The next day, Henry visited Anne. She was in a playful mood, resisting his attempts to kiss her, but with a wicked smile.

"I have a new motto," she told him. "I invented it myself."

Henry was intrigued. "What is it?"

Anne gave an enigmatic smile. "You'll have to find it."

Still more intrigued, Henry murmured, "Where is it?"

Anne slanted him a laughing glance. "On a piece of ribbon . . . hidden somewhere." She glanced downward.

Smiling, Henry touched the silk on her shoulder. "Is it in here?"

"No." She smiled, teasingly.

Henry grabbed her and peered into her bodice. "Down there?" He tried to put his hand inside. They tussled, laughing.

He lifted her skirts and burrowed underneath. "Where is it?" Henry asked, his voice muffled by her clothing.

Anne gasped as his search became more passionate but she managed to focus on the problems uppermost in her mind. "But . . . there are fresh delays! Nobody can see Campeggio!"

"There are just things he has to do."

"Are you sure?"

His head emerged from under her skirts, the search for the motto temporarily forgotten. "What do you mean?"

"What if someone is deliberately delaying matters. Making excuses."

He paused. "Who—Campeggio?"

"No—someone else," she said. "Someone much closer to you."

He frowned. She took his hand and seductively started to slide it up her leg toward the thigh. His hand stopped. "Aha! I have it." He smiled and pulled out a length of ribbon with words stitched on it. He read the motto aloud, "Thus will it be, grumble who will," and smiled.

He leaned forward to kiss her and to resume their game, but she pulled back, her expression serious.

"It's someone much closer to you," she said.

Soon afterward, Henry summoned Wolsey for a stroll in his private gardens.

"I want to ask you, frankly, about Campeggio," Henry said. "Do you trust him? Do you think he's compromised in any way? Who knows—he might be getting a pension from the emperor."

Wolsey shook his head. "As I know it, Lorenzo is the least prejudicial of men. And he has personally suffered at the hands of Charles's soldiers. When they entered Rome, they ransacked his house. I don't believe he bears any love for the emperor."

"Then why is he delaying the trial?"

"There are some technical matters that have to be resolved, that's all. Your Majesty has no reason to be concerned."

Henry stopped and swung around. "God damn it. It's not Campeggio at all. It's *you*! You're the one who's delaying things!" He stared at Wolsey. "You've gone cold on the divorce. Perhaps you never believed in it in the first place. Just lied to me. Pretended you were on my side."

Wolsey went white as a sheet. He dropped to his knees before Henry. "Majesty, before you and before God, I swear on my honor that I am your most loyal servant, and that there is nothing on earth I covet so much as advancing your divorce. To bring it to pass is my continual study and my most ardent desire, for which I am ready to expend my body, my life, and my blood, so help me God."

There was a short silence. Henry stared down at Wolsey. His face suddenly cleared. He smiled and raised Wolsey back to his feet. "Your Grace mustn't be so dismayed. You understand my impatience. But I know it's not you. I've known you a long time. I trust you."

He took Wolsey's arm. "Come. Let's talk of other things."

In an upstairs window, Norfolk and More stood observing the scene. "By God's body, Master More," Norfolk said. *"Indignatio princips mor est."*

More translated the Latin. "The anger of the prince means death."

Chapter Seventeen

"So you've returned to court, Mr. Wyatt?" Thomas Tallis said, having found the poet Thomas Wyatt sitting and writing in a quiet alcove at court.

"Difficult to stay away." Wyatt sighed. "More difficult to stay." Two very beautiful young women walked slowly past, paused, and caught Wyatt's eye.

He quoted: "'And now again I fear the same / The windy words, the eyes' quaint game / Of sudden change make me aghast / For dread to fall I stand not fast.'"

He gave Tallis a rueful look. "Why is it that when I'm away from court, I can behave perfectly normally. But when I'm here, I desire to possess every woman I see?"

Tallis smiled. "You were right about your brunette. She has indeed put the world in a roar."

"But I'm surprised to hear that the king still calls it his secret matter!" Wyatt said. They both laughed.

Tallis said, "I heard someone the other day offer the opinion that, despite all his experience of the world, the king had still proved foolish enough to become enslaved by his passion for a girl."

Wyatt shook his head emphatically. "No. That man is a fool. Not the king. Why should he not be a slave to passion? What else do we live for? Why do we breathe? So we can live sensibly and then die? When you desire someone so much that it consumes you utterly, body and soul, and you would give your life for a single kiss, or a touch of their flesh, or to feel their faint breath close upon your cheek—then, Mr. Tallis, and only then, are you really and truly alive. The rest is all waste."

"Except when you write it!"

Wyatt inclined his head. "Or, in your case, blow your own trumpet!"

Suddenly the king came striding down the corridor like an angry lion. He paused, scowling at them. Wyatt and Tallis hastily rose to their feet and bowed. The king glared at Wyatt for a long moment, his jaw set, then walked on.

He turned the corner, shouting, "Mr. Cromwell! Mr. Cromwell!"

Cromwell came running.

"You will go to Rome," Henry ordered him. "You will force his fucking Holiness into submission, if necessary by telling him that, if he fails to grant my fucking annulment, then England will withdraw its submission to Rome, and I my fucking allegiance to him. And make him understand that this is no idle threat. I mean it! And I *will* do it if he will not satisfy me!"

"Majesty." Cromwell bowed himself out.

Henry shouted after him, "Send the Duke of Suffolk in. I want to see him." He paced like a caged beast until Brandon entered.

"I want you to go to Paris and talk to King Francis," Henry said. "Question him closely about what he knows of Campeggio. What kind of dealings has he had with him? What kind of a man is he? Is he honest? Does he have ambitions to be pope? Or secret relations with the emperor? Just anything he knows!"

Brandon nodded. "I'll leave at once." He started to leave.

"And Charles—ask him about Wolsey, also. What he knows about Wolsey. You understand? Whose side is Wolsey is on?"

Katherine was surprised when Thomas More brought Bishop Fisher to her private apartments in the palace. "Sir Thomas?" she greeted More cautiously. She had never been sure whose side he was on. He had a reputation as a man of principle, but he had also been Henry's tutor and had always seemed fond of the king.

More fell to his knees in front of her. "Most gracious sovereign lady. I have brought Bishop Fisher to see you. I believe that he can offer you true and devoted counsel."

"Thank you, Sir Thomas."

More bowed and left. Katherine offered her hand to Fisher. "My lord Bishop." She gestured him toward some cushioned chairs, then said, "Are you certain that you wish to act for me? You must know the dangers and difficulties you may face." Looking at the old man, she added gently, "I would understand if you would prefer peace and tranquility."

But though he was old, Fisher had a sinewy strength that applied both to his body and his mind. "Gentle madam, what peace or tranquility can there be without justice and the blessing of God?"

He went on, "I have considered the case against you very carefully. They will no doubt press the fact that the pope's dispensation for you to marry the king was technically faulty—and therefore invalid. But the obvious way of resolving any technical deficiency is not to declare the marriage null and void but to issue fresh and more perfect dispensations." He gave her a shrewd look.

"In any case, the continuance of so long space has made the marriage honest, and the principle of *supplet ecclesia*—let the church provide— would itself have made good any defects in the pope's dispensation."

Katherine stared at him, impressed. She had not imagined that an elderly man of the cloth would exhibit the sharp brain of a lawyer.

She said, "Then, you suppose we may win?"

There was a long silence. "We may win the argument, yes," he said. "But I cannot pretend that it will avail us much."

Seeing the look in her eyes, he hastened to reassure her. "We shall still try. Be of good cheer, madam, for we are on the side of the angels."

Brandon had reached the French court and was dining with King Francis and his lovely wife, Queen Claude.

"We entertained the pope's legate as he passed through France on his way to England," Francis told Brandon. "I spoke personally to Campeggio. He was very careful. But even in the few words he spoke, I thought he dissembled. And I have talked to others who felt the same."

"In what way dissembled?" Brandon asked.

"I think he shows one face but conceals another. He has been asked to deal with a matter he secretly despises."

Francis gestured for Brandon's glass to be refilled, then leaned closer. "My advice to the king, my brother, is to be careful, and not put too much trust in any man, in case he should be deceived." He leaned back, smiled, and sipped his wine. "Do you say the same about Cardinal Wolsey?" Brandon asked.

Francis's expression changed subtly. He and Claude exchanged glances. Francis said carefully, "I have nothing against His Eminence."

"Of course not," Brandon assured him. "But what do you think his attitude is to the divorce?"

Francis shrugged. "As far as I could tell, he wanted the divorce to go through. He has no love for the queen. But . . . at the same time . . ." He paused thoughtfully.

"At the same time?" Brandon prompted.

Francis steepled his fingers as if to deliver a verdict from on high. "It is also my impression that he has marvelous intelligence with the pope; they understand each other. And in Rome, and also with Cardinal Campeggio." He paused again.

Brandon frowned, trying to follow his drift.

Francis continued, "Therefore, if he has such understanding with them—and they are not themselves minded to advance the king's matter—then to speak frankly to you, I think the king himself should take a closer interest in it himself, and not leave it to dissemblers."

He set down his glass. "That is my advice." He briefly touched his wife's hand, rose, and departed, leaving Brandon staring thoughtfully after him.

He turned back to the queen and caught a bleak look in the queen's eyes.

"Where has he gone?" he asked her.

She shrugged. "To service his latest mistress, I'm sure."

"Why would he do that when he has such a beautiful wife?" Brandon said softly.

"Perhaps you could ask him."

Brandon saw the sheen of unshed tears in her eyes. "Don't you ever want to pay him back?"

Claude shrugged again. "Of course, always. I'm a woman."

"Then go to bed with me," he said.

She said nothing for a long time, just twirled her wine glass in her fingers. Then she looked at him. "Perhaps, if you like. But tell me first— how is your beautiful wife?"

"She—"

Claude cut him off. "She is just like me, no? You have affairs, and she ignores it."

He said nothing. Claude gave a sad little smile and said softly, "To make love for pain or revenge—what is that? It hurts the mind, and the soul it . . . shrinks. Yes? You understand, sir? The soul grows smaller . . . Perhaps it even dies."

Brandon dropped his eyes.

Henry and Anne were playing cards in Anne's chambers. Henry seemed moody, and though Anne was winning, that was only part of the problem.

"What is it?" Anne asked quietly.

After a moment he said, "I have heard from Cromwell. He was eventually allowed access to the pope, but wrote in desperation."

Anne played a card. "Why?"

"He doesn't believe Clement will do anything for me. He said . . . he said of the pope: 'It might be in his paternoster, but it's nothing in his creed!'"

Anne looked up. "What does that mean?"

"He means the pope might pray that I will solve my problems, but he won't personally commit to doing anything about it!" Henry explained irritably. He looked at the cards. "Show!"

Anne tried to turn in her cards unseen. But Henry caught her hand. "Show me!" he demanded and turned her hand over. She held the ace and king of hearts.

He let go her hand and, with a petulant gesture, pushed the rest of his money over to her.

Their eyes met. Both were full of hurt.

When Brandon returned from Paris, he made a point of seeking out his coconspirators, Norfolk, Boleyn, and a few of their trusted affiliates. They met in a private room in Norfolk's quarters in the palace.

"My lords," Brandon said. "It's clear enough now that Wolsey is secretly acting against the king. He has lost that affinity he used always to enjoy with His Majesty. The king is suspicious of his first minister, and we must encourage his suspicions."

"It's time to bring him down," Norfolk agreed.

Boleyn placed a sheet of paper on the table. "Here is a pamphlet. You see it mocks his period in office as a time of pride, waste, repression, and ineffectual policies. It's ready to distribute."

"We have drawn up a plan of action," Norfolk explained to Brandon. "It calls for the immediate arrest of Wolsey and his agents, the impounding of their papers, and a thorough examination of his administration. His corruption will be exposed—his treason guaranteed."

Brandon nodded. "I will make sure that I have men keeping watch on all the channel ports, in case His Eminence—despite his bulk—should try to run."

They exchanged grim smiles of satisfaction, enjoying a moment so long anticipated. Norfolk turned to Boleyn. "All that remains is for your daughter to prove to the king that all his suspicions are justified."

"And then," Brandon added with gleeful anticipation, "the cardinal will be naked to his enemies!"

* * * *

Wolsey was desperate. He could feel the wolves of ambition closing in on him. By luck one day, he spied Campeggio making his agonizingly slow progress down a corridor. For once the pope's envoy was unattended by his son, only by a single servant. Wolsey seized his chance.

Grabbing the old man by the arm, he shoved him into a nearby chamber and pushed him up against a table.

"The trial is coming," he said.

"Indeed . . . Your Grace," stammered Campeggio.

"I want to make it plain to you again," Wolsey said, his hands biting into the old man's arms. "If you refuse to grant the divorce, you will provoke a wave of opinion against the pope, the papal courts, and the papacy itself!"

Campeggio stared at him through watery eyes, but his will stood firm. "I am obliged, by the Holy Father, to seek truth and justice in this matter. And that, Your Grace, I will attempt to do, as God is my witness."

Furiously, Wolsey tightened his grip. "You still don't seem to understand. I will spell it out to you again: If you fail to find in the king's favor, then you will not only lose the king and the devotion of his realm to Rome—*you will also destroy me—utterly and forever!*"

Their eyes locked. There was a short silence.

"I understand completely," Campeggio said at last. "You must have faith, Cardinal Wolsey."

Wolsey stared at him in disbelief. The pope and Campeggio were tossing him to the wolves. He was helpless against such obdurance. He loosened his grip and watched the old man stagger to a chair.

"Then God help me," Wolsey muttered, and turned away.

The day of the trial had arrived. Outside the Great Hall at the Priory of Blackfriars Church in London, there was huge excitement. Never before had a king and queen of England been summoned to appear in court together.

Pushing and jostling to get a better view, they watched as the various players in the drama walked into the church: Warham, the archbishop of Canterbury, and Bishop Tunstall, with a host of other priests. Many of the great nobles of the realm were there also: the Duke of Norfolk, Brandon, the Earl of Suffolk, and the Earls of Oxford and Arundel.

Seventy-year-old Bishop Fisher, the queen's representative, stumped in alone, a solitary but somehow charismatic figure.

Then, to a stir of excitement, the king arrived, flanked by Cromwell and Boleyn. The king was magnificently dressed for the occasion in all his pomp and beauty.

The crowd, craning their necks in restless anticipation speculated aloud about whether or not the queen would come.

Finally, escorted by Griffith ap Rhys, a loyal man who had served the queen since she first arrived in England, Katherine appeared and walked toward the church doors. She was greeted by warm and thunderous applause. She smiled, nodding her head in acknowledgment to the people who so readily and openly showed their love and affection for her.

A man in the crowd called out, "Good Katherine! How she holds the field! She doesn't give a fig!" The cheers and clapping rose even louder.

Katherine entered the Great Hall, the applause still sounding in her ears. The beautiful chamber had been arranged like a solemn court, with carpets on the floor and tapestries on the wall. Henry and Katherine were seated on chairs under regal canopies of gold brocade, the queen's set slightly lower than the king's. They were divided by the banks of spectators.

Facing them at the head of the hall were the presiding churchmen, Campeggio and Wolsey, in their scarlet robes. Campeggio had to be helped, slowly and in pain, to his chair.

Campeggio blessed the court, making the sign of the cross and saying, "*In nomine Patris, et Filii, et Spiritus Sancti.* I declare this legatine court, commissioned by His Holiness, Pope Clement, is now in session, and that all that is said here is said under oath and in the presence of God Almighty."

He paused and looked at the king. "I call upon His Majesty to speak first as to this matter."

Everyone turned to look at the king.

"Your Eminences," Henry said. "You know well what cause I have to be here. It concerns some scruples I have concerning my marriage, which prick my conscience. I did not have them at first—until the Bishop of Tarbes raised queries concerning the legitimacy of my daughter Mary. And after that, I consulted widely to discover the truth, and read in Leviticus that it was against God's law, and a sin, for me to marry my brother's wife."

He paused. "Your Eminences, I am not alone in questioning the validity of my marriage. All of my bishops share my doubts and have signed a petition to put this matter in question—"

Suddenly, Bishop Fisher was on his feet, saying, "My lords, I tell you now that I never signed my name to any such document. And if it appears there, then Archbishop Warham wrote it without my consent!"

There was a stir among the galleries.

Henry, irritated, made a dismissive gesture. "Well, well. I'm not going to argue with you now. You are but one man. As to the main issue, if I am asked why I have waited so long to bring this question to trial, then I can truthfully say that it was the great love I bore the queen that prevented me. Nor did His Eminence Cardinal Wolsey ever raise this issue with me. It is I myself who bear all responsibility, and my own conscience that troubles and doubts me. And so I ask this court for one thing only: justice."

He looked at Campeggio, but the old man's expression was inscrutable.

Wolsey announced, "In a moment the court will ask the Queen's Majesty to reply to His Majesty's statement."

He looked around the room, then added, "But first I must tell the court that the queen, through her advisers, has sought to question the competence of this court to try her case. Further, she questions the impartiality of her judges. And finally, she contends that this matter is already in the hands of a higher authority—namely, the pope—and can only therefore be tried in Rome."

Again, he took in each man in the court. "For the first part, as duly appointed legates, Cardinal Campeggio and I can confirm that we have the necessary authorization from His Holiness to try the matter here. Secondly, I firmly deny any prejudice on my part. I have simply been appointed by the pope to find out the truth of this marriage. Finally, since this court is properly constituted and legal, we reject the queen's applications and will continue to try this case as we have been appointed to do."

He paused, then said, "Now I call upon Her Majesty, Queen Katherine, to address the court."

Katherine rose to her feet. Threading her way through the spectators with some difficulty, she reached Henry's chair—and flung herself down at his feet. The spectators recoiled in shock.

Henry, looking embarrassed, quickly and gently raised her up. Almost immediately, Katherine knelt once more in supplication before him.

"Sir," Katherine said, "I beseech you for all the love that has been between us, let me have justice and right, give me some pity and compassion, for I am a poor woman, and a stranger, born out of your dominion. I have here no friend and little counsel. I flee to you as head of justice within this realm."

She looked up at him. "I take God and all the world to witness that I have been to you a true, humble, and obedient wife, ever comfortable to your will and pleasure. I loved all those whom you loved, for your sake, whether I had cause or not, and whether they were my friends or enemies."

She paused. In the courtroom the spectators sat absolutely silent and spellbound. Henry stared at her, seeming to be caught in the spell of her eyes.

Katherine continued, "By me you have had many children, although it has pleased God to call them from this world. But when you had me at first, I take God as my judge, I was a true maid, without touch of man. And whether this be truth or not, I put it to your conscience."

Then, in the absolute silence of the courtroom, Katherine rose to her feet. Sweeping the king a low curtsy, and leaning upon the arm of Griffith ap Rhys, she moved in a dignified manner toward the exit.

Henry, belatedly realizing what was happening, gestured quickly to the court crier, who hurried after her, shouting, "Katherine, Queen of England, come back into the court!"

Katherine made no sign she had heard. Head held high, she continued her slow and graceful exit.

The court crier shouted more loudly still, "Katherine, Queen of England, come back into the court!"

All around the audience buzzed with amazement and speculation. The court crier tried for a third time to bring her back, bellowing, "Katherine, Queen of England, you are ordered to return to the court!"

Katherine's supporter, Griffin ap Rhys, hesitated. "Perhaps Your Majesty should turn back! You are called again."

"On, on," Katherine told him. "It makes no matter, for it is a meaningless court for me. Therefore I'm not going to stay. Come on." She swept through the doors and stepped outside.

Her reappearance was greeted with a fresh eruption of cheering and applause, which made her smile.

Inside the hall, Henry could hear all the cheers for his wife. They filled the hall. He rose to his feet, flung an angry look of blame at Wolsey, then stormed out through a back door.

Wolsey, rising to bow to him, froze as he saw the king's expression.

Chapter Eighteen

Despite the notable absence of the queen, the trial continued. It was a sweltering day and the hall seemed airless. The audience fanned themselves as best they could. Campeggio's discomfort was acute and visible. Henry sat, listening intently, flanked by Norfolk, Cromwell, and Boleyn.

Wolsey addressed them. "My lords, in the absence of the queen herself, whom this tribunal has pronounced contumacious, since she does not appear when summoned, we are trying to determine whether or not her first marriage to Prince Arthur was consummated with Carnal Copula. We call a witness: Sir Anthony Willoughby."

Willoughby, a man of about Henry's age, stood before the legates.

"I understand you were among the escort taking Prince Arthur to the nuptial bed?" Campeggio said.

"I was, sir," Willoughby replied. "My father was at the time steward of the king's household. So I was present when the prince was inserted into the Lady Katherine's bed, and also when he woke in the morning."

"And did the prince say anything to you when you saw him in the morning?"

"Yes, sir. He said, 'Willoughby, I'm thirsty. Bring me a cup of ale. Last night I was in the midst of Spain.'"

For a moment, the galleries were silent. And then one man snorted with helpless laughter. It was infectious, and the courtroom erupted with laughter.

The court crier banged his staff on the ground. "Silence! Silence in court!" The laughter subsided.

"Anything else?" Campeggio asked.

Willoughby nodded. "Yes, sir. Later that day he said to us, 'Masters, it's a good pastime to have a wife.'"

There was more laughter in the court.

Wolsey said, "I believe we may have the bloodstained sheets that would corroborate my lord's story."

Campeggio gave Wolsey an opaque look. "That would be most useful, Your Eminence. Most useful."

That evening in church, Wolsey and Cromwell watched Katherine praying. Wolsey's fingers drummed impatiently. Finally she finished and began to walk away from the altar, down the aisle with her ladies. Wolsey and Cromwell stepped out into the aisle to intercept her.

Katherine's brows rose. "Gentlemen?"

"His Majesty asks why you are not in court," Wolsey said.

"I have already given answer to that."

Wolsey glanced at her retinue of ladies, all avidly listening. "May we go somewhere private?"

"Why?" Katherine gave him a contemptuous look. "I have nothing to hide. Let my ladies and all the world hear what you have to say."

Wolsey tried to force a mask of politeness over his face. This stubborn woman would be the death of him. Beads of sweat stood out on his brow. "His Majesty commands that you surrender this whole matter into his hands. Otherwise you will be condemned by the court."

Katherine produced a shocked look. "I am surprised to hear such a request from such noble and wise men as you are. I am only a poor woman, lacking both wit and understanding. How can I respond to a request made to me out of the blue?"

Wolsey flushed angrily at her sarcasm. "You know only too well what the king desires—and must have."

Katherine glared back at him. Cromwell watched the exchange unemotionally.

"All I know, Eminence," said Katherine, "is that you, for your own purposes, have kindled this fire. All this time, all these years, I have wondered at your high pride and vain glory. I have abhorred your voluptuous life, and had no regard at all for your presumptuous power and your tyranny!"

Her mouth curled with disdain. "I know also your malice against my nephew the emperor. You hate him worse than a scorpion. And why? Because he would not satisfy your ambition and make you pope by force."

She smiled. Wolsey's face was suffused with rage. He struggled to control himself. "Madam, you are so wrong to suppose—"

She cut him off. "My only satisfaction is this: that in frustrating you I hasten your fall from the king's good graces—an outcome I desire above all others!" With that, she sailed past him, her ladies scurrying after her.

Wolsey was furious. He started to go after her, but Cromwell took his arm. "Hold, your Eminence. You will not get your divorce this way."

Wolsey stared at him. "There is no *other* way!" He shook off Cromwell's hand, and stormed out.

The court that evening was more crowded than ever, with everyone in London for the trial. Henry swept in, dressed magnificently in cloth-of-gold lined with lynx skins. At his side came Anne Boleyn, looking beautiful, bedecked with dazzling jewels.

They moved through the court with everyone bowing before them. Anne was aware of the sneers and the coldness behind the courtiers' false smiles, but she refused to acknowledge them. She carried herself defiantly and with pride.

At the doors to the king's private chambers, in a place of honor, stood her father and her uncle, the Duke of Norfolk, as well as her young brother, George. Henry paused to smile graciously upon them. Anne kissed them warmly.

As Anne and Henry passed inside, Norfolk said to Boleyn. "My sources tell me that the emperor blames Wolsey for instigating the divorce. He believes that the people of England will rise up and bring that creature to the scaffold."

"His end is surely approaching," Boleyn agreed. "After which, Your Grace will be the first man at council—as you ought to be."

Norfolk preened himself and said, "In which case, Boleyn, I shall not fail to promote your family's interests. It's true you have risen high." He smiled. "But you will rise higher yet!"

In the king's private chambers, Henry and Anne sat down to dine—Anne in Katherine's chair. Grooms and servants swarmed around them, bringing food and pouring wine. Henry signaled and the musicians began to play a ballad Henry himself had composed for Anne.

Henry could not take his eyes off Anne. "Did you see? They were all looking at you. I'm glad. I want them to look at you. I want them to be envious. I want them to know how much I love you."

"Then, like my family motto, am I 'the most happy.'" She smiled and rested a jeweled hand over his. "How did it go in court today?"

Henry's face tightened. "Well enough."

"Yet Katherine still refuses to attend?"

"It will make no difference," Henry said shortly. "Wolsey promises that I will have my divorce by the summer."

Anne looked down at her plate. "Promises are easy."

Henry gave her a warning look. She ignored it, saying, "And what if Wolsey's promise is false?"

In a rough London dockside tavern, crowded with apprentices, sailors, and whores, all the talk and laughter was about the court case.

A man banged on the bar and loudly assailed the barman. "Friend! Give me a drink! I'm thirsty! If you'd been to Spain as often as I went there last night, you'd be fucking thirsty too! In and out, in and out, in and out . . ."

Everyone roared laughing at the joke.

And then a tough-looking sailor raised his tankard. "A toast, I say! A toast to Queen Katherine, the queen of England—who doesn't give a fig!—God bless her!"

As one, they all stood, and repeated the toast, "To the queen of England! Katherine—God bless her!" And they drank their ale.

Brandon woke in the middle of the night. Margaret had left the bed and stood in her nightgown, her arms wrapped around herself, looking out of the window of their home in the country.

"Margaret?" he said. "What is it?"

"I couldn't sleep."

"It's cold. Come back to bed."

She shook her head. "Not yet."

He watched her for a moment, then said, "I'm going to court tomorrow. Will you come? Your brother has asked again for your presence."

Margaret shook her head. "I've told you. Not as long as he makes love in public to that Boleyn girl. It's offensive and it makes him look like a fool. Everyone else can see how proud and grasping the Boleyns are. Why can't he?"

"What if the king commands you?"

"He won't. But you go to court if it worries you. I know you miss it."

"And what if I miss my wife?"

She walked slowly over to the bed, and gave him a sweet smile. She reached down and stroked his face.

Puzzled, Brandon frowned. "What is this?"

"Only a wife to a husband," she said softly, leaning down and kissing him softly on the lips. "Sleep now, my sweet darling. My sweet Charles. I pray you, sleep." She touched his eyelids with her fingers . . . and his eyes closed.

Margaret left the bedchamber and, holding a candle high, began walking down a flight of stairs. Halfway down she started coughing, a hand-kerchief to her lips.

When the bout was over, she opened her linen handkerchief and looked at it the candlelight, at the vivid specks of blood bright against the purity of the cloth.

The court in Blackfriars reconvened. "In the absence of the queen," Campeggio announced, "her council, Bishop Fisher, will make a statement to this court."

Fisher slowly got to his feet. He looked very frail, but his voice, though quiet, was all the more powerful and compelling because it issued from such a frame. He addressed the court: "Your Honors, you are asked to give verdict on the validity of the royal marriage. Sirs, it is my contention that this marriage of the king and queen can be dissolved by no power, human or divine."

He paused theatrically. The audience stirred, anticipating stronger things to come. The king's party exchanged glances.

Fisher continued. "Indeed, let me give you, if I might, a biblical parallel. You will remember, I am sure, the tyrant Herod Antipas, who disembarrassed himself of his wife in order to take his brother's wife. And who then executed John the Baptist when he dared to criticize the royal couple."

There were gasps of incredulity in court at his comparison of the king to a famous biblical tyrant.

Fisher continued, "But just as John the Baptist, so I, in all humility, say to you all today that I am ready to lay down my life to defend the sanctity of marriage and to condemn adultery!"

Pandemonium broke out in court at this. Henry was furious. Fisher was forced back to his seat.

Bishop Tunstall, supporting the king, leaped to his feet and shouted above the turmoil, "Your Honors, I accuse Bishop Fisher of arrogance, temerity, and disloyalty! I demand that you disregard every vile word!"

But the damage was done. Enraged, Henry swept out of court with his entourage. Only Cromwell stayed behind—a calculating decision on his part.

Wolsey stood and watched the shambles, appalled.

Sir Thomas More was shown into Wolsey's chamber in the evening. Wolsey looked up from his desk, which, as usual, groaned under piles of official documents and reports.

"Ah, Thomas. Come in! Drink?"

More shook his head. "Not for me, thank you."

Wolsey poured himself a drink. His hand trembled as he poured. "I have a mission for you." He drank. "The French and the imperial forces have halted their aggression. There is to be some sort of conference at a place called Cambria, in France, between their negotiators, and representatives of the pope."

He drank some more wine. "I have been trying to persuade His Majesty to allow me to attend the conference . . . but His Majesty insists my presence is needed here."

More inclined his head in acknowledgment of an obvious truth. Wolsey was actually sweating, though the evening was not noticeably warm.

"The vital thing, Thomas, is that there must be no agreement between the other two parties. I have received private assurances from the king of France—who, after all, is our ally—that he will never make peace with the emperor, under any circumstances. Similarly, there must be no rapprochement between the emperor and the Holy Father. You must understand that, in those circumstances, it would be impossible for the pope to grant the king his desire."

"I understand," More said.

"You have principles; I understand that too. But, for the love we both have for the king, your job at Cambria is to be as obstructive as possible. Don't let Francis renege on his commitment to us—and don't let the pope forget that it was Charles's forces that invaded and sacked Rome!"

Wolsey paused, drank again, his hand shaking. "And there is one other thing. By subtle means, try to discover from his agents if the emperor means to use force to support his aunt."

More frowned. "You think he might invade England in support of the queen?"

Wolsey waved a hand. "I don't *think* anything. But I imagine *everything*."

Campeggio had become so weak that he had to be brought to court in a canvas litter carried by servants. Outside the court, the servants set down the litter and the old man struggled to climb out of it. It was raining, and a young man, seeing his distress, hurried over and helped him toward the porch.

"Thank you, kind sir," Campeggio said.

Unnoticed by all around, the young man slipped a letter into the cardinal's pocket and whispered, "From His Holiness."

Once out of the rain, Campeggio found a private moment to scan the letter quickly, then return it to his pocket. Then he shuffled through the doors and into the court.

At the same time, the king and Knivert entered through another door. They noticed Campeggio being helped to a seat next to the fire.

"Look! He is always leaning on someone," Henry commented.

"Perhaps someone ought to lean on him," Knivert said.

"Perhaps." Henry approached Campeggio, who rose painfully to his feet, his head drooping. "Eminence."

"Your Majesty."

Henry gave him a hard look. "I trust you will soon reach a verdict."

"Indeed," Campeggio responded, promising nothing.

Henry said coolly. "We hear with distress of events in Germany. Of the destruction of churches."

Campeggio shook his head. "Melancholy events, Majesty."

"But why is it happening?" Henry said meaningfully.

"Majesty?"

"I will tell you. The Lutherans attack what they see as the wickedness of Rome. They say that the corrupt are rewarded, but that the faithful are abandoned and badly treated." He let his words sink in. "I am a man of faith, Eminence. God forbid that the Holy Father should turn his back on me!" Henry turned on his heel and strode off.

Henry dined with Katherine once more, demonstrating that he shared her board. Servants and grooms hurried back and forth. Music played. The king ate. The dinner was punctuated by long silences.

After one such silence, Katherine said, "Have you no kind things to say?"

"Kind?" Henry said.

"To your wife. The mother of your child. You treat me so unkindly. And in public neglect me."

Henry bridled. "Katherine, you must accept the inevitable. The weight of academic opinion is against us. We were never legally man and wife. The court's decision will go in my favor." He wiped his mouth. "And if it doesn't, I shall denounce the pope as a heretic and marry who I please."

"That's not a legal argument," Katherine said. "Merely an assertion."

"Of course it's legal! I've read every book on canon law that exists."

"Your whole case rests on my virginity. And I swear to you I was a virgin when I married you."

Henry looked uncomfortable again. He said nothing.

"Sweetheart," Katherine said softly, "I swear by all the angels that I was intact when I came to your bed."

It was too much. Henry's temper flared. He stood up abruptly. "All right! So you were a fucking virgin. It's not the point!" And he walked out on her.

He headed straight for Anne Boleyn's apartments, seeking solace. He told her of the argument with Katherine, but for once, Anne showed him scant sympathy.

"Didn't I tell you that if you argued with the queen she would be sure to have the upper hand?"

"Yes, but—" He tried to embrace her, but she was having none of it.

She moved away from him, visibly distressed. "I see now that one fine morning you will succumb to her reasoning, and cast me off."

"What? What do you mean? Of course I won't!" He tried again to embrace her. "I love you, Anne!"

"Let me go," she said furiously. "Let me go!" Tears welled from her eyes. She struggled free of him and said in a rising voice, "Don't you see? Don't you understand? I've been waiting so long. And for what?" She flung her arms out in a frantic gesture. "In the meantime I could have contracted some advantageous marriage, and borne sons—which is a woman's greatest consolation in this life. But now I see I've been wasting my time and my youth. For no purpose. For nothing!" She was almost hysterical.

Henry had no idea what to do. "Anne, Please. Please! You will have sons by me!"

Anne thrust him off. "No! It's too late. Your wife won't let you go. I should have realized."

He stared, confused and upset as she ran about the room collecting her things.

"Where are you going?" Henry said when she moved toward the door.

"Home!"

"No, stay. I beg you. Stay. I love you. I am . . ."

Anne left.

"The King of England," Henry finished. But Anne had gone.

The day of judgment had come. Henry waited tensely, flanked by Norfolk, Brandon, and Boleyn. The court was packed, the people waiting, expectant and quiet. All eyes were focused upon the two figures in their red cardinal robes.

Time stretched. Still Campeggio did not move.

"This is beyond endurance," Brandon muttered.

Henry heard him. "Hush!"

The king's proctor made his way toward the two cardinals and bowed.

"Eminences, in accordance with the laws and rules of this tribunal, and the wishes of His Majesty, I ask you officially to deliver your judgment."

He bowed again, and retreated. Everyone waited.

Slowly, painfully, Campeggio got to his feet, leaning on a stick. There was a long silence, then finally he said, "Your Majesty . . . my lords . . . after much deliberation, it has been decided that this great matter is too important to be here decided without consultation with the Curia at Rome."

He licked his dry lips . . . sensing the menacing mood developing around him. "Unfortunately, the Curia is now in summer recess. In which case there is no alternative but to prorogue this tribunal until October first. That is our judgment."

It took a few seconds for the meaning of his words to sink in. Then, the court erupted into shouting. Wolsey, devastated, swore at Campeggio.

Henry stared in shocked disbelief. He'd been cheated! He'd lost! His face working with fury, he got up and stalked out. Norfolk followed.

Wolsey, too, tried to leave, but Brandon grabbed him, saying in a loud voice, "By the Mass, it was never merry in England while we had *cardinals* among us!"

Wolsey turned on him in fury. "Are you so stupid you think that was *my* doing?" He gave Brandon a scornful look and added, "And of all men in this realm, *you* have least cause to be offended with cardinals! For if I, a simple cardinal, had not been, you would now have no head upon your shoulders!" Wolsey pushed angrily past Brandon and left the court.

Behind him all was pandemonium.

Chapter Nineteen

Queen Katherine smiled as the Spanish ambassador, Señor Mendoza, kissed her hand. "Happy day, Majesty," he said in Spanish, for although there were only a few of Katherine's ladies present, one of them at least was a spy for Wolsey,

"Indeed it is, Señor Mendoza. I was so surprised—and delighted—by the decision."

In a whisper he told her, "Campeggio received secret instructions from His Holiness, who has advocated the matter back to Rome."

Katherine smiled. "So, I was not abandoned."

"The emperor worked tirelessly for your cause," he assured her.

Katherine switched to English. "Is it true you are leaving?"

"Yes, Majesty. Ambassador Chapuys will replace me."

"I know him."

"He is a very trustworthy person, and sure to take up your defense with all fidelity and diligence."

"As you have done, Señor Mendoza. Take this, in memory of me." She removed a large jewel from her bodice and gave it to him.

Mendoza, touched by the gesture, bowed deeply again, and kissed her hand. "Majesty."

Despite the precarious position he was in, Wolsey continued to work at his desk, plowing through a mountain of paperwork, as if nothing had changed. However, recent events had taken a physical toll on him. He looked strained, he'd lost weight, and there were dark rings under his eyes. He hadn't slept well in a long time.

He signed a document and sealed it with the great seal of the chancellor's office, just as the door opened and a servant announced the arrival of Wolsey's erstwhile protégé, Mr. Thomas Cromwell, now the king's secretary.

Wolsey looked up at Cromwell with a hopeful expression. "Thomas, how is the king?"

"His Majesty has decided to go on a progress. Immediately." Cromwell seated himself, then added, "He is going with the Lady Anne."

Wolsey's face fell at the bad news. Anne Boleyn, he knew, would use the time to further poison Henry's mind against Wolsey. He cast about in his mind for something he could do to win back the king's grace.

"Tell His Majesty that I am handing over to him at once the revenues of the See of Durham," he said. "It is one of the richest in England."

Cromwell inclined his head.

"And tell His Majesty that I shall not cease to work for his great matter," Wolsey continued. "Tell him that both His Eminence Cardinal Campeggio and myself will gladly accomplish his lawful desire."

"I shall tell him."

"And Thomas . . ." Wolsey paused, breathing heavily, and wiped some sweat from around his mouth. "Thomas, tell me I can trust you to advocate my interests to His Majesty." He fixed Cromwell with an anxious look.

"You may, Your Eminence," Cromwell assured him. "For without you, I should still be a lowly clerk, without profit or future. I owe you my life."

At Cromwell's words, Wolsey managed a small smile.

Henry was was accustomed to making regular progresses around his kingdom. It served a variety of purposes: It allowed Henry to keep in touch with his subjects, it ensured that the costs of the feeding and maintaining the large number of people at court was spread about, it made life more interesting, and it was a precaution against the accumulation of dirt and disease.

This time, traveling with Anne, Henry was enjoying a new sense of excitement. He and Anne rode out ahead of the rest of the party, galloping fast together across the landscape, enjoying the sense of freedom.

As they breasted a hill, the breeze sharpened and strengthened and the sky ahead darkened. Henry's mood changed abruptly. He reined in, and said bitterly, "I have been summoned to Rome. I must appear before the pope to answer for myself!" He made a gesture of suppressed rage. "Can you imagine? Me! The king of England! Who recognizes no superior but God!"

"As it should be," Anne agreed softly. "No superior but God!"

"Wolsey should have had this matter sorted months ago."

"Perhaps Wolsey puts his pope before his king."

He stared at her and his face hardened. "Then damn him! Damn him to hell!" He galloped in a circle around Anne, never taking his eyes off her. Then he slowed, put his hand behind her head and crushed his mouth against hers in a passionate and lingering kiss.

After a few minutes they rose on again, slowly. The rest of the party were still far behind and out of sight.

"May I speak plainly?" Anne said after a while.

"Of course, my love. Say anything. From your lips it will be sweet to me."

"There are some who, on good authority, care not for popes." She gave him a quick sideways look and continued. "These writers say that the king is both emperor and pope absolutely in his own kingdom."

Henry gave her a sharp look. This was dangerous territory—heresy— and they both knew it. But Henry had reached the limit of his patience with popes. If there was indeed another way to get his divorce, without depending on the pope, he would consider it.

For a moment, he said nothing; then he asked cautiously, "Which . . . writers?"

"I have a book I could show you—with your permission."

He thought for a minute, then nodded. "Very well, show it to me."

They reached Grafton House just as thunder rumbled and rain began to pelt down. They hurried inside, laughing at their escape, while servants raced to unpack their belongings.

Later that afternoon, Anne brought the promised book to Henry. It was a small, slim, volume—the same book that Cromwell had given to her—a radical, Lutheran creed.

Henry took it cautiously, but did not immediately open it. To open it, to read a book he knew to be heretical, was a huge step. He had written a total denunciation of Luther and his beliefs not so long ago. He ought not even to consider such a thing.

The pope—and Wolsey—had driven him to this point.

But once he opened this book, once he considered the notion that perhaps the pope was not his master . . . anything might be possible. The world could change forever.

He put the book down on a small table and paced restlessly about. The storm rattled and shook the house. Though it was not late, candles had been lit early because of the darkness caused by the storm.

Henry paced around the room, brooding. He passed the table and stopped abruptly, his attention caught. The room was full of dark shadows, but the book sat in a pool of golden candlelight.

He stared at it for a long moment, then he opened it, and began to read.

At Brandon's house in the country, Margaret sat in an upstairs room, dressed only in her nightgown. It hung about her frame, now gaunt and ravaged by consumption.

She gazed sadly at a letter from her husband, then moved with painful slowness to a table. Her breathing was harsh and labored. She took out a piece of paper, dipped a quill in ink, and began to write.

No, Charles, I will not come back to court. Not while my brother
disports himself with that woman—as you no doubt disport your-
self with the pretty young sluts that attract you so easily.

She picked up a small looking glass and stared at her reflection. She'd
once been spoken of as a beauty: now she could no longer be called even handsome. She was all bones and pasty, ashen complexion. Her eyes were huge,
sunken, and red-rimmed. She looked like an old witch—or the ghost of one.

A bitter laugh escaped her and she choked on it, coughing blood into
her already well-bloodied handkerchief. It would not be long now before
she was a ghost. But she would not allow him to see her like this. She
would have him remember her young and beautiful, and passionate.

She closed her eyes for a second, as if in pain, then forced them open
and continued writing.

You are welcome to your women. I have no need of you here—I
have more important matters to concern myself with.

She lifted her heavy lids and looked out toward the graveyard on the
hillside.

She sanded the letter, folded it shut, and sealed it with red sealing wax.
The melted wax dripped onto the paper like bright, thick blood. Again,
a harsh laugh escaped her—a laugh that turned to a sob, then became a
coughing fit. Once the paroxysm had passed, she picked up the letter and
held it gently against her cheek.

"Farewell, my dearest love," she whispered, and kissed the bright,
bloodlike seal. "Grieve not for me."

She rang for a servant. "Have this sent to my husband immediately,"
she said, handing him the letter.

The man left. Margaret watched the messenger through the window
as he galloped away. She watched until he had disappeared over the hill,
then she stood, wiping away her tears.

She walked slowly and painfully toward the top of the stairs. Her body jerked, and her eyes widened as her mouth suddenly filled with blood. She stared, as if watching it happen to someone else, as blood spurted from her mouth, spilling down her nightgown and splashing onto the stone floor. It dripped on her pale, narrow feet and ran between her toes. Her body sagged abruptly, and she buckled forward.

"Mistress!" a maid shouted, and ran toward her, seeing her start to fall, but then she saw the streams of blood and began to scream.

"Thomas! You sent no word ahead that you'd returned from Italy," Wolsey exclaimed. "Come, come! Tell me what happened? I take it you arrived at Cambria in time for the negotiations?"

More grimaced. "Not exactly. We were a week late."

"A *week*?" Wolsey looked horrified. "Then how could you contribute to the substantive arguments?"

More shrugged. "We couldn't. We were not party to the main discussions. Instead, we were only able to enter into peripheral negotiations with the major parties."

Wolsey stared at him. The word "peripheral" seemed to hang in the air. Wolsey pulled out a crumpled handkerchief and mopped his brow. It was not a hot day. "What negotiations?"

"I am happy to say that we secured a return to mutually beneficial trade relations between ourselves and the Low Countries. We also obtained guarantees regarding long-standing payments owed to the king by the emperor."

"But the major disputes, Thomas. What happened? Did the king of France refuse to make peace?"

"On the contrary. He settled all his differences with the emperor—and both of them then settled their differences with His Holiness Pope Clement," More told him, apparently quite pleased with the news.

Wolsey swallowed. If the emperor, the pope, and the king of France had all joined forces, then there was no possibility of a divorce for Henry. And Wolsey knew full well whom Henry would blame. "In other words, we were deliberately sidelined."

More shrugged, apparently unconcerned. "If you put it like that."

"Now there is no chance that the pope will agree to the divorce."

More looked down and remained diplomatically silent.

His response angered Wolsey. "Tell me, Thomas: What exactly do you think you achieved at Cambria, that makes you look so smug?"

"For the most part, it wasn't for me to achieve anything—and yet I consider this diplomacy to be a success."

Wolsey looked at him with incredulity.

More continued, "Once more, there is peace in Europe—which should please each and every humanist. England is once more at peace with the empire but, more importantly, papal authority has been restored and recognized. That is what I believe in."

Wolsey rose from his seat, increasingly agitated by the abyss he saw growing in front of him. "Francis betrayed me."

More shook his head. "No. He saw the futility of war. He recognized the need for tradition."

"Thomas," Wolsey said, "you have destroyed me."

More looked back at him, unblinking. "It was not my intention," he said slowly. "Our purposes are different."

The court was now assembled at Henry's place at Grafton in Northamptonshire, a modest establishment, but a favorite with Henry for the fine hunting it provided.

Henry was presiding over a council meeting when Brandon burst in, looking distracted.

"Your Grace?" Henry addressed him with icy disapproval.

"Majesty . . . forgive me." Brandon paused and looked around, seeming lost for words.

Finally he faced the king and said baldly, "Margaret is dead."

There was a shocked silence.

"How?" Henry asked after a moment.

"She . . ." Brandon looked down, then turned a troubled face to Henry. "She was . . . ill."

Henry looked back at him. There was a long silence, then Henry said in a hard voice, "And you never even told me that she was sick?"

Brandon hung his head, unable to explain. How could he admit that he hadn't known himself, that it had been such a long time since he'd seen his wife?

Henry said nothing for a long moment, then he rose and, without saying a word, strode from the room.

The door closed behind him, and, hidden from sight, Henry sagged against the wall. His face crumpled. "My little baby sister," he muttered brokenly, and covered his face with his hands.

The rain poured down, cold and relentless on the day of Margaret's funeral. Her coffin was carried in solemn procession along the path between the wheat fields and the briar patch, past the ancient sycamore tree, through the intricate iron gates and into a churchyard lined with stone tombs and intricate medieval crosses.

The Duke of Norfolk, as the king's representative, led the procession, dressed in funereal clothing, the unrelieved black of which did not detract from its richness. Brandon followed, his face grave and unemotional. After him came many others, representatives of most of the noble families of the kingdom, including Knivert and Boleyn, Derby and More.

Villagers and servants lined the route; the men bareheaded, despite the rain. Many of the women were weeping.

A young boy stood with his father, watching solemnly. "If the lady was the king's sister, why isn't the king here?" he asked.

"The king cannot go to funerals," the father told him in a hushed voice.

"Why not?"

"Because no one is allowed to think of the king and death together," the father explained. "Even to imagine the king's death is treason, so hush now, and say not another word."

The ornate coffin was carried toward the Brandon family vault. Brandon's face was blank, seemingly untouched by the death of his wife, as the coffin was carried inside.

The archbishop of Canterbury presided over the ceremony. Latin orisons were sung by choir boys, and the coffin was placed upon a marble slab.

Its top was then removed, revealing the body of Margaret, dressed in a simple white shift. The skin of her face was pale and waxen, her long, narrow hands folded as if in prayer.

A final prayer was said, delivering her soul into the hands of God, then everyone departed, leaving Brandon alone with the body of his wife.

The last footsteps retreated, the last murmurs of people talking in hushed tones faded, and finally there was just the sound the drumming, steady rain.

Brandon stared down at the body of the wife he treated so negligently, of Margaret, whom he had loved so passionately—passionately enough to risk his neck for—and whom . . . somehow . . . he had lost, without understanding why . . . or even realizing.

The loss hit him there; his throat was choked with unspoken words, and he started to weep in great, gasping, painful sobs. It was then he spoke the words he had not uttered while she was alive, the words of love and farewell, regret and anger. Finally, kissing her cold lips and closed, waxy eyelids, he begged her forgiveness.

Campeggio and Wolsey had been summoned to attend the king at Grafton. They arrived together, Campeggio in a horse-drawn litter, and Wolsey riding a horse. They were met in the yard by the king's grooms and men—a deliberate insult, as Wolsey noted, for there was not a single great lord to greet them.

As Wolsey and Campeggio dismounted, one of the grooms, rather pointedly, singled out Campeggio, bowing to him and saying, "This way, Your Excellence." He led the old man inside the house.

Wolsey, having no greeting or any groom so much as look at him, followed, doing his best not to show the disquiet he felt at such blatant lack of respect.

The groom showed Campeggio to a chamber. "Your Honor's chamber," he said. As Campeggio entered, the groom turned to leave.

"Wait!" Wolsey detained him. "Where is my chamber?"

"There is none prepared for you, Your Eminence," the man said in a bored voice.

"But I need to change from my riding clothes," Wolsey said.

The man shrugged. "Then you had best ask elsewhere." With a hard-faced, smug expression, he walked off.

Wolsey, reeling in shock from the implications of this treatment by a menial, stumbled along the gloomy corridor, looking for a place to change his clothing, a place to regroup.

"Your Eminence," a quiet, respectful voice spoke from behind. Wolsey turned and squinted in the poor light. It was an old retainer, a man he had not seen in some time.

"Mr. Norris?"

Norris nodded. "Yes, Your Eminence. Here, you can use my room. It's not much, but . . ." He gave Wolsey a rueful look and showed him to a small, cramped room: the room of a servant, not anyone important. "I'll have your trunk sent up, Eminence. When you've changed, you are to go to the Presence Chamber."

Wolsey said with difficulty, "I am grateful to you, Norris."

The man's kindly face softened. "Sir, many people here have cause to be grateful to you. Though, alas, they do not show it."

A short time later, Norris escorted Wolsey to the Presence Chamber—so called simply because the king was present there. He and Campeggio waited. No chair had been provided, not even for the aging, infirm old Italian.

After a long wait, they were admitted. It was a small room and, on this occasion, was packed with people. Many of the nobles of the kingdom were present—mostly those who despised Wolsey.

Wolsey saw the situation at a glance; his enemies had come to gloat over his downfall. They'd come to witness his humiliation.

He looked toward where the king was sitting, under a cloth-of-gold canopy. Henry rose and came forward, looking very stern. Both Campeggio and Wolsey fell to their knees.

Henry stood, frowning down at them, then suddenly his face cleared. He bent and raised Wolsey up, took his arm and led him across the room to a window. Wolsey went warily, unsure of what was happening, but then he caught the looks of surprise and consternation on the faces of Boleyn and his daughter, and on Brandon's face. It gave him heart.

Brandon looked at Boleyn accusingly as the king embraced Wolsey with obvious affection.

"What, in the name of God, is he doing?" Brandon muttered. "How can he forgive him?"

Boleyn shook his head, bewildered. "I am as much at a loss as Your Grace. I never thought . . ."

Wolsey saw their astonishment and obvious concern and basked in the sun of the king's attention, temporary as he suspected it to be. He had another chance.

"They tell me you have been unwell," Henry said sounding concerned. "Is it true?"

"Majesty, when have I ever been unwell enough to serve you?"

Henry gave a vigorous nod. "That's what I thought! People tell me such lies! Whom can I trust?" He laughed, slapping Wolsey on the back. "We've been through a lot together, Wolsey, have we not? Do you think I could ever forget?"

Wolsey was very moved, and did not care who saw it. In a choked voice, he said, "And there is still a great deal more to do."

Henry smiled, but catching sight of the Italian cardinal, he became distracted. "I know, I know. But look at Campeggio! Now there's a man who is sick! How do you catch gout? Perhaps he won't last the journey! I suppose I have to speak to him." He frowned irritably, then looked back at Wolsey and lowered his voice. "Don't be afraid. Tomorrow we'll talk properly."

Wolsey nodded, his heart filled with love and gratitude, but as the king moved off, Wolsey saw Boleyn give him a malevolent stare. As he watched, Boleyn bent over and whispered something in his daughter's ear. Anne looked up and stared straight across the room at Wolsey. She nodded slowly, and Wolsey's joy froze in his veins.

That evening, Henry dined with Anne. Henry ate with great gusto, clearly in a good mood.

"How can you be so friendly to Wolsey?" Anne said. "After he's failed you."

Henry paused, chewing meditatively. "It's not all his fault."

"He's your chief minister. He controls everything—you know he does. But Wolsey is the cardinal of a church that will *never* free you, a church that keeps you in its toils like a serpent."

"Wolsey works tirelessly in my interests," Henry told her. "I know him better than you."

Anne sighed. "Then you are blinded by affection. If he had truly wanted you to be free of Katherine, do you think he would not have achieved it?" She placed her hand over his and said, "You know—deep down—whose fault it is that you can't get a divorce."

Henry looked at her, and frowned.

Later that night he paced about his room, turning over what Anne had said. Wolsey did control everything. And though he had always served Henry well, in this, he had put the pope first. Henry was sure of it. There was not a single other thing he had asked of Wolsey that Wolsey had not been able to do.

He walked to the window and, seeing movement, peered down into the yard. Wolsey stood there in a small knot of people, talking quietly by torch light.

Henry stared down at his long-time friend and chancellor and brooded. At one time, Wolsey had been like a father to him.

But times had changed. In the morning they would move on to the next house in his progress.

A mist hung over the house and yard in the morning. Anne, Henry, and his party were already dressed and mounting their horses as Wolsey and

Campeggio came out of their lodgings. A small crowd of local people had gathered to cheer the king on his way.

Wolsey tried to make his way across the crowded yard to greet the king. At a signal from Norfolk, guards forced him back, away from the monarch, as if Wolsey were one of the common folk.

Henry didn't seem to notice. Wolsey waved and tried to catch the king's eye. Henry, flanked by Norfolk and Boleyn, did not look at all in his direction. Anne Boleyn gave Wolsey a smug look, and Wolsey realized that the king was, in fact, studiously avoiding looking in his direction at all.

Nobody understood better than Wolsey the actual and symbolic importance of not being allowed into the king's presence. It was vital he re-establish contact, remind the king that Wolsey was his old friend and loyal servant.

He tried to force a passage through the guards. They stopped him. "Majesty! Your Majesty!" he called out.

The guards pushed him back, but hope flared in him as he saw that Henry had heard his desperate call. Wolsey saw the king hesitate and glance back at him. His heart fell as he saw the brief struggle in Henry's face.

Then the king's face hardened and, with Anne beside him, he turned his back on Wolsey and rode off.

The usual gaggle of onlookers who hung around the gates of Whitehall fell back nervously as Brandon and the Duke of Norfolk rode into the palace grounds. They looked as ferociously serious as if they had come to commit a murder. Dismounting, they entered the palace together and stalked menacingly through the court.

The pair made their way to Wolsey's private chambers. Wolsey had just entered. He was closing the door behind him when Norfolk shoved it back open, and he and Brandon strode in, leaving the door open. A crowd quickly gathered outside, peering curiously in.

Wolsey turned to face his enemies.

"Cardinal Wolsey," Norfolk said. "You are here charged with praemunire: That is, exercising your powers of papal legate in the king's realm, thus derogating the king's lawful authority."

"You are dismissed of all your offices, and all your goods shall be taken into the king's hands," Brandon added.

There was a fraught silence. "Do you have the king's written authority and seal to do this?" Wolsey asked, even though he knew they would not have acted so publicly if they had not.

With grim satisfaction, Norfolk produced the warrant, and held it up so that Wolsey and then the watching crowd could see that it bore the king's seal.

"You are commanded to hand over the Great Chain of your office," Norfolk said.

Slowly Wolsey unclasped the heavy chain from around his neck. He held it in his hands, and hesitated, reluctant to hand it over. Brandon leaned forward and ripped it from his grasp.

Wolsey swallowed. "Where am I to go?"

"To the king's house at Jericho," Norfolk told him. "To await the verdict of the court." He gestured to Wolsey to leave.

Wolsey took a deep breath. It was over then. Trying to summon his dignity, he stepped out of his chambers and into the large crowd that had gathered to witness his humiliation.

A man cried mockingly, "Make way for His Lord's Grace there! Make way! Make way!" and the crowd laughed.

Shoulders hunched against their hostility, Wolsey pushed his way through the jeering throng. Someone threw an orange at him. He made no sign he noticed.

He made the journey to Jericho in numb misery, but his fertile brain jolted back into action as he was pushed into a small, dark room. "Writing materials and a candle," he requested with an echo of his old authority, and by some miracle, they were produced.

Wolsey sat down to write a letter.

*My own eternally beloved Cromwell, I beseech you, as you love
me and will ever do anything for me, come here today, as soon as
your work is finished, and forgetting everything else—*

Cromwell looked up from Wolsey's pathetic letter and, distracted by
the light of torches, glanced out of the window. The king was returning
to the palace. Cromwell returned to the letter.

*for I would not only communicate things to you for my own
comfort and relief. But would also have your good, sad, discreet
advice and counsel.
In haste, this Saturday, with the rude hand and sorrowful heart of
your assured friend and one-time patron, Wolsey, who loves you.*

Cromwell looked at the letter for a long moment, then slowly and
deliberately, he tore it up.

Wolsey's trial was over, and Henry was walking in his private gardens
with Thomas More. It was a beautiful day, and Henry was in a good
mood.

"You know that Wolsey pleaded guilty to the charges against him,"
Henry told More.

"So I heard. And sentenced to imprisonment."

They strolled on for a moment. "I have rescinded the punishment,"
Henry told him. "I am even allowing him to keep the Bishopric of York,
with a pension of three thousand angels."

More looked at him, surprised. An angel was a gold coin worth ten
shillings—it was a very generous allowance. Henry laughed and clapped
More on the shoulder. "You see what a monster I am?"

More smiled, but made no comment. They walked on for a few moments
in silence. Henry grew serious again. "I need to appoint a new chancellor,
Thomas. Someone I can really trust." He gave More a meaningful look.

Still, More said nothing.

Henry continued, "You have been trained as a lawyer and in royal service. You have an international prestige. The friend of Erasmus, the greatest humanist in England. You have a fine, keen mind."

More gave him a sharp look. "No."

Henry stopped short. "No—what?"

"No—Your Majesty," More said. "I don't want to be chancellor."

Henry's face slowly flushed with anger. "You will do as I command!"

They stared at each other, neither giving way. Then Henry suddenly laughed, and put his arm around More's shoulder. He pulled him forward, walking on again. "Listen," he said. "I know you have scruples about the Great Matter. So I swear to you that it will be handled only by those whose consciences can agree with it."

He gave More a quick look. More's expression was pained, reluctant. They walked on.

"I promise I'll use you for other things and never let that matter molest your own conscience," Henry continued. He looked at More intently. "Tom, I say this to you. I want you—no, I command you!—in all things you do, to look first to God, and only then look to me." He waited for More's response.

After a long pause, More, knowing he had little choice in the matter, said, "Very well. I accept. Your Majesty."

Chapter Twenty

"My lords and councillors, there is a great deal for us to do," Henry addressed the council meeting. "In the past, those who had the reins of government in their hands"—he contemplated Wolsey's empty chair—"deceived me. Many things were done without my knowledge or my approval. But such proceedings will be stopped in the future." He looked around at them all, at his new chancellor, Sir Thomas More, at the Duke of Norfolk, at Brandon, Derby, and the other nobles of the kingdom.

His gaze settled on Norfolk and he said, "Your Grace is hereby appointed president of council . . ."

Norfolk inclined his head, smiling with satisfaction at his elevation, until Henry added, "Jointly with the Duke of Suffolk." Norfolk could not suppress a grimace of displeasure. Brandon grinned.

Henry continued, "We shall convene again very shortly, to consider those matters that remain close to our heart." He rose and left.

The councillors drifted back into court, discussing the events in low voices, but Norfolk intercepted Brandon with a hand on his arm. He waited until the other councillors had all left, then said, "Although it pleases me greatly that Wolsey is no longer here among us, even in his absence, he causes me disquiet."

Brandon smiled a little. "How so?"

"Don't smile! He was never attaindered for treason. So he still lives. And so long as he lives, he remains a danger both to us—and to this realm."

Brandon frowned. "But . . . he is far away in York. He is in disgrace. I think you exaggerate the danger."

"And I think you don't understand it!" Norfolk glanced around the room to check for listening ears, and then continued: "The king could easily change his mind. And if he did so, and if Wolsey ever came back to court . . . we should both have cause enough to fear his vengeance."

Henry paced about his private chamber reading aloud in an excited voice from the small volume that Anne had given him.

"'This belief . . . that the pope and the clergy possess separate power and authority is contrary to scripture. The king is the representative of God on earth and his law is God's law! The ruler is accountable to God alone and the obedience of his subjects is an obedience required by God!'"

He stopped and grinned at Anne. He finished reading the text with quiet conviction: "'For the church and the pope to rule the princes of Europe is not only a shame above all shames—but an inversion of the divine order. One king, and one law in God's name in every realm.'" He slammed the book down in satisfaction. "This book is a book for me, and for *all* kings."

Anne smiled, delighted at his satisfaction, and at the direction of his thinking. "And there are other books like it," she told him. "Books that detail the abuses of power, the privileges, and greed of the clergy in Your Majesty's realm. Books that Wolsey deliberately kept hidden from you."

"Yes," Henry said, "he would have called them heresy."

"Since when is the truth heretical?" Anne said.

He looked thoughtfully at her, then nodded. "I would like to read them," he said, then added, "but I shouldn't like ordinary people to get hold of them. I doubt they would understand."

He was silent for a short while, clearly thinking. Anne waited, saying nothing as he paced about the room. After a few moments, Henry continued. "Wolsey left my kingdom in chaos. I had no idea. But now I have taken the power unto myself, and I will work day and night, if necessary, to resolve things." He swung around and looked at her. "Including my annulment. Wolsey wasn't strong enough to achieve it. He threatened action against Rome—but he never meant to take it! Now, I swear to you, everything will be different."

His eyes were fixed on Anne's. She gave a halfhearted shrug of acceptance but looked away. It was clear she no longer believed it would happen.

Henry hated to see that look in her eyes. "Will you kiss me?"

She hesitated, then leaned toward him and kissed him quickly on the cheek. It was not a lover's kiss. It was the kiss of duty.

Henry's despair grew. If he didn't marry her soon, he would lose her!

In Wolsey's old chambers in the palace, Thomas More used the great seal of the chancellor's office to seal a document. Thomas Cromwell watched. The room looked very different from the richly luxurious interior of Wolsey's time. It was now spare, even austere.

Thomas Cromwell said, "I notice you have allowed yourself none of the trappings of your great office, Sir Thomas."

More shrugged. "I won't be wearing that chain of office for any but official occasions. I'm not vain enough to display its power, Mr. Cromwell. Yet I mean to use it."

"May I ask to what effect?" Cromwell enquired casually. It was not simply polite conversation. As a reader and distributor of Lutheran-inspired texts, Cromwell was concerned. Sir Thomas More was well known for his beliefs about heretics. In the past he had pursued a vigorous policy of book burning, but now he was in a far more powerful position. Books might not be the only thing he burned. . . .

More picked up a paper from his desk. "Here is a report of a sermon recently delivered in Cambridge by a certain Hugh Latimer—a senior member of that university."

He read from the paper: "'Mr. Latimer said that Holy Scripture ought to be read in the English tongue of all Christian people, whether they were priests or laymen'!" More shook his head in outrage. "He also raged against the gilding of images, the running of pilgrimages, and superstitious devotion! He said that all men were priests—and that we had no need for priests or popes on earth!"

He dropped the report in disgust. "The world has changed, Mr. Cromwell. It was once undoubtedly a good thing to tolerate religious extremism, to acknowledge clerical abuses, and encourage the theologically naive. But now I see plainly the risk and the danger involved in such a policy of tolerance toward all these new, dangerously erroneous sects. Wolsey was far too soft on them. I intend not to be."

"You will condemn all reformers as heretics?"

"I will protect all those men who do not deliberately desert the truth . . . but are seduced by the enticements of clever fellows."

"And those clever fellows?" Cromwell asked. "Will you burn them?"

More reached for the next document. The question hung in the air, unanswered.

The frigid Yorkshire rain pelted down steadily. In the church house that had been assigned to Wolsey in his exile, the rainwater leaked through the ceiling, dripping into the numerous pans Wolsey's mistress, Joan, had placed strategically through the house, and running down the walls. The bitter wind rattled the old house, sweeping through cracks and under doors.

Compared with the glories of Wolsey's former homes, this house was utterly wretched—cold, drab, and damp. Wolsey, shorn of his magnificence, sat huddled at a table by the fire, writing a letter.

"This is intolerable." Joan put down another pan to catch a new leak. "We must have the roof mended."

"With what?" Wolsey asked her. "And by whom? We have no money and most of our servants are gone."

Joan gave him a distressed look. "Surely the king never meant you to live so wretchedly? After all, you are still archbishop of York!"

"Perhaps it is not the king's fault," he said. He looked up from his letter writing. "I have had cause to remember an old prophecy: *When the cow rideth the bull, then, priest, beware thy skull.*"

"You mean that cow, Anne Boleyn?"

Wolsey smiled. "Indeed so . . . which is why I'm writing her this letter."

"What?" Joan was shocked. "But she is the cause of all our misery."

"I know. But since she is the cause, she can also be the cure. If I could only persuade her that I am not her enemy but her friend." He patted a leather-bound document folder. "I still have the letter in which she promised to reward me for all my pains and efforts on her behalf, when she came to be crowned."

Joan said wryly, "I seem to remember that, at the time, you thought her promises rather amusing."

"I may have done," Wolsey admitted. "But since then, I have lost my sense of humor." He returned to his writing.

"The king!" the palace chamberlain announced in a loud voice. Henry entered the court, followed by Cromwell, his arms full of papers. Courtiers bowed and curtsied as the king passed.

On his way toward his private chambers, he noticed Chapuys, the imperial ambassador, in a huddle with the Earls of Derby and Arundel. They looked almost conspiratorial.

Henry beckoned to Chapuys. "Ambassador Chapuys, we have not talked much since your appointment. A pity. I hear you are a very able and intelligent diplomat."

Chapuys inclined his head at the compliment.

Henry continued. "Like me, you must be aware of all the new religious controversies."

Chapuys said cautiously, "I know of some new heresies that have sprung up here and there, certainly."

Henry said in a teasing voice, "If only the pope and his cardinals could set aside vain pomp and ceremony, and start living according to the precepts of the Gospels and the early Fathers. That way, a great deal of scandal, discord and heresy could have been avoided. Don't you agree?"

Chapuys tried to be diplomatic. "I am well aware that Your Majesty is in the midst of an argument with His Holiness."

Henry shrugged. "Oh, I'm not talking about myself." He gave Chapuys a searching look. "You see, Excellence, when Luther attacked the vices and corruption of the clergy, he was right. And had he stopped there, and not gone on to destroy the sacraments, and so on, I would gladly have taken up the pen in his defense, rather than attacking him."

Chapuys looked unsure. "I—"

"It's true, there is a good deal of heresy in Luther's books."

"Indeed there is!" Chapuys agreed.

"On the other hand," Henry said, "that shouldn't obscure the many truths he has brought to light. The need to reform the church is manifest. The emperor has a duty to promote it. And I must do likewise in my own domains."

Chapuys stared at the king, unsure of how to respond or react.

Henry smiled, perfectly aware of the ambassador's dilemma. "I'm glad we've had this opportunity to exchange opinions," he said.

Chapuys bowed as Henry moved on to his private chambers.

A few moments later, Anne Boleyn entered the court, wearing a beautiful purple dress. There was a collective gasp of shock followed by a buzz of speculation.

"What is it?" Chapuys asked a neighbor. "What has she done?"

"She is wearing purple. Purple is the color reserved for the exclusive use of royalty!"

The whole court watched as Anne progressed in a queenly manner through the court. She came across two of Queen Katherine's Spanish ladies standing outside the queen's apartments, and people crowded forward, craning their necks, anxious to see the confrontation.

They were not disappointed. The ladies spoke in Spanish, clearly disparaging Anne and refusing to acknowledge her.

Anne paused before them, flicking them with a contemptuous look. In a clear voice she said to her companion, "You know, I wish sometimes that all the Spaniards in the world could be drowned in the sea!"

The jaws of Katherine's high-born ladies dropped in shock and outrage at such a crude and blatant attack.

"Mistress Boleyn," one of them said. "You should not abuse the queen's honor with such language."

Anne raised a disdainful eyebrow. "I care nothing for Katherine. In fact, I would rather see her hanged than acknowledge her as my mistress!"

The court rippled with shock. Anne had crossed an unspoken boundary. The queen was still the queen, after all. And though Anne may be in the ascendant, Katherine still deserved respect.

Anne moved off, head held high, but her heart was beating fast. She was determined to put an end to this endless stalemate. She had thrown down the gauntlet.

Chapuys, distressed on the queen's behalf, sought an audience with her. He hoped she had not heard of what Anne Boleyn had said, hoped that her ladies had preserved their discretion on her behalf, to spare her further distress.

When he was admitted into her presence, he was shocked by the change in her appearance. She looked older, pale, and unwell, her complexion muddy and thick-looking. Her dark eyes were pouchy and ringed with dark shadows.

Chapuys bent to kiss her hand. "Sweet madam, how are you?"

Katherine wearily tried to summon a smile. "You must forgive me for not seeing you more often. I have been sick and very low. I have had fevers, and the physicians have bled and purged me too often."

Chapuys regarded her with tenderness and concern. "But tell me, please tell me you are not losing hope?"

There was a long silence, then Katherine said, "It's true. I . . . I had always believed that the king, after pursuing his course for some time, would turn away, would yield to his conscience." She gave Chapuys a helpless look. "He has so often done so before, you see. He is not . . . not a constant man in his . . . fancies. I believed with all my heart that he would return to reason. But now—" Her voice broke, and she turned her face away from him, to hide her distress.

"Madam, I pray you, don't give way."

She took a deep breath. "No, Excellence," she said in a firmer voice. "I shall *never* give way. I shall never let them make of my beloved daughter a bastard!" She looked at him with steel in her gaze. Her thin, aristocratic nostrils flared as she added, "And I shall never give way to *that woman!*"

Henry leaned back from his desk and groaned. The hour was late, and he had spend the better part of the day on matters of state. Since Wolsey's fall from grace, the work seemed to have doubled. Tripled. He rubbed his tired eyes, sighed, and picked up the next document. Wearily he read it through, then signed.

His secretary, Cromwell, picked up the document. He hesitated, opened his mouth, then shut it.

Henry noticed. "Something on your mind, Mr. Cromwell?"

Cromwell looked awkward. "Your Majesty, I . . . I . . . ."

"Spit it out, Mr. Cromwell!"

"I had cause, recently, on a visit to Waltham Abbey, to speak to a learned friend there, Thomas Cranmer," Cromwell told him. "We spoke . . . about Your Majesty's Great Matter." Cromwell darted the king a glance, as if he expected a rebuke. But Henry, looking interested, just leaned in a little closer.

Cromwell continued, "We . . . we came to the conclusion that Your Majesty's advisers were not, perhaps, approaching the Matter in the most convenient way to solve it."

Henry, intrigued, said, "You mean through the courts?"

"Yes. We all know how the law operates—all those tedious processes and endless delays! And in the end, there is often no conclusion."

Henry nodded. "That's true. But if the Matter is not to be settled in law . . ."

"What is the law?" Cromwell said. "As Your Majesty well knows, kings are set above the law. They are answerable to God alone, who anointed them."

He glanced at the king's face, then, emboldened by his expression, went on. "So it seems to us that the issue is not and never has been a legal one. It is a *theological* one."

Henry was much struck by this argument. "In that case, who should pass a verdict upon it?"

Cromwell spread his hands in a gesture. "We would suggest that Your Majesty canvas the opinions of theologians at colleges around Europe. Their sentence would be soon pronounced, and could be implemented with little enough industry. But by that simple measure, I trust Your Majesty's troubled conscience might be pacified."

"Will you write me a paper showing your arguments?"

Cromwell bowed. "If Your Majesty trusts me to do so."

"No, I *demand* that you do so," Henry said with new energy. "And then I command that, as a royal agent, you go to Europe. Visit the universities. I would have the opinion of their theological faculties as soon as possible!"

In his renewed flush of hope, Henry threw a lavish party, with music and feasting and dancing. The queen did not attend.

The Norfolks, Brandon, More, Chapuys, and others watched as Henry escorted Anne to the high table and invited her to sit in the queen's empty chair. Anne, glittering with jewels, looked radiant. The musicians played one of the songs Henry had written for Anne.

Thomas Boleyn was invited to sit at the king's other side. The seating put several noses severely out of joint: Both Boleyn and his daughter had been raised above all others—above the Duke of Norfolk, who was the head of their family clan, above his wife, above the king's brother-in-law and close friend, Brandon.

Henry kissed Anne's hand. To Boleyn, he said, "I have something to tell you. I have decided to ennoble you and your family. You are to be created Earl of Wiltshire and Ormonde, and I am also appointing you Lord Privy Seal. George will become Lord Rochford, and be made a member of council."

Boleyn managed to look astounded. "Your Majesty. I am lost for words. Your bounty is unceasing."

Henry smiled and said quietly, "We have great hopes for Mr. Cromwell."

"I'm very glad," Boleyn said. "He is a friend of the family."

"You know his thesis," Henry said. "I want you to visit the emperor and the pope at Bologna and put to them our new case."

Boleyn inclined his head in obedience. Henry feeling ever more hopeful, turned to Anne and forgot all about the company. They gazed into each other's eyes.

"Well, well, I see that the gossip is right," the Duchess of Norfolk, newly come to court, said to her husband. "She is the king's whore, and the bitch's father is raised above all!"

"Let them feast and fatten themselves," Norfolk told her bitterly. "For one day they will be harvested." He watched the Boleyns fawning about the king. The Boleyns were no longer obscure kinsmen, dependent on Norfolk's goodwill—and it rankled.

Brandon drew Norfolk aside with a smile. "Everything seems to move in your favor, Your Grace," he murmured with irony.

Norfolk gave him a cold look. "I have bad news. I happen to know that the king has sent Wolsey an intaglio portrait of himself."

Brandon said nothing for a moment, then shrugged. "So?"

Norfolk rolled his eyes. "It is a sign of goodwill," he explained. "It may presage a reconciliation."

Brandon made a dismissive gesture. "A small gift to ease the king's conscience is hardly a sign that the Bishop of York is to be restored to his former glory. Think of it this way: After Satan fell from Heaven, was he ever invited back?"

"I don't know about Satan," Norfolk said, "but *you* were."

Brandon gave him a sharp look, then laughed uneasily and moved off.

Chapuys and More, sitting close together, also watched the king and Anne Boleyn making what amounted to public love.

"It is everything now for the Lady Anne!" Chapuys observed. "Sir

Thomas, does this not remind you of a wedding feast? It seems to me that nothing is wanted but for the priest to give away the nuptial ring and pronounce the blessing."

"God forbid it should ever come to that," More said. "But it is none of my business. My job as chancellor is to root out the new false sects. I will do my utmost to contend for the interests of Christendom."

Chapuys looked across at Henry, then at the Boleyns, then back at More. "Perhaps the King's Majesty is more inclined toward the reformers than you know."

"I don't think so. I know him better than you, Excellence," Thomas More told him comfortably. "The king's deepest instincts are traditional and faithful. He may *threaten* to break with Rome, but I can't believe he will ever do so."

Chapuys frowned, unconvinced. "I hope so. I truly hope so," he murmured. "The consequences would be . . . unthinkable."

At the high table, Henry was tenderly feeding Anne morsels of meat. "Thank you for what you have done for my father—for my whole family," she told him.

"There is more, my love. I have ordered alterations to be made to Wolsey's old palace at York Place." Pleased with her amazement, Henry explained. "Well, you told me how much you liked it, so I am giving it to you."

Anne, delighted, then suddenly overwhelmed, lowered her eyes. Henry put a hand over hers. "What is it, my love? Have I made you unhappy?"

She raised her face, and gave him a loving look. "No. I would only be unhappy if you stopped loving me."

"London would have to melt into the Thames first," he told her, and, in full view of the court, he leaned forward and kissed her on the lips.

Watching from a distant table, Tallis sat with his friend, the poet Thomas Wyatt. "I hear that you have accepted the patronage of Mr. Cromwell, Mr. Wyatt."

"How very transparent the world is!" Wyatt gave a wry smile. "But was I wrong to do so, Mr. Tallis?"

"I . . . I think so, yes," Tallis said seriously. "You should be your own man."

Wyatt snorted. "Don't be a fool, Tallis. You never will survive long in this slippery world without the support of a great man."

Tallis raised his brows. "You think Mr. Cromwell a great man?"

Wyatt winked and said confidentially, "I think him a coming man! You mark my words."

Tallis wrinkled his brow. "When I first came to court, I received a piece of advice that I thought very wise."

"Indeed? And what was this gem?"

"He told me, 'We poor folk must seek the light of great men, as the moth seeks the flame.'"

"Yes, which is why—"

"I'm not finished," Tallis told him. "He then told me, 'But take heed of the moth, for if we venture too close, we risk burning our wings.'"

Wyatt shrugged. "I am no moth." They both looked across again at Henry and Anne, caressing each other in public. Wyatt leaned closer to Tallis and whispered into his ear, "And for what it's worth, I did fuck her!"

Tallis gave him a warning look. "I'd keep that to myself if I were you."

Sir Thomas More was pursuing his perceived duty as the King's chancellor—battling the spread of heresy that he so abhorred and that was in danger of destroying the very foundations of society, and sorting innocent dupes from "clever fellows."

He was questioning a thin, ordinary-looking, middle-aged former lawyer named Simon Fysh. Fysh sat at a plain wooden table. In front of him were various radical tracts and books.

"You have been in exile, Mr. Fysh?"

"Yes, sir. It was Cardinal Wolsey's pleasure to keep me in Holland, for fear I might speak the truth."

More raised an eyebrow. "So why did you try to return?"

"I thought, sir, that with the cardinal fallen and sent away, that circumstances in this country would be changed for the better." He gave More a clear look and added, "I had supposed that people in England might be more tolerant. I have read your book *Utopia*."

More did not react. "You have friends in this country, Mr. Fysh?"

Fysh frowned. "Of course, sir, as an Englishman."

"At court?" Fysh said nothing. More repeated, "Do you have friends at court?"

Fysh looked away, refusing to answer.

After a moment, More picked a pamphlet up from the table. "Do you deny that you are the author of this work: *A Supplication for the Beggars*?

"No, sir, I do not deny it. It is an appeal to His Majesty to redress many of the terrible and scandalous abuses of the Church."

More opened the pamphlet. "You describe the leaders of the Church as thieves! They are 'ravenous, cruel and insatiable'—for collecting the tithes that are owed to them!" He looked at Fysh, who said nothing.

More continued, "You suggest that the real aim of the church is to seize all power, lordship, obedience, and dignity from the king, for themselves. Indeed, you go further, and claim that the Church fosters disobedience and rebellion against the king!" He leaned closer and said to Mr. Fysh's face, "Do you not, Mr. Fysh?"

Still, Fysh said nothing.

More circled the table slowly, thoughtfully, looking through the pamphlet. "And here, Mr. Fysh . . . if I may. You say that the exactions taken from the people are not given to a kind temporal prince but to 'a cruel, devilish bloodsucker, drunken in the blood of the saints and martyrs of Christ.'"

He let the pamphlet slip through his fingers. "For shame, Mr. Fysh! And who are these cruel, devilish bloodsuckers, but the anointed priests of our Holy Church, who show us the way to Heaven!"

Fysh didn't respond.

More moved closer to him. "But then, you don't believe that, either, do you, Mr. Fysh?" He thrust his face in Fysh's and asked, "Who are you, Mr. Fysh?"

Fysh finally raised his head. "The answer to that question is: I am a Christian man, the child of everlasting joy, through the merits of the bitter passion of Christ. That is the joyful answer."

There was a short silence, then More said in a cold voice, "It is also heresy."

Thomas More decided not to make the execution of Simon Fysh a public spectacle. Too often in the past, such events had attracted vulgar crowds, as if the solemn duty of burning a heretic was some sort of public entertainment.

Today, since it was a solemn and official ceremony, he consented to wear all the rich trappings of his office, rather than his usual plain dress. Bishop Fisher and attending clergy stood by, all wearing their full ecclesiastical garments.

The executioners completed the job of tying Simon Fysh to the stake. He stood there, pale but calm as they piled kindling all around his feet. A burning brazier stood nearby.

More looked compassionately at Fysh, who wore only a simple smock. "There is still time to recant of your heresy, Mr. Fysh. If you will only acknowledge that your opinions were misguided, evil, and contrary to God's law . . . then you will be spared the great pains you must otherwise endure."

Fysh turned his head and met More's gaze. But he said nothing.

One of the executioners picks up a burning brand and held it near to the piles of kindling.

"I beg you, Mr. Fysh," More said. "Acknowledge your sins, and God will welcome you back to his fold. Recant! You still have a moment."

He waited. Fysh stared at him, then began to recite the Twenty-third Psalm—defiantly in the forbidden English translation. "'The Lord is my shepherd, I can want nothing. He feedeth me in a green pasture, and leadeth me to fresh water . . .'"

Bishop Fisher tried to drown out Fysh's heretical act by praying loudly in Latin. More gave the signal, and the flames were put to the kindling.

Fire began to crackle around Fysh's feet. Fysh raised his voice. "'Though I should walk now in the valley of the shadow of death, yet I fear no evil, for thou art with me.'"

As the flames suddenly leaped up, More could watch no longer. He turned his back on the scene, wishing he could drown out the terrible sound of the flames roaring and the burning man shouting out his heretical prayer.

"'Oh let thy loving-kindness and mercy follow me all the days of my life, that I may dwell in the house of the Lord for ever!'" The last word ended on a terrible scream as Fysh's blood vessels burst with a popping noise. The fire roared.

At last, More turned back, forcing himself to look. What was once Fysh was now just a ragged shape dancing and whirling like a blackened puppet in the flames.

Chapter Twenty-one

Henry was in a foul mood. The assembled members of his council shifted uncomfortably and waited for him to speak.

"My lords, every day I am forced to read new reports of dissatisfaction, confusions, and delays throughout my kingdom. I hear that my exchequer is empty and that we are borrowing money at a biting rate!"

He glared at Brandon and Norfolk. "Your Graces are presidents of this council. Yet I hear *nothing* from you on these matters—nor on any *other* matter."

Brandon cleared his throat. "Your Majesty must forgive me. I—"

Henry cut him off. "I know! I must *always* forgive Your Grace!" he said sarcastically. "But I grow tired of it. I have given you everything—including the right to call yourself a prince!" He followed that with a hard look. "But what do I get in return?"

Brandon's eyes dropped.

Henry continued. "I used to think Cardinal Wolsey vain, self-serving, and greedy—just as you all told me he was! Now I understand the burden he carried. Uncomplainingly!"

Brandon and Norfolk exchanged looks. Norfolk said quickly, "Your Majesty should not forget that he also stole from you—and served the interests of the French even above those of England."

Henry looked at Sir Thomas More. "Is that what you think, Thomas?"

More chose his words with care. "It is true that the cardinal was vainglorious above all measure. And that was a very great pity. It did him harm and made him abuse the many great gifts that God gave him."

Many of the councillors nodded. Henry said nothing for a long time. Then, suddenly he smashed his fist on the table and shouted, "And yet he was a better man than any of you for managing this kingdom's matters!" He stormed from the chamber.

The councillors looked at one another in consternation. The king's temper was notoriously short these days—prolonged celibacy did that to a man, but this was serious! They left the room, falling into clumps of earnest discussion.

Norfolk sought out Brandon. "I did warn you! I will speak to the king."

"Yes. Yes, you must!" Brandon agreed, as Norfolk left. The king's personal attack on him had shaken him severely.

Sleep eluded Wolsey. After tossing and turning for some time, he sat up in bed, disturbing his mistress, Joan, who had been trying to sleep.

She turned over and looked at him. "What is it, Thomas? Is it that letter you received?"

Wolsey sighed. "Yes, she sent a reply."

"Mistress Boleyn? What did she say?"

"That she would *not* promise to speak to the king for me."

There was a short silence. "Then . . . our hopes are over," Joan said. She leaned against him in silent comfort.

Wolsey looked down at her, his expression softening. "No," he said thoughtfully. "They don't have to be. There is another I can write to; a lady much greater in every way than that mischievous whore—and more likely to be kind. . . ."

"I have a letter for Your Majesty." Ambassador Chapuys produced a letter from the folds of his clothes. Once again, Katherine had chosen to receive him in the privacy of her chamber.

Katherine's eyes brightened. "From the emperor?"

Chapuys grimaced, apologetically. "No. From Cardinal Wolsey."

"From Cardinal Wolsey?" she repeated, amazed. She opened the letter and quickly read it. "This is . . . so strange," she exclaimed when she had finished. "Do you know what it says?"

Chapuys inclined his head. "The cardinal is offering to create a rapprochement between you and he, the emperor, and Rome. The coup would be signaled by the arrival of a papal edict ordering Henry to leave Anne Boleyn and return to his marriage. The emperor would offer his financial and moral support, and insist that Wolsey be reinstated as chancellor."

There was a short silence, then Katherine said, "Do you think it could work?"

"The cardinal is nothing if not ingenious," Chapuys said noncommittally. "And there are many rumors that, in any case, the king intends to restore him to favor."

"Oh, how fast my heart beats," Katherine exclaimed in Spanish. "Can we pray together, Excellence?"

Together they knelt before her private altar, and offered prayers to the Virgin.

"I want you to summon a new Parliament," Henry instructed Sir Thomas More. He had sent for More to walk with him in his private gardens. "There are important things that need to be done. My exchequer is empty, for one thing."

More nodded. "I will do as Your Majesty commands. But I must warn you that you may not find the new Parliament as . . . compliant as those before."

Henry frowned. "How so?"

"Well, though I confess to being amongst those who once called for greater tolerance and freedom of speech, I fear that the freedom so granted by Your Majesty's kindness is now openly abused. There are many dissenting voices in Your Majesty's kingdom—especially in matters of religion." He glanced at the king. "There are many calls for a reformation."

Henry nodding, walked on, then suddenly stopped. "How many have you burned, Thomas?"

"Six." Then he added, "It was lawful, necessary, and well done."

Henry stared at him. "Well done?"

More met his gaze. "Yes, Your Majesty."

Anne Boleyn was walking along a corridor when she noticed one of the king's personal grooms heading for the the queen's private apartments, carrying several folded length of what looked like new white linen.

"Wait a moment!" she called to the servant. She examined the linen. It was the finest quality.

"Where are you taking this?" she asked the groom.

"To the Queen's Majesty, Lady Anne."

"What for?"

"For the queen—to make shirts for His Majesty, my lady," he said, adding, "She has always made them, my lady."

Anne stared at him, speechless.

The groom looked at her questioningly. "Lady Anne?"

She waved him impatiently away, and he was admitted to the queen's private chambers. Anne turned on her heel and went to find Henry.

"She still makes your shirts?" she demanded furiously.

Henry blinked. "Yes. Yes, she still makes my shirts." He was baffled by her apparent outrage.

"I can't believe it!"

Henry searched her face for a clue to her anger. "Can't believe what?"

Anne glared at him. "You told me—you told me there was nothing intimate between you anymore!"

Henry tried to move closer to her. "Sweetheart, they're just shirts."

Anne angrily dashed his hands away from her. "No, they're not just shirts! They are *you and me*! They are *you and she*!

"I—"

"Has nobody told you that I'm a fine seamstress too?" She bit her lip, on the verge of tears. For a long moment they stared at each other.

Henry made a helpless gesture. "I'm sorry. I didn't think."

At that, Anne burst into tears. "No, no, no, no . . . I'm sorry. I'm really sorry," she muttered, hiding her eyes from him. "I'm so sorry. I'm sorry."

"Sweetheart." He pulled her into his arms, then raised her tear-stained face and kissed her. "I love you."

"Your Majesty will be pleased to know that the greatest prize of all, the University of Paris, has declared in your favor." Cromwell and Boleyn had returned from their tour of the great universities of Europe, where they had canvassed opinion on the theological basis of Henry's divorce. Henry had received them at the palace and was listening to their report in his private chambers.

"And Italy?" Henry asked.

"I confess that the universities there are divided," Cromwell said. "But Padua, Florence, and Venice have all declared for Your Majesty."

"And Spain?"

"Spain is against," Cromwell told him.

Henry smiled wryly. "What a surprise!" He turned to Boleyn. "And you, my lord, did you meet the emperor and the pope? How were they?"

Boleyn shifted uncomfortably. He had contributed little to the conversation so far. He swallowed and admitted, "Your Majesty, the emperor refused to see me."

Henry frowned. "And His Holiness?"

Boleyn swallowed again. "The pope simply gave me this edict, to bring to Your Majesty." He produced a piece of rolled parchment with the papal seal and, after brief hesitation, handed it to Cromwell.

"What does it say?" Henry demanded.

Cromwell unsealed and opened it. He began to scan the contents, then stopped, glancing from Henry to Boleyn, then back to Henry. Clearly it was not good news.

"Tell me!" Henry demanded impatiently.

"The edict instructs Your Majesty to order Lady Anne Boleyn to leave your court," Cromwell told him. "It—it refuses to allow Your Majesty to remarry while the papal Curia is still considering your Majesty's case."

There was a long silence. Henry looked grim, furious, and very disturbed. Without a word, he stormed from the room.

Boleyn and Cromwell followed him from the room, watching as he strode down the corridors heading for the outside. They exchanged glances. "I will go and tell Anne what has happened," Boleyn said quietly, and headed toward his daughter's apartments.

Turning a corner, he was suddenly intercepted by Ambassador Chapuys, who bowed to him.

"Your Excellency," Boleyn said with restrained impatience. "What can I do for you?

"My lord, I would ask a very great favor of you." Chapuys gave Boleyn an anxious look. "These are troubled times. It seems to me that, in certain quarters here, there is now a blatant and open hostility to our Holy Church. As we discovered in Germany, this—"

Boleyn interrupted him brusquely. "What do you expect me to do?"

"You are a great man, a man of much influence in England," Chapuys told him. "I beg you to use the great influence you have, here at court, to pull England back from the brink of catastrophe and ruin—for the love we all bear for Christ and his Apostles."

Boleyn regarded Chapuys with faint scorn for his naivety. His mouth twisted. "What apostles?" Boleyn said harshly. "I don't believe that Christ had Apostles—not even Saint Peter! Those men were liars and charlatans who pretended to follow Christ and speak in His name. And they built a church upon their lies!"

He walked off, leaving Chapuys crossing himself in horror and dismay.

Boleyn was not the only one who was waylaid on his way back from the audience with Henry. Cromwell had not gone fifty paces when the poet Thomas Wyatt stepped out in front of him and bowed.

Cromwell said impatiently, "Not now, Mr. Wyatt. I'm busy."

"There is someone I think you should see," Wyatt said in a low conspiratorial tone.

"I said not now, Mr. Wyatt!" Cromwell kept walking.

"It concerns the cardinal," Wyatt told him.

Cromwell stopped dead, then turned back. "Very well."

"This way," Wyatt said, and led Cromwell toward a far corner of the palace.

Wyatt led Cromwell to a chamber where a balding, nervous, middle-aged man was waiting. As Cromwell entered, the man leaped to his feet and bowed low and repeatedly. "Your Honor, Your Honor . . . so grateful . . ."

He was not a particularly prepossessing creature. Cromwell looked inquiringly at Wyatt.

Wyatt said, "Sir, this is Augustine de Agostini. I knew him from when he was physician to the Boleyn family." He added silkily, "Dr. Agostini has been, of late, acting as private physician to Thomas Wolsey, archbishop of York."

Cromwell, suddenly all ears, turned back to Agostini.

"What do you know about Wolsey?"

Agostini stammered, "Sir, I kn-kn-know that W-Wolsey sought the help of the emperor, and the po-po—"

"The pope?" Cromwell prompted him.

Agostini nodded wildly. "Yes, Your Honor. His H-H-Holiness. The p-pope. A-against His M-Ma-Majesty."

Cromwell leaned forward. "They communicated?"

"Y-yes."

"And whom else did Wolsey communicate with?"

"W-Wolsey c-c-conspired with Queen K-Katherine, sir . . . because he s-said it w-was the only wa-wa—"

"It was the only way he could be restored to power," Cromwell finished impatiently.

Agostini nodded again. "He s-sang the t-tune as they w-w-wished him to d-do."

"We have to tell the king," Cromwell decided.

As Cromwell left, Agostini peered anxiously across at Wyatt, who gave him an approving nod.

The Yeomen of the Guard smashed in the door of Church House in York. A couple of young servants screamed.

"Hold! You within! Stop, in the king's name!" a guard shouted. They were armed and expecting resistance.

Wolsey stood waiting, standing in the middle of the room, all alone, except for his mistress, Joan. As the guards entered, brandishing their weapons, she ran to him and put her arms protectively around him.

The guards almost did not recognize Wolsey. He looked like an old man now, unshaven, and dressed in faded and threadbare clothing. He had lost a lot of weight and looked haggard, his skin gray, his hair thin and unbrushed.

The Renaissance prince of the Church was just a faint memory. Only his bright, intelligent eyes recalled the old Wolsey.

Brandon entered after the guards. He regarded Wolsey with considerable satisfaction. "Thomas Wolsey, you are arrested by order of the king, and charged with High Treason. You will be taken from here to London, where you will be tried."

Joan burst into tears and clung to Wolsey.

"There, there, Joan," Wolsey told her gently. "No tears for me, I beg of you." With a smile he eased her arms away. He cupped her cheek tenderly, saying, "Forgive me, that you have not much to remember me by."

"No," she said, tears running down her face. "I have a life and everything in it to remember you by." Ignoring the guards, she kissed him.

Then, with dignity, Wolsey put her to one side and walked toward Brandon. "If I had served God as diligently as I served the king, He would not have given me over in my gray hairs," he said.

"Take him outside," Brandon said roughly.

Outside a crude, dirty farmer's cart was waiting, the sort of cart used to transport livestock. Brandon half-smiled as the guards pushed Wolsey roughly into it. The cart had not even been cleaned out; it was deliberately degrading.

Wolsey affected not to notice. Joan, weeping, watched from the steps as Brandon and the armed escort mounted their horses, and the cart moved slowly away.

As Wolsey looked back in what he knew to be a final farewell, Joan suddenly collapsed.

"Joan! Joan!" he called to her. He watched as a servant ran to her, but the cart rolled relentlessly on. There was nothing he could do.

The party escorting Wolsey to London for his trial reached Leicester by the evening and stopped for the night in a monastery there. A monk with a candle led Wolsey and Brandon to a monk's cell.

"You will stay here the night," Brandon informed Wolsey. "There will be a guard always outside the door." He waved toward a table where food and water had been laid out. "There is food there for you. It is plainer than you are no doubt accustomed to, but there is meat, at least, and bread. Be thankful you are being fed."

Wolsey glanced at the meal and slowly nodded. The monk set down the candle, then, without ceremony, he and Brandon withdrew. The door closed behind them, and Wolsey heard the sound of a bolt being drawn.

He looked around his little kingdom. Beside the crude wooden table and chair there was an iron cot, and on a stone shelf a large wooden crucifix. Wolsey knelt and gazed up at the image of the suffering Christ.

"We have not spoken, Lord, as long or as often as we should," he said quietly. "I have often been about other business. If I wanted forgiveness, I should ask for it . . . but for all I have done, and am yet still to do, there can be no forgiveness." A quiver passed over his face, and he struggled for composure.

"And yet, I think, I am no evil man, though evil men pray louder, and do penance, and think themselves closer to Heaven ever than I am. I shall not see its gates, nor yet hear, Lord, your sweet words of salvation and joy. I swear I have seen Eternity, but only in dream, and in the morning all was lost."

He was silent for a moment. "I know myself for what I am. I throw my poor soul upon your mercy—and yet I know I deserve to receive none at your loving hands, O Lord."

He made the sign of the cross, then slowly rose. He walked over to the table. He looked down at the small plate containing a chunk of boiled meat. A half loaf of dry bread and a cup of wine accompanied it, but Wolsey had eyes only for one thing—he'd noticed it the moment he'd entered the cell: the small, well-honed knife left for him to cut his meat with.

The innocent, unworldly monks would never conceive of any other use for a knife. Nor that a priest could commit such an unholy act.

Picking up the knife, Wolsey stabbed the blade into his throat and drew it sideways. . . .

A monk, bringing a bowl of porridge to the prisoner, was the first to discover the body in the morning. Ripples of shock and consternation spread through the monastery.

Brandon pushed his way through the small crowd of monks and

guards. He looked down at the figure lying dead beneath the crucifix, in a large pool of congealed blood.

Angry, balked of his triumph, he kicked the body contemptuously. "Damn you! Damn you to Hell and back, Wolsey!"

The news was brought to Henry as he was practicing with bow and arrows in the shooting gallery at the palace. He and Knivert stood taking turns. Cromwell approached.

"Mr. Cromwell? What is it?" Henry said impatiently.

Cromwell bowed. "Your Majesty, Cardinal Wolsey is dead."

"I'm sorry to hear it," Henry said after a moment. "I wish he had lived." He looked away in the direction of the target pinned on the butt. "How did he die?"

Cromwell looked uncomfortable. "He . . ." Cromwell leaned forward and whispered into Henry's ear.

Henry stared at him, appalled. "No one must *ever* know that," he ordered in a quiet, forceful voice. "Do you understand? *No one. Ever!*" Suicide was a mortal sin. A suicide would have to be buried in unconsecrated ground.

Cromwell nodded, then Henry said, "I will finish my game, then I will talk to you."

Cromwell bowed and moved off. Knivert strung an arrow, and prepared to aim. "Go!" Henry told him abruptly. "Leave me!"

Knivert bowed and left. Fighting for composure, Henry walked slowly toward the butt, until he was out of sight of guards and courtiers alike.

Then, in private, he silently wept for Wolsey, bitter, genuine tears of love and remorse—and of loss. For Henry knew he wept not just for Wolsey, but for himself, and his future. . . .

"Have you heard?" Bishop Fisher burst into Sir Thomas More's chamber in a state of agitation. The room was dark, and More had been standing pensively by the window.

"I just heard it myself!" Fisher said. "By His Majesty's orders, fifteen senior clergymen have been arrested for recognizing Wolsey's authority!"

For a moment, More continued staring out of the window. Then he turned. "I know." His face was filled with pain and anger. "There is also a statute before Parliament that recognizes that, in all matters, temporal and spiritual, the king is above the law and shall give account to God alone!"

Fisher's jaw dropped. He could not take in the enormity of it.

More pounded his fist against the paneled wall.

"What can be done?" Fisher exclaimed.

There was a long silence. More, striving for calm, shook his head. "I remember, once, that Cardinal Wolsey said I should always tell the king what he ought to do, not what he could do. He said, 'For if the lion once knows his own strength, then nobody will be able to control him.'" He stared at Fisher a moment, then turned away, and looked hard at an image of the Blessed Virgin.

"I fear that Wolsey's prophecy has come true," he said quietly. "I think we are standing on the edge of the abyss . . . and God knows what shall become of us!"

In the palace, the reformers were out in force to watch a specially commissioned performance. Norfolk, Brandon, Thomas, and George Boleyn, Cromwell, Cranmer, Gardiner, Foxe, and others sat, drinking, watching, and laughing as, in the gallery above them, a grossly obese and ridiculous-looking character playing Cardinal Wolsey slavered kisses on the cross, heaped money into his pockets, and ogled semi-naked women.

To roars of delight, the winged figure of death sprang onto the stage and dramatically cut his throat with a scythe. Fake blood sprayed out in ribbons and, making great play of his own distress, the cardinal died.

Two horned devils then seized Wolsey and began to drag him toward the stairs. Wolsey tried to fight them off, but to no avail. The delighted audience jeered, cheered, and clapped as curtains parted, revealing a world beneath filled with fire and acrid smoke. The naked bodies of the damned writhed in eternal torment. Devils tortured the damned in every fiendish way, with fire, with hooks and knives. A horrified Wolsey cowered, slavering with terror as he scrabbled desperately to escape his fate.

The audience, loving it, jeered at him, yelling encouragement to the devils. When at last Wolsey turned to prayer in a vain attempt to escape his fate, the watchers—Norfolk, Brandon, Cromwell, the Boleyns and the rest—shouted with laughter, clapping and roaring with approval as Wolsey burned.

Two members of the court were not there to watch the play; Henry and Anne had gone out riding in the balmy summer's evening.

They rode slowly through the trees. Henry couldn't keep his eyes off Anne. He was burning inside. She stared back at him, knowing they were on the brink. . . .

Without a word, Henry suddenly stopped and dismounted. He moved restlessly between the trees, always looking at her, coiled like a spring and almost mad with desire.

The time had come; she knew it, felt it too, an irresistible force. She slipped off her horse and walked slowly toward him.

"I want you," he said. "And I will not be denied."

"I will deny you nothing, my love," she said, and his mouth crushed hers, and their passion, so long damned, burst free.

With frantic hands, Henry dragged at Anne's clothes, unlacing, ripping, pulling them awry and apart to get at her, his Anne. With equal fervor, Anne pulled apart his doublet, shirt, and codpiece, clawing at laces and buttons and ties, to bare his skin to her. And at the first touch, taste, sight of flesh, they fell on each other, for their need was too great to wait.

Half-naked they rolled over the soft-leafed forest floor, finally touching, kissing, mouth-to-mouth and skin-to-skin, hands seeking and caressing, learning and knowing, making love like lovers through the ages.

Soft rain fell, and leaves clung to their wet, gleaming skin, but Henry and Anne clung and rolled and writhed and arched as they made love, unaware of rain above or earth below, rutting like beasts, soaring like angels, a carnal love . . . but also beautiful, a passion overwhelming. Cruel and tender in equal measure. Temporal and spiritual. Flesh and blood transfigured. And as the climax built, they cried aloud to the gods of love and, at last the two became one. And their world changed forever.

About the Author

Anne Gracie is an award-winning writer of historical romance novels. She grew up in Australia, Scotland, Greece, and Malaysia, as her family moved a lot. She grew up in a house with no TV, lots of books, and animals. She developed her love of history in childhood, reading historical novels by authors such as Henry Treece, Rosemary Sutcliff, and Georgette Heyer.

She completed her education at Melbourne University, majoring in English literature and historical geography, and later, linguistics. As a young adult she traveled, and she still remembers the day she was sitting on a bus bound for Scotland when it started to snow. She watched in awe as plain green fields were revealed as medieval strip fields, their ancient boundaries clearly etched in snow.

Anne taught for a number of years in inner metropolitan secondary schools, and in tertiary institutions, until a year of backpacking around the world helped her rediscover her love of writing fiction.

Anne now writes full-time, keeps bees, and travels when she can.

Her website is www.annegracie.com.